Sally Pratt McLean

Cape Cod Folks

A Novel

Sally Pratt McLean

Cape Cod Folks
A Novel

ISBN/EAN: 9783743303225

Manufactured in Europe, USA, Canada, Australia, Japa

Cover: Foto ©Andreas Hilbeck / pixelio.de

Manufactured and distributed by brebook publishing software
(www.brebook.com)

Sally Pratt McLean

Cape Cod Folks

Making him look like a man of thirty.—Vide p. 92.

CAPE COD FOLKS

BY

SALLY PRATT McLEAN,

BOSTON
A WILLIAMS & COMPANY
OLD CORNER BOOKSTORE
1881

EIGHTH EDITION.

TO

M. Y. G.

CONTENTS.

—:•:—

Frontispiece:

GRANDMA GETS GRANDPA READY FOR SUNDAY SCHOOL.

CHAPTER I.

ON A MISSION.

" Lo, on a narrer neck o' land,
'Twixt two unbounded seas, I stand! "

UNT Susan was not sporting, now, in the airy realms of metaphor. Aunt Susan stood upon Cape Cod, and her voice rang out with that peculiar sweep and power which the presence of a dread reality alone can give. Something of the precariousness of her situation, too, was expressed in the wild, alarming, though graceful, gesture of her arms.

It was before the long projected canal separating Cape Cod from the main land had been put under active process of preparation.

It was at an evening meeting in the Wallencamp schoolhouse. A row of dingy, smoking lanterns had been set against the wall and afforded the only light cast upon the scene. Aunt Susannah Cradlebow the speaker, was tall and dark-eyed, with an almost super-human litheness of body, and a weird, beautiful face.

" And, oh, my dear brothers and sisters and oncon-varted friends !" she continued, " how little do we realize

the reskiness of our situwation here on the Cape ! Here
we stand with them ar identical unbounded seas a rollin'
up on ary side of us ! the world a pintin' at us as them
that should be always ready, with our lamps trimmed and
burnin' ! and, yit, oh my dear brothers and sisters and
onconvarted friends !—as fur as I have been inland, and I
have been a consid'able ways inland, as you all know,
whar it would seem no more than nateral that folks should
settle down kind o' safe and easy on a dry land univarse —
I say as fur as I have been inland, I never see sech
keeryins on and carnal works, sech keerlessness for the
present and onconsarn for the futur' as I have amongst
the benighted critturs who stand before me this evenin', a
straddlin' this poor, old, Hopeforsaken Pot Hook !"

Clearer and louder grew Aunt Susan's tones ; her eyes
lightened with terrible meaning ; her words flowed with
an unction that was unmistakable, and, at length, "Oh,
run for the Ark, ye poor, lost sinners," she exclaimed.
"Oh, run for the Ark, my onconvarted friends ! Don't
ye hear the waves a comin' in ? They 're a rollin' swift
and sure ! They 're a rollin' in sure as death ! Run for
the Ark ! Run for the Ark !"

Now, there was in Wallencamp a literal Ark, otherwise
this exhortation would have lacked its most convincing
force and significance. But Aunt Susan paused.
Among the usually restless audience, there was a moment
of almost breathless suspense. Not half a mile away,
behind a strip of Cedar woods, we could plainly
hear the surf rolling in from the bay, breaking hard
against the shore with its awful monotonous moan, moan,
moan.

My heart was already faint with homesickness. The

effect of that waiting moment was as sombre as anything
I had ever experienced. Much to my distaste, I found
myself sympathizing with the vague terror and unrest around
me. I can hear it still, the voice that then rose, singing,
through the sullen gloom of the school room, a strangely
sweet and rapturous voice —— Abagail's. I learned to
know it well afterwards. I listened with rapt surprise to
the pathos with which it thrilled the simple words of the
song.

> " Shall we meet beyond the River
> When the surges cease to roll,
> Where, in all the bright forever,
> Sorrow ne'er shall press the soul?"

A keenly responsive chord had been touched in the
simple, agitated breasts of the Wallencampers and they
joined in the chorus—these rough people—not with their
usual reckless exuberance of tone, but plaintively, tremblingly even, as though whatever the words, they would
make of them a prayer in which to hide some secret doubt
or longing of their souls.

> " Shall we meet, shall we meet,
> Shall we meet beyond the River?"

The strain was repeated with a most pathetic quaver in
the rendering, and then big Captain Sartell broke
down, with a helpless gulp in his voice, and I, who
believed myself of too superior and refined a nature
to be moved by such tawdry sentiment, was further
dismayed to feel the tears gathering fast in my own eyes.

After the meeting, on the schoolhouse steps, the big
Captain, as if to atone for any unmanly exhibition of
feeling into which he might have been betrayed inside,
took little Bachelor Rae up by the shoulders, and gently

and playfully held him suspended in mid air, while he put to him the following riddle :

"I'll wager a quarter,in a good, squar' guess, Bacheldor. Why is — why air' Aunt Susan's remarks like this 'ere peninshaler, eh, Bacheldor?"

"Because — ahem ! — because they 're always a runnin' to a p'int, eh?" inquired the keen little bachelor.

"No, by thunder !" exclaimed the discomfited Captain, setting the magician down promptly. "As near as I calk'late," he continued, endeavoring to resume his former air of cool and reckless raillery ; "as near as I calk'late, Bacheldor, — yes, sir, as near as I calk'late, — it 's — it 's — by thunder ! it 's because they 're both liable to squalls in fa'r weather !"

Amazed, and almost frightened at the unexpected brilliancy of his evil success, the Captain yet kept a rueful and furtive eye on the little bachelor.

Bachelor Rae coughed slightly and smiled. "Very true," he drawled, cheerfully, in his small, thin voice, "I 'm — ahem ! — I 'm not a married man myself, you know, Captain. However," he added, "you should have given me another try. I had the correct answer on my tongue's end."

During this brief exchange between the stars of the Wallencamp debate ground, murmurs of appreciative applause arose from the group of bystanders, and " Pretty tight pinch for you, Captain !" and "'Three cheers for Bacheldor ! ye can't git ahead of Bacheldor !" sprang delightedly from lip to lip.

Aunt Susan had scented from within this buoyant resumption of the Wallencamp mirth, and now appeared on the scene, bearing a burning lantern in her hand.

She first turned the .glare of its full orb on the late sin-convicted Captain, who stood revealed with a guilty grin frozen helplessly on his alarmed features, and next directed the beams of disclosing justice towards the form of the little bachelor, who, in pronounced meekness, was engaged in re-adjusting the collar of his coat.

"At it ag'in!" Aunt Susan exclaimed, with slow and cutting emphasis. "At it ag'in! I do believe you 're all possessed of the devil!"

Then, with one sweep of the lantern, she took a com-prehensive survey of the shivering group, and passed on without another word, while in the breast of every guilty Wallencamper then present, there rested a deep sense of merited condemnation.

Aunt Susan was soon followed by the other lantern bearers, who dispersed homeward, along the four roads diverging from the schoolhouse, and, the night being starless, the children of the darkness followed meekly in their wake.

The longest route lay before those who took the River Road leading to the Indian Encampment. Bachelor Rae was the hindmost in this receding column. Bachelor Rae, though too withered and brown of visage to afford enlightenment as to his species, was held to be of un-questionable white descent. Yet he kept house, alone, at the Indian Encampment.

Then there was the Stony Hill Road, up which a few pilgrims toiled; and the Cross Lot Road to the beach — thither went the Norrises. Last of all, there was the Lane, and it was somewhat in the rear of the lane proces-sion that I musingly wended my way, led by the beams of Grandma Spicer's slowly swaying lantern.

I was the Wallencamp school teacher. I had come to this "rock-bound coast" imagining myself impelled by much the same necessity as that which fired the bosoms of the earlier pilgrims. Not that I had been restricted in respect to religious privileges, but I sought for a true independence of life and aim ; and, furthermore, it should be said, I had come to Wallencamp on a mission. "On a mission !" how the thought had tickled my fancy and roused my warmest enthusiasm but a few short days before ! Indeed, I had not been yet a week in Wallencamp , and now, as I walked up the lane in a mood quite the reverse of enthusiastic, I was painfully trying to gather from my small and scattered sources of information what the exact meaning of the phrase might be.

I had entered on the performance of my errand to Wallencamp under circumstances not usual, perhaps, among propagandists ; nevertheless, I had been singularly free from misgivings.

A girl of nineteen years, I had a home endowed with every luxury ; a circle of family acquaintance, which, I admitted, did me great credit ; congenial companions ; besides, I was particularly well pleased with Nature for the uncommon beauty which she seemed to me to have poured out in my behalf. As for my education, I was pleased to call it completed. My career at boarding schools had been of a delightfully varied and elective nature, for I would never have deigned to peg along with squalid studiousness, or even to sail with politic and inglorious ease through the prescribed course of study at any institution. Any misadventures necessarily following from this course, my friends had gilded over with the flattering insinuation that I was "too vivacious" for this sort of discipline, or "too fragile" for that, though I am bound to say that, in such cases, my "vivacity" had generally sealed my fate before the delicacy of my constitution became too alarmingly apparent.

I had, to be sure, a few commendable aspirations, but I had started out fresh so many times with them, only to see them meet the same end!

Though not by nature of a self-depreciatory turn of mind, I had occasional flashes of inspiration, to the effect that, in spite of the soft flattery of friends, I really was amounting to very little after all.   It was in a mood induced by one of these supernatural gleams that I stood on one occasion, leaning a pair of very plump arms on the graveyard wall, looking wistfully over into the place of tombs, and thinking how nice it would be to have done forever with the fret and turmoil of a life! And it was at such a time, too, that I received from a school friend, Mary Taite, the letter which was the moving cause of my mission to Wallencamp.

Mary Taite, by the way, was one of those "prosy, ridiculous girls" — so I had been compelled to classify her, although I was secretly troubled by a sincere admiration of her virtues, — who had made it an absorbing pursuit of her school days to probe her text books for useful information, and was also accustomed to defer to her teachers as high authority on matters of daily discipline.   She was not in "our set."   She was poor, and studious, and obedient, yet a friendship had sprung up between her and me, and I was moved to forgive her, in many respects, the grovelling tendencies of her nature. I even ascended occasionally to her room on the fourth floor to shock her with my sentiments, when there was nothing livelier going on.

She wrote :

" My dear S—— : Are you still perfectly happy, as you used to try to have me think you were always — the old restlessness, the better longings unsatisfied, do they never come up again ? [That was Mary's insidious way of stating a difficulty.] 'Don't you believe you would be happier to *do* something in real earnest ? Something for people *outside*, I mean. [I flushed a little at that. An insinuation of that sort can 't be put too delicately.] I have tried to imagine how the proposal I am going to make will strike you — but never mind. I am teaching, you know, in Kedarville. I leave here, at the close of the term, for another field of labor, and now I want you to apply for the Kedarville school. Yes, it is a remote, poverty-stricken place. It contains no society, no church, no library, not even a little country store ! It would seem to you, I dare say, like going back to the half barbarous conditions of life. The people are simple and kind-hearted ; but they need training — oh, how much ! — physically, mentally and morally. I can assure you, here is scope for the most daring missionary enterprise, and you,— I believe that you could do it if you would. * * * * * Consider the matter seriously ; consult with your friends about it, and if you do decide to try the experiment, write as legibly as you possibly can to the Superintendent of Schools, Farmouth, Mass., stating your qualifications, etc., etc."

The idea struck me with such strange and immediate favor, that I quite forbore to consult with my friends in regard to it. I resolved to go on the instant, and wrote my friend Mary to that effect, congratulating her, with an undercurrent of mischievous intention, on having been the happy means of setting my powers drifting in the right direction at last ; and reproached her gently with having seemed to imply, once, in her letter, some occult reason why I had not been regarded, heretofore, as specially designed to work in the cause of missions, whereas I had always felt myself drifting inevitably towards that end.

I wrote to the Superintendent of the Farmouth schools. But here I had an earnest purpose to serve, and a real desire to succeed, and here met with a difficulty.

I had not the art of presenting my earnest purposes in the most assuring and credible manner. They *would* wear, in spite of me, an uneasy air of novelty; yet I aimed nobly.

I dilated largely on some of the evils existing in the present system of education, and hinted at reforms not yet meditated by the world at large, but skilfully forgot to mention my own qualifications.

On reading the letter over, I was astonished at the flattering nature of the result, and, with the buoyant pride of one who believes he has suddenly discovered a new resource in himself, I sent a copy of my application to Mary Taite.

She answered in the language of sorrowful reproach:

" Oh, S., how could you ! " I was forced to conclude that, as usual, I had somehow made a mis-step, and sought to conceal my mortification as best I might, by persuading myself and my friend that I had only regarded the matter as a joke all through. Nevertheless, I was bitterly disappointed.

What was my surprise, then, a few days afterwards, to receive this communication from the Superintendent of Schools:

" You are accepted to fill the position of teacher in the Kedarville school." Then followed terse directions as to the best way of reaching Kedarville, and, finally : " Mrs. Ithamer Spicer will board you for two dollars and fifty cents per week."

As I read this last clause everything that had made a sudden tumult in my mind before was lulled into a mysterious calm.

It was not the low value set upon the means of subsistence in Kedarville. Mercenary motives were, with me, as yet, out of the question. It was not the oppressive charm of Mrs. Ithamer Spicer's name that effected me so strangely.

It was the expressive combination of the whole, at once so clear cut and unique.

I murmured it softy to myself on my way home from the Post-Office.

" Han," said I, quite gravely, to my elder sister, on entering the house, " Mrs. Ithamer Spicer will board me for two dollars and fifty cents per week," and handed her the letter in pensive, though triumphant, confirmation of my words.

" When did you do this? " she gasped, and, before I could answer — " how are you going to get out of it? " she faintly demanded.

" Simply by getting into it, my dear," I answered, with that unyielding sweetness of demeanor for which I fancied I had ever been distinguished in the family circle.

I began to make my preparations for departure without delay.

Tender remonstrances, studied expostulations, were alike of no avail, and they helped me to pack, finally—

those dear good people at home — putting as brave a face as they could upon it, and hoping for the best.

My father assured my mother, though with trembling lip and tearful eye, that " God would temper the wind to the shorn lamb."

I smiled at the part I was meant to play in this cheerful allegory, though it seemed to me rather inappropriate, as I had a new sealskin cloak that very winter.

At the last, I gathered from the new and sprightlier form which the family submissiveness assumed, as well as from certain inadvertent disclosures of Bridget's, that I was confidently expected home again " in the course of a week or two." And I thereupon doubly confirmed myself in the resolve to see this thing through or die in the attempt.

I can not define the motives which actuated me at this time. They do not appear to have flowed in a clear and pellucid stream. I discover a thirst for the surprising and experimental, for situations, dilemmas, and emergencies, sustained by the most sublime recklessness as to consequences. Then I see a dread of sinking into humdrum — the impulse never to be at rest ; deeper than all this, I find a secret dissatisfaction with myself, a vague longing to use the best that is in me to some true purpose, a desire to leave the tangled skein, and " begin all over again."

It was early in January when I set out on my mission to the distant shores of Cape Cod. It was also, I remember, very early in the morning, and John Cable occupied a seat in the car. I had reason to know that John shared in the family disapproval of my sublime conduct. He sat, looking very glum, behind his paper, and appeared not to notice me when I came in.

Having finished reading his paper, he gnawed his moustache and gazed, still with glaring unconsciousness of my presence, out of the window. But as we neared Hartford, where I was to take the train for Boston, he came over to where I sat.

"I hope you 'll enjoy yourself at Sandy Creek, this winter," he said.

Now, I knew that John had designed this as sarcasm the most scathing, but he was himself conscious of failure, and the thought filled him with deeper gloom. He sought to reveal his baffled intentions in a scowl, which lent to his manly and intelligent features the darkness of spiritual night. And I replied, that "the recollection of his face, as it then appeared to me, would be, in itself, an inspiration through all the days to come."

There was silence for a space, and then John continued.

"Have you found it on the map, yet?"

"What, please?"

"Kedarville!" with bitter e nphasis.

"Oh! certainly not."

"It may be a little island out there somewhere, you know," delivered with the effect of a masterpiece.

"Yes; or a lighthouse, possibly."

I saw that John wished he had thought of that himself. He became dejected again. Then, presently, he threw off the cloak of bitterness which sat so ill on him, and, resuming his usual kindliness and benignity of manner, succeeded in making himself unconsciously tantalizing.

"If you do find it," he said, "and if you — if you conclude to stay for any length of time, I think I will go down sometime this winter and hunt you up."

"If you do, John Cable," I answered, with unaccountable warmth, " I 'll never forgive you as long as I live — never ! "

At Hartford, John took the train for Boston, too. We were very old friends. Latterly, we had read Shakespeare together at the Newton Literary Club. We concluded not to quarrel for the rest of the way. I had an influx of gay spirits, and John was almost without exception " nice."

There were several hours to wait in Boston before the train on the Old Colony Road would go out. We had dinner (I little realized how long it would be before I should eat again), and John tamely suggested driving about to look at some of the places of interest. I assured him that there was nothing so dispiriting as looking at places of interest, and he answered, cheerfully, after some moments of thought, that we could " shut our eyes when we went by them, then."

I had reason to dread a decline of spirits. Mine were rapidly on the wane. By the time we stopped at the Old Colony dépôt they were low, indeed. And the hardest of all was, that I would not, for my life, let my companion know. It was four o'clock in the afternoon, and already quite dark. The atmosphere was heavy and chill ; the sky ominous with clouds. I had an unknown journey yet to take in search of an unknown destination. The car into which I got on the Cape-bound train was dismal and weird-seeming enough.

" I wish, if you must go, you would let me see you to the end of this," said John.

I answered, laughing, with an unnecessary tinge of defiance in my tone. It would have been so much easier to have cried. I thought, " If John would only try to

look cross again !" as he did in the morning — anything
but that expression of grieved and compassionate disapproval with which he sat, talking so earnestly to me, for
the last few moments, in that dark car.   I thought he was
cruel.   He was trying to make me *think*, and I was trying
so hard *not* to think !   I felt a childish desire to scream
out.   Then, when the signal for starting rang, and John
took my hand an instant, in parting, looking down at me
with his kind, familiar eyes, the impulse swept up strong
within me to beg him to take me out of that dreadful car
and take me back home, and I would be good, oh, so good,
and " prosy," yes, and " humdrum," and never ask to
go on any more missions to forlorn pieces of land sticking
out into the water.

So there must have been a wild extravagance in the
airy recklessness of tone with which I bade John " good-
bye."   A sense of utter helplessness came over me as
as he turned and went out.

I observed, particularly, but two passengers in the car.
One was a man, very much bandaged as to his head, who
sat gazing into the coal stove, which occupied the centre
of the car, with weakly meditative, burnt-out eyes.   The
other was a girl, occupying the seat directly in front of
me.   She might have been nine years old, but she had a
singularly faded and mature countenance.   As the train
started, she turned to me with some excitement.

" There !" said she, pointing towards the window.
"your beau 's walking off I   He 's walking fast !   He
ain 't looking back ! "

"'Thank you," said I, in a low, expressionless tone, not
intended as an inducement to further conversation.

This girl had a parcel of confectionery, the con

tents of which she occasionally took out, and ranged in a row on the window ledge, selecting therefrom the smallest and least inviting fragment, and having eaten it with the hasty air of one who treats herself under protest to the luscious prerogatives of childhood, put the rest back in the paper bag, carefully replacing the string every time. She selected and handed to me the very largest specimen in her collection, which I had the gracelessness to refuse, though without show of disgust. Afterwards, she asked if she might come and sit in the seat with me. I thought she was very disagreeable. Besides, I was so miserable I wanted to commune apart with my own loneliness. However, I made room for her.

She proceeded to confide to me all of her past history. She was returning home from a visit to her aunt. Her mother had died a good many years ago, "when Johnnie was a mere baby." She "kept house for father and took care of Johnnie." She "tried hard not to have father feel his loss. It was very hard," she added, gravely, "for a man to be left alone so." She had bought a little book for Johnnie, but she never had much time to read ; besides, she was n't quick to learn. She could pick the words out, to be sure, but, somehow, it did n't make good sense, and would I read the book to her?

Oh to take counsel of my own despair ! How dark and wild it was growing outside ! Where was I going? whom should I meet there ?

And so I read, at the foot of gorgeously-illuminated pages, how

"Henny Penny and Ducky Lucky got started for the fair,
When Goosie Poosie and Turkey Lurkey went out to view the air,"

etc., the range of characters swiftly widening as the

narrative increased in power.   To my surprise, the mature
child listened to this nonsense with the utmost gravity and
interest.   No shadow of derision played on her attentive
features.   When I had finished — it was soon finished —
she said :

"Oh, that sounded so good; it made such good
sense," and sighed, very wistfully.

"Do you want me to read it again?" I exclaimed, in
despair.

Would I read it again? she asked.

I read it again.

After that she was silent and thoughtful for some time.
Then she said, looking gravely into my face :

" Do you love Jesus? "

" No, my dear," said I, surprised into much gentleness.

The faded blue eyes filled with tears.   She had no
notion of harrassing me on the subject, but spoke quietly
and at length of her own religious convictions.

The East wind crept in through the window, and once
my little companion shivered.   I noticed that she was
rather thinly clad.   I unstrapped my shawl and wrapped
it around her.   She let her head fall at my side, and went
to sleep.

Slowly, I was constrained to draw her up closer and
put my arm around her as support.   In so doing, I
received from some source an unaccountable strength and
calm of spirit.

At Braintree, which the child had told me was her
home, I woke her up, and she got off.

I was to stop at West Wallen, the railway station least
remote from Kedarville, and expected there to meet Mrs

Abagail Spicer, or some member of that mysterious family, to convey me to Wallencamp.

It seemed as though the train had had time to travel the whole interminable length of the Cape and plunge off into the ocean beyond, when, in fact, we were just entering upon that peculiar body of land at West Wallen.

There was no one there to meet me. The little dépôt was held by a strange night brigade of boys and girls, playing "blind-man's buff." They shouted like cannibals, and bore down on all opposing objects with resistless force. I did not attempt an entrance. A rough, good-natured looking man stood on the platform outside.

I put on my glasses (I was sadly and unaffectedly near-sighted), and having further assured myself of his seeming honesty, enquired if there was such a place as Kedarville in the vicinity.

"Waal, no, miss, thar' ain 't," said he, with a noon-day smile, which informed me that there was yet something to hope for. "Thar 's no Kedar*ville* that I know on. Thar 's a Wallencamp some miles up yender. We do n't often tackle no Sunday go-to-meeting names on to it, but I reckon, maybe, it 's the same your alookin' for."

He had spoken with such startling indefiniteness of the distance that I asked him how far it was to Wallencamp.

"Waal, thar' you 've got me," said he, beaming on me in a broadly complimentary way, as though I had actually circumvented him in some skilful play at words. "Fact is, thar' ain't never been no survey run down in that direction that I know on. We call it four miles, more or less. That 's Cape Cod measure — means most any-thin' lineal measure. Talkin' 'bout Cape Cod miles," he continued, with an irresistible air of raillery. "Little

2

Bachelder Rae lives up thar' to Wallencamp, and they do n't have no church nor nothin' thar'; so Bachelder and some on 'em, they come up here, once in a while, tu Sunday-school. Deacon Lancy, he 'd rather see the Old Boy comin' into Sunday-school class any time than Bachelder, for he 's quiet, the little bachelder is, but dry as a herrin'. So the Deacon thought he 'd stick him on distances. The Deacon is a great stickle ·on distances

" ' How fur, Bachelder,' says he, ' did Adam and Eve go when they was turned out of the garden of Eden?' says he.

" ' Wall,' says Bachelder, coughing a little, so — that 's Bachelder's way o' talking — ' we have sufficient reason to cenfer, Deacon, that, in all probabeelity, they went a *Ceape Cod mile.*' "

My informant's delight at this reminiscence was huge. It yielded to a more subdued sense of the ludicrous when I asked him if there was any public conveyance to Wallencamp He made a polite effort to restrain his mirth, but the muscles of his face twitched violently.

" Wall, no, miss," said he, " we do n't run no reg'lar express up to Wallencamp; might be a vary healthy oc'pation, but not as lukertive as some, I reckon — not as lukertive as pickin' 'tater bugs : that 's what they do, mostly, down thar'. Fact is, miss," he concluded, with considerable gravity, " we do n't vary often go down to Wallencamp unless we 're obliged to."

On my proposing to make it lucrative, he immediately called, in a loud voice, to one of the playful occupants of the dépôt :

" Hi, thar ! 'Rasmus ! 'Rasmus ! Here 's a lady wants

to be conveyed down to Wallencamp ; you run home and tackle, now ! You be lively, now ! "

'Rasmus was lively. In a very few moments something of an unusual and ghostly appearance — so much only I could discover of what afterwards became a very familiar sort of vehicle — was waiting for me alongside the platform. The only means of getting into it was through an opening directly in front. Towards this I was encouraged to climb over the thills, but met with an obstacle, in the form of my trunk, which seemed effectually to block up the entrance.

"Thar', now ! I told ye so," exclaimed one of the bystanders, a large number of whom mysteriously gathered about the scene. " You 'd orter got *her* in first."

A disconsolate silence prevailed. The trunk had been elevated to its present position through the most painful exertions.

" Perhaps I can climb over it," I said, and bravely made the attempt.

No one knew in the voiceless darkness, of the suddenly helpless and collapsed condition in which I landed on the other side. I groped about for a seat and finally succeeded in finding one at the extreme rear of the vehicle.

'Rasmus drove. He was situated somewhere, somehow — I could not tell where nor how — in the realm of vacancy on the other side of the trunk ; I only know that he seemed a long way off.

Under these circumstances, conversation was rendered extremely difficult. I learned that Mr. Ithamer Spicer was away at sea ; that Mrs. Ithamer Spicer lived at the

Ark, with Cap'n and Grandma Spicer, and the two little Spicers.

'Rasmus was the unmistakable son of his father.

"And it ain't no *got-up* ark, neither ! " he yelled at me, in a tone which pierced through the distance and the darkness, and every intervening obstacle. " It 's the reg'lar old *Ark !* It 's what Noer, and the elephant, and them fellows come over in ! "

I did not wonder, as we journeyed on, that my inform- ant of the dépôt platform had used his "ups" and "downs" indiscriminately in indicating the direction of Wallencamp·

In the inky blackness by which I was surrounded I was conscious, clearly, of but one sensation—that of going *up* and *down*. The rumbling of the wheels reached me as something far off and indefinably dreadful.

Then we stopped, and I crawled out like one in a dream. There was no light at the Ark to make it a dis- tinguishable feature of the gloom. 'Rasmus found the door and knocked loudly. I became dimly conscious of the knocking, and followed 'Rasmus.

" I reckon they 're to bed," said he, and knocked louder.

Pretty soon a clear, feminine voice, startled into musical sharpness, issued from a room quite near, with,— " Who 's there ? " and was followed by two small, squeal- ing voices, in unison,— " Who 's there ? "

Then other sounds arose — sounds from some quarter mysterious and remote — a low, mumbling, comfortable refrain, and ominous snatches of an uneasy grumble ; then a roar that shook the Ark to its foundations :—

"Who the devil 's making such a rumpus out there at this time in the mornin'?" (It was nine o'clock P. M.)

'Rasmus sent back an intrepid yell:

"It 's the *tea-cher!* It 's pretty late," he said, aside, to me. "I guess I won't go in. I reckon they won't have much style on. I seen ye pay father; that 's all right. I 'll tip yer trunk up under the shed, and the old Cap'n 'll see to gettin' it in in the mornin'. Here 's a letter the postmaster sent down to the Cap'n's folks. Good night."

'Rasmus, my only hope! I made a convulsive grasp for him in the darkness, but he was gone.

It was she of the soothing, comfortable voice who took me in; and Grandma Spicer's *taking in* I understand always in the divinest and fullest sense of the term.

Further than that, I was conscious that there were white-robed and night-capped figures moving about the room.

So unearthly was their appearance, that I had, at last, a confused notion of having become disengaged from the entanglements of the flesh, and fallen in with a small planetary system in the course of my wanderings through space. The centre of attraction seemed to be a table, to which the figures were constantly bringing more *pies.*

The letter which 'Rasmus had directed me to hand to the "folks" was read with interest, being the one I had dispatched from Newton, a week or two before, informing them as to the time of my arrival.

Abagail rendered the brief and business-like epistle with the full effect of her peculiarly thrilling intonation, and Grandma listened with rapt attention; but, meanwhile, Grandpa Spicer and the two little Spicers found time surreptitiously to dispose of nearly a whole pie, with the serious aspect of those who will not allow a mere fleeting diversion to hinder them in the improvement of a rare opportunity.

Having declined to partake of pie, through Grandma Spicer's kind interposition, I was not further urged.

"Thar', poor darlin'," said she, "fix her up a good cup o' your golden seal, pa, and she shall go to bed right in the parlor to-night, seein' as we did n't get the letter and hain't got her room fixed upstairs. It's all nice and warm, and thar', darlin', thar', we 're r'al good for nussin' folks up."

In the parlor, I saw only one great, delicious object — a bed. My weary brain hardly exaggerated its dimensions, which could not have failed to strike with astonishment even the most indifferent observer. It was long; it was broad; it was deep; and, alas! it was high. I disrobed as best I might, and stood before it, gazing despairingly up at its snowy summit.

Then, remembering my experience with the trunk, I approached at one extreme, scaled the headboard, fell over into an absorbing sea of feathers, and, at that very instant it seemed, the perplexing nature of mortal affairs ceased to burden my mind.

CHAPTER II.

I BLOW THE HORN.

ORNING dawned on my mission to Wallencamp. My wakening was not an enthusiastic one. Slowly, my bewildered vision became fixed on an object on the wall opposite, as the least fantastic amid a group of objects. It was a sketch, in water colors, of a woman in an expansive hoop and a skirt of brilliant hue flounced to the waist. She stood, with a singularly erect and dauntless front, over a grave on which was written "Consort." I observed, with a child-like wonder, which concealed no latent vein of criticism, the glowing carmine of her cheeks, the unmixed blue of her pupilless eyes, from a point exactly in the centre of which a geometric row of tears curved to the earth. A weeping-willow — somewhat too green, alas ! — drooped with evident reluctance over the scene, but cast no shade on its contrasting richness. The title of the piece was "*Bereavement.*" By some strange means, it served as the pole-star to my wandering thoughts.

As I gazed and wondered, my life took on again a definite form and purpose. The events of the preceding

day rose in gradual succession before me, and I proceeded
to descend from the heights I had scaled the night before.

I looked at my watch.   It was eight o'clock, and school
should begin at nine.   Yet the occasion witnessed no
feverish display of haste on my part.   I saw that the
difficulties which I was destined to endure in the performance of my toilet that morning called either for
philosophy or madness.   I chose philosophy.

The portion of the Ark surrounding my bed was cut
up into little recesses, crannies, nooks,— used, presumably,
for storing the different pairs of animals in the trying
events which preceded the Flood.   In one of these, I
had a dim recollection of having secreted my clothes, in
the disordered condition of my brain the night before.
So I cast desultory glances about me for these articles on
the way, having first set out on a search for a looking-
glass.   In one dark recess I came into forcible contact with a hanging shelf of pies.   I thought what a
moment that would have been for Grandpa Spicer and
the little Spicers ! but I had been brought up on hygienic,
as well as moral, principles, and moved away without a
sigh.   In another sequestered nook, I paused with a sinful
mixture of curiosity and delight before a Chinese idol
standing alone on a pedestal.   .

There was a strangeness and a newness about things at
the Ark that began to be exhilarating.   I was reminded,
in a negative sort of way, that I had intended to begin
my work on this new day with a prayer to the true God
for strength and assistance.   I had found it necessary to
make this resolve because, although I had a " fixed habit
of prayer," it was reserved rather for occasions of special

humiliation than resorted to as an everyday indulgence ; practically, I had wellnigh dispensed with it altogether.

However, I started back in an intently serious frame of mind to find my couch. I lost my way, and stumbling against a swinging door which opened into a comparatively spacious apartment, what was my joy to discover my trunk, with the portmanteau containing my keys on top of it.

I then proceeded to array myself with an absorbing ardor and devotion, doing my hair before a hand-glass with rare resignation of spirit. I began to feel more and more like an incorporated existence, and admitted a sudden eagerness to join the Spicer family at breakfast.

I had no hesitation which direction to take, being guided by the sound of voices and wafts of penetrating odors.

It was a fortunate direction, for I discovered on the way my lost apparel artfully concealed under a small melodeon, and, strangely enough, I was again brought face to face with my deserted couch and the weeping lady on the wall. She held me a moment with the old fascination. As I put up my glasses, I thought I detected in her face a hitherto unnoticed buoyancy of expression ; and not having wholly escaped in my life from ideas of a worldly nature, I reflected that, probably, her regretted consort had left her with a sufficient number of thousands.

In this same connection, I was reminded that I, myself, had started out on an independent career, and wondered if it would be unkind or undutiful in me to start a private bank account of my own. I concluded that it would not.

When I entered the little room where the Spicer family was assembled :

"Why, here 's our teacher!" exclaimed Grandma Spicer in accents of delight, and came to meet me with outstretched arms. "We could n't abear to wake ye up, dearie," she went on, "knowin' ye was so tired this mornin'; and there 's plenty o' time — plenty o' time. My Casindana come home!" she murmured, with a smile and a tremble of the lips, and a far-away look, for the instant, in her gentle eyes.

In fact, the whole Spicer family received me with outstretched arms. If I had been a long-lost child, or a friend known and loved in days gone by, I could not have been more cordially and enthusiastically welcomed.

The best chair was set for me; glances of eager and enquiring interest were bent upon me.

I accepted it all coolly, though not without a certain air of affability, too, for I had a natural desire to make myself agreeable to people, when it was n't too much trouble; but I was quite firm, at this time, in the conviction that there was little or no faith to be put in human nature. On the whole, I was much entertained and interested.

The two children came to climb into my lap; but this part of the acquaintance did not progress very fast. I thought they must have been struck by something in my eye (I was merely wondering abstractedly if their heads were not out of proportion to the rest of their bodies), for they paused, and Mrs. Ithamer called them away sharply.

Mrs. Ithamer was a frail little woman — she could not have been over thirty or thirty-two years old,— not pretty, though she had a very airy and graceful way of comporting herself. Her eyes were large and dark, with a strange, melancholy gleam in them.

I never knew the secrets of Mrs. Ithamer's heart. She had often a tired, tense look about the mouth, and seemed often sorely discontent; but she had the sweetest voice I ever heard. She was familiarly called Abagail.

Grandpa or Cap'n Spicer was over eighty years old. He had a tall, powerful frame — at least, it spoke of great power in the past — and I thought his eye must have been uncommonly dark and keen once.

From his manly irascibility of temperament and his frequent would-be authoritativeness of tone, one might have inferred, from a passing glimpse, that Grandpa Spicer was something of a tyrant in the family; but I soon learned that his sway was of an extremely vague and illusory nature.

Grandma Spicer was twenty years his junior. She had not married him until she was herself quite advanced in life, and had had one husband.

"To be sure," I heard her say once, "I ain't quite so far advanced as husband, but, then, it do n't make no difference how young the girl is, you know."

She used to sit down and laugh — one of Grandma's "r'al good laughs" was incompatible with a standing posture — until the tears rolled down her cheeks, and she had to wipe them off with the corner of her apron.

She had been thrown from a wagon once — how often and thrillingly have I heard dear Grandma Spicer relate the particulars of that accident! She had broken at that time, I believe, nearly every bone in her body. Long was the story of her fall, but longer still the tale of her recuperation.

In due course of time, she had grown together again; could now use all her limbs, and was in superabundant flesh. There was an unnatural sort of stiffness about her movements, however, her way of walking particularly. She advanced but slowly, and allowed her weight to fall from one foot to another without any perceptible bend of any joint whatever.

I have stood at one end of a room and seen Grandma Spicer approaching from the other, when it seemed as though she was not making any progress at all, but merely going through with an odd sort of balancing process in order to maintain her equilibrium.

As for Grandma Spicer's face, there was enough in it to make several ordinary scrimped faces. Besides large physical proportions, there was enough in it of generosity, enough of whole-heartedness, a world of sympathy. The great catastrophe of her life had affected the muscles of her face so that although she enunciated her words very distinctly, she had a slow, automatic way of moving her lips.

The room where the breakfast table was set was the same that I had entered first, on my arrival at Wallen -camp. It was low and small, but capable, as I learned afterward, of holding any amount of things and people without ever seeming crowded. There was a cooking stove in it, and many other articles of modest worth, so artlessly scattered about as to present a scene of the wildest and richest profusion.

Art was not entirely wanting, however. There was a ray of it on the wall behind the stove pipe, the com-panion-piece to " Bereavement," entitled " Joy," and represented my heroine of the bed-chamber, reclining on a rustic bench in rather an unflounced and melancholy condition. In one place there hung a yellow family register, which was kept faithfully supplied from week to week with a wreath of fresh evergreens. It was headed by a wood cut representing a funeral, Grandma Spicer said, but Grandpa Spicer afterwards informed me, aside, with much solemnity, that it was a "marriage ceremony." Near the foot of the list of births, marriages and deaths, I saw "Casindana Spicer; died, aged twenty."

We sat down at the table. There was a brief altercation between Dinslow and Grace, the little Spicers, in which impromptu missiles, such as spoons and knives and small tin cups were hurled across the table with unguided wrath, and both infants yelled furiously.

Grandma had nearly succeeded in quieting them, when Abagail remarked to Grandpa Spicer in her lively and flippant style,

"Come, pa, say your piece."

"How am I going to say anything?" enquired Grandpa, wrathfully, "in such a bedlam?"

"Thar, now, thar!" said Grandma Spicer, in her soothing tone, "It's all quiet now and time we was eatin' breakfast, so ask the blessin' pa, and do n't let's have no more words about it."

Whereupon the old sea-captain bowed his head, and, with a decided touch of asperity still lingering in his voice, sped through the lines :

> "God bless the food which now we take,
> May it do us good, for Jesus' sake."

"Now, Dinnie," said Grandma Spicer, beguilingly, but it was not until after much coaxing and threatening and the promise of a spoonful of sugar when it was over, that Dinslow was induced to solicit the same blessing, in

the same poetical terms, and with an expedition still
more alarming.

Then Gracie, with tears not yet dried from the late
conflict, lifted up her voice in a rapture of miniature
delight, " Dinnie says, ' gobble the food ' ! Dinnie says,
' gobble the food ! ' "

" Did n't say ' gobble the food ! ' " exclaimed Dinslow,
blacker than a little thunder cloud.

Abagail anticipated the rising storm, and stamped
her foot and cried,

" *Will* you be still ? "

It was Grandma Spicer, who quietly and adroitly restored peace to the troubled waters.

The Wallencampers including the Spicer family, were
not accustomed to speak of bread as a compact and
staple article of food, but rather as one of the hard means
of sustaining existence represented by the term " hunks."
At the table, it was not " will you pass me the bread ? "
but — and I shall never forget the sweet tunefulness of
Abagail 's tone, in this connection,— " Will you hand me
a hunk ? "

The hunks were an unleavened mixture of flour and
water, of about the size and consistency of an ordinary
laborer's fist.

I was impressed, in first sitting down at the Spicers'
table, with a sense of my own ignorance as to the most
familiar details of life, but soon learned to speak confidently of " hunks," and " fortune stew," and " slit herrin',"
and " golden seal."

Fortune stew was a dish of small, round, blue potatoes,
served perfectly whole in a milk gravy.

I cherish the memory of this dish as sacred, as well as

that of all the other dishes that ever appeared on the Wallencamp table. They were the products of faithful and loving hands to which nature had given a peculiar direction, perhaps, but which strove always to the best of their ability.

Slit herrin' was a long, dried, deep-salted edition of the native alewife, a fish in which Wallencamp abounded. They hung in massive tiers from the roofs of the Wallen camp barns. The herrin' was cut open, and without having been submitted to any mollifying process whatever, not one assuaging touch of its native element, was laid flat in the spider, and fried.

I saw the Spicer family, from the greatest to the least, partake of this arid and rasping substance unblinkingly, and I partook also. The brine rose to my eyes and coursed its way down my cheeks, and Grandma Spicer said I was " homesick, poor thing ! "

The golden seal, a " remedy for toothache, headache, sore-throat, sprains, etc., etc.," was served in a diluted state with milk and sugar, and taken as a beverage. The herrin' had destroyed my sense of taste ; any thing in a liquid state was alike delectable to me, and while I drank, I had a sense of having become somehow mysteriously connected with the book of Revelations. " We used to think," Grandma proceeded mildly to elucidate, " that it had ought to be took externally, but husband, he was painin' around one time, and nothin' did n't seem to do him no good, and so we ventured some of it inside of him, and he did n't complain no more for a great while afterwards." I appreciated the hidden meaning of these words when I saw how sparingly Grandpa Spicer partook of the golden seal. " So then we tried some of it ourselves, and ra'ly begun to like it, so we 've got into the habit of drinkin' it along through the winter, it's so quietin' and may not be no special need of it, so far as we can see, but then, it's allus well enough to be on the safe side, for there's no knowin'," concluded Grandma, solemnly, "what disease may be a growin' up inside of you.

"My brother invented on 't," said Grandpa Spicer, looking up at me from under his shaggy eyebrows with questionable pride. He went on more glowingly, however, "There's a picter of my brother on every bottle, teacher." (Abagail immediately ran from her chair, went into an adjoining room and brought out a bottle to show me.) "Ye see, he used to wear them air long ringlets, though he was a powerful man, John was; but his hair curled as pretty as a girl's. Oh, he was a great dandy, John was; a great dandy." Grandpa Spicer straightened himself up and his eyes brightened preceptibly.

"Never wore nothin' but the finest broad-cloth; why, there 's a pair of black broad-cloth pants o' his 'n that you 'll see, come Sunday, teacher!"

"Wall thar now, pa," said Grandma Spicer, reprovingly, "I would n't tell everything."

"Le' me see," continued Grandpa, "I had eight brothers, teacher, yis, yis, there was nine boys in all," nodding his head emphatically, and proceeding to count on his fingers.

Grandma Spicer laid her knife and fork aside, as though she felt that the occasion was an important one, and that she had a grave duty to perform in regard to it.

"Thar was Philemon, he comes first, that makes one, do n't it? and there was Doddridge—"

" Sure **he comes next**, pa?" interposed Grandma, "for now you air namin' of 'em, you might as well git 'em right."

" Yis, yis, ma," replied the old man, hastily. "Then there was Winfield and John, they 're all dead now, and Bartholomew, he was first mate in a sailin' vessel, fine man, Bartholomew was, fine man ; he—"

" Wall, thar now," said Grandma," you 'll never git through namin' on 'em, pa, if you stop to talk about 'em."

" Yis, yis," continued Grandpa, hopelessly confused, and showing dark symptoms of smouldering wrath, "there was Bartholomew. That makes a, — le' me see, Bartholomew, — "

" How many Bartholomews was there?" enquired Grandma, with pitiless coolness of demeanor.

" Thar, now, ma, ye 've put me all out !" cried Grandpa, taking refuge in loud and desperate reproach, "I was gittin' along first-rate, why could n't ye a kept still and let me reckoned 'em through? "

" Yer mus n't blame me, pa, 'cause yer ca' n't carry yer own brothers in yer head." There was a touch of gentle reproach in Grandma's calm voice. "Why, there was my mother's cousin 'Statia, that was only second cousin to me, and no relation at all, on my father's side, and she had thirteen children, three of 'em was twins and one of 'em was thrins, and I could name 'em all through, and tell you what year they was born, and what day, and who vaccinated 'em. There was Amelia Day, she was born April ninth, eighteen hundred and seventeen, Doctor Sweet vaccinated her, and it took in five days." And so on Grandma went through the entire list, gradually going more and more into particulars, but always coming out strong on the main facts.

The effect could not have failed to deepen in Grandpa's bosom a mortifying sense of his own incompetency.

When I got up from the Spicers' breakfast table there was something choking me besides the herrin' and golden seal, and it was not homesickness, either; but as I stepped out of Mrs. Ithamer's low door into the light and air, all lesser impulses were forgotten in a sudden glow and thrill of exultation. I wondered if that far, intense blue was the natural color of the Cape Cod sky in winter, and if its January sun always showered down such rich and golden beams. There was no snow on the ground; the fields presented an almost spring-like aspect, in contrast with the swarthy green of the cedars. The river ran sparkling in summer-fashion at the foot of "Eagle Hill." From the bay, the sea air came up fresh and strong. I drank it with deep inspirations. At that moment it seemed to me that I had indeed been born to perform a mission. It was so hopeful to turn over an entire fresh leaf in the book of life, and I was resolved to do it heroically, at any cost. I reflected, not without a shade of annoyance, that I had forgotten to say my prayers, after all. At the same time I had a sort of conviction that it was n't so unfortunate a remissness on my part as it would have been for some less qualified by nature to take care of themselves.

I discovered the school-house at the end of the lane. The general air of the Wallencamp houses was stranded and unsettled, as though, detained in their present position for some brief and restless season, they dreamed ever of unknown voyages yet to be made on the sea of life. They were very poor, very old. Some of them were painted red in front, some of them had only a red door, being otherwise quite brown and unadorned. There was one exception, — Emily Gaskell's — that stood on the hill, and was painted all over and had green blinds.

I heard a mighty rushing sound mingled with whoops and yells and the terrible clamp of running feet, and was made aware that a detachment from my flock was coming up the lane to meet me.

A girl, taller than I, with stooping shoulders and a piquant and good natured cast of features, seized my hand and swung it in childish and confiding fashion. She had warts. I wondered, uneasily, if they would be contagious through my gloves.

I was struck with the uncommon beauty of one sturdy little fellow. He was barefooted (on Cape Cod, in January), and ragged enough to have satisfied the most crazy devotee of the picturesque. His shapely head was set on his shoulders in an exceedingly high-bred way, while its bad archangel effect was intensified by rings of curling black hair and great, seductive black eyes.

The children walked back, in comparative quiet, toward the school house, except the boy. To him care was evidently a thing unknown. He managed, while keeping the distance undiminished between himself and me, to perform a great variety of antics, in which, by way of an occasional relief, his head was seen to rise above his heels.

Emily's wash had been left out to dry during the night. The wind had torn various articles from the line and carried them down in the direction of the lane fence.

My gymnastic performing imp vanished through the bars. In an incredibly short space of time he reappeared clothed—but, alas ! I cannot tell how the imp was clothed, except to say that Emily being a tall woman and the imp but a well grown boy of ten, the effect was voluminous, and oriental.

This part of the lane was marked by some insignificant though very abrupt depressions and elevations of the surface. Occasionally he of the floating apparel was lost to sight ; then he would appear all glorious on some small height, while the mind was compelled to revert irreverently to the picture of Moses on Mt. Pisgah. He was the personification of impudence, withal, looking back and showing his teeth in superlative appreciation of his own sinfulness. He descended, and I looked to see him arise again, but I saw him no more.

I had a faint and fleeting vision, afterwards, of an apostolic figure flying back across the fields. It was so indistinct as to remain only among the ephemera of my fancy.

In a fork of the roads, opposite the school-house, stood a house with a red door. It was loaded, in summer with honeysuckle vines. Aunt Pucinda sat always at the window. Sometimes she had the asthma and sometimes she sang. This morning, her favorite refrain from the Moody & Sankey Hymnal was wafted in loud accents up the lane :

> "Dar' to be a Danyell !
> Dar' to be a Danyell !
> Dar' to make it known ! "

As I entered the school-house, the inspiring strains still followed me.

There was a large Franklin stove within, which exhibited the most enormous draught power, emitting sparks and roaring in a manner frightful to contemplate.

Aunt Patty, who acted the part of janitoress of the

school-house at night and morning, had written on the blackboad in a large admonitory hand, "No spitting on this floor, you ninnies!"

The bench, containing the water pail, occupied the most central position in the room. At one side of the bench hung a long handled tin dipper; on the other, another tin instrument, resembling an ear trumpet, profoundly exaggerated in size.

"That's what you 've got to blow to call us in," exclaimed a small child, with anticipative enlivenment.

I went to the door with the instrument.

"Dar' to be a Danyell!
Dar' to make it known."

The stirring measures came across from Aunt Pucinda's window. Then the singer paused.

There were other faces at other windows. The countenances of the boys and girls gathered about the door were ominously expressive. I lifted the horn to my lips. I blew upon it what was intended for a cheerful and exuberant call to duty, but to my chagrin it emitted no sound, whatever. I attempted a gentle, soul-stirring strain; it was as silent as the grave. I seized it with both hands and, oblivious to the hopeful derision gathering on the faces of those about me, I breathed into it all the despair and anguish of my expiring breath. It gave forth a hollow, soulless and lugubrious squeak, utterly out of proportion to the vital force expended, yet I felt that I had triumphed, and detected a new expression of awe and admiration on the faces of my flock.

"I do n't see how she done it," I heard one freckled-faced boy exclaim, confidingly to another, "with a hull button in thar."

"Who put the button in the horn?" I enquired of the

youngster, afterwards, quite in a pleasant tone, and with a smile on which I had learned to depend for a particularly delusive effect; at the same time I put up my glasses to impress him with a sense of awe.

"Simmy B.," he answered.

"And which is Simmy B.?" I questioned, glancing about the school room.

"Oh, he ain't comin' in," gasped my informer, "he run over cross-lots with Emily's clo's on."

I had planned not to confine my pupils to the ordinary method of imbibing knowledge through the medium of text books, but by means of lectures, which should be interspersed with lively anecdotes and rich with the fruitful products of my own experience, to teach them.

My first lecture was, quite appropriately, on the duty of close application and faithful persistence in the acquisition of knowledge, depicting the results that would inevitably accrue from the observance of such a course, and, here glowing and dazzled by my theme, I even secretly regretted that modesty forbade me to recommend to my pupils, as a forcible illustration, one who occupied so conspicuous a position before them.

My new method of instruction, though not appreciated perhaps, in its intrinsic design, was received, I could not but observe, with the most unbounded favor.

After the first open-mouthed surprise had passed away from the countenances of my audience, I was loudly importuned on all sides for water. I was myself extravagantly thirsty. I requested all those who had "slit herrin'" for breakfast to raise their hands.

Every hand was raised.

I gravely enquired if slit herrin' formed an ordinary or

accustomed repast in Wallencamp, and was unanimously assured in the affirmative.

After dwelling briefly on the gratitude that should fill our hearts in view of the unnumbered blessings of Providence, I inaugurated a system by which a pail of fresh water was to be drawn from one of the neighboring wells, and impartially distributed among the occupants of the school-room, once during each successive hour of the day. The water was to be passed about in the tin dipper, in an orderly manner, by some member of the flock, properly appointed to that office, either on account of general excellence or some particular mark of good behavior, though I afterwards found it advisable not to insist on any qualifications of this sort, but to elect the water-bearers merely according to their respective rank in age. This really proved to be one of the most lively and interesting exercises of the school, was always cheerfully undertaken, executed in the most complete and faithful manner, and never on any account forgotten or omitted.

I drank, and continued my lecture, but the first look of attractive surprise never came back to the faces of my audience. They sought diversion in a variety of ways, acquitting themselves throughout with a commendable degree of patience until they found it necessary gently to admonish me that it was time for recess.

After recess, as the result of deep meditation, in which I had concluded that the mind of the Wallencamp youth was not yet prepared for the introduction of new and advanced methods, I examined my pupils preparatory to giving them lessons and arranging them in classes, in the ordinary way. I found that they could not read, but they could write in a truly fluent and unconventional style;

They could not commit prosaical facts to memory, but they could sing songs containing any number of irrelevant stanzas. They could not cipher, but they had witty and salient answers ready for any emergency. There seemed to be no particular distinction among them in regard to the degree of literary attainment, so I arranged them in classes, with an eye mainly to the novel and picturesque in appearance.

They were a little disappointed at the turn in affairs, having evidently anticipated much from the continuation of the lecture system, yet they were disposed to look forward to school-life, in any case, as not without its ameliorating conditions.

CHAPTER III.

"WE have our r'al, good, comfortin' meal, at night," Grandma Spicer had said, and the thought was uppermost in my mind at the close of my first day's labor in Wallencamp. I had taken a walk to the beach, a strong east wind had come up, and the surf was rolling in magnificently; a wild scene, from a wild shore, more awful then, in the gathering gloom. The long rays of light streaming out of the windows of the Ark, guided me back across the fields. Within, all was warmth and cheer and festive expectation. Grandma Spicer was in such spirits; a wave of mirthful inspiration would strike her, she would sink into a chair, the tears would roll down her cheeks, and she would shake with irrepressible laughter. It was in one of her serious moments that she said to me:

"Thar, teacher, I actually believe that I ain't made you acquainted with my two tea-kettles." They stood side by side on the stove, one very tall and lean, the other very short and plump. "This 'ere," said Grandma, pointing to the short one, "is Rachel, and this 'ere," pointing to the tall one, "is Abigail, and Abigail's a graceful creetur' to be sure," Grandma reflected admiringly, "but then, Rachel has the most powerful delivery!"

I was thus enabled to understand the allusions I had already heard to Rachel's being " dry," or Abigail's being as " full as a tick," or *vice versa*.

The table was neatly spread with a white cloth ; there was an empty bowl and a spoon at each individual's place. In the centre of the table stood a pitcher of milk and a bowl of sugar. Grandpa Spicer having asked the blessing after the approved manner of the morning, there was a general uprising and moving, bowl in hand, towards the cauldron of hulled corn on the stove. This was lively, and there was a pleasurable excitement about skimming the swollen kernels of corn out of the boiling, seething liquid in which they were immersed. Eaten afterwards with milk and sugar and a little salt, the compound became possessed of a truly " comforting " nature.

I stood, for the second time, over the kettle with my eye-glasses securely adjusted, very earnestly and thoughtfully occupied in wielding the skimmer, when the door of the ark suddenly opened and a mischievously smiling young man appeared on the threshold. He was not a Wallencamper, I saw at a glance. There was about him an unmistakable air of the great world. He was fashionably dressed and rather good looking, with a short upper lip, and a decided tinge of red in his hair. He stood staring at me with such manifest appreciation of the situation in his laughing eyes, that I felt a barbarous impulse to throw the skimmer of hot corn at him. It was as though some flimsy product of an advanced civilization had come in to sneer at the sacred customs of antiquity.

"I beg your pardon," the intruder began, addressing the Spicer family with exceeding urbanity of voice and manner, " I fear that I have happened in rather inoppor-

tunely, but I dared not of course transgress our happy
Arcadian laws by knocking at the door."

"Oh, Lordy, yis, yis, and the fewer words the better.
You know our ways by this time, fisherman," exclaimed
Grandpa Spicer. "Come in ! come in ! Nobody that
calls me friend need knock at my door."

"Come in ! come in, fisherman ! Won't you set, fisherman?" hospitably chimed in Grandma Spicer.

"Ah, thank you ! may I consider your kind invitation
deferred, merely," said the fisherman, suavely, "and
excuse me if I introduce a little matter of business with
the Captain. We carelessly left our oars on the banks,
yesterday, Captain Spicer, they were washed off, I have
ordered some more, but can't get them by to-morrow. I
hear you have a pair laid by, I should like to purchase."

"What, is it the old oars ye want?" interrupted Grandpa, "why, Lord a massy ! you know whar they be, fisherman, alongside that old pile o' rubbish on hither side o'
the barn, and do n't talk about purchasin'—take 'em and
keep 'em as long as ye want, they ain't no account to me,
now."

" I am very much obliged to you, Captain," the fisherman said, "I am very sorry to have interrupted this
— a —"

"Why, no interruption, I 'm sure," said Grandma Spicer,
good naturedly, " we 've kep' right along eatin'."

"Want a lantern to look for 'em, eh?" enquired
Grandpa Spicer, for the fisherman lingered, hesitating,
on the threshold.

"'This is our teacher, fisherman," said Grandma, in her
gentle, tranquilizing tones, "and this 'ere is one of

Emily's fishermen, teacher, and may the Lord bless ye in
yer acquaintance," she added with simple fervor.

The fisherman saluted me with a bow which reflected
great credit on his former dancing-master. He murmured the polite formula in a low tone, at the same time
shooting another covertly laughing glance at me out of
his eyes. As the door closed behind him, " Ah, that 's
a sleek devil ! " said Grandpa Spicer, giving me a meaning
glance from under his shaggy eyebrows.

" Wall thar now, pa, I would n't blaspheme, not if
I 'd made the professions you have," said Grandma, with
grave reproval.

" A sleek dog," continued Grandpa Spicer, " tongue
as smooth as butter, all ' how d' yer do ! ' and ' how
d' yer do ! ' but I do n't trust them fishermen much,
myself, teacher."

" Who are the fishermen ? " I enquired.

" They board up to Emily's," said Grandma. " They
come from Providence and around, and they stay here off
and on, a week or two to time, along through the winter,
some of 'em. They fish pickerel on the river, and sometimes they 're blue fishin' out in the bay, and quite
generally they 're just kitin' round as young men will, I
suppose. Sometimes they have vittles sent to 'em, and
Emily she cooks for 'em."

" Why, they 're off on a spree, that 's all," said Grandpa
Spicer, comprehensively, giving me another significant
glance, " they 're off on a spree, and ye see, they think
this 'ere is jest a right fur enough out the way place for
'em. This 'ere red haired one that was in here this
evenin', Turner, his name is, he 's a dreadful rich one, I
suppose, dreadful rich ! I 've heered all about him.

He 's an old bachelder, I reckon, that is, he keeps mighty spruce, but I reckon he 's hard on to thirty. Emily's got a cousin that works for some 'o them big folks down to Providence, and she 's heered all about him, this red-haired one, and how he keeps a big house down thar, and sarvants enough, massy! and half the time he 's hither and yon and a throwin' out money like water. His father and mother they 're dead, so I 've heered, and he used to have gardeens over him, but he haint kep' no gardeens lately, I reckon," said Grandpa, with grim facetiousness.

"Why, he's been a waitin' on Bede's daughter, down here—Ethel. She goes to school to you, teacher," the old man added, presently, brightening with a senile predilection for gossip.

"Ethel's a very sensible girl," said Grandma Spicer, "and don't cast no sheep's eyes, but goes right along and minds her own business. Ethel plays very purty on the music, too."

"Yes. But you know Eliot Turner wouldn't any more think of marrying Ethel Kent than he would of marrying me," cried Mrs. Ithamer. "Of all the fishermen that have come down here, not one of them ever married in Wallencamp. He's just trifling, and she thinks he's in real earnest; anybody can see that. You've only to mention his name to see her flush up as red as a rose. I tell you this is a strange world," Abagail snapped out, sharply, "and Eliot Turner, I suppose, is one of the gentlemen."

"We ain't no right to say but what he's honest," said Grandma Spicer, " Ethel she's honest herself, and she takes it in other folks. She's more quiet than some of our girls be, and higher notions, and she's young and haint never been away nowhere, and no wonder if he waits on her she should take a kind o' fancy to him."

"You know, ma," continued Abagail, "that Eliot Turner would never take her home among his folks, never; and if I was Ethel's mother, I'd shut the door in his face before I'd ever have him fooling around my house, and she should never stir out of the house with him, never!"

"I don't suppose there's much use in talking to the girl," said Grandma, "Emily was in here the other day, and Ethel, she happened to come in the same time, and I did n't see no use in Emily's speaking up in the way she did for says she, ' What do you have that El' Turner flirtin' around you for, Ethel? What do you suppose he wants o' you 'cept to amuse himself a little while when he ain't nothin' better to do and then go off and forgit he's seen ye!' And Ethel didn't say nothin', but she give Emily a dreadful long, quiet kind of a look out of her eyes."

"She hasn't lost quite all of Bede's temper since she's been seeking religion," said Abagail, in a strangely light and vivacious tone. Grandma and Grandpa Spicer, by the way, were good Methodists, but Abagail was not a "professor."

"Seekin' religion, eh?" inquired Grandpa Spicer. "She'd better let Eliot Turner alone, then," he added.

"Let us hope that we shall all on us be brought to a better state of mind," concluded Grandma Spicer, with solemn pertinency.

Before the meal was finished and the table cleared away, the latch of the ark had been often lifted.

On all occasions, afterwards, there was a marked and cheerful variety in the nature of the droppers-in at the ark — the children and all the young men and maidens making their appearance with a promiscuousness which precluded the possibility of design — but to-night the Wallencamp mind had evidently aimed at some great system of conventionality, and had been eminently successful in evolving a plan.

The callers were young men exclusively — the native youth of Wallencamp. Their blowzy, well favored faces which ever afterward appeared to beam with good nature, to-night expressed a sense of some grave affliction heroically to be endured.

Their best clothes, it was obvious, had been purchased by them, "ready made," and had been designed, originally, for the sons of a less stalwart community.

The young men were especially pinched as to their expansive chests, the broad-cloth coming much too short at this point. and shrugging up oddly enough at the shoulders, while the phenomenally slick arrangement of their hair was calculated to produce a depressing effect on the mind of the observer.

As they came in one by one, in a matter of fact way, and Grandma Spicer announced hopefully to each in turn — "and this is our teacher!" they accepted the fact with no more flattering sign than that of a dumb and helpless resignation to the inevitable. They seated themselves about the room in punctilious order. assuming positions painfully suggestive of a conscientious disregard for ease, and seemed to draw some silent support and sympathy out of their hats, which they caressed with lingering affection, touching to behold.

Grandma beckoned me aside into the pantry which immediately adjoined the kitchen, and informed me in one of her reverberating whispers, that I "must n t mind the boys being slicked up, for they'd sorter dropped in to make my acquaintance, and, if we wanted the pop corn, it was in a bag down under where the almanac hung, to the furthest corner of the wood-box."

I pondered these mysterious injunctions in silence and realizing the fact that the Wallencamp beaux had appeared in a body for the express purpose of making my acquaintance, I essayed to show my appreciation of this amiable design by an attempt to engage them in conversation.

My various efforts in this line proved alike futile, and they seemed but to grow impressed with a deeper sense of misery.

I had a vague intention of going in search of the pop-corn, when, to my sudden dismay, Grandma Spicer and Abagail, who had been noiselessly clearing off the table, emerged from a brief consultation in the pantry, bearing with them a lighted candle, and having given Grandpa Spicer a nod of unmistakable force and significance, disappeared through the door which led into that indefinite extension of the ark, beyond.

But Grandpa Spicer remained wilfully indifferent to these broadly insinuating tactics. He fancied, poor, deluded old man, that here was a choice opportunity to tell a tale of the seas after a fashion dear to his own heart, unshackled by the restraints of family surveillance.

A singularly child-like and unapprehensive smile played across his features. He drew his chair up closer to the stove and began: "Jest after I was a roundin'

Cape Horn the fourth time, I believe, — yis, yis, Le'me see — twenty times I 've rounded the Horn, wall, this ere — I recken, was somewhere nigh about the fourth time."

Scarcely had Grandpa arranged the merest preliminaries of his tale when ominous footsteps were heard returning along the way whither Grandma and Abagail had so recently departed, and he was interrupted by a strangely calm though authoritative voice from behind the door, "Pa ! "

"Wall, wall, ma ! what ye want, ma?" exclaimed Grandpa, turning his head aside, with a slight shade of annoyance on his face.

No answer immediately forthcoming, that wofully illusory smile returned again to his features. He moved still nearer to the stove, and was just at the point of resuming the thread of his narrative when —

"Hoggarty Spicer !" came from behind the door in accents still calm, indeed, but freighted with a significance which words have faint power to express.

"Yis, yis, ma ! I'm a coming, ma !" replied Grandpa, rising hastily and shuffling toward the door, "I'm a coming, ma ! I'm a coming !"

The door opened wide enough to receive him and then closed upon him in all his ignominy.

The sound of his voice in irate expostulation mingled with the steady flow of those serener tones grew gradually faint in the distance, and I was left alone with the sepulchral group of young men.

They arose, still maintaining the weighty aspect of those elected to honor, and abruptly opened their lips in song.

There was no repression now; the Ark fairly rang with the sonorous strains of that wild Jubilate.

They sang:

> " Light in the darkness, sailor,
>   Day is at hand.
> See o'er the foaming billows,
>   Fair Haven stands."

Their voices rolling in at the chorus with the resistless sweep of the ocean-waves:

> " Pull for the shore, sailor,
>   Pull for the shore.
> Heed not the rolling waves
>   But bend to the oar."

and with a final " Pull for the shore," that sent that imaginary life-boat bounding high and dry on to the strand at the hands of its impulsive crew.

Then, they sat down and wiped the perspiration from their faces which had become transfigured with a sudden zest and radiance.

I recovered myself sufficiently to express a bewildered sense of pleasure and gratitude.

" Do you sing, teacher?" asked Noah Alden, a round faced youth with an irrepressible fund of mirth in his eyes, who had broken in on the former silence with an un-guarded little snicker.

Noel Norris, he of the dignified countenance and spade shaped beard, had faintly and helplessly echoed that snicker, and now repeated Noah's words:

" Ahem, certainly — Do you sing, teacher? Do you, now? Do you sing, you know?"

I had some new and seriously awakened doubts on the subject. However, the degree of attainment not being brought into question, I felt that I could answer in the affirmative.

The countenances of the group brightened still more perceptibly.

"And do you sing No. 2?" enquired Noah, eagerly.

I tried to assume, in reply, a tone of equal animation.

"Is it something new? I don't think I've heard of it, before."

"Why, it's the Moody and Sankey hymn book!" exclaimed Noah, looking suddenly blank.

I strove to soften the effect of this blow by a lively show of recognition.

"Oh, yes, I know perfectly now. It's "Hold the Fort," "Ring the Bells of Heaven," and all those songs, is n't it?"

"'Hold the Fort' 's in No. 1," said George Olver, a new speaker, with beautiful, brave, brown eyes and a soldierly bearing.

He spoke, correcting me, but with the tender consideration which a father might display toward an unenlightened child.

"There's three numbers," said Noah Alden, "and you ought to learn to sing 'em, teacher. We sing 'em all the time, down here."

"You are fond of singing?" I questioned.

Dick Peterson, of lithe figure and straight black hair, a denizen of the Indian encampment, started up, flushing through his dark skin.

"I lul-love it!" he said.

Dick Peterson sang with the most exquisite smoothness, but stumbled a little in prosaical conversation.

A silent Norwegian, Lars Thorjon, who had sat

gazing at me and smiling, flushed also at the words, and murmured something rapturous with a foreign accent.

" Yes, we're rather fond of singing." I heard George Olver's resolute tones.

Noah Alden gave a low, expressive whistle.

" I like it, certainly, ahem ! *I* do. *I* like it, you know," said Noel Norris.

" We have a singin' time generally every night," said Noah. "Sometimes Abagail plays for us on her music, and sometimes we go down to Ethel's. Abagail's melodeon is very soft and purty, but George, he e, he likes the tone of Ethel's organ best, I reckon. Eh, George ? "

Noah winked facetiously at George Olver, who reddened deeply but did not cast down his eyes.

" If I was you, George," continued the merciless Noah, — " I'd lay for that Turner. Gad, I'd set a match to his hair. I'd nettle him ! "

" I'd show him his p-p-place ! " stammered Dick Peterson, with considerable warmth.

" *I* would, certainly," reiterated the automatic Noel. " I'd show him his place, you know ; *I* would, certainly."

The big veins swollen out in George Olver's forehead knitted themselves there for an instant, sternly.

" I don't interfere with no man's business," said he. "So long as he means honorable and car'ies out his actions fa'r and squar' I don't begrudge him his chance nor meddle in his affa'rs."

Our attention was suddenly diverted from this subject, which was evidently growing to be a painful one to one of the company, by the sound of a violin played with singular skill and correctness just outside the window.

"Glory, there's Ben!" exclaimed Noah, bounding ecstatically from his chair.

"Come in, Ben, come in?" he shouted, "and show us what can be got out of a fiddle!"

"Let him alone," said George Olver, but the group had already vanished through the door, Noel following mechanically.

"That's Ben. Cradlebow fiddlin' out thar," George Olver explained to me. "I don't want 'em to skeer him off, for it ain't every night Ben takes kindly to his fiddle. There's times he won't touch it for days and days. Talkin' about Ben's fiddlin' — I suppose it's true — there was some fellers out from Boston happened to hear him playin' one night, up to Sandwich te-own, and they offered him a hundred and fifty a month — I reckon that's true — to go along with some fiddlin' company thar to Boston, and he'd a got more if he'd stuck to it, but Ben, he come driftin' back in the course of a week or two. I don't blame him. He said he was sick on't.

I tell you how 'tis, teacher. Folks that lives along this shore are allus talkin' more'n any other sort of folks about going off, and complainin' about the hard livin', and cussin' the stingy sile, but thar's suthin' about it sorter holt's to 'em. They allus come a driftin' back in some shape or other, in the course of a year or two at the farderest."

The door was thrown wide open and my recreant guests reappeared half dragging, half pushing before them a matchless Adonis in glazed tarpaulin trousers and a coarse sailor's blouse.

I recognized at once in the perfect physical beauty of the eccentric fiddler only a reproduction in a larger form, of that sadly depraved young cherub who had danced before me in ghostly habiliments on the way to school. It was the imp's older brother.

"Here's Ben, teacher!" cried Noah, "he would n't come in 'cause he was n't slicked up; but I tell him clo's don't make much difference with a humly dog, anyway. Come along, Ben, and put them blushes in your pocket to keep yer hands warm in cold weather. Teacher, this is our champion fiddler, inventor, whale-fisher, cranberry picker, and potato bugger,— Benney Leonard Cradlebow!"

The youth of the bird-like name dealt his tormentor a hearty though affectionate cuff on the ears, and being thus suddenly thrust forward, he doffed his broad souwester, took the hand I held out to him, and, stooping down, kissed me, quite in a simple and audible manner, on the cheek.

It was done with such gentle, serious embarassment, and Benney Leonard Cradlebow was so boyish and quaint looking, withal, that I felt not the slightest inclination to blush, but I heard Noah's saucy giggle.

"Gad!" said he, "hear the old women talk about Ben's being bashful and not knowin' how to act with the girls! Now I call them purty easy manners, eh, Noel? what do you think, Noel?"

"Ahem, certainly,—" responded Noel, smiling in vague sympathy with the laughing group. "*I* call them so,— certainly, —*I* do."

Only George Olver turned a sober, reassuring face to the blushing Cradlebow.

"Give us a tune, Bennie," said he. "Lord, *I'd* laugh if I could get the music out o' them strings that you can."

The Cradlebow sat down, drew his bow across the strings with a full, quivering, premonitory touch, and, straightway, the fiddle began to talk to him as though they two were friends alone together in the room. How it played for him,—the fiddle—as though it were morning. How it shouted, laughed, ran with him in a world of sunshine and tossing blossoms !

How it hoped for him, swelling out in grander strains, wild with exultation, tremulous with passion !

How it mourned for him, with dying, sweet despair, until one almost saw the night fall on the water and the lone sea-birds flying, and heard the desolate shrieking of the wind along the shore.

I heard a real sob near me, and looking up saw the tears rolling down Noah's rosy cheeks.

It was in the midst of a simple melody,—I think it was the " Sweet Bye and Bye "—that the player stopped and turned suddenly pale.

"That was a new string, too !" he said, "and only half tight." Then he blushed violently, seeking to hide the irritation of his tone under a careless laugh.

" Oh, I do n't mind the string," he went on ; "that 's easy mended, but I happened to think it 's a bad sign, that's all—to break down so in the middle of a tune."

" Darn the sign !" exclaimed Noah, " I wanted to hear that played through."

"You remember Willie Reene?" Benney turned his eyes, still unnaturally bright with excitement, towards George Olver.

"Aye, I remember," said George Olver. "I was goin' mackerelin' with ye myself that time, only I wrinched my wrist so."

"We was out on deck together," Benney continued. "I was lying down,—it was a strange, warmish sort of a night—and Willie played. He played a long time. It was just in the middle of a tune he was playin' that — snap ! the string went in just that way. I never thought anything about it. I tried to laugh him out of it and he laughed, but says he 'It 's a bad sign, Ben. Likely it had nothin' to do with it, but I think of it sometimes, and then it seems as though I must go to that same place and look for him again. I never done anything harder than when I left him there."

"You done the best you could," George Olver answered stoutly. "They said you dove for him long and long after it was n't no use."

"No use," Benney repeated, shaking his head sadly and abstractly, "no use."

"There 's naught in a sign, anyway," George Olver affirmed.

"They don't worry me much, you can depend — " the player looked up at length with a singularly bright and gentle smile. "But Grannie, she believes in 'em, truly. She's got a sign in a dream for everything, Grannie has, so I hear lots of it."

Noah Alden had quite recovered by this time, from his tearfully sentimental mood.

"Now it's strange," he began with an air of mysterious solemnity, "there was three nights runnin' that I dreamed I found a thousand dollar bill to the right hand corner of my bury drawer, and every mornin' when I woke up and went to git it — it wa'n't there, so I know the rats must a carrried it off in the night, and a pretty shabby trick to play on a feller, too — but then you can't blame the poor devils for wantin' a little pin money.

"Did I ever tell ye how Uncle Randal tried to clear 'em out o' i is barn? Wall, he traded with Sim Peck up to West Wallen, a peck o' clams for an old cat o' hisn, that was about the size, Uncle Randal said, of a yearlin' calf, and he turned her into the barn along o' the rats, and shut the door, and the next mornin', he went out and there was a few little pieces of fur flyin' around and devil a — devil a cat! Uncle Randal said!"

"You're the D — d — d — you're it, yourself, Noah!" stammered Dick Peterson.

"You'd better look out, Dick," Noah giggled, "'we're all a little nearer'n second cousins down here to Wallencamp. Dick's mother didn't use to let him go to school much, teacher," Noah added, turning to me; "it used to wear him out luggin' home his 'Reward o' merit cards.' "

"I n-n-never got any," Dick retorted, blushing desperately through his dark skin, " n-n-nor you either!"

"I guess that's so, Noah," said Noel Norris, quite gravely, " I rather think that's so, Noah — ahem, I guess it is."

When my visitors rose to depart they formed in line, with George Olver and Benney at the head.

George Olver was the spokesman of the group. He offered me his strong brown hand in hearty corroboration of his words, "We 're a roughish sort of a set down here, teacher, but whenever you want friends you 'll know right whar to find us; we mean that straight through and fair and kindly.

I thanked him, and then Benney gave me his hand, but did not kiss me, in departing.

Each member of the phalanx gave me his hand in turn, with a hearty "Good night," and so they passed out. The door closed behind them. I meditated a space and when I looked up there was Noel Norris's pale face peering into the room.

"Ahem — Miss Hungerford !" he murmured, in awful accents : "Miss Hungerford !"

Could it be some telegram from my home thus mysteriously arrived? The thought flashed through my mind before reason could act.

"What is it?" I gasped, hastening to meet the informer.

Noel Norris handed me a picture; it was a small daguerrotype in which the mild and beneficent features of that worthy being himself shone above his own unmistakable spade-shaped whiskers.

"Would you like it, Miss Hungerford?" said he, still with the same deeply impressive air, "would you, now, really, Miss Hungerford? would you like it now?"

"Why, certainly," I exclaimed, with intense relief, and before I could fully appreciate the situation. Noel Norris cast a cautious glance about him, leaned his head forward, and whispered hoarsely, "I've got some more, at home — ahem! I've got six, Miss Hungerford. Mother wants to keep two and she's promised Aunt Marcia one ; but you can have one any time, Miss Hungerford. Ahem ! ahem ! *You* can, you know."

"Thank you," I murmured, while it seemed as though my faculties were desperately searching for light on a hitherto unsounded sea. "I think this will do for the present."

Noel nodded his head with a grave good night and disappeared.

Meanwhile, Grandma and Grandpa Spicer and Abagail were absorbing this last impressive scene as they slowly emerged from that unknown quarter of the ark whither they had retreated.

Grandpa looked at me with a peculiar twinkle in his eye.

"So Noel came back to give ye his picter, eh, teacher?" said he.

I returned Grandpa's look with cheerful and unoffended alacrity; but Grandma interrupted, "Thar, now, pa! Thar, now! We mustn't enquire into everything we happen to get a little wind on. Ye see, teacher," she continued, in tones of the broadest gentleness, "we knew they'd be sorter bashful gettin' acquainted, the first night, and so we thought it 'ud be easier for 'em if we should leave 'em to themselves, and we knew you was so — we knew you would n't care."

As Grandpa resumed his accustomed seat by the fire, an expansive grin still lingered on his features.

"Ah, he's a queer fellow, that Noel," said he, "but he's quick to larn, they say, larns like a book. I'll tell ye what's the trouble with him, teacher. He's been tied too long to his mother's apron strings. He don't know no more about the world than a chicken. He's thirty odd, now, I guess, and I reckon he ain't never been further away from the beach than Sandwich te-own!"

"I don't know as we'd ought to blame him," said Grandma Spicer, "though to be sure, Noel's more quiet

natured than some that likes to be wanderin' off as young
folks will, generally; but he was the only one they
had, and Noel's allus been a good boy. Pa and me, when
we go to meetin' we most allus come acrost him a carryin'
his Sunday School book under his arm, and may be,"
concluded Grandma Spicer, "there'll be a time when
we shall more on us wish that thar wan't nothin' wuss
could be brought against us than being innocent."

We pondered these suggestive words a few moments in
silence ; then Grandpa Spicer boldly interposed :

"That   Ben   Cradlebow— he's   a   handsome   boy,
teacher.   Ah, he's a handsome one.   They're a handsome family, them Cradlebows.

"There's the old grannie, Aunt   Susan   they   call
her. Lord, she's got a head on her like a picter ! They're
high bred, too, I reckon.   To begin with, why, Godfrey —
Godfrey Cradlebow — that's Ben's father, teacher ; he's
college bred, I suppose !   He had a rich uncle thar, that
took   a   shine   to   him   and   kind o' 'dopted him   and
eddicated him, but Godfrey, he took   a   shine   to a poor
girl thar, dreadfully handsome, she was, but yet they
was both on em young, and it did not suit the old uncle,
so he left him to shift for himself.   And Godfrey, he tried
one thing and another, and never held long to nothin', I
guess, and finally he drifted down this way and here he
stuck.

" He's got a good head, Godfrey has, but he was n't
never extry fond o' work, I reckon, and he's growed
dreadful rheumatiky lame, and   he   has   his   sprees,
occasionally.

" Liddy, that's his wife, teacher, she was full good
enough for him when ye come to the pint.   Oh, she's a

smart wife and she's had a hard row, so many children
and nothin' to do with, as ye might say. Why, they've
had thirteen children, ain't they, ma?

" Le'me see — four on 'em dead, and three on 'em —
no ! four on 'em married, and three on 'em — How is't,
ma ? "

Grandma then took up the tangled thread of the
old captain's discourse, with calm disdain, and proceeded
to disclose an appalling array of statistics not only in
regard to the Cradlebow family, but including generations
of men hitherto unknown and remote.

When I signified a desire to retire for the night,
Abagail informed me with a brisk and hopeful air, that
my room was " all ready now."

She led the way up a short and narrow little staircase
into a low garret where, amid a dark confusion of objects,
I was forcibly reminded of the rows of hard substances
suspended from the rafters.

Turning to the left, the rays of the candle revealed
a small red door framed in among the unpainted boards of
the wall.

There, Abagail bade me a flippant and musical good
night, and I entered my room, alone.

Within, the contrast between the door and the brown
walls was still more effectively drawn.

The bed, neatly made, stood in a niche where the roof
slanted perceptibly downward, so that the sweetly unconscious sleeper (as I found afterwards) perchance tossing
his head upward, in a dream, was doomed to bring
that member into resounding contact with the ceiling.

I judged something of the restless preclivities of
the last occupants of the room by the amount of plastering

of which this particular section had been deprived. In this, and in other places where it had fallen, it had been collected and tacked up again to the ceiling in cloth bags which presented a graceful and drooping, though at first sight, rather enigmatical appearance.

The chimney ran through the room forming a sort of unique centrepiece.

This and more I accepted, wearily, and then sank down by the bed and cried. Outside, before the one small window, stood a peach tree. Afterward, when this had grown to be a very dear little room to me, I looked out cheerfully through its branches, warm with sunshine, and fragrant with bloom; but now it was bare and ghostly, and, as the wind blew, one forlorn twig trailed back and forth across the window.

For an hour or more after my head touched the pillow, I lay awake listening to the unaccustomed sound of the surf and those skeleton fingers tapping at the pane.

CHAPTER IV.

THE TURKEY MOGUL ARRIVES.

I STUDIED Ethel in school, the next day, with special interest. She was a girl of seventeen or eighteen, with the stately, substantial presence of one of nature's own goddesses. She had a fresh, constant color in her cheeks, a pure, low forehead, and eyes that were clear, gray, and large, but with a strangely appealing, helplessly animal expression in them, I fancied, as she lifted them, oft times, to mine. She was distinguished among my young disciples by the faithful, though evidently labored and wearisome attention, she gave to her books.

Her glance, bent on some small wretch who was misbehaving, had a peculiarly significant force. The little ones all seemed to love her and to stand rather in awe of her too.

Entering the school-room in the morning, she discovered a network of strings, which one Lemuel Biddy had artfully laid between the desks, intending thereby to waylay and prostrate his human victim, and stooping down, she boxed the miscreant, not cruelly, but effectively, on the ears. I was surprised to see that the boy seemed to regard this infliction as the simple and natural award of justice, bowed his head and wept penitently, and was subdued for sometime afterward.

To me, whose earliest years had been guided and

illuminated on the principle that reason and persuasion alone are to be used in the training of the tender twig, this little occurrence afforded food for serious wonder and reflection.

I doubted if the logic of the sages or the wooing of the celestial seraphim would have wrought with such convincing power on the min l and ears of Lemuel Biddy.

If Ethel perchance, after painfully protracted exertions, succeeded in working out some simple problem in arithmetic, her slate containing the solution was freely handed about amo· g her unaspiring comrades, so that I judged her to be "weakly generous" as well as "plodding," — qualities not of a high order, I esteemed, yet by no means insuperable barriers to friendship when found to enter more or less largely into the composition of one's friends.

There was something in my novel relation to the girl as her teacher peculiarly fascinating to me. At recess, she remained in her seat and kept quietly at her work.

I went down and stood over her. "Can I help you, my dear?" I said.

Whatever might have been the pedantic or obtrusively condescending quality of those words, Ethel seemed to find nothing distasteful in them. She looked up with a "Thank you," and a pleased, trustful face like a child's. "I can't do this one," said she. "I've finished the rest, but this would n't come right, somehow."

It was a sum in simple addition. I could not help a feeling of deep surprise and commiseration that one of Ethel's age should have stumbled at it at all, but I essayed to examine it very closely and worked it out for her as slowly as possible. "Do you see your mistake?" I said.

She blushed painfully. The tears almost stood in her eyes.

"Yes, and I knew you'd have to find out how dull I was," she said, "but I dreaded it. When Miss Taite was here, mother was sick and I didn't go to school at all, and Miss Taite took me for a friend; and I told mother I'd most rather not go to school to you, for Miss Taite said you'd be a real friend and I knew you wouldn't want me when you found how dull I was."

I looked at the girl and a bright, hesitating smile woke in her face.

"Do you know, Ethel," I said, "I don't choose my friends for their mental qualifications — for what they know; I select them just as people do horses — by their teeth. Let me see yours."

Ethel laughed most musically, thus disclosing two brilliant rows of ivories. I had noticed them before.

"You'll do!" I exclaimed, lightly. "I take you into my heart of hearts. Now what is your standard of choice? What charming characteristic do you first require in a friend, Ethel?"

"Oh!" said she, gasping a little and speaking very slowly, "I — don't — know. I — don't — think — I've got any."

"Don't be afraid lest you shall guess something that I have not, my dear," I said, "you can hardly go astray. Begin with modesty, if you please, truly the chief of virtues."

Ethel caught quickly the meaning in my tone and answered with a low ripple of laughter. When I urged her, she grew gravely embarassed.

"Well," said she, "I don't think I should want any-

body that I thought I could n't ever help them any, you
know. That would n't ever need me, I mean, and I
know," she went on more hastily, "it seems funny to
say that to you because it seems as though there was n't
anything that I could ever do for you — because you —
you seem — not to need anybody —but I did n't know
but sometime — there might be something — I thought —
maybe — sometime."

Ethel paused and looked up at me with that pitifully
beseeching expression in her eyes.

"Oh yes," I answered, still carelessly, "no doubt
I shall be a great burden to you in time. But you do
help me, now, dear, by your conduct in school. You
helped me this morning when you boxed Lemuel Biddy's
ears. I shall have to take boxing lessons of you."

"You be the scholar," Ethel answered quickly, her lips
parting again with a merry outburst of laughter.

"Wretch!" said I, well pleased but affecting a tone of
deep severity, "You must not be saucy to your teacher !
I shall keep you in the rest of your recess for that.

"Do you like to study, Ethel?" I added, presently.

"No-o," said she, much abashed at the admission, and
yet evidently incapable of speaking otherwise than according to the simple dictates of her conscience. "I don't
think I should care anything about it if it did n't
make you so dull not to. I mean," she continued, "perhaps
I might a liked it if I'd been to school right along, but we
never did. And I was to the mills up to Taunton. I
did n't stay long there. Then mother was sick. They
don't any of the scholars be let to go very regular. Sometimes they're wanted to work out. So they forget. So
they don't care much, I think. They get to dreading it

I wanted to tell you so you would n't think it so much blame — our bein' so backward."

"It is the faithful improvement of what opportunities we have, Ethel," I began, and then paused, somewhat confused by the throng of lively reminiscences which suddenly crowded my mental horoscope. "You are young yet, my dear," I concluded gravely, with a resigned sigh for my own departed youth, " you can make up for lost time. It is pleasant to give, but there may be circumstances in which it is our duty imperatively, to receive. You must let me do all I can for you this winter. I do want you for a friend, but I would rather it should be on these plainly implied conditions."

Ethel had been studying my face, thoughtfully, with a still expression of wonder.

" I'll try to learn," said she, slowly. " I'll do anything you want me to."

" Do you like to read?" I enquired, in a brighter tone.

" Stories?" said Ethel, a sparkle waking in her eyes.

" Stories mixed with other things," I insisted, gently, and was then compelled to wonder how many of those "other things" had found their way into the literary appointment of my trunk.

" I'll try," said Ethel.

"Come to the Ark, after school, and look over the books I have. We will talk some more about it and you shall select as you please, or I will select for you, if you desire," I said, looking at Ethel with kindly though severe penetration.

" I'd rather you would," said Ethel, obediently.

To inflict this particular sort of patronage was a delightfully new experience for me. The glaring inconsistencies

which confronted me at every turn only gave a heightened
zest to the pursuit.

When I went to the door to blow the horn I felt that
Ethel already regarded me as her patron, guide and spiritual
mentor, and I was seriously resolved to fill these positions
hopefully for her and with credit to myself. With respect
to the rest of my flock, I felt a different sort of interest —
the wide awake concern of one who finds himself suddenly
perched on the back of a mettlesome, untried steed.

Any one member of that benighted corps, taken as the
subject of pruning and cultivating effort, would have
occupied, I believed, the faithful labors of a life time.
Considered as a gloriously rampant mass, the aspect of the
field was appalling.

I was especially impressed with this view of the case
when I went to toot them in from those free and reckless
diversions in which their souls expanded and their bodies
became as the winged creatures of the earth.

The horn was still an object of terror to me, though experience had made me wise enough to institute, on all
occasions, a careful preliminary search for buttons.

Its blast, freighted with baleful meaning to the ears
of sportive innocence, found a melancholy echo among
the deeper woes of my own heart, and, if it chanced to be
one of Aunt Pucinda's singing days, the " Dar'to be a Dan-
yell ! Dar' to be a Dan-yell ! " which floated across
the lane, had but a doubtfully inspiriting effect.

I felt, indeed, like a Daniel doomed to convocate
my own lions, and lacking that faith in a preserving
Providence which is believed to have cheered and elevated
the spirit of the ancient prophet, I confidently expected,
on the whole, to be devoured.

Gathered into their den, my lively herd gasped some moments as though suffering the last loud agony of expiring breath, and then, bethinking them of that only one of their free and native elements now obtainable, they sent up a universal cry for "water!"

Ah! what to do with them through the long hours of the day — beautiful creatures! by no means unlovable, with their bright, clear eyes, their restless, restless feet, their overflowing spirits; their bodies all alive, but with minds unfitted by birth, unskilled by domestic discipline to any sort of earnest and prolonged effort. Long, weary hours, therefore, not of furnishing instruction to the hungry and enquiring mind — ah, no! — but of a desperately sustained struggle in which, with every faculty on the alert to discover the truest expedients, with every nerve strained to the utmost, I strove for the mastery over this antic, untamed animal, until I could throw the reins loose at night, and drop my head down on my desk in the deserted school-room, tired, tired, tired!

The parents of the children " dropped in " often at the Ark, and savored the lively and varied flow of their discourse with choice dissertations on methods of discipline.

" I want my children whipped," said Mr. Randal Alden. "That's what they need. They git enough of it at home. It won't skeer 'em any — and I tell the folks if they'd all talk like that, they would n't be no trouble in the school."

" Ye can't drive Milton P. ," said that hopeful's mother. " He's been drove so much that he don't take no notice of it. If coaxing won't fetch him, nothin' won't; and I tell 'em if they was all like that, they would n't be no trouble in the school."

" Well," said Emily Gaskell, the matron of the painted

house, a tall, angular woman, with the hectic ot the
orthodox Yankee consumption on her cheeks, and the
orthodox Yankee twinkle in her eye, "ye can manage
my boys whatever way ye please, teacher. I ain't per-
tickeler. They've been coaxed and they've been whipped,
but they've always made out to mind by doin' pretty
much as they was a mind to. They 're smart boys, too,"
she added, with sincere pride, "but they don't take
to larnin'. I never see sich boys. Ye can't git no larnin'
into 'em, no way. They'd rather be whipped than go to
school. Sim had a man to work on our cranberry bog,
and he found out that he was first rate in 'rithmetic, this
man was, and so Sim, says he, 'I'll give ye the same
ye git on the bog,' says he, 'to stay up to the house and
larn my boys 'rithmetic,' says he, and the man, he tried
it, and in the course of a day or two, he come around to
Sim, and wanted to know if he could n't go back to clarin'
bog again."

Emily took in the broadly contemplative expression on
Grandma Spicer's benign features, and then winked at me
facetiously: "I tell 'em if they was all like that," said
she, "and I guess they be, pretty much, they might
as well be out o' doors as in, and less worryin' to the
teacher."

It might have been the third day of my labors in
Wallencamp that a man, having the appearance of a
lame giant, entered the school-room, and advanced to
meet me with an imposing dignity of mien. He held
captive, with one powerful hand, a stubbornly speech-
less, violently struggling boy. I recognized the man as
Godfrey Cradlebow, the handsome fiddler's father, and
the boy was none other than the imp whose eyes, scorch-

ing and defiant now, had first sent mocking glances back
at me while their light-limbed owner kicked out a jaunty
rigadoon from under the encircling folds of his sacerdotal
vestments.

"Miss Hungerford, I beg your pardon," said the elder
Cradlebow, with a distinct, refined enunciation foreign
to the native element of Wallencamp whose ordinary
locution had something of a Hoosier accent. "After a
good deal of trouble in catching him, I have finally
succeeded in bringing you in this — a — this little dev"
— he made an impressive pause, patted his fiery offspring
on the head with fatherly dignity, and eyed him, at once
doubtfully and reflectively.

I was interested in observing the aspect of the two
faces.

"The little boy resembles you, I think," I said.

The lame man struck his cane down hard upon the
floor and laughed immoderately.

"If you knew what I had in my mind to say!" he
exclaimed — "Ah! that was well put, well put! — though
but dubiously complimentary, but dubiously so, I assure
you, either to father or son!"

The idea still continuing to tickle him, he laughed
more gently, beating a sympathetic tattoo with his cane on
the floor.

"To pursue directly the cause of my intrusion here,"
he went on, at length, "this little —— well, for present
purposes, we will call him the *Phenomenon*. I confess it
is a name to which he is not totally unused. This little
phenomenon, whom you see before you, is the youngest but one in a flock of thirteen. Some of that
beautiful band — " here Mr. Cradlebow raised a very

shaky hand for an instant to his eyes, and although
a fitting occasion for sentiment, I was compelled
to think of what Grandpa Spicer had said about Godfrey
Cradlebow's "sprees" — "Some of that beautiful
band rest in the grave-yard, yonder.   Some of them
already know what it is themselves to be parents.
Some of them still linger in the poor, old home
nest.   I see you have here, my Alvin, and my
Wallace, and my youngest, the infant Sophronia.
Well, you find them good children, I dare say. Ah!
they have an estimable mother."   Again, he lifted his
hand to his eyes.   "Mischievous enough, you find them,
probably, but amenable — there it is, amenable, — but
this lad," Mr. Cradlebow paused again, shaking his
head with a meaning to which he gravely declined further
expression.

"What is your name?" I enquired of the little boy,
hopefully.

"Simmy B.," he answered revengefully in a tone of
alarming hoarseness.

"Such colds as that boy has!" exclaimed the paternal
Cradlebow.   "They're like all the rest of him — they're
phenomenal.   There are times when that boy appears to
be nothing but one frightful, perambulating cold! Well,"
he sighed, "and yet it's a strange fact, that the more
depraved and miserable a little devil is, the more his
mother 'll coddle him.

"Now there's this one and my Ben — Benney Leonard — a good boy, but lacking all capacity for rest —
always lacking the capacity for rest — uneasy, both of
them — always uneasy! but how the mother would give
her own rest for them and seem to love them the better

for it! strange! They have always been her idols, too.
Well, I have captured Simeon and brought him in. I
hope you may keep him. The rest you must learn
for yourself. The Lord help me!" he groaned, as
he picked up his cane, with evident physical pain, and
hobbled out of the room.

Within the school-room, things resumed their customary, Niagara-like roar, until a lamentable voice rose
above the others, and was straightway followed by another
voice in indignant explanation.

"Teacher, can't Simmy B. stop? He's puttin' beans
down Amber G.'s neck!"

"Simeon!" I exclaimed, in accents calculated to melt
that youthful heart of stone, and then added, "I will speak
with you a few moments alone, at recess."

Simeon looked no longer helplessly angry as when his
father brought him in. He appeared, on the whole, well
pleased, but I scanned his angelic features in vain for any
trace of repentance.

There followed a few moments of comparative quiet.
Then came a startling, sickening sound as of some
one undergoing the tortures of strangulation. Then,
a long, convulsive gasp. I looked down upon a sea
of round eyes and uplifted hands.

"Teacher, Simmy's swallered a slate-pencil! Simmy's
swallered a slate-pencil!"

"He's swallered most a hull one!" cried the owner of
one pair of protruding orbs.

"It wa'n't!" retorted Simeon, flaming with righteous
indignation — "It wa'n't but harf a one!"

"He t-t-told me," cried a young scion of the stammering Peterson race, all breathless with excitement, "that

he was a going to p-p-put it into his m-m-mouth and
t-t-take it out of his n-n-nose, and he did and it t-t-t—
and it slip-p-ped !"

" Wall, jest you keep your eyes peeled and your
ears cocked," replied the sturdy Simeon, in hoarse and
jarring accents, "and see if I don't take it out of my
nose, yet."

The signs of that painful struggle slowly faded out of
Simeon's face and there was an unusual calm in the
school-room.

Perhaps a quarter of an hour elapsed. I was thoughtfully engaged in hearing one of my classes when startled
by the sound of a window closed with a sharp bang. At
the same time arose the universal voice :

"Simmy B.'s got out o' the winder !   Simmy B.'s got
out o' the winder ! "

I looked out across the snowless fields, and there, having
already scaled two fences and put many a good rod
between himself and the scene of his brief imprisonment, I
beheld, borne as on the wings of the wind, the form
of the retreating Simeon.

An incident at the close of my first week in Wallencamp was the visit of the " Turkey Mogul." Such
was the name given by the Wallencampers to Mr. Baxter,
the Superintendent of Schools.

Mr. Baxter lived miles away in Farmouth, and was,
properly, the visitor of the schools in Farmouth County.
Wallencamp was not in Farmouth County. Nevertheless,
Mr. Baxter had charge of the Wallencamp school. I
had been informed that he drove over at the beginning
and close of each term, put the scholars through the
most " dreadful examins," and gave an indiscriminate

"blowin' up" to persons and things in the place. So I looked forward to his coming with a curiosity not unmingled with more doubtful emotions.

It was Friday, and so near the close of the afternoon session, that I had quite dismissed from my mind the contemplation of any dread advent for that day. It was just at that trying hour of Friday afternoon when only the spelling classes remained to be heard, and teacher and scholars both were conscious, the one with a deep inward sense of relief, the others with many restless demonstrations of impatience, that the week was near its close, and that "tomorrow" would be Saturday and a holiday.

Estella — the raven-haired, familiarly known as the "Modoc," a long and ungainly creature, with arms and legs so seemingly profuse and unmanageable, that they reminded one of the tentacles of a cuttle-fish — Estella was " passing around the water."

She was performing this accustomed office with a grin of such supreme delight and satisfaction as seemed actually to illuminate the back of her head, when the door of the school-room opened, and there, without any previous warning, appeared a grim, fierce looking little man, whom I knew at once to be the "Turkey Mogul."

The extreme exigency of the case inspired me with a certain calmness of despair. Having advanced to meet this august personage, conducted him to the desk and placed for him the official chair, which he shortly refused, I lifted my eyes, "prepared for any fate," to observe what might be the condition of my turbulent flock, and lo — all the tops, and Jews-harps, and apples, and whirligigs, and miniature buzz saws had disappeared, and there was an array of pallid faces bent over another array of books—many of the latter were upside down, but the effect was unbroken. Even Estella, moved by some sudden divine sense of the fitness of things, had ceased her desultory wanderings about the room with the tin dipper, and, not having had time to procure a book, was working out imaginary problems on her fingers with the air of a Herschel, and I became slowly conscious that there was such a stillness in that room as had not been — no, nor anything like unto it,— since the first time I entered there.

I think Mr. Baxter must have observed something of the look of helpless astonishment which transfixed my features. I certainly saw the shadow of a smile lurking in his steel grey eyes.

"Yes," he snarled, addressing the school, "yes, if I did n't know you, now, and if your books were not most of 'em, bottom side up, and if I should n't be compelled in two minutes to prove the contrary, I might possibly imagine that you were studying — yes — Humph ! "

I said to Mr. Baxter, as cheerfully as possible, that "we were nearly through with our usual routine of classes for the day, but I should be happy, of course, to repeat any of the recitations which he might care to hear."

" Would you ? " said he, looking at me not unpleasantly. " Do you really ask me to believe that ? um-m-m," he murmured, resuming his stern aspect. " Let me see — Geography — yes, Miss Hungerford, you may call the first class in Geography."

I did not accuse the Superintendent of Schools of malevolent intentions, but I could honestly have affirmed that of all the divisions and subdivisions of my empire the first class in Geography was the one least calculated to shine on an occasion like the present.

I groaned, inwardly, and called them forth. Their forlorn and wilted appearance as they formed in line went to my heart. I was resolved to defend them at whatever cost.

"Now," said Mr. Baxter, planting himself firmly, with his legs rather far apart, thrusting his hands in his pockets and staring steadily at the shivering group from under his awful brows, "what is Geography? to begin with. That's the first thing. What is Geography? "

For a moment there was no reply. I almost began to hope that there would be none. I felt that here " Silence was golden," and if maintained, all might be comparatively well, when, to my dismay, there was a sort of flank movement in the ranks and the ill-starred Estella raised her hand.

"Well," said Mr. Baxter, pointing his finger steadfastly at her as if to impart a vein of concentration to her palpably loose and floating appearance, " You ! you ought to know. What is Geography, eh? "

Some fair wreck of an idea, formerly appropriated in this connection, floated through the brain of the " Modoc." She opened her mouth and in those loud and startling accents, for which she was ever distinguished, gave utterance to these memorable words :

" A — round ! like a ball ! "

Mr. Baxter glared fiercely at her, for a moment, and then permitted his scorn to escape in a long, sarcastic hiss.

" Yes-s-s," said he, "yes-s-s ! around like a ball ! Do

you find it much in your way, eh? Do you often give it such a kick as that, eh? Well, take your seats ! take your seats ! "

The Superintendent of Schools seemed disinclined to evoke any further catastrophes of this sort, but proceeded to discourse to me, aside, in a confidential growl, on the peculiar and erratic natures of the benighted Wallencampers.

"Their minds," he said, with a grim smile, "have no receptivity. They must originate, or they are naught. Parents and children — they are all the same. I am convinced that there is no scholarship to be established here. It has been tried and the attempt has failed a hundred times. It's not in the nature of things. Get on the good side of them, that's all. That has failed sometimes, but it is not among the impossible things. Get on the good side of them."

Finally, he turned to address the children. The "examins" had certainly not been severe, but the " blowin' up " was faithfully and liberally performed.

Never before had I felt so drawn to my poor, wondering, wolf besieged flock, and in proportion to my tenderness for them waxed my indignation toward the " Turkey Mogul."

"You can't learn," said he. "That's a sufficiently established fact, but if you don't behave, your teacher is going to write to me, mind ! and I shall come down here in my buggy and take you right up and off to Farmouth, where we have a place to keep all such naughty boys and girls."

This last was evoked as a benediction. Mr. Baxter looked at his watch and remarked that it was a long drive to Farmouth, and he must be going. "Dismiss your school, Miss Hungerford," he said.

Now the children were accustomed — it was a special privilege they had requested — to sing, before the school closed at night, one of the hymns with which they were all so familiar in Wallencamp.

I would have dismissed them, on this occasion, without further ceremony, but before I had time to tap my ruler on the desk as a signal for dismissal, they all struck up as with one voice :

> " What a friend we have in Jesus,
> All our griefs and woes to share!
> What a privilege to carry
> Everything to God in prayer."

At first I was a little amused at the incongruity of the thing. Then it began to seem to me inexpressibly touching.

The Superintendent of Schools stood with a cold, supercilious grin on his face, a stern, self-sufficient man, not one likely to echo the spirit of these simple words.

I stood beside him, weary and perplexed enough, but ever taking council of the pride of my own heart. And those poor children, with their hard, toilsome, barren lives before them, how they sang! their clear, young voices ringing out fearlessly, carelessly — they knew the words.

I wondered if any one in the room appreciated the song as having inner truth and meaning.

As I was locking my desk, before leaving the room, I discovered this little note, which Ethel had dropped in it.

" dere teecher,

" I wanted to do sumthyng to help yu wen I seen him combing in To Day fur I new jus howe yu felt but thay wasent no wours than thay always was,

and he nose it I and thay studdid more fur yu I think
than thay did for any but I think it mus be harrd for yu
not bein' use to us.   I think yu was tired.   Wen
we was singin' I thot howe tired yu was, but thar
was always won to help.   Excus writin pleas but I wanted
to let yu no for yu was good to me and I lov yu.

Ethel."

Some how, the little note rested and comforted me,
more than I would have imagined, a week before,
any expression of this humble disciple of mine could
have done.

I held the letter crumpled in my hand going up the
lane.   Going up the lane, too, I met Emily's fisherman
coming gayly home from the river.

Mr. Turner stopped and gallantly requested the
pleasure of carrying a small book which I held in
my hand.   He walked back to the ark with me, talking
very fluently the while.

"Do you know," he began, "I think I'm awfully
fortunate meeting you here in the lane.   I've been wishing for an opportunity to speak with you for two or
three days past, but the Ark is such a popular resort for
the youth of Wallencamp, and the children seem to be
always following you.   Well, they regard the school teacher
as their special property, and would consider me worse
than an intruder if I should go in to take even the lowest
seat in the synagogue.   I've been wanting to speak with
you, ever since that first night — when I stared at you
so stupidly at Captain Spicer's — when I went up to
borrow the oars, and you were engaged, you remember," said Mr. Turner, laughing gently, "in wresting
particles of hulled corn from the ocean depths of that
kettle."

"I remember," I said, trying to smother what annoyance I still felt at the recollection. "I admit that it was a very striking scene. It was very good," I added, religiously, referring to the corn. Mr. Turner ought to know, I thought, that I had come to Wallencamp on a mission, and that if he wished to scoff at the ways of its defenceless inhabitants, he should n't look to find a confidante in me.

"The hulled corn? Oh! yes, indeed!" he answered with a sprightly air. "We have it served in the same way at Emily's, and we think it's just — a — rich, you know. But I wanted to tell you. If you could have known how confoundedly . struck up I was when I went into the Ark that night, you would n't think it so strange my standing staring there like a fool. You see, we fellows picking up everything of interest down here to amuse ourselves with, heard that there was a new school teacher coming, so we gave our imaginations free rein. We were laughing it over among ourselves, and Smith said, 'she'd probably have hair like Turner's,' and Jake said 'she'd wear spectacles, and have a nose like the Clipper in the *Three Fates*,' and all that sort of thing. So I went up that night to see, just for the deuce of it, and not to get the oars at all, and I was deucedly well paid for it, too. In fact, Miss Hungerford," said the fisherman, darting a keen glance at me from his laughing eyes, "I did go up to scoff, but I remained to pray."

My ears had never been conscientiously closed to the voice of idle praise, but with this, for some reason, I was not well pleased.

"Your attitude was certainly devotional," I answered,

without haste. "Your friend," I added, "must be something of a seer. Here are the literal glasses ! "

" Nonsense ! " said Mr. Turner, coloring slightly, "you know I did n't mean that — just being a little near sighted. I said spectacles. Besides," and the fisherman looked me full and unblushingly in the face — " if I had such eyes as yours, by Jove, I would n't mind whether I could see anything out of 'em or not ! "

" You will hardly expect me to thank you for that," I murmured, with a sincere flash of indignation, not that I was unmindful of certain reckless moods of old, when I had found it not impossible to listen even with calmness, to vain demonstrations of this sort, but I felt that I was a different person now, in a different sphere of action.

Mr. Turner knew nothing of me except that I was the Teacher of the Wallencamp school — a doubtful position to his mind.

He fancied that he might "pick me up," to "amuse" himself with, I thought, and at the reflection, I felt an angry glow rising from heart to cheek.

Meanwhile the fisherman gnawed his moustache ruefully. This idle worldling could assume, occasionally, a whimsical helplessness of expression, with an air of aggrieved and child-like candor, somewhat baffling to the stern design of justice.

" Now I've offended you," he began, exchanging his tone of easy nonchalance for one of slow and awkward dejection. "And you think I've had the impudence — well, if either one of us two is going to be taken in, Miss Hungerford, I can tell you it's a blamed sight more likely to be me ; but you 're prejudiced against me, I can see. You were prejudiced against me that first night. I know

how those old women talk. They've got an idea, some
how, that I'm a scapegrace, and a desperate character.
And, on my word, Miss Hungerford, I'm considered
a real model chap there at home, and make speeches
to the little boys and girls in Sunday School, and all that
sort of thing. On my word, I do."

Mr. Turner spoke quite warmly. I could not help
laughing at his droll self-vindication.

"I should like to ask you to speak to my little
boys and girls!" I said, "but it's too harrowing to
the feelings. I listened to one address this afternoon."

"The 'Turkey Mogul?' Oh, that isn't my style!"
said Mr. Turner. "I don't sear their young vision
with the prospect of eternal flames. I entice them
with the blandishments of future reward." Let me go
in some day, and I promise you in one brief half hour
to destroy the cankering effect of all that the 'Turkey
Mogul' has ever said. At least, I shall serve as an
antidote — a cheerful and allaying antidote to the
wormwood of censorious criticism."

Thus the voluble fisherman ran on with an air of
simple and charming ingenuousness, while I reflected
that here possibly was a light and aimless creature
whom I had mentally convicted of ungracious designs,
that, although his presence in Wallencamp, as a
representative of the great world I believed I had left
behind me, was rather *mal a propos*, it might be that
I ought to consider him providentially included in my
field of labor, and as one of the objects of my regenerating care.

Whether Mr. Turner detected anything of this philan-

thropic intention, I do not know. When we got to
the gate he said :

" Will you go with me for a drive to-morrow, Miss
Hungerford? You know what the Wallencamp equipages
are. They furnish entertainment, at all events. The
drive to West Wallen is really beautiful — even at this
season of the year, with such uncommonly fine weather,
and you have a holiday, and the mail has n't been brought
from West Wallen for nearly a week."

I thanked the fisherman almost eagerly, thinking,
at that instant, of the longed-for letters that I knew were
waiting for me in the West Wallen Post Office.

Then, suddenly, I felt Ethel's little note grow heavy
in my hand.

To act voluntarily for others — to consider as serious
any obstacles in the way of following out my personal
inclinations — these were experiences too new to me,
and my resolve was not a natural one, but forced and
impatient.

"You are very kind," I said, "but I can't go to-morrow."

The two little Spicers came running out of the Ark
to meet me. I was secretly relieved. Mr. Turner had
been watching me narrowly, his lips curled, and his eyes
flashed with a half angry, half scornful light. He cast an
unloving glance at the little Spicers.

" I can't, of course, question the justice of your
decision," he said shortly, and touched his hat and walked
away without another word.

I considered this as one of the least among my many
trials and perplexities. Oftentimes I sighed for
the light hearted   irresponsible" days of yore when
" missions " were, as yet, to me unknown.

School was the greatest perplexity. Grandma Spicer's tenderness grew more impressive each day.

"It seems to me you're a growin' bleak and holler-eyed, teacher," she would say to me when I came home at night.

So I indulged more and more in a deeply sentimental self-pity and felt a growing satisfaction in the conscious-ness that I was enduring martyrdom. It was more by reason of a stubborn and desperate pride, I think, than from higher motives, that, in my letters home, I said nothing of the discomforts and discouragements which attended my course. I chose to dilate on the beautiful scenery of Wallencamp, and the quaint originality of its inhabitants.

CHAPTER V.

GRANDMA SPICER GETS GRANDPA READY FOR SUNDAY SCHOOL.

SUNDAY morning, nothing arose in Wallencamp save the sun.

At least, that celestial orb had long forgotten all the roseate flaming of his youth, in an honest straightforward march through the heavens, ere the first signs of smoke came curling lazily up from the Wallencamp chimneys.

I had retired at night, very weary, with the delicious consciousness that it would n't make any difference when I woke up the next morning, or whether, indeed, I woke at all.

So I opened my eyes leisurely and lay half dreaming, half meditating on a variety of things.

I deciphered a few of the texts on the scriptural patchwork quilt which covered my couch.

There were — "Let not your heart be troubled," "Remember Lot's wife," and " Abagail Spicer," traced in inky hieroglyphics, all in close conjunction.

Finally, I reached out for my watch, and, having

ascertained the time of day, I got up and proceeded to dress hastily enough, wondering to hear no signs of life in the house.

I went noiselessly down the stairs. All was silent, below, except for the peaceful snoring of Mrs. Abagail and the little Spicers, which was responded to from some remote western corner of the Ark by the triumphant snores of Grandma and Grandpa Spicer.

I attempted to kindle a fire in the stove, but it sizzled a little while, spitefully, as much as to say, " What, Sunday morning? Not I ! " and went out. So I concluded to put on some wraps and go out and warm myself in the sun.

I climbed the long hill, back of the ark, descended, and walked along the bank of the river. It was a beautiful morning. The air was — everything that could be desired in the way of air, but I felt a desperate need of something more substantial.

Standing alone with nature, on the bank of the lovely river, I thought, with tears in my eyes, of the delicious breakfast already recuperating the wasted energies of my far away home friends.

When I got back to the house, Mrs. Abagail, in simple and unaffected attire, was bustling busily about the stove.

The snores from Grandma and Grandpa's quarter had ceased, signifying that they, also, had advanced a stage in the grand processes of Sunday morning.

The children came teasing me to dress them, so I fastened for them a variety of small articles which I flattered myself on having combined in a very ingenious and artistic manner, though I believe those infant Spicers went weeping to Grandma, afterwards, and were re-modelled by her all-comforting hand with much skill and patience.

In the midst of her preparations for breakfast, Abagail abruptly assumed her hat and shawl, and was seen from the window, walking leisurely across the fields in the direction of the woods. She returned in due time, bear-ing an armful of fresh evergreens which she twisted around the family register.

When the ancient couple made their appearance, I remarked silently, in regard to Grandma Spicer's hair, what proved afterward to be its usual holiday morning arrangement.

It was confined in six infinitesimal braids which ap-peared to be sprouting out, perpendicularly, in all directions from her head.

The effect of redundancy and expansiveness thus heightened and increased on Grandma's features was striking in the extreme.

While we were eating breakfast, that good soul observed to Grandpa Spicer : " Wall, pa, I suppose you'll be all ready when the time comes to take teacher and me over to West Wallen to Sunday school, wont ye ? "

Grandpa coughed, and coughed again, and raised his eyes helplessly to the window.

" Looks some like showers," said he. "A-hem ! a-hem ! Looks mightily to me like showers, over yonder."

" Thar, r'aly, husband ! I must say I feel mortified for ye," said Grandma. "Seein' as you 're a perfessor, too, and thar ain't been a single Sunday mornin' since I've lived with ye, pa, summer or winter, but what you've seen showers, and it r'aly seems to me it's dreadful inconsistent when thar ain't no cloud in the sky, and don't look no more like rain than I do." And Grandma's face, in spite of her reproachful tones, was, above all, blandly sunlike and expressive of anything rather than deluge and watery disaster.

Grandpa was silent a little while, then coughed again. I had never seen Grandpa in worse straits.

"A-hem! a-hem! 'Fanny' seems to be a little lame, this morning," said he. "I should 'nt wonder. She's been goin' pretty stiddy this week."

"It does beat all, pa," continued Grandma Spicer, "how 't all the horses you've ever had since I've known ye have always been took lame Sunday mornin'. Thar was 'Happy Jack,' he could go anywhers through the week, and never limp a step, as nobody could see, and Sunday mornin', he was always took lame! And thar was 'Tantrum'——"

"Tantrum" was the horse that had run away with Grandma when she was thrown from the wagon, and generally smashed to pieces. And now, Grandma branched off into the thrilling reminiscenses connected with this incident of her life, which was the third time during the week that the horrible tale had been repeated for my delectation.

When she had finished, Grandpa shook his head with painful earnestness, reverting to the former subject of discussion.

"It's a long jaunt!" said he, "a long jaunt!"

"Thar's a long hill to climb, before we reach Zion's mount," said Grandma Spicer, impressively.

"Wall, there's a darned sight harder one on the road to West Wallen!" burst out the old sea captain desperately, "say nothin' about the devilish stones!"

"Thar now," said Grandma with calm though awful reproof, "I think we've gone fur enough for one day; we've broke the Sabbath, and took the name of the Lord in vain, and that ought to be enough for perfessors."

Grandpa replied at length in a greatly subdued tone.

"Wall, if you and the teacher want to go over to Sunday school to-day, I suppose we can go if we get ready," a long submissive sigh—"I suppose we can."

"They have preachin' service in the mornin', I suppose," said Grandma. "But we don't generally git along to that. It makes such an early start. We generally try to get around, when we go, in time for Sunday school. They have singin' and all. It's just about as interestin' I think, as preachin'." "The old man ra'ly likes it," she observed aside to me, "when he once gets started, but he kind o' dreads the gittin started."

When I beheld the ordeal through which Grandpa Spicer was called to pass, at the hands of his faithful consort, before he was considered in a fit condition of mind and body to embark for the sanctuary, I marvelled not at the old man's reluctance, nor that he had indeed seen clouds and tempest fringing the horizon.

Immediately after breakfast, he set out for the barn, ostensibly to "see to the chores," really, I believe, to obtain a few moments' respite, before worse evil should come upon him.

Pretty soon Grandma was at the back door calling in firm though persuasive tones.

"Husband ! Husband ! Come in, now, and get ready."

No answer. Then it was in another key, weighty, yet expressive of no weak irritation that Grandma called— "Come, pa ! pa-a ! pa-a-a !" Still no answer.

Then that voice of Grandma's sung out like a trumpet, terrible with meaning—"Hoggarty Spicer!"

But Grandpa appeared not. Next, I saw Grandma slowly but surely gravitating in the direction of the barn, and soon she returned bringing with her that ancient delinquent who looked like a lost sheep indeed and a truly unreconciled one.

"Now the first thing,"—said Grandma, looking her forlorn captive over,—"is boots. Go and get on yer meetin' gaiters, pa."

The old gentleman having invested himself with those sacred relics, came pathetically limping into the room.

"I declare, ma," said he, "somehow these things — phew! Somehow they pinch my feet dreadfully. I don't know what it is,— phew! They're dreadful oncomf'table things somehow."

"Since I've known ye, pa," solemnly ejaculated Grandma Spicer, "you've never had a pair o' meetin' boots that set easy on yer feet. You'd ought to get boots big enough for ye' pa," she continued looking down disapprovingly on the old gentleman's pedal extremities, which resembled two small scows at anchor in black cloth encasements, "and not be so proud as to go to pinchin' yer feet into gaiters a number o' sizes too small for ye."

"They're number tens, I tell ye!" roared Grandpa, nettled outrageously by this cutting taunt.

"Wall, thar, now, pa," said Grandma, soothingly, "if I had sech feet as that, I wouldn't go to spreadin' it all over town, if I was you — but it's time we stopped bickerin', now, husband, and got ready for meetin'; so set down and let me wash yer head."

" I've washed once this mornin'. It's clean enough,"
Grandpa protested, but in vain. He was planted in
a chair, and Grandma Spicer, with rag and soap and a
basin of water, attacked the old gentleman vigorously,
much as I have seen cruel mothers wash the faces of
their earth-begrimed infants.   He only gave expression
to such groans as :

" Thar, ma ! don't tear my ears to pieces ! Come, ma !
you've got my eyes so full o' soap now, ma, that I can't
see nothin'.   Phew ! Lordy ! ain't ye most through with
this, ma ? "

Then came the dyeing process, which Grandma Spicer
assured me, aside, made Grandpa " look like a man o'
thirty," but, to me, after it he looked neither old nor
young, human nor inhuman, nor like anything that I had
ever seen before under the sun.

" There's the lotion, the potion, the dye-er, and the
setter," said Grandma, pointing to four bottles on the
table.   " Now whar's the directions, Abagail ? "

These having been produced from between the leaves
of the family bible, Abagail read, while Grandma made a
vigorous practical application of the various mixtures.

" This admirable lotion"—in soft ecstatic tones Aba -
gial rehearsed the flowery language of the recipe—
" though not so instantaneously startling in its effect as our
inestimable dyer and setter, yet forms a most essential
part of the whole process, opening, as it does, the
dry and lifeless pores of the scalp, imparting to them
new life and beauty, and rendering them more easily
susceptible to the applications which follow. But we
must go deeper than this ; a tone must be given to
the whole system by means of the cleansing and rejuvenat-

ing of the very centre of our beings, and, for this purpose, we have prepared our wonderful potion." Here, Grandpa, with a wry face, was made to swallow a spoonful of the mixture. " Our unparallelled dyer," Abagail continued, "restores black hair to more than original gloss and brilliancy, and gives to the faded golden tress the sunny flashes of youth." Grandpa was dyed. " Our world renowned setter completes and perfects the whole process, by adding tone and permanency to the efficacious qualities of the lotion, potion, and dyer, &c.," while on Grandpa's head the dye was set.

" Now, read teacher some of the testimonials, daughter," said Grandma Spicer, whose face was one broad, generous illustration of that rare and peculiar virtue called faith.

So Abagail continued : " Mrs. Hiram Briggs, of North Dedham writes : — ' I was terribly afflicted with baldness, so that, for months, I was little more than an outcast from society, and an object of pity to my most familiar friends. I tried every remedy in vain. At length, I heard of your wonderful restorative. After a week's application, my hair had already begun to grow in what seemed the most miraculous manner. At the end of ten months, it had assumed such length and proportions as to be a most luxurious burden, and where I had before been regarded with pity and aversion, I became the envied and admired of all beholders."

" Just think !" said Grandma Spicer, with rapturous sympathy and gratitude, " how that poor creetur must a' felt ! "

"' Orion Spaulding of Weedsville, Vermont,' " Abagail went on — but, here, I had to beg to be excused, and went to my room to get ready for the Sunday school.

When I came down again, Grandpa Spicer was seated, completely arrayed in his best clothes, opposite Grandma, who held the big family bible in her lap, and a Sunday school question book in one hand.

"Now, pa," said she, "what tribe was it in sacred writ, that wore bunnits?"

I was compelled to infer from the tone of Grandpa Spicer's answer that his temper had not undergone a mollifying process during my absence.

"Come, ma," said he, "how much longer ye goin' to pester me in this way?"

"Why, pa," Grandma rejoined calmly, "until you git a proper understandin' of it. What tribe was it, in sacred writ, that wore bunnits?"

"Lordy!" exclaimed the old man. "How d'ye suppose I know! They must a' been a tarnal old woman- ish lookin' set, any way."

"The tribe o' Judah, pa," said Grandma, gravely. "Now, how good it is, husband, to have your under- standin' all freshened up on the scripters!"

"Come, come, ma!" said Grandpa, rising nervously, "It's time we was startin'. When I make up my mind to go any where I always want to git there in time. If I was goin' to the Old Harry, I should want to git there in time."

"It's my consarn that we shall git thar before time, some on us," said Grandma, with sad meaning, "unless we larn to use more respec'ful language."

I shall never forget how we set off for church that Sabbath morning, way out at one of the sunny back doors of the Ark, for there was Abagail's little cottage that fronted the highway, or lane, and then there was a long backward extension of the Ark, only one story in height. This belonged peculiarly to Grandma and Grandpa Spicer. It contained the "parlor" and three "keepin'" rooms opening one into the other, all of the same size and general bare and gloomy appearance, all possessing the same sacredly preserved atmosphere, through which we passed with becoming silence and solemnity into the "end" room, the sunny kitchen where Grandma and Grandpa kept house by themselves in the summer time, and there at the door, her very yellow coat reflecting the rays of the sun, stood Fanny, presenting about as much appearance of life and animation as a pensive summer squash.

The carriage, I thought, was a fac-simile of the one in which I had been brought from West Wallen on the night of my arrival. One of the most striking peculiarities of this sort of vehicle was the width at which the wheels were set apart. The body seemed comparatively narrow. It was very long, and covered with white canvas. It had neither windows nor doors, but just the one guarded opening in front. There were no steps leading to this, and, indeed, a variety of obstacles before it. And the way Grandma effected an entrance was to put a chair on a mound of earth, and a cricket on top of the chair, and thus having climbed up to Fanny's reposeful back, she slipped passively down, feet foremost, to the whiffle-tree ; from thence she easily gained the plane of the carriage floor.

Grandpa and I took a less circuitous, though, perhaps, not less difficult route.

I sat with Grandpa on the "front" seat — it may be remarked that the " front " seat was very much front, and the "back" seat very much back—there was a kind of wooden shelf built outside as a resting place for the feet, so that while our heads were under cover, our feet were out, utterly exposed to the weather, and we must either lay them on the shelf, or let them hang off into space.

Abagail and the children stood at the door to see us off.

"All aboard! ship ballasted! wind fa'r! go ahead, thar, Fanny!" shouted Grandpa, who seemed quite restored in spirits, and held the reins and wielded the whip with a masterful air.

He spun sea yarns, too, all the way — marvelous ones, and Grandma's reproving voice was mellowed by the distance, and so confusedly mingled with the rumbling of the wheels, that it seemed hardly to reach him at all. Not that Grandma looked discomfited on this account, or in bad humor. On the contrary, as she sat back there in the ghostly shadows, with her hands folded, and her hair combed out in resplendent waves on either side of her head, she appeared conscious that every word she uttered was taking root in some obdurate heart. She was, in every respect, the picture of good will and contentment.

But the face under Grandpa's antiquated beaver began to give me a fresh shock every time I looked up at him, for the light and air were rapidly turning his rejuvenated locks and his poor, thin fringe of whiskers to an unnatural greenish tint, while his bushy eyebrows, untouched by the hand of art, shone as white as ever.

In spite of the old sea-captain's entertaining stories, it seemed, indeed, "a long jaunt" to West Wallen

To say that Fanny was a slow horse would be but a feeble expression of the truth.

A persevering "click! click! click!" began to arise from Grandma's quarter. This annoyed Grandpa exceedingly.

"Shet up, ma!" he was moved to exclaim at last. "I'm steerin' this craft."

"Click! click! click!" came perseveringly from behind.

"Dum it, ma! thar, ma!" cried Grandpa, exasperated beyond measure. "How is this hoss goin' to hear anything that I say, ef you keep up such a tarnal cacklin'?"

Just as we were coming out of the thickest part of the woods about a mile beyond Wallencamp, we discovered a man walking, in the distance. It was the only human being we had seen since we started.

"Hullo, there's Noel!" exclaimed Grandpa. "I was wonderin' why we had n't overtook him, before. We gin'ally take him in, on the road. Yis, yis; that's Noel, ain't it teacher?"

I put up my glasses, helplessly.

"I'm sure," I said, "I can't tell, positively. I have n't seen Noel but once, and at that distance I should n't know my own father."

"Must be Noel," said Grandpa. "Yis, I know him! Hullo, thar! Ship ahoy! ship ahoy!"

Grandpa's voice suggested something of the fire and vigor it must have had when it rang out across the foam of waves and pierced the tempest's roar.

The man turned and looked at us and then went on again.

"He don't seem to recognize us," said Grandma.

"Ship a-hoy! Ship a-hoy!" shouted Grandpa.

The man turned and looked at us again, and this time
he stopped and kept on looking.

When we got up to him, we saw that it wasn't Noel at
all, but a stranger of trampish appearance, drunk and fiery,
and fixed in an aggressive attitude.

I was naturally terrified. What if he should attack us
in that lonely spot! Grandpa was so old! And moreover, Grandpa was so taken back to find that it wasn't
Noel that he began some blunt and stammering expression of surprise, which only served to increase the
stranger's ire. Grandma, imperturbable soul! who never
failed to come to the rescue even in the most desperate
emergencies—Grandma climbed over to the front, thrust
out her benign head, and said in that deep, calm voice of
hers :

"We're a goin' to the house of God, brother, wont you
git in and go too?"

"No!" our brother replied, doubling up his fists and
shaking them menacingly in our faces :—"I won't go to
no house o' God. What d 'ye mean by overhauling me
on the road, and askin' me to git into yer d——d old
traveling lunatic asylum !"

"Drive on, pa," said Grandma, coldly : "He ain't in
no condition to be labored with now. Drive on kind o'
quick !"

'Kind o' quick' we could not go, but Fanny was
made to do her best, and we did not pause to look
behind.

When we got to the church, Sunday school had already
begun. There was Noel looking preternaturally stiff in
his best clothes, sitting with a class of young men. He
saw us when we came in, and gave me a look of deep

meaning. It was the same expression — as though there was some solemn, mutual understanding between us — which he had worn on that night when he gave me his picture.

" 'There's plenty of young folks' classes," said Grandma, "but seein' as we're late maybe you'd jest as soon go right along in with us."

I said that I should like that best, so I went into the "old folks'" class with Grandma and Grandpa Spicer.

There were three pews of old people in front of us, and the teacher, who certainly seemed to me the oldest person I had ever seen, sat in an otherwise vacant pew in front of all, so that, his voice being very thin and querulous, we could hear very little that he said, although we were edified in some faint sense by his pious manner of shaking his head and rolling his eyes toward the ceiling.

The church was a square wooden edifice, of medium size, and contained three stoves all burning brightly. Against this and the drowsy effect of their long drive in the sun and wind, my two companions proved powerless to struggle.

Grandpa looked furtively up at Grandma, then endeavoured to put on as a sort of apology for what he felt was inevitably coming, a sanctimonious expression which was most unnatural to him, and which soon faded away as the sweet unconsciousness of slumber overspread his features. His head fell back helplessly, his mouth opened wide. He snored, but not very loudly. I looked at Grandma, wondering why her vigilance had failed on this occasion, and lo! her head was falling peacefully from side to side. She was fast asleep too. She woke up

first, however, and then Grandpa was speedily and adroitly
aroused by some means, I think it was a pin; and
Grandma fed him with bits of unsweetened flagroot, which
he munched penitently, though evidently without relish,
until he dropped off to sleep again, and she dropped off
to sleep again, and so they continued.

But it always happened that Grandma woke up first.
And whereas Grandpa, when the avenging pin pierced
his shins, recovered himself with a start and an air of
guilty confusion, Grandma opened her eyes at regular intervals, with the utmost calm and placidity, as though she
had merely been closing them to engage in a few
moments of silent prayer.

Our class occupied a humble place in the sanctuary,
near the door. Behind the pew in which Grandma,
Grandpa and I were sitting, there was one more, vacant.
Presently the door opened, admitting a delightful waft of
fresh air, and some one entered that pew, and bowed his
head forward on the desk in a devotional attitude.

After the brief excitement caused by the advent
of this new and very late comer had subsided,
the Sunday school resumed its former lethargic
condition, and then I heard my own name whispered
very softly in my ear.

I had to turn my head but a little to meet the depre-
cating, though evidently irreverent eyes of Emily's
fisherman.

" How do you do, Miss Hungerford?" he murmured
brightly. " Please don't consider me in the light of
an intruder. I know I'm rather young for the class,
to which you are admitted by reason of some extraordinary acquaintance with biblical lore."

"But it's an excellent opportunity for you' to address the little boys and girls," I said.

"Nonsense!" said Mr. Turner, reddening. "I only meant that for a joke, you know."

Without pausing to reflect at all on the moral consequences of the act, I welcomed the appearance of this voluble, fashionably dressed young man among the "ancient and fish-like" odors of the West Wallen meeting house with a positive sense of relief.

"If I might venture to suppose," Mr. Turner continued, whispering, "that I came here, to-day, clothed, in any sense, as an angel of light — and, indeed, I feel a good deal like that sort of thing to-day — so sweet are the solaces of an approving conscience, and the consciousness of having resisted temptation. You see I was — yes, I was going fishing this morning, but I saw Captain Spicer go by to church — observe too, the beauty of setting a good example — and I persuaded myself that it was wrong to go fishing on Sunday, and so I concluded to come to church, too."

At the light mockery of the fisherman's tone, the bolder flattery of his eyes, I felt the same quick flash of resentment that his words had occasioned when he walked with me up the lane. I turned my head away with the noble resolve to keep it there persistently.

Then I heard the whisper, "Miss Hungerford, you are driving me to the last extreme of idol worship. I shall keep on addressing my petitions to that ostrich tip in your hat until you give me at least, the benefit of your profile."

"I don't see why you should say such irreverent things

to me, Mr. Turner," I said, quite seriously, turning, and looking him full in the face, for an instant.

"Heaven forbid!" he replied in an almost inaudible tone. "And if I could have conceived of such a thing, I would beg your pardon. You have brothers, Miss Hungerford?"

"Yes," I answered, nodding my head slightly with my eyes fixed steadfastly on the ancient instructor of our class.

"How would you feel if your brother was off, alone, in some wild country, in need of good and gentle influences, and some young lady should treat him as you are treating me? Please turn your head a little this way. But, on the whole, I'm very glad I'm not your brother. Shall I tell you why? Miss Hungerford," the fisherman continued, after a pause, "do you know I've always heard that auburn haired people come, by right, into possession of the worst tempers. Your hair is brown — dark brown, and mine is red, almost — don't you think so? — And yet my mind is all peace within, and hope and joy, and

'What is the blooming tincture of the skin,
To peace of mind and purity, within?'

Miss Hungerford, it has been full two minutes, by my watch, since I caught the last beam from your eye. Let us forget the idle wranglings of the hour, and compose our minds to the great subjects which agitate eternity. One of those insects which infest ancient church edifices has been hovering about Captain Spicer's mouth. It has been drawn in. It has disappeared. Such are we, hovering on the vortex of eternity. How calm and undisturbed the old captain's face! how utterly unconscious

of the tragedy just enacted ! So eternity swallows us
and leaves no trace behind, and no ripple marks its
surface. How infer—— how more than odd the old
captain looks, any way ! I say, she ought to have touched
up his eye-brows a little, you know, while she was
at the nefarious business, Miss Hungerford ? "

" Yes," I answered, listening deliberately.

" Do you suppose that the time will ever come when
she to whom I once gave the love of my young heart, and
all that sort of thing, you know, will take me in hand, and
dye my hair, and rig me up, and make such an infernal
looking old guy of me ? "

" I don't see how you can escape," I said.   " But you
won't care so much, then."

" No, that's true." Mr. Turner sighed deeply; " I
shall be old, then ;

> ' When I am old, I shall not care
> To deck with flowers my faded hair.' "

The idea of Mr. Turner's decking his hair with flowers
was a specially entertaining one to me.

Presently, he continued :

" To descend for a moment to secular subjects — I've
got my own horses here, now, Miss Hungerford.   I
had my man Bob bring them down from Providence.
They got here last night, and they 're a pair of spankers,
too, if I do say it that should n't, as the phrase is.   That
was one of the inducements which led me to follow your
— to follow Captain Spicer's example in coming to
church this morning.   And, now, I have a calm, serious,
and reasonable proposal to make.   No doubt, we are
both familiar with the small conventionalities of life,

but on such a day as this, and with such a glorious air outside, and such a unique framework of society — everything delightfully pagan — scruples worthy only of small consideration at any time, should be thrown aside. I don't know what perils you encountered on your way to church this morning, in the canvas-covered vehicle. But, if you will drive back to Wallencamp with me, I promise to take you there fleetly and safely, and you may have the consciousness, besides, if you care for it, that you have made the day one of spiritual reclamation to an erring fellow creature."

The Sunday school had risen to its feet and was slowly droning " yield not to temptation, etc." The situation was odd enough. Mr. Turner's repressed laughing voice was in my ear "will you yield?" and I yielded.

At the close of the Sunday school, as we were going out of the church, I told Grandma that I should drive home with Emily's fisherman.

She drew me gravely to one side. "We shall be very sorry to lose your company, teacher," she said, " only we had n't ought to lose no precious opportunity, and I do hope as you 'll labor for that young man's soul." I felt hopelessly conscience stricken.

We drove home through "Lost Cedars"—a good many miles out of the ordinary course—and I was cheerfully consenting to the divergence.

Wild and tenantless, in the midst of a wild and tenant-less landscape, Lost Cedars wore that air of lovely, though utter, desolation, which might easily have suggested its name.

There was a still unfrozen lake, which the setting sun

more like the sun of an Italian winter than of rugged New England, was painting in gorgeous colors, when we reached the place.

"We come fishing here, sometimes," said Mr. Turner; "I keep a little boat down there under the bush, and I happen to have the key of the boat here in my pocket. It looks awfully tempting, does n't it?"

I had always been passionately fond of out door life, and prided myself in having acquired no little skill at the oar. We were out on the painted lake, and I was rowing the light boat, and taking much selfish enjoyment out of the scenes around me, when I became conscious that the fisherman was leaning far forward from his seat in the boat, addressing me in a low tone.

"To discuss a topic appropriate to the day, Miss Hungerford:— I suppose you 've read about that fellow who was looking for the pearl of great price, have n't you? —that is, as I take it, you know, it was something that was going to be of more value to him than anything else in the world,—well, now, I believe that every man thinks he 's going to be lucky enough to fall in with something of that sort some day—don't you?"

Mr. Turner's tone was unusually serious and even slightly embarrassed. I looked up with curious surprise from my dreamy observation of the water. Then I thought of what Grandma Spicer had said to me about laboring for this young man's spiritual good.

"I think we all ought to seek it," I observed tritely, giving a long studied artistic stroke to the oars. "I don't see why you should n't find it, I'm sure—if you ask. I wish that I were good enough to talk to you real helpfully on this subject."

I was startled at the inspiriting effect my brief exhortation seemed already to have produced on the soul of Emily's fisherman.

"To ask! is that all!" he exclaimed in the same low breath. And looking at the glowing, though rather unsanctified light on his features, my interest suddenly expanded to take in the possible drift of his words. I concluded that it was time for me to show myself eminently discreet; having departed so far from the immediate object of my mission as to spend a considerable part of the Sabbath driving and rowing with a strange young man, miles from every place of refuge.

"I'm tired," I said. "Please row back now, I should like to go home."

I rose to give Mr. Turner my place at the oar. He held out his hand to assist me, and whether by any malicious design of his or not, at that moment the boat gave a sudden lurch, and I was precipitated helplessly forward into his arms. I felt his kiss burning on my lips.

With anger at the fisherman's unfairness, and bitterness at what I felt to be the mortifying result of my own folly and indiscretion—"Oh," I exclaimed, "I hate you! I wish you would never speak to me, again! I wish I had fallen into the water."

The fisherman sent the boat leaping on with long strokes. "D——n it!" he muttered softly: "I wish you had, and I after you!"

We drove for several miles on the way homeward in silence. Then Mr. Turner spoke. I had been meditating upon Ethel upon my determination to make my life in Wallencamp one of supreme self-sacrifice and devotion to duty, and had concluded, in a deeply repentant mind, that this unpleasant incident at the close of the day was only the natural consequence of my error in departing from the prescribed limits of my self-appointed task.

I felt that after this experience it would be unwise for me further to extend my mission work in Mr. Turner's behalf.

So I answered him but briefly, and in a tone of martyr-like composure, which I could not help observing perplexed and irritated him more than anger or the most frigid silence would have done.

I was strengthened in this frame of mind when we parted at the little gate in front of the Ark, and Mr. Turner proposed another drive for the ensuing week.

Then I revealed to the fisherman the grave burden of my soul.

" Mr. Turner," I said, " if I had come to Wallencamp merely in search of my own pleasure and diversion I should doubtless find it very easy to do some things which I do not consider harmful in themselves, but which it is wrong for me to do, under the circumstances. I may tell you that I have been very reckless, very thoughtless in my life, but I came here resolving to devote myself to an earnest, serious work. I hoped to do these people good. They do seem to believe in me. They trust me. I can not bear that they should think me in any way unworthy of their trust. When you asked me to drive, this evening,— it was just as it used to be — I did not think. You were very kind. It was pleasant and I thank you,—but I ought not to have gone — don't you see? I believe, now, that it would have been so much better if I had not."

" I don't see." said Mr. Turner, "why should you leave

me altogether? Don't I believe in you? Don't
I need to be done some good to?"

At this last childishly whimsical appeal, I was in sore
danger of being diverted from the serious channel of
my thoughts. Then the door of the Ark softly opened a
little way, and there, night-capped in white, like a
full, benignant moon, appeared the head of Grandma
Spicer, as she peered blindly out into the night.

"Poor old soul!" I said. "She has probably been
'waiting and watching.' Don't you see already one
of the results of my sinning? Good night," I said, extending my hand to the fisherman, who had fixed on that
innocent and unconscious night-cap a darkly withering
gaze.

"Oh, never mind me," he muttered, turning abruptly.
"Only take care of this infernal old nest of Hoosiers, and
respectable people may go to the devil!"

CHAPTER VI.

ETHEL AND THE CRADLEBOW.

"TEACHER'S got Eth's beau!"

"'Teacher's got Eth's beau!'" I heard it whispered among the school children Ethel heard, too, and paled a little, but looked up at me and smiled as frankly as ever.

Seeing her alone afterwards, I took occasion to remark, incidentally, "how kind it was of her friend, Mr. Turner, to bring me home from church. Fanny was so slow! And I thought he was a very pleasant young man, but even the most estimable people, you know," I added, laughing, with an undertone of studied significance, "are not just fitted to enjoy each other's society always."

Then I blushed under the girl's clear, trustful gaze.

"You don't think I mind what the children talk!" she said.

Every day Ethel appealed more and more, unconsciously, to what was most generous and grave and heed-
ful in my nature.   She seemed to be demanding of me,
with mute, gentle importunity to make real my ideal
of life, to be what I knew she believed me to be.   Her
faith in my superior wisdom and goodness, her slow,
timid way of confiding in me, with tears and blushes,
even ; it was all very flattering, very captivating to
one who had but so lately risen to occupy the pedestal of
a moral instructress, and " my child," " my dear child,"
I said to her in many private discourses, with more
than the tranquil grace and dignity with which such terms
had been applied to me, only a year before, by the august
principal of Mt. B—— Seminary.

Ethel read my books, and I drew her out to talk
with me about them.   She prepared her lessons, with me,
out of school.   She knew that she might come whenever
she chose to my little room, at the Ark, which the
chimney kept comfortably warm, and often I heard
her footsteps on the stairs, and her gentle knock at the
door.

If I was troubled or perplexed on any account,
Ethel always seemed to understand in that quiet,
unobtrusive way of hers, and followed my movements
with a grave, restful sympathy in her eyes.   On several
occasions I had asked her, playfully, to walk up the lane
with me, after school.   So it became a matter of course,
that she should wait for me.   Often we took longer walks,
for it was an " open winter," with   only one or two
light falls of snow.

Then I believed the " Tempter " came to me, in the
form of another invitation to drive, from Mr. Turner.

Occupied with my duties in the school-room, one afternoon, I was startled to observe these characters as suddenly and mysteriously raised as if by the unseen hand of a modern sibyl on the black-board :

"teecher's Bo is a setting On the Fens."

Involuntarily raising my eyes to the window, I was unable to discover on the fence opposite, anything of the nature indicated in those words. I concluded that the whole was to be taken as one of those deeply allegorical expressions in which the Wallencamp tongue abounded.

Shortly afterward, a boy who had been playing truant and the Jews' harp at the same time, in a subdued and melancholy way under the window, and who had, doubt-less, been bribed to undertake his present commission through some extraordinary means, entered the school-room, and laid on my desk a note from the auburn-haired fisherman. It was hastily scrawled in lead pencil, on a leaf torn from a memorandum.

The fisherman confessed to all the meekness and long suffering, without the cheerful intrepidity of Mary's little lamb ! He would do all his waiting outside. Mr. Levi was down from West Wallen to-day, and said that he had heard somebody say that there were four letters came for the teacher in last night's mail. Would I like to drive over to West Wallen and get them? The fisherman did not believe that I had been in earnest in the prudish and unreasonable notions I had propounded when he left me the other evening.

"Prudish!" In my newly acquired elevation of mind, I hugged the term with a deep, intense, and mysterious delight. Oh, if my mother could only know—if my elder sister could only know that I had actually been accused of prudishness ! It was in the glow and inspiration of this idea that I indited the answer to Mr. Turner's missive : — "why would he make it unpleasant and disagreeable for me to do what seemed to me so plainly my duty ?"—and despatched the same by the pensive and unpunished truant, who was soon heard again revelling in the stolen sweets of his Jews' harp beneath the window.

After this I had no further intercourse with the fisherman for some days. If I chanced to meet him in the lane, Ethel was always with me. He came one evening to the Ark. The young people were there, singing.

Then I heard, from time to time, of his taking Ethel to drive, and congratulated myself that through my composed wisdom and forethought, the little world of Wallencamp was destined to move very smoothly, on the whole.

" I wonder why Mr. Turner don't go home," observed Grandma Spicer complacently, on one of those rare occasions when the Spicer family circle held quiet possession of the Ark before the songful company had arrived. " He did n't use to stay but a week or two at a time, and all the rest o' the fishermen have been gone some time, now ; and he keeps them horses down here, and goes loungin' around with no more object than a butterfly in December."

" I tell ye he's a makin' up to Eth." said Grandpa Spicer, with the knowing air of an old man accustomed to fathom mysteries of this peculiar nature.

A spark shot out of Abagail's great, black eyes. Then she laughed unpleasantly. " There's something in the wind besides Eth." said she.

" Why, I don't know," said Grandma, " He don't hang

around there very much, may be, but they say he takes her to ride, and, I'm sure, he don't wait on nobody else. But I should think, if he was a goin' to speak out, he'd ought to do it, and not waste his time a keepin' a puttin' it off. Why, my fust husband was n't but a week makin' up his mind, and pa," she continued, referring openly to Grandpa Spicer, "he wan't quite so out-spoken, to be sure ; but he came around to it in the course of a month or two, and kind o' beat around the bush then, and wanted to know what I thought on't, and — wall, I told him ' yes,' — I did n't see no use in bein' squeamish so long as I'd once made up my mind to it."

" I asked ye as soon as I could ! " exclaimed Grandpa, bristling on the defensive. "I wanted to be sure o' gittin' a house, fust."

"There !" said Abagail briskly, putting down her foot, and tossing her head as she addressed the old couple. "Be good, children ! Be good ! — and, now, do you mark my words, it is n't Ethel Kent that Eliot Turner is hanging around here for. There's some folks to be made up to, and there's some folks, jest as good, to be stepped on. And Eliot Turner — what does he think of Wallencamp folks, any way? He would n't take the trouble to kick 'em out of his road ; he'd jest step on 'em, and he's steppin' on Eth. Kent. He don't care enough about her to let her.alone."

" Wall, I — don't — know !" said Grandma. " What's he stayin' for, then?"

"Staying ! Lord, ma ! " said Abagail sharply, with a strange cold glitter in her eye. " How do I know what he's stayin' for? Oh," she added, in a tone of lighter bitterness, "It's a mild winter and open roads. He's sketching they say, and exploring the Cape. Let him explore from one end to the other, he won't find such another fool as himself."

"We can't help nothin' by talkin' that way," said Grandma Spicer, a little pale, though calmly cognizant of Abagail's emotion.

"You know I had an experience of my own, once, ma," said Abagail, terribly white about the lips.

"I wouldn't rake up old wounds, daughter." There was nothing unfeeling in Grandma Spicer's tone.

The daughter shut her lips together tightly, as though more than she had intended to reveal had already escaped them, and applied herself desperately to her sewing.

I fancied that I had detected a personally aggressive quality in Abagail's indignant tone.

"I don't see why we should feel that way about **Ethel**," I said. "The more one gets acquainted with her, the more lovable and worthy of respect she seems. I knew a great many girls, at school — girls with every advantage of wealth and culture, too, who had not half of Ethel's grace and refinement, nor a tenth part of her beauty!"

Abagail said nothing, bending to her work with the same bitter compression of the lips.

"It's right you should stand up for her, teacher," said Grandma Spicer, pleasantly. "Miss Taite, she begun by makin' a kind o' pet o' her, but I don't think Ethel ever set her heart on her as she has on you, and it's easy to see you've took lots o' pains with her. She's a gittin' them same kind o' sorter interestin' high flowed ways — why, she used to be jest like the rest of 'em jest sich a rompin', roarin' thing as Drussilly Kent is now."

"Goodness gracious, ma!" Abagail put in again, sharply. "What good is it going to do Eth. Kent to put on airs? Better stick to her own ways, and her own folks, she'll find they'll stand by her best in the end, I guess, than to be fillin' her head with notions to hurt her feelin's over by and by. She's a fool, I think, for treatin' George Olver as she does. He's worth a dozen Eliot Turners, if his coat don't set quite so fine, and would work his fingers off to suit her if she'd only settle down to him, and be sensible."

"Wall," said Grandma Spicer, in a tone that was a curious contrast to Abagail's, "our feelin's won't always go as we'd ought to have em. daughter."

"No, they won't!" Abagail snapped out excitedly, "but, ma, you know I'm in the right of it just as well as I do, and there's Benney Leonard's got to dreamin' and moonin' around in the same way. Took it into his head he wanted to get an education—well, what has n't he took into his head! So he must begin recitin' to teacher. Well, he had in his mind to study I don't doubt, to begin with, and used to come two or three times a week, and rattle off a string, and, now he's here every day of his life, and, if there's any reciting going on, I don't hear it—not that I want to meddle with other folk's business, but I've known those boys a good many years, and I hate to see anybody hurt and run over, even if they be young and ignorant, and making fools of themselves. Some folks are none too good, I think, for all their airs, and had better look out to see where they're going!"

"Why, thar, Abagail!" said Grandma with a decided touch of disapproval in her voice. " R'a'ly, seems to me you 're kind o' out.   I'm sure Benney Leonard seems to be a gittin' along finely with his Latin and Algibbery — I'm sure, I've heard a lot of it, when I've been goin' through the room, if you ain't; and if he's took it into his head to git book larnin', and maybe scratch enough together to go away somewheres to school, why I'm sure, there's older boys than him, and not so bright, have ketched up if they set their minds to it, and as for our teacher — Abagail ! "

" Oh, I've no doubt but what Miss Hungerford meant kindly," said Abagail with the lightness she could so suddenly assume. " It's a mighty queer world, that's all ! " she added presently, rising and putting on her bonnet, "and managed very queerly, for I suppose it is managed. I'm going out, ma. Those children have split my head with their noise to-day, and I promised Patty I'd come in and sit awhile. Now, if I've been cross and crazy, don't you and teacher talk me over," she said, looking back and trying hard to smile — and she did look very tired and white, as though she had been suffering—" and if those children wake up and begin to squall "— with a glance towards the little bed-room — " Let 'em squall. If I've wished it once to-day, I have a hundred times—that they was the other side of sunset ! "

" I wish you'd step into Lihu's — such a poor, sufferin' creetur as he is—with these," said Grandma, appearing from the pantry with some eggs in her apron. " I wish you could take the consolations of religion with you, Abagail ," she continued gravely, as Mrs. Ithamer was closing the door.

"Lord, ma! my pocket's full now!" exclaimed Abagail. "Besides, they might break the eggs!" And the latch fell down with a click.

"I wish Abagail was a believer," Grandma sighed, purposely rattling about the cover of the stove to wake up Grandpa, who had fallen asleep in his chair.

Grandpa looked at me, and smiled feebly, then roused himself to meet this supposed challenge like a man.

"Believer, ma?" said he, "why ain't I a believer? As old Cap'n Gates said to me on his last voyage" — Grandpa yawned alarmingly (poor old man! he was but half awake), as this unlucky reminiscence of his seafaring life flitted through his brain — "says he, 'I read my almanick and my bible, both, Hoggarty'" says he "I read 'em both, and I believe there's a great deal o' truth in both on 'em."

"Thar, pa!" said Grandma, solemnly, "you'd *better* go to sleep! you'd *better* close your eyes, Hoggarty Spicer! What if you should never open 'em again on earthly scenes, and them words on your lips,—and you a perfessor!"

Grandpa scratched his head in drowsy bewilderment, passed his hand once or twice over the coarse stubble on his face, and again committed himself helplessly to the sweet obliviousness of slumber.

I drew my chair up confidentially close to Grandma Spicer's and rested my arms on the table as I looked into her face.

"Grandma!" I said, for I knew that she was better pleased to have me call her that, "I begin to think that I ought never to have come to Wallencamp on a mission, that perhaps it would be just as well, if I had never come

to Wallencamp at all, I mean.   I did n't think.   At first,
it seemed more than anything else, like something very
new to entertain myself with.   I did n't think enough of
the responsibility.   Then, perhaps I thought too much of
it.   I don't know.   I wish I were out of it all.   Grandma, I never tried to do the right thing so hard before in
my life.   I never worked so hard before — and I don't
mind that ; but I meant it all for the best, and its no use,
its just like all the rest.   I'm tired.   I wish I were out of
it."

"Wall, thar now, darlin'," said Grandma, employing to
the full her tone of infinite consolation.   "You ain't
the first one as mistook a stump for a livin' creetur in the
night, and don't you talk about givin' up nor nothin' like
it, darlin', for we could n't do without you noways — nor
you without us, for yet a while I'm thinkin', though it does
seem strange — and never you mind one straw for what
Abagail   said, for she was kind o' out to-night, anyway,
not having got no letter from Ithamer I suppose.   But
then, she ought not to feel so.   Why there was time and
time agin that I did n't git no letter from Hoggarty Spicer
when he was voyagin', and to be sure, they was n't much
better than nothin' when they did come, for pa "—Grandma cast a calmly comprehensive glance at her unconscious
mate — "pa was a man that had a great many idees in
general, but, when he set down to write a letter, somehow
he seemed to consider that it was n't no place for idees, a
letter was n't — seemed as though he managed a'most a
purpose not to get none in."

"Grandma," I said, leaning forward, laughing, and
folding my hands in her lap, "you 're the best comforter I
know of."

"Wall, thar," said she, "it's a good deal in feelin's, and Abagail ain't r'al well, so she kind o' allows 'em to overcome her sometimes."

"And what did she mean by saying that about Ethel?" I asked.

"Oh, she just meant girls will be girls, that's all!" replied Grandma, "why mercy! I know all about that. I don't feel like nothin' much more than a girl myself, half the time ; and we all have to have our experiences, to be sure. They ain't nobody else can wear 'em for us, but, dear me ! the Lord ain't goin' to let our experiences hurt us, they're for our betterin'."

"And Benney, Grandma?" I said, "what did she mean about him?"

"Oh, she just meant boys will be boys, that's all — especially big ones — but, thar ! I've known 'em to get over it a hundred times and not hurt 'em none. If you'r always lookin' at human natur' on the dark side, it seems kind o' desp'rit. My first husband, he wasn't a fretful man, but, he was always viewin' the dark side o' things. I suppose one reason was he did n't have no father nor mother, and so he kind o' begun life as a took-in boy, but Pollos Slocum, he done very well by him, for he had n't no children of his own, but his brother — that was Daniel Slocum — he had six. There was two boys and four girls. Mary she came fust. She was born February nineteenth."

I was sorry that Grandma's thoughts had drifted into this hopeless and interminable channel.

I had considered carefully what Abagail nad said, and determined on a little new advice for my friend, Ethel. So the next time we were alone in my room together, I directed the conversation with a view to this end :

"And I would n't trust any one, my dear," I said with cheerful earnestness, "then if people prove true, why, it's all the more delightful; and if not, one is n't disappointed, so you can hold the scales quite indifferently in your own hand, and are always master of the situation. Oh, I would n't trust people! It would be very nice if this were the sort of world that you could do it in, but it is n't. It's a very deceitful world."

"But I can trust you, can't I?" Ethel held me with her gravely questioning eyes.

"Well, I don't know." I began with the determination to be severely true to my text, but the look in Ethel's eyes hurt me.

"Oh, yes! little girl," I continued, falling into the half tender, half playful tone that it was always easiest to assume with her, "of course, you must trust me! Have n't I been a good teacher to you, so far?" And I sought by smiling in the girl's face, to chase the grieved expression away from it. "What I meant was that I would n't trust people generally, because it's a selfish world, and such is the depravity of the human mind that if it appears at all convenient, we are apt, you know, to sacrifice other people to our own interests; so, with all the little kindnesses and politenesses which are current in society, it is still the common practise—and it is best that it should be so—to keep, in the main, a sharp look out for 'Number One!'"

Having proceeded so far, it occurred to me that the occasion was favorable for the discharge of another duty which I had been meditating in regard to Ethel

"You are what Grandma Spicer calls a believer, are you

not, dear?" I said. with the same composedly dictatorial manner, " in distinction from a professor, I mean."

Ethel gave a little gasp, and turned her head away, for an instant. When she looked back, there were tears of distress in her eyes.

I felt a vague wonder and regret.

" No," she said, " I thought, once — I wanted — I hoped —— "

" Why, child ! " I hastened to exclaim. "I did n't ask you because I had any reason to doubt that you were one — quite the contrary — but simply for this. It seems to me it would be such a desirable thing for you, situated as you are, here, with so few surroundings of a refining and elevating nature, if you could attach yourself, if it were merely for a feeling of fellowship and sympathy — for of course, you could not attend, often — to some simple Orthodox body of believers — like the Methodist church at West Wallen for instance. It seems to me, that, in your case, believing simply and unquestionably, as I have no doubt you do, it would be a sort of assurance, a sort of continual rest and support to you. It would be a great relief to me if I felt that you were so guarded. Not that I consider it essential at all ; to some people, in- deed, of a deeply thoughtful and inquisitive mind, such a course would appear impossible You have never troubled yourself, Ethel," I continued, in a tone of reassuring light- ness, " you have never troubled yourself with doubts and speculations on religious subjects ? "

" I don't know," Ethel replied, the look of perplexity and distress deepening in her eyes.

" Why should you ? " I murmured, softly stroking her hair, " He carries the lambs in His bosom." I had been little in the habit of quoting scripture — the words coming to mind, struck me as particularly beautiful and applicable on this occasion, "and so what I have suggested, would be the easiest, and most natural thing in the world for you to do. I suppose it might be necessary for you to have come to some conclusion in regard to the first principles of Theology, but probably you have already satisfied yourself as to these in your own mind."

Ethel looked little like one who had arrived at the calm plane of philosophical conclusion of any sort.

" I don't know," she gasped.

" Well, take the Trinity, for instance," I continued, in a tone highly suggestive of calm and supreme forbearance with helpless ignorance. " Probably you believe in the Trinity ? "

" Oh, I don't know," said Ethel. " I don't know what it means. Nobody ever told me ; nobody ever talked to me about those things before."

" It's simply," I said, " a term implying the existence of three persons in the God-head. So, the Trinitarians are distinguished from the Unitarians who believe that it consists of one. I'm not particularly informed as to the Methodist credentials of faith. You will always hear that they believe that salvation is free to all who will accept of it. Some people believe that man is a free agent, and may accept or refuse the means of grace, and if he refuses, is eternally lost. And then, again, there are the Universalists, who believe that all will be eventually saved. There is the Calvinistic element — those who believe in predestination — that is —— "

Ethel had laid her head down on the bed, and was quietly sobbing.

" My poor child," I exclaimed, with swift compassion,
" don't think anything more about what I have said
to you. Let it go. It is n't vital."

" You don't hate me for not knowing anything? "
sobbed Ethel. " Nobody ever tried to have me understand. before."

" You know enough ; quite enough, dear ! " I remarked
hastily, producing from my trunk a quantity of illustrated
magazines. These we looked over together, and when
Ethel went away, the tears were dried in her eyes, and
she was laughing as merrily as ever.

With the severely implied reproach of Abagail's words
still in my mind, I took pains to assume toward Benney
Leonard a more elder-sisterly air even than before.

It was true, I felt that I had been unjustly stung, having,
amid the press of other duties, undertaken the advance-
ment of that bright youth, from motives, I believed, of
an ideal and disinterested nature. It was also true, that,
after the first enthusiasm with respect to his lessons had
passed away, as well as the natural diffidence he had at
first felt in my presence, Benney Leonard, though
punctual to the hour of recitation, had gradually
fallen into a habit of more lively and discursive inquiry
than that furnished within the dull range of his text books.
He had a singularly fearless manner of challenging the
inexplicable in thought and life, with a light conversa-
tional flow of much brilliancy. Moreover, he was a
delightful dreamer.

We had our recitation, for quiet, in one of Grandma's
gloomy and mysterious keepin'-rooms. The only object
inviting to sedentary posture in this room, was Grandpa's
huge " chist," which occupied a position " alongside "

the East window. Those sacred window curtains, of green paper, flowered with crimson roses, were never rolled up; but as the light strayed in at one side, and fell on the Cradlebow's fine head, often I reflected that under certain other conditions of life, meaning conditions more favorable to Benney Leonard, I might have regarded him very tenderly, and invested the strength and beauty of his young manhood with heroic meaning.

As it was, I assumed that I was years beyond him in the gravest respects. And if there was any truth in what Abagail had intimated, possibly I had been at fault for not impressing this fact more deeply on his mind.

"So you are getting sadly behindhand with your lessons, Benney," I said. "I wish you would make a brave effort to catch up. There is no true attainment to be reached without a corresponding degree of effort — of perseverance."

I spoke with a serious and gracious air, as though this sentiment, gleaned from a profound experience, had occurred to me as an idea peculiarly my own.

"Never mind the lessons!" replied my audacious pupil, brightly. "Teacher," he added presently, having fallen into a gently musing attitude, "how shiny those crimples in your hair look, with that streak of sun lighting on 'em!"

"Benney," said I, very gravely, "you ought not to talk to me about my hair. Suppose we give our attention to these books. Now you were getting along so fast, I'm very sorry ——,"

"Do you think I'm to blame, teacher!" exclaimed Benney earnestly. "There was n't a stick of wood to be had in our house this morning! And I've had to be off,

all day, chopping, with Scudder—you ought to have seen
the black snake we killed this morning. It was six feet
long. If you don't believe it, Scudder's got the carcass.
It was lying all curled up in the bushes, with its head up
so —'you watch him, Ben,' says Scudder, 'and I'll run
and get the axe !' I couldn't help laughing. The axe
was over the other side of the bog, and the snake began
to stretch himself out and slide along. I brought my
boot-heel down once or twice on his head, about as quick
and strong as I could make it. I killed him. It's a good
sign to kill a snake, teacher. It's a good sign to dream
of killing one ; but you come across one so, accidentally,
and kill it, and it's sure to bring good luck, Granny says."

"That's more significant than a great many of your
signs and symbols," I said. "That means that you will
slay the tempter in your path, and be successful in over-
coming difficulties. In short, it means that whatever
there has been to divert you, you are coming back to the
resolve to study and improve yourself, to be all the
stronger for having a few chance obstacles to dispose of."

Benney's head began to drop a little. I thought it
was time that the melancholy atmosphere of the room
should have begun to exercise its usual depressive
effect on his spirits.

"You think I don't like the books, teacher," he said.
"I do, but there's most always something else to be
doing. Father's lame. He can't do any work, and
there's the rest to take care of. First, I sat up nights to
study, then I got so sleepy I couldn't. But, I'd got so
in the habit of coming in to talk a little while after you
got home from school, teacher, that I — I forgot to forget
it. Have I been a great bother to you? You've been

real good. I don't want you to think I forget that. And
if I'd had a chance at the books early, or to push right
along with 'em now, I might make out something in that
line."

Benney did not speak complainingly, nor even with
hopeless regret. He rose and stretched himself, with
solemn satisfaction, to the extent of his goodly proportions.

" But, I'm a man now, teacher," he said. " I shall be
twenty in June, and life is short. A man has n't got time
for everything. He'd be a fool to waste it crying for
what he did n't happen to have. He'd better push along
and work for the best. I meant to tell you. I'm going
to sea, teacher ! I'm going trading. I was down to New
Bedford, to see Captain Sparhauk yesterday, for I was
out with him once before, and got a good deal of the
hang of the business then, and he offered me a place on
his ship next time he sails."

Benney stood with flushed face, regarding me with a
bright restless look of inquiry in his eyes.

" Are you going away, really, **Benney**? I'm very
sorry !" I said.

" You don't care ! what do you care?" he exclaimed
almost rudely, with an unnatural touch of hardness in his
laugh. " It's the way you talk to all the rest. A fellow
might get to thinking too much about it. A fellow might
get to caring — if he believed it — I don't."

" What makes you think I should n't care if you were
going away?" I continued, with the dispassionately gentle
and reproving tone I considered it wisest to assume on
the occasion. " I should care, I should be very sorry.
Come and sit down here, please, and tell me all about it,

when you are going, and where, and what you are going
for?"

Benney came slowly back to the light. He seemed
verily to have grown older and handsomer in a moment.
I experienced a deeper feeling of regret than ever before,
that the circumstances of his life could not have been
conducive to heroism.

"The Captain could n't tell me just when he should
sail," said he, "and I'm going to get money. I know a
good deal of the Spanish and Portugal, I learned to talk
them before — and I shall go to a great many places, I
may not come back when the ship does, — Say, what
strange eyes you've got, teacher, now they're brown —
and now, they're black, and now, they're a sort of — a —
purplish grey."

"Oh, my dear boy," I exclaimed, with a sudden accession of wisdom, sighing deeply, "you ought not to talk to
me about the color of my eyes." At the same time to
deepen the effect of this condescending tenderness, I
pushed back lightly from his forehead a stray lock of hair
that was hanging there.

"Don't do that!" the boy cried with startling im-
petuosity. "Don't call me that again ! I mean, teacher,"
he went on in a gentler tone, though none the less excitedly, —"If you should know somebody, that had set
his heart on something, very much, and did n't want anything else if he could n't have that, and if he should know
that he had n't any right to ask for it now, but go off and
work for it real tight, and, maybe come back lucky in a
few years, with a right to ask for it then, — do you think,
teacher, that there 'd be any chance of his finding — of
his getting wnat he wanted most? If you were in any-

body's place, now, teacher, would you give him a word of encouragement to try?"

"I think that the person you speak of would be much more likely to succeed in a practical undertaking, without any hallucination of that sort before his eyes — and if, as you say, it isn't right that he should ask for it now, can we predict that it would be any more reasonable and expedient in the future? These idle fancies of ours soon pass away, Benney, and will look laughable and grotesque enough to us, by and by. Life is so full of changes, and people change, oh, so much!"

In spite of the vanity of my soul, I comforted myself with the reflection that Benney would not care long. I did not really believe that he would go to sea. I stood with him a moment in the door of Grandma's kitchen. He looked over to the woods, behind which the water lay, and the fire and impatience had all gone out of his manner. His gentleness touched me deeply, yet I was determined not to feel his hurt, nor—"if only the circumstances of his life had been different"— what might have been mine also!

"Hark! It's high tide. It's making quite a fuss, over there," he said. "I think a man feels more quiet, somehow, when he's out there, teacher. Father says I'm a wild chap and uneasy. I guess that's so. I can take care of them just as well too if I go, and better. Only if I should die—" there was nothing affected or forlorn in the Cradlebow's tone—"I should like to be buried on the hill, with father's folks. You've been across there. You look one way, and there's the river, oftenest still—and the other way, you hear the old Bay scouring along the sand. I like it, being used to hearing it go always. Granny says it makes a difference then, where you lie, about the resting easy. I don't know. Sometimes it seems as though I should rest easier there."

" A dissertation on the graveyard," I began in a tone of affected lightness, and then paused, convicted of untruth by the solemn light in the Cradlebow's strange, grand eyes.

CHAPTER VII.

BENNEY KISSES THE TEACHER.

ALLENCAMP had its peculiar seasons. After the season of hulled corn, came the reign of baked beans. It was during this latter dispensation that my courage failed considerably.

Abagail used to remark, throwing a rare musical halo about her words, " These beans are better than they look. Ain't they, teacher? "

And I was wont to reply conscientiously enough, though with a sweetly wearied glance at the familiar dish, " Certainly, they do taste better than they look."

Occasionally, we had what Randal Alden called, "Squash on the shell," an ingenious term for the last of the winter pumpkins boiled in halves, and served *au naturel.*

Grandpa, too, pined and put away his food. He used to look across the table at me, with a feeble appeal for sympathy in his expression. Oftentimes he sighed deeply, and related anecdotes redolent of "red salmon" and "deer flesh," "strawberries as big as tea cups" and "peaches as big as pint bowls," in places where he had sailed.

Once, he ventured to remark, apologetically, referring to the beans and pumpkins, that "bein' sich a mild winter, somehow he did n't hanker arter sech bracin' food, and he guessed he'd go over to Ware'am, and git some pork."

"Wall, thar now, pa!" said Grandma; "seems to me we'd ought ter consider all the fruits o' God's bounty as good and relishin' in their season."

"I call that punkin out of season," said Grandpa, recklessly. "Strikes me so."

"I was talkin' about fruits. I was n't talkin' about punkins," said Grandma, with derisive conclusiveness.

"Wall," said Grandpa, very much aroused, "if you call them tarnal white beans the fruits of God, I don't!"

"Don't you consider that God made beans, pa?"

"No, I don't!"

"Who, then—" continued Grandma, in an awful tone—"do you consider made beans, pa?"

Grandpa's eyes, as he glared at the dish, were large and round, and significant of unspeakable things.

"Hoggarty Spicer!" Grandma hastened to say, "my ears have heard enough!"

As for Grandma, neither her appetite, nor her spirits, flagged. In spite of her confirmed habit of tantalizing Grandpa — and this was from no malevolence of motive, but simply as the conscientious fulfilment of a sacred religious and domestic duty—she was the most delightful soul I ever knew.

At supper, it was a habit for her to sit at the table long after we had finished our meal, and to continue eating and talking in her slow, automatic, sublimely philosophical manner, until not a vestige of anything eatable remained, and then as she rose, she would remark. simply, with a glance at the denuded board:

"It beats all, how near you guessed the vittles to-night, daughter!"

Then Grandma resorted to an occasional pastime, harmless and playful enough in itself, yet intended as a special means of discipline for Grandpa, and certainly, a source of great torment and anxiety to that poor old man.

Between the hours of eight and nine P.M., Grandma would deftly glide out of the family circle, and be seen no more that night. At bed time, Grandpa would begin the search, while Abagail and I ungenerously retired.

In the privacy of my own chamber, I could hear the old captain tramping desolately about the Ark, calling, "Ma! ma!" Could hear the outside door swung open, and, imagine Grandpa's wild face peering into the darkness, while still he called, "Ma! ma! where be ye? It's half after ten!"

Then, from the foot of the stairs would arise his distressed, appealing cry, "Come, ma, where be ye? It's half after ten!" Silence everywhere. With a mighty groan, Grandpa would come shuffling up the steep stairs, and what was most remarkable, Grandma was invariably found secluded amid the rubbish in the old garret. Then the whisperings that arose between those two would have pierced through denser substances by far than the little red door which separated me from the scene.

"How'd I know, ma, but what you'd gone out and broke yer leg, or somethin'? Come, ma—" with exasperated persuasiveness—"What do ye want to pester me this way for?"

"Why, pa," arose the calm, mellifluous accents of Grandma Spicer, "so't you might know how you'd feel if I should be took away!"

Next, the little stair-case would resound with loud creaks and groans, as this reunited couple cautiously — and I have no doubt that they believed the whole affair had been conducted with the utmost secrecy — made their way down in their stocking feet.

Grandma — Heaven bless her, always devoted, though original — never saw a human ill that she did not long to alleviate. So, as Grandpa and I daily refused our food, she affirmed, as her opinion, that the one need of our deranged systems was a clarifier ! And she forthwith prepared a mixture of onions and molasses, with various bitter roots, which latter, she, upon her knees, had wrested from the frosty bosom of the earth in an arena immediately adjoining the Ark. Thus I beheld her one wintry day, and wondered greatly what she was at. When I came home from school at night, through a strangely permeated atmosphere, I beheld the clarifier simmering on the stove.

Grandpa already stood shivering over the fire. He smiled when I came in, but it was a faint and deathly smile — the smile of one who has returned, per force, to weak, defenceless infancy.

Grandma pressed me kindly to partake. I preferred to keep what ills I had, rather than fly to others that I knew not of. So I gently and firmly declined. But for several days in succession, Grandpa was made the victim of this ghastly remedy.

His sufferings went beyond the power of mad expostulation to express, and came nigh to produce upon his features the aspect of a saintly resignation.

Never shall I forget his appearance during this clarifying period — his occasional faint and fleeting attempts at

wit — his usually hopeless and world-weary air. The
wonder to me was that he did not then enter upon a
celestial state of existence, being eminently fitted to
go, as far as the attenuation of his mortal frame was
concerned.   It was at this time that I wrote home
that I had never had such an appetite before in my life as
now in Wallencamp (which, in one sense, I felt to
be perfectly true), that the food was of a most
remarkable variety (which I also felt to be true),
but that it was rather difficult to procure oranges
and the like.   Whereupon, I received from home a
large box, containing all manner of pleasant fruits,
and thus poor old Grandpa Spicer and I were enabled
to take a new lease of life.

I found that it was considered indispensable to
the proper discharge of my duties in Wallencamp that I
should make frequent calls on the parents of my flock,
throughout the entire community.   If I failed in any
measure in this respect, they reproached me with being
" unsociable," and said, " Seems to me you ain't very
neighborly, teacher."

I had called myself a student of human nature.   It
seemed to me, now, that in those dingy Wallencamp
houses, I stood for the first time, awed and delighted
before the real article.   Sometimes the men sent out great
volumes of smoke from their pipes, in the low rooms, that
were not delightful, but as far as they knew, they exerted
themselves to the utmost, men and women both, to make
their homes pleasant and attractive to me.

Godfrey Cradlebow's place was as small and poor
as any.   There was one room that served as kitchen,
dining-room, and parlor, with a corresponding medley of

furniture. A very finely chased gold watch hung against the loose brown boards of the wall — a reminder of Godfrey Cradlebow's youth. But what distinguished this house from all the others, was the profusion of books it contained. There were books on the tables, books under the tables, books piled up in the corners of the room.

Godfrey Cradlebow himself was confined in-doors much of the time with the rheumatism. He made nets for the fishermen. I used to like to watch his fingers moving deftly while he talked.

Things having gone wrong with him, and he having suffered much acute physical pain, besides — (that was evident from the manner in which his stalwart frame had been bent with his disease) he had "taken to drink," not excessively, but he seemed to be, most of the time, in a lightly inebriated condition. He was a strange and fluent talker, often ecstatic.

"It is commonly believed, Miss Hungerford," he said to me, once, "that we start on the summit of life, that we descend into the valley, that the sun is westering; but as for me, I seem to look far below there on the mists and dew of earlier years. I walk among the hills. The horizon widens. The air grows thin. I see the solemn streaks of dawn appearing through the gloom. Ah," he murmured, again, "weak and erring though I undoubtedly am, I have a kinship with the living Christ. Yes, even such kinship as human worthlessness may have with infinite perfection. People will say to you about here, Miss Hungerford, ' Oh, never mind Godfrey Cradlebow. He's always being converted, why, he has been converted twenty times already!' very true, aye, and a hundred times, and I trust I shall taste the sweets of conversion many times more before I die. I do not believe the soul to be a barren tract, so far removed from the ocean of God's love, that it may be washed by the waves only once in a life-time, and that, in case of some terrible flood. But I rejoice daily in the sweet and natural return of the tide. How the shore waits for it ! Strewn with weeds and wreck, scorched by the sun, chilled by the night, how it listens for the sound of it's coming ! until it rushes in — ah ! roar after roar — all covering, all hiding, all embracing ! "

Godfrey Cradlebow shook his head rapturously, tears rolled down his cheeks, and all the while he went on rapidly with his netting.

He had the natural tact and grace of a gentleman, and was especially courteous to his wife. This brought down upon him the derision of the Wallencampers, whose conjugal relations were seldom more delicately implied than by a reference — " my woman, thar ! " or " my man over thar ! " with an accompanying jerk of the thumb.

Lydia, Godfrey Cradlebow's wife, was tall and slight, with dark hair and eyes — a perfect face, though worn and sad. She invariably wore over her cotton gown on occasions when she went out, a very fine, very thin old fashioned mantilla, bordered with a deep black fringe. This pathetic remnant of gentility, borne rudely about by the Cradlebow winds, with Lydia's refined face and melancholy dark eyes, gave her a very interesting and picturesque appearance, though I never thought that she wore the mantilla during the winter for effect. She was shy, though exceedingly gentle in her manners. At first, I had thought that she avoided me. But one time, when, making the round of my parochial calls, I stopped at the Cradlebow's, and Mr. Cradlebow discoursing fluently on the Phenomenon, recommended a severe method of discipline as best adapted to his case, I replied, laughingly, that he had better be cautious about making any suggestions of that sort, for Simeon and I were getting to be great friends; the mother, on whose heart I had had no design, took my hand at the door, when I went away, in a clinging, almost an affectionate way.

"You are good to my boys, teacher," she said, "and I thank you for it. They make you a great deal of trouble."

"Oh, no," I answered lightly, returning with a sense of pleasure the pressure of her hand, and it was not until afterwards, walking slowly down the lane that I sighed gently, thinking of that troublesome boy who had told me he was going to sea.

Removed from the world of newspapers, the ordinary active interest in the affairs of church and state, there was a great deal of the lively gadding about, neighborly dropping-in element in Wallencamp. This applied to the men equally as well as to the women. I remember that Abbie Ann once put out her washing and this fact kept the whole social element of Wallencamp on the *qui vive* for a number of days.

The caller would appear at the door at any time during the day with a good natured matter-of-fact "I was a passin' by, and thought I'd drop in a minit, jest to see how ye was gittin' along."

"Won't you set?" would be the cordial response. "Do set."

"Wall, I don't know how to spend the time, anyway,"

the visitor would reply, "thar's so many things a drivin' on me."

But this care belabored victim of fate usually concluded by sitting quite complacently for any length of time.

When such visitations occurred out of school hours, and I remained up in my room, as I frequently did at first. the droppers in felt very much aggrieved, as though I had wittingly offended the instincts of good society.

Besides all which, seldom an evening passed that the young people did not come to the Ark *en masse* to sing.

Then Abagail or Ethel, or (very rarely) I, propelled a strain of doubtful melody from Abagail's little melodeon, while the singers —boys and girls together—chimed in, joyfully rendering with a perfect fearlessness of utterance and deep intensity of expression such songs as " Go, bury thy sorrow, the world hath its share," and " Jesus keep me near the cross," and " Whiter than snow, yes, whiter than snow ; now wash me, and I shall be whiter than snow."

They knew no other songs.   They would sing through a large proportion of the Moody and Sankey Hymnal in a single evening.

At first I listened half amused or thoroughly wearied. But, as the strains grew more familiar and I sang occasionally with the others, I felt each day more tired and more conscious of my own incompetency.   And still the words rang in my ears : " I hear the Saviour say, thy strength indeed is small," with much about trusting in Him, and his willingness to bear it all.   As the wind beat against the Ark on wild nights, so that we could hardly tell which was the wind and which was the roar of the maddened sea, and still those voices chanted hopefully of the "stormless home beyond the river," etc., the words began to strike on something deeper than my physical or intellectual sense, and that not rudely.

I smiled to catch myself humming them over often, and in the school-room when I felt that my patience was fast oozing, and I experienced a wild desire to loose the reins and let all go, unconsciously I took refuge in repeating those same simple words, going over with them, again and again, beneath my breath, holding on to them as though they possessed some unknown charm to keep me still and strong.

I went to the evening meetings. They were held in the school-house, and were very popular in Wallencamp.

By some provision of the Government on behalf of the Indians, a small meeting-house had been built for those in the vicinity of Wallencamp, and they were also provided with a minister for several months during the year. On this account the Indians rather set themselves up above the benighted Wallencampers whom Government had not endowed with the privileges of the sanctuary, while they in turn, made derisive allusions to the "Nigger-camp" minister, and regarded with contempt its pre-scribed means of grace.

The Indians enjoyed, for part of the time that I was in Wallencamp the ministrations of a Baptist clergyman, a truly earnest and intelligent man, gifted with a most force-ful manner of utterance, but so lean as to present a phenomenal appearance.

This good man feared nothing but that he should fail in some part of the performance of his duty. He be-lieved that it was his duty to come over and preach to the Wallencampers also, in their school-house, and he did so.

I think that the Wallencampers regarded this, on the whole, as a doubtful though entertaining move.

I do not think that they took any particular pains to harass or annoy the Rev. Mr. Rivers. But they certainly did not restrict themselves in that natural freedom which they always enjoyed on the occasions of their spiritual feasts.

They attended, as usual — the old and the young, the good, the bad, the indifferent, with a lively sprinkling of babies.

Though not a cold night, they kept the stove gorged with fuel. It roared furiously. They were restless. They made signs audibly expressive of the fact that the air of the room was insufferably close, and very audibly slammed up the windows. They whispered and giggled; they went out and came in, as they pleased. They drank a great deal of water. I remember particularly, how at the most earnest and affecting part of the Rev. Mr. Rivers discourse, the immortal Estella, alias the "Modoc," arose in gawky innocence and all good faith from her seat immediately in front of the speaker, and walked to the back part of the room to regale herself with a draught.

The Baptist minister discharged a withering and conscientious reproof at them through his nose.

Now, for the Wallencampers to be reproved, however scathingly, by some zealous and inspired individual of their own number, was considered, on the whole, as an apt and appropriate thing, but to be reproved by the "Nigger-camp" minister! When, after the meeting he walked with the Spicer family back to the Ark, where he had been hospitably entertained, the Wallencamp boys saw us depart in silent wrath, and I feared that treachery lay in wait for the Rev. Mr. Rivers.

He sat and talked with us at the Ark for an hour or more, perhaps, before bidding us good night, and during that time, I caught frequent glimpses of faces that appeared at the window, and then vanished again instantly — familiar faces, expressive of much scornful merriment. Now and then I heard a smothered giggle outside, and a scrambling among the bushes. It was a dark night. When the Rev. Mr. Rivers finally rose to depart. and had got as far as the gate, he became helplessly entangled in a perfect net-work of small ropes. He could neither advance nor recede. In a pitiable and ignominious condition, he called to us for help.

"Those devilish boys!" said Grandpa, with religious fervor of tone, at the same time glancing at me with a delighted twinkle in his eye. "I knew they was up to something. I heered 'em out there," and he patiently lit his lantern, and went out to cut the minister free, but the Rev. Mr. Rivers did not come to the Wallencamp school house to preach again.

Among those who looked on with quiet approval at this childish and barbarous performance of the Wallencamp youth, I learned afterwards, were staid Noel Norris and little Bachelor Rae.

Left to their own spiritual devices, the Wallencampers carried on their evening meetings after methods formerly approved. They rose and talked — or prayed — or diverted themselves socially — or sang. Everything they were moved to do, they did.

The lame giant, Godfrey Cradlebow, at seasons when the tide came in, would pour forth the utterances of his soul with the most earnest eloquence. At other times, he was morbid and silent, or made sceptical and sneering remarks, aside.

Noel Norris, though generally regarded as a believer, had never so far overcome his natural modesty and reserve, as to address the Wallencamp meeting. But one night, spurred to make the attempt by some of his malicious and fun-loving compatriots, he surprised us all by rising with a violent motion from his seat, and making a sudden plunge forward as though his audience were a cold bath, and he had determined to wade in.

"Boys!" he began, with a most unnatural ferociousness. Then I felt Noel's eyes fixed on my face. "And girls, too," he added, more gently, "and girls, too, certainly, *I* think so," he continued, "*I* think so." His tone became very feeble. He glanced about with a wild eye for his hat, grasped it, and went out, and I saw him afterwards, through the window, standing like a statue, in the moonlight, with his arms folded, and with a perfectly cold and emotionless cast of countenance.

Among the professors, Godfrey Cradlebow's mother, Aunt Susan, with quite as much fire and less delicacy of expression than characterized the speech of the strange lame man, was always ready to warn, threaten, and exhort.

Grandpa Spicer, too, though not subjected to the renovating and rejuvenating processes of the Sabbath, but just touched up a little here and there, enough to give him a slight "odor of sanctity," and a saving sense of personal discomfort, was always led to the meeting, and kept close by Grandma Spicer's side on the most prominent bench.

When there was one of those frightful pauses which sometimes occurred even in the cheerful concourse of the Wallencampers, casting a depressing influence over all hearts, Grandma Spicer by a series of covert pokes and nudges, would signify to Grandpa that now was the appointed moment for him to arise and let his light shine.

And Grandpa Spicer was not a timid man, but·since the event of his clarification, he had shown a stronger dislike than ever to being pestered, and was abnormally quick to detect and resist any advances of that kind. So his movements on these occasions were marked by an angry deliberation, though the old sea-captain never failed in the end, to arise and "hand in his testimony."

His remarks were (originally) clear cut and terse.

"There's no need o' my gittin' up. You all know how I stand" (an admonitory nudge from Grandma), "What's the matter now, ma?" I could hear the old man swear, mentally, but he went on with the amend ment, "or try to. I'm afeered that even the best on us, at some time or nuther, have been up to some devil "—(sly, but awfully emphatic nudge from Grandma) "ahem! we're all born under a cuss!" persisted Grandpa, with irate satisfaction. "I've steered through a good many oceans," he continued, more softly, "but thar ain't none so — misty—as this—a—"(portentious nudge from Grandma,) "as this pesky ocean of Life! We've got to keep ι sharp look out" (another nudge from Grandma), "ahem, steer clear of the rocks," (persistent nudges from Grandma), "ahem! ahem! trust in God Almighty!" admitted Grandpa with telling force, and sat down.

As for Grandma, she was herself always prompt and

faithful in the discharge of duty, however trying the
circumstances.   She was no hypocrite, this dear old
soul !   She could not have feigned sentiments which she
did not feel, yet it was invariably the case that, as she
rose in meeting, her usually cheerful face became in the
highest degree tearful and lugubrious.   The thought
of so many precious souls drifting toward destruction
filled her tender heart with woe.   She besought them
in the gentlest and most persuasive terms to "turn
to Jesus."   She dwelt long upon His love, standing
always with hands reverently clasped before her, and eyes
downcast with awe.

I used to long to hear her speak.   The sound of that
low, tender monotone was in itself, inexpressibly soothing.
But Grandma's tongue had its mild edge, as well.

Once, when she was speaking, a number of the
young people — it was a common occurrence — rose
to go out.

Grandma went on talking without raising either her
voice or her eyes ; but, when they had reached the door,
" What —" said she, in that tone which, though so mild,
somehow unaccountably arrested their progress, " what —
poor, wanderin' creeturs — if your understandin's should
give out !" meaning, what if you should suddenly be
deprived of the use of your legs !   " Have you never
heered," she continued, "the story of Antynias and
Sapfiry ? "

But she did not recount the tale.   If possible, she
would rather use words of love than of malediction.

I shall never forget the faithful manner in which
she narrated Abraham's intercession with the Lord
for Sodom and Gomorrah.

"And Abraham said to the Lord, 'Periodventure there be fifty righteous found,' he said, 'willest thou destroy the city, and them in it? Oh, no! that ain't like the Lord,' he says 'for to slay the righteous and the wicked together — fur be it.' And the Lord says, 'No. If I find fifty righteous I'll spare all the rest,' he says, 'on account o' them fifty,' he says, and Abraham says, 'Oh Lord, now I've begun,' he says, 'and you don't seem so very much put out with me as I expected, I've a good mind to keep on askin' ye a little more, jest to see what ye'll say,' he says, 'Oh Lord, periodventure what if there should n't be but forty-five?' he says."

Grandma went through the list of "periodventures," depicting Abraham's growing fear and obsequiousness in the most tragic manner until she got to the hypothetical ten.

"And Abraham said, 'Oh Lord, I know you won't like it this time, but I've gone so fur now, that I'm going to out with 't, and don't — don't git put out, oh Lord! and I won't put it one mite lower. Period-venture, oh Lord, what if there should n't be but ten?' and the Lord said, 'If there was n't but ten, he would n't destroy them wicked cities.' Now," continued Grandma, with tearful impressiveness, "if Abraham had even a ventured to put it down one five more, what more chance do you think there'd be for us here in Wallencamp?"

After the meeting, Captain Sartell and Bachelor Rae held their usual theological levee, outside the school-house.

"Wall, Bachelder," said the Captain, who always took the initiative with extreme recklessness, "if it was a goin' to take ten to clear Sodom and Germorrer, how many righteous men do you calkilate it ud take ter lift the mortgage off'n this ere peninsheler, eh?"

Bachelor Rae was unusually thoughtful.

" Heh !" said he, in his thin drawl. " The Lord knew he was seafe enough — knew he'd a been seafe enough if he'd a said tew; knew he'd a been seafe enough if he'd a said eone, for there's his own statement to the effect — heh ! — that there was n't a righteous man eany-where, no, not eone."

" Not much leeway, that's a fact, Bachelder," said Captain Sartell, who had an embarrassed way, particularly when discussing subjects of a religious nature, of twisting his powerful blonde head about, and swallowing very hard. " D——d little leeway, I must confess,— wall — all the same for you and me, Bachelder."

Bachelor Rae smiled a little.

" Heh ! What was it about that couple, Almiry (Grandma Spicer) was tellin' about — Antynias and Sapfiry — heh, Captain? What streuck 'em eany way? It was n't because they went out o' meetin' was it? I think it would be a satisfaction to the company, Captain, if you would relate the circumstance."

The brave and honest captain craned his neck about with several hard gulps.

" Wall, to tell the truth, Bachelder, I ain't quite so well posted with the Old Testament as I be with the New, but," he continued, resolutely, " if it would be any favor to the company — as near as I calkalate, this ere Antynias heered that the Lord was a goin' by, and, as near as I calkalate, he clim' up in a tree to see him pass." The captain writhed fearfully, but did not flinch. " And, as near as I calkalate, he got on to a rotten limb, and it let him down. That is," he remarked, with concluding agony, "as near as I calkalate."

" Heh ! yees, much obleeged, I'm sure," said Bachelor Rae. " I, heh ! I recall the anecdote now, perfectly, but wheere — wheere was Sapfiry ? "

" Wall," the captain gave a gulp that actually brought the tears to his eyes, " as near as I calkalate, Sapfiry was under the limb."

" Certainly," said Bachelor Rae, " certainly ! and a veery unfortunate poseetion for Sapfiry it was, too. I weesh you would be so kind as to eenform the company in what part of the Sacred Writ this little anecdote is recorded, Captain, as I for one, should very much leike to look it up."

Captain Sartell took a determined step forward. " Look y' here, Bachelder," said he, " I don't want no hard words betwixt you and me, for there never has been. But a man's word is a man's word, and a man's friends had ought to stick by it, and I want you to understand that, on this ere point, I ain't agoin' to have no lookin' up."

" Heh ! " Bachelor Rae smiled and nodded his head, cheerfully. I'd be willin' to waeger my life, Captain, that if anybody's made a mistake on this point — heh — it ain't you." And with this amicable conclusion, the two stars withdrew.

George Olvc, sometimes rose in meeting and made a few remarks indicative of a manly spirit and much sound common sense. He was very fond of Ethel, that was plain. Her continued indifference to him made him sore at heart, and the people in Wallencamp suggested that on this account he was more serious than he would other- wise have been.

As for Ethel, they said that she had given up "seekin' religion," and had returned to the world. She did not rise for prayers any more and she did not "lead the singin'" any more. And it was true that she seemed to me to have changed, somehow. I knew that she was as girlishly devoted to me as ever, as thoughtful as ever to please me. One Saturday morning, knowing that I had letters in the West Wallen Post Office, which I was anxious to get before Sunday, she walked the whole distance alone to get them, and sent them up to me by one of the school children, so that I should not know who went after them. She was careful lest I should notice any change in her. But I caught a reckless, mocking gleam in her eyes, at times, that had never shone there when I knew her first. She associated more with the "other girls," now. I heard her talking and laughing with them in as loud and careless a tone as their own. She even whispered and laughed in the evening meetings. And this after all the earnest, serious discourse I had had with her, the "refining," "elevating" influences I had tried to throw around her, having first taken her so graciously under my wing! She knew what belonged to agreeable manners, and the advantage of paying a graceful obedience to the dictates of one's moral sense! Something must be very innately wrong in Ethel, I thought something I had not hitherto suspected, else why should she fail in any degree under so admirable a method!

"My dear," I said to her. "I am often tempted to do wrong — especially because my life has been hitherto so vain and thoughtless — but, having resolved to struggle with temptation, and to repel my own selfish inclinations, I will not be content until I come off conquerer; I will not fall out or loiter by the way; I have trials and perplexities, but I will not submit to them, nor be driven from my purpose. Now, are you struggling to resist the little temptations that come to you day by day? Are you striving to make the very best of yourself, Ethel?"

I knew how easily I could move Ethel, either to laughter or tears, so I was not surprised to see her lip tremble, and her eyes fill; but I was surprised at the look of intense anguish, almost of horror, that came into her face. I had not supposed that she was capable of such strong emotion and I marveled greatly, what could be the cause.

"Oh," she said, "you don't know, teacher, you don't know! It never seemed so bad before I knew you. I was different brought up from you, and I loved you, and when I knew, oh, then I could die, but I couldn't tell you! Oh, you wouldn't kiss me again, ever, if you knew, and I wish you would n't, for it hurts, it hurts worse than if you did n't!"

Ethel had turned very pale, and drew her breath in long gasping sobs.

"Baby!" I said reassuringly, stroking her hair, "I don't believe you have done anything very wrong." But Ethel drew away from me.

"You don't know," she said. "I was brought up different — and it was before you came, and I never knew that, what you told me about not trusting people. I thought it was all true, and oh! — there ain't anybody to help! Oh, I wish I was dead! I wish I was dead!"

"Ethel," I said, a little frightened and convinced that the girl had some serious trouble at heart. "Tell me what the trouble is? Has anyone deceived you? And why should any one wish to deceive you, child?"

Ethel only moaned and shook her head.

"But you must tell me," I said, "I can't help you unless you do."

She drew herself farther away from me, with only these convulsive sobs for a reply. I did not attempt to get nearer to her, to comfort her as it had been my first impulse to do. She had repulsed me once. "You are nervous and excited, my dear," I decided to say, "and something of little consequence, probably, looks like a mountain of difficulty to you. At any rate, when you get ready to confide in me, you must come to me. I shall not question you again."

So I left her, less with a feeling of commiseration for her, than with a deep sense of my own pressing burdens and responsibilities.

I had another ex-pupil (Ethel had been out of school for several weeks), who was a source of considerable anxiety to me — Benney Leonard. He had ceased coming to the Ark to sing with the others. He had not played on his violin since that first night when his string broke.

I heard that he had gone to New Bedford, and it was a day or two afterwards that, coming out of the schoolhouse after the meeting, I saw him standing on the steps alone. I knew that an escort from among the Wallencamp youths was close behind me. I hastened to put my hand on Benney's arm.

"Will you walk home with me?" I said, looking up in his face and smiling. I knew that the face lifted to his then, was a beautiful one, that the hand resting on his arm was small and daintily gloved, unlike the bare coarse hands of the Wallencampers. I knew that my dress had an air and a grace also foreign to Wallencamp, that a delicate perfume went up from my garments, that my voice was more than usually winning. I experienced a dangerous sense of satisfaction in the conquest of this unsophisticated youth — a conquest not wholly without its retributive pain and intoxication.

I felt the Cradlebow's arm tremble as we walked up the lane.

" I have a little private lecture to give you, Benney," I said. " Of course you have been very much absorbed in your own affairs lately, but, is that an excuse for forsaking your old friends entirely? Especially if you are going away. Are you going away?"

"Yes," said Benney.

"When?" I asked.

"In April," he answered briefly.

" And were n't you ever coming to see me, again?" I murmured with designing soft reproach.

"I was coming up by and by, to say Good-bye," said Benney, brokenly.

"Only for that?" I questioned, and sighed with a perfect abandonment of rectitude and good faith to the selfish gratification of that moment.

"What else should I come up for?" he exclaimed breaking out into sudden passion. "Except to tell you what you don't want to hear, that I love you, teacher, I love you."

" Oh, hush !" I cried with a little accent of unaffected pain. " It is n't right for me to let you talk to me in that way, Benney. Oh, don't you see? you're nothing but a boy to me !"

"That's a lie !" the boy replied, with face and eyes

aflame. "And because I am poor and because I am more ignorant than you, you make it an excuse to trifle with me —and you look only to the outside, but you know I have lived as long as you — a boy's head, you mean," he went on with choking, fiery bitterness. " And it may be, and you are very kind, God knows ! But I can tell you one thing, teacher, it is n't a boy's heart for you to put your foot on ! "

It was not a boy's strength in the quivering frame and tense, drawn muscles. In his rare passions I admired Benney.

The greater meekness and patience which always followed, I attributed to a lack of perseverance or a too easy abandonment of purpose.

" I hope you will be very happy all your life through, teacher," he said, as we stood at the door of the Ark ; and he spoke very gently, and as though he was going away then forever.   Abagail had the key;   she and her companions had lingered at the school house, as usual, after the meeting.   I murmured something about being very happy to have such a kind, true friend ;   that I should probably leave Wallencamp before he went to sea, but I hoped he would write me about his wanderings over the world, and I should always be happy to answer and give him my sisterly advice.

Benney continued, thoughtfully, almost smiling :

" You remember that night, teacher, ever so long ago it seems, before I knew you, when the boys dragged me into the Ark and I kissed you? I've always kissed the girls when they come home from anywhere, and I never thought, you know. I did n't mean anything by it."

"Yes," I said. I think I must have looked amused. Benney answered the laugh in my eyes with quiet appreciation.

" Well, teacher," he said, " I should like to kiss you just once to-night, and mean it."

" That's a remarkable request," I said, " to come from my oldest pupil; but it is my privilege to bestow, just once. If you will bend down from your commanding height, and put yourself in a humble and submissive attitude before me."

The Cradlebow knelt on the doorstep. I would have stooped to his forehead, but he put up his arm with an extremely boyish, inoffensive gesture, almost with a sob, I thought, to draw me closer.

I would have had that kiss as passionless as though it had been given to a child. The Cradlebow's breath was pure upon my cheek — but I was compelled to feel the answering flame creep slowly in my own blood.

" Never ask me to do that again ! " I exclaimed, in righteous exculpation of the act. " Never ! "

CHAPTER VIII.

FESTIVITIES AT THE ARK.

P from the beach, lightly tripping, capacious reticule in hand, came Mrs. Norris to spend the day at the Ark, unexpectedly! The inspired and felicitous customs of the Wallencampers admitted of no rude surprises; rational joy, alone, pervaded the Ark at this matutinal advent.

Mrs. Norris, Noel's mother, presented a charmingly antique appearance — antique not in the sense of advanced years, but the young antique — the gay, the lively, the never fading antique. She had even a girlish way of simpering and uttering absurdly rapturous exclamations. Her face might have struck one at first as being of a strangely elongated cast, but for its extreme prettiness and simplicity of expression. Her nose was marked by a becoming scallop or two. Her eyes were of the ocean blue. Her dark hair was arranged, behind, in the simplest and most compact manner possible ; but, in front, art held delightful play. There, it was parted, slightly to the left, over a broad, high forehead, and disposed in braids of eight strands each, gracefully and lovingly looped over Mrs. Norris's ears

The tide of cheerful converse was at its full when I came home from school to lunch. Amid this preponderance of female society, my friend, Grandpa, shone with an ardent though faintly tolerated light, giving to the lively flow of the discourse, an occasional salty and comprehensive flavor, which dear Grandma Spicer held herself ever in calm and religious readiness to restrain.

I listened, intensely interested, to the conversation, quite content for my own part, to keep silence, but I caught Mrs. Norris's eye fixed on me as if in abstracted, beatific thought. Soon was made known the result of her meditation. She had concluded that I was incapable of descending to subjects of an ordinary nature. Leaning far forward on the table, with a smile more ecstatic than any that had gone before, she directed these words at me in a clear, swift-flowing treble :

"Oh, ain't it dreadful about them poor delewded Mormons?"

"Why?" I exclaimed, involuntarily, blinded by the absolute unexpectedness of the question, and not knowing, in a dearth of daily papers, but that the infatuated people alluded to had been swallowed up of an earthquake, or fallen in a body into the Great Salt Lake.

"Oh, nothing!" said Mrs. Norris, "only I think it's dreadful, don't yew, settin' such an example to Christian nations?"

"Dreadful! certainly!" I murmured, with intense relief, and allowed my glasses to drop into my lap again.

Thus the conversation turned to subjects of a religious nature.

"Oh, I think it's so nice to have direct dealin's with

the Almighty; don't yew?" said Mrs. Norris.   " Oh, I
think it is !   Brother Mark Norris says he can hear
the Lord speakin' to him jest as plain as they could in
Old Testament times; oh, yes, jest as plain exactly;
Abraham and all them, yew know !   And brother Mark
Norris generally means to go to Sunday school. He
says he thinks it's so interestin'; but it's sich an awful
ways.   Don't yew think it is?   Oh, yes, it's a dreadful
ways ! He don't always.   But yew remember that Saturday we had sich a dreadful storm? oh, was n't it dreadful !
Oh, yes !   Well, the next day, that was Sunday, brother
Mark Norris said he heard the Lord sayin' to him, jest as
plain as day, ' Mark Norris, don't you go to Sunday
school to-day !   You stay home and pick up laths ! ' and
he did, and oh, he got a dreadful pile ! most ten dollars
worth ; but I think it's so nice, don't yew, to have direc'
dealin's with the Almighty ! "

The Norrises, by the way, were regarded with a sort of
contemptuous toleration by the Wallencampers in general,
on account of their thrift and penuriousness, the branded
qualities of sordid and unpoetic natures.

I was sorry when the brief hour of the noon intermission
was over, and I had to go back to school.   .

But at night the Ark became alive.   Soon after supper,
Mr. Norris arrived and "brother Mark Norris" and Noel.
Then the little room began to fill rapidly.   We adjourned
to the "parlor " and the melodeon.

" Oh, I do think them plaster Paris picters are so
beautiful, don't yew?" said Mrs. Norris, enraptured
over a statuette or two of that truly vague description,
which adorned the mantel-piece.   But she became perfectly lost in delight when Noel began to sing.

Noel's was the one execrable voice among the Wallen-campers — if anything so weak could be designated by so strong a term — and his manner of keeping time with his head was clock-like in its regularity and painfully arduous, yet, out of that pristine naughtiness which found a hiding place in the hearts of the Wallencamp youth, Noel was frequently encouraged to come to the front during their musicals, and if not actually beguiled into executing a solo, was generously applauded in the performance of minor parts. There was comfort, however, in the reflection that if Noel had indeed possessed the tuneful gift of a Heaven-elected artist, he could not have been so supremely confident of the merit of his own performances, nor could his mother have been more delighted at their brilliancy. She sat with hands clasped in her lap and gazed at her manly offspring.

"Oh, I do think it's so beautiful !" she murmured occasionally to me, aside. " Oh, yes, ain't it beautiful ? "

Once, she remarked in greater confidence, " Oh, he's dreadful wild ! "

"Noel ? " I enquired, with impulsive incredulity.

" Oh, dreadful ! " she continued. " I don't know what he'd a ben if we had n't always restrained him. But somehow, I think there's something dreadful bewitchin' about such folks. Don't yew ? "

" Very," I answered with vague, though ardent sympathy.

" Oh, dreadful ! " she responded.

Meanwhile the perspiration stood out on Noel's grave countenance, and his head like a laborious sledge hammer was swaying mechanically backward and forward.

" Sing bass, now, Noel," said Mrs. Norris ; and the expression of awed delight and expectancy on her face, as she uttered these words, was a rebuke to all cynics and unbelievers of any sort whatever.

"Yes'm so I will, certainly," said Noel, "so I will, and if I had n't got such a cold, I'd come down heavy on it too."

"What do you think," Mrs. Norris went on in the same confidential aside to me. "He's took it into his head that he wants to get married! Oh, yes, he has really! and I think it's a wonder he never got set on it before. But he never has so but what we could restrain him. But William and I, we're beginning to think he might as well if he wants to. Oh, yes, I think it will be so nice. Don't yew? I think it will be just splendid! And I tell William, Noel's wife shan't do nothing but set in the parlor and fold her hands, if she don't want to, and she shall have a music, and everything. When we built our new house, you know we used to live in that little house that brother Mark Norris lives in now, oh, yes, and I think it's so nice to have a new house, don't yew? I had 'em make the window seats low on purpose, so that Noel's children could sit on them! Oh, I think it will be so pleasant, don't yew?"

Mrs. Norris turned her enraptured gaze on me.

"Noel's wife," I hastened to reply, toying with my glasses, "whoever she may be, is certainly to be envied — and Noel's children too"— I added, induced by that transcendently beaming smile, "who will have such a broad window seat to sit on."

Never an evening began in heartier fashion at the Ark.

George Olver, standing next to Ethel, rolled out a grand and powerful bass.

Lars Thorjon, the Norwegian, maintained a smiling silence, except when he was giving utterance in song to his inspiring tenor.

Abagail played the " music."

I saw her wince sometimes, when the fine though un-tutored voices around her took on a too wild and exuberant strain. The little woman's own voice was exceedingly gentle and refined, more than that, it had a passionately sweet sad tone, a rare pathos. I used to wonder what there was in Abagail's heart — what there had been in her life — to make her sing so. Then I remembered how easy it was for her to get out of temper, and how often she slapped the children, and I concluded that it was only a voice after all, and not necessarily indicative of any inward sentiment or emotion.

And the mischievous Noah — could it be the same youth who stood there now with tearful eyes, chanting his longings to be pure and sanctified and heavenly. This merry youth had a predilection for those religious songs which contained the deepest and saddest sentiment.

" Now, what's the matter with you, Noah ? " said Emily Gaskell, who had but just dropped in.

" You know you'll go along hum to-night stunin' my cats ! You know what a precious nice time you're calcu-latin' to have about two months from now, up in my trees stealin' my peaches, you young devil. 'Wash you from your sins ! ' Humph ! Yes, you need it bad enough, Lord knows ! A good poundin', and boilin', and sudzin', you need — and a good soakin' in the bluein' water over night, too."

Emily's eyes sparkled with keen though good natured satire. There was a flood of crimson color in her cheeks,

not entirely the effect of her brisk walk in the open air.
She had a spasm of coughing which she endured as
though such discomforts had become quite a matter of
course, merely remarking when she had recovered herself
sufficiently to speak :

" Thar, that ' ll last me for one spell I guess."

" Won't you set, Emily ? " said Grandma.

" No," said Emily. " I can't. I jest come up to tell
my man, there, to go home ! Levi is over from West
Wallen, and want's to see him. Lord, I did n't know
you'd got a party, Miss Spicer ! " she continued, glancing
with an irresistibly comical expression about the room.

" Oh, no ! we ain't got no party," said Grandma Spicer,
pleasantly. " They jest happened to drop in along."

" Wall now, I should think there'd ben a shower and
rained 'em all down at once," again surveying the
occupants of the room with a comprehensively critical air
that was hardly flattering.

" I don't see what on 'arth ! " she went on. " Half the
time you might ransack Wallencamp from top to bottom
and you'd find everybody a'most somewhere, and nobody
to hum ! It ain't much like the cake Silvy made last
week — she's crazier than ever —'Where's the raisins
Silvy ? ' says I — I always make it chock full of 'em, and
there was n't one,— ' Oh,' says Silvy, ' I mixed 'em up so
thorough you can't a hardly find 'em.' ' I guess that's
jest about the way the Lord put the idees into your head,
Silvy,' says I. ' Bless the Lord ! ' says that poor fool, as
slow and solemn as a minister."

" We've been a singin'," interposed Grandma Spicer in
a voice that contrasted with Emily's, like the flow of a
great calm river with the impatient fall of a cataract.

"It seems a' most as though I'd been in Heaven. They was jest a singin'—'The Light of the World is Jesus.' I shall never forgit, when I was down to camp meetin' to Marthy's Vin'yard a good while ago — there was a little blind boy stud up on a bench and sung it all alone, and it made me cry to see him standin' there with his poor little white face, and eyes that could n't see a' one of all the faces lookin' up to him, a singin' that out as bold and free, and he did pronounce the words so beautiful so as everybody could hear — I can hear him a singin' of it out, now — 'The Light of the World is Jesus.' And I suppose we git to thinkin' that the light's in our eyes, maybe, or the light's in the sun, or the light's in the lamp, maybe. But you might put out my eyes,"— said Grandma Spicer, closing her eyes as she spoke, and looking very peaceful and happy —"and you might put out the sun, and you might put out the lamp, and say — 'Thar, Almiry's all in the dark room, she can't see nothin' now '— but the Light of the World 'ud be thar jest the same, you could n't put out the light — 'The Light of the World is Jesus.'"

"Oh, I did n't know ye was havin' a meetin'," said Emily Gaskell, mockingly.

"No more we ain't, Emily "— said Grandma Spicer. "We was jest cheerin' ourselves up a little, singin' about home. Come you, now, and sing with us:"

"We're goin' home
No more to roam."

With eyes still closed, with head thrown back, and a heavenly serene expression on her face, Grandma began the refrain, while Abagail struck the cords on the melodeon and the singers took up the words with a hearty cheer:

11

> " We're goin' home
> No more to roam,
> No more to sin and sorrow,
> No more to wear,
> The brow of care,
> We're going home to-morrow." .

Then the chorus, "We're going home," joyfully
repeated, died away at last, more plaintively, "We're
going home to-morrow."

"Wall, I'm goin' home to-night," said Emily, and,
as I looked up at her, I caught the same mischievous
gleam in her unsoftened eyes. "So strike up something
lively, now, and I 'll waltz down the lane to it. 'Are Your
windows open towards Jerusalem?'—Lord, can't you think
o' something warmer than that for this weather?"

But the singers were going on gloriously :

> " Are your windows open towards Jerusalem?
> Though His captives here a little while stay,
> For the coming of the King in His glory,
> Are you watching, day by day ?"

Emily tightened the shawl around her neck with a
quick motion. In going out, she took an indirect
course through the room, purposely to pass by where
I was sitting.

"Are your windows open towards Jerusalem?" said
she, stooping and whispering in my ear, " El' Turner's
out there hangin' onto the fence one side the bushes, and
Ben Cradlebow the other, and they don't see each
other no more than two bats."

"Are your windows open towards Jerusalem," was
a favorite with the Wallencampers. On this occasion,
they repeated it several times. Captain Sartell and
Bachelor Rae, who had been engaging in a game of
checkers, in the little kitchen, left the board as the well-

loved strains greeted their ears, and came in to join the group.

Grandpa had been consigned to the kitchen stove, with a corn-popper. I do not think that he regretted being removed, somewhat, from the more inspiring scenes which animated the Ark. I was amused to follow, with my ear, the old gentleman's progress in the successive stages of his corn-shelling and corn-popping operations, with certain contingent misfortunes, as when he went into the pantry to look for a pan, and brought down a large quantity of tin ware clanging about his ears, and rolling in all directions over the floor, while I immediately inferred from the tones of his voice that he was enjoying a little unembarrassed colloquy with the powers of darkness. Once, in his shuffling peregrinations, he tipped over the little bench which sustained the water pail. A deep sigh of horror and despair escaped his lips, and was followed by a "What the Devil!" borne in upon the song-laden air with unmistakable force and distinctness.

"For Heaven's sake, ma," said Abagail, looking up, sharply, "what can pa be a' doin' ?"

"Oh," calmly said Grandma Spicer, "I guess he's only settlin' down."

And with Grandma, indeed, the turmoils of this sublunary sphere implied only a vast ultimate settling down.

But if such deep rest came to Grandpa, it was only as a dream from which he was soon to be rudely awakened.

The sound of his footsteps had ceased. I knew that he was seated in his chair by the fire, and I heard the long-handled popper shaken back and forth upon the stove, at first as if moved by the power of a steadfast purpose. But the sound grew fainter, the motions less regular. They were several times desperately renewed, and then ceased altogether, so quickly had Grandpa soared beyond the low vicissitudes of a corn-popping world. Soon a burning smell arose. Then the door of the kitchen opened. Grandpa was startled. I knew the catastrophe. The corn-popper with its contents had been precipitated to the floor. Then I heard a courteous male voice, with just a touch of suppressed merriment in it :

" Never mind, Captain ! small business for you, steering such a slim craft as that, eh? On a red hot stove, too ! "

" Humph ! Top mast heavier than the hull," replied Grandpa, accepting with gratitude, in this extremity, the sympathy of the new comer.

The other gave a low laugh.

" Never mind, Captain ! " he repeated, "we'll have it slick here in a minute. Let me take the broom. You've got it wrong side up. By Harry, we've got the deluge inside the Ark, this time, Captain ! "

" Tarnal water pail slipped moorin's," confessed Grandpa.

Then followed a vigorous sound of corn rattling, and water swashing against the sides of the room, and I knew that Mr. Turner, the elegant, was sweeping out the kitchen of the Ark.

" I guess they's somebody else come," exclaimed Grandma, with hospitable glee. " Wall, I declare for't. I guess I'll go out into my kitchen, and git that little no-back cheer. Seems to me as though we'd got all the rest on 'em in use, pretty much."

"I'll go, ma," said Abagail. "Teacher'll be wanted to play now, and may be she will, though she can't be got to do it for common folks."

I did not enjoy playing on Abagail's melodeon. Any performances of that kind which I had undertaken had been confined exclusively to an audience of the Wallen- campers. I had certainly never made an exception for the amusement of the fisherman. But I flattered myself that there was no trace of resentment in my tone, when I said, "Sit still, Abbie, please, I know where the chair is. Don't I, Grandma?" and was groping my way out through the green curtained "keepin'" rooms, towards Grandma's culinary apartment, thankful for a momentary escape from the heated atmosphere of the "parlor," when I heard just behind me, a voice of the most exquisite smoothness :

"Miss Hungerford, allow me."

"Mr. Turner!" I exclaimed, with an overwhelming sense of the ludicrousness of the situation, "How dare you come through the room where they were all sitting, and follow me out here! Did Grandma tell you that I had gone after a little no-back chair for you to sit on?"

"She did," replied Mr. Turner, with impressive gravity, "and I took it as most divinely kind of you, too ; though, if I might be allowed any choice in the matter, I think I should be likely to assume a much more graceful and more easeful and natural position in a chair con- structed after the ordinary pattern, Miss Hungerford, especially as after my exertions in the kitchen, I feel the need of entire repose."

"But this is the only one left," I answered, with

suppressed laughter. "Do you think you can find it, Mr. Turner?"

" If you should leave me, now," replied the fisherman "I should have positively no idea whither to direct my steps."

"Then I shall be very happy to get it for you," I said.

" But I could not think," he continued, "of allowing you to pursue your way through this utter darkness to the extreme rear of the Ark alone. I beg you to show me the way."

I was not disposed to commit so gross an impropriety as to linger with Mr. Turner in "Grandma's kitchen," which we had reached, and through whose broad, un-curtained windows the moonlight was pouring in with a clear, fantastic radiance.

" Is n't this glorious !" exclaimed the fisherman in a tone nearly as rapturous as Mrs. Norris's own. "Oh, you don't think of going back, now, Miss Hungerford ! After I've mopped the kitchen floor, and braved all Wallencamp in its lair, and groped my way out through these infernally black rooms, for the chance of having a few quiet words with you."

Mr. Turner's eyes were not snaky, nor his manner suggestive of dark duplicity, yet I always felt a certain unaccountable discomfort while in his presence, as though there was need of keeping my own conscience particularly on the alert.

I knew that the group in the parlor would be counting the moments of our absence.

" How can you ask me —" I began, in a tone of cheerful remonstrance," at the same time re-adjusting my glasses to glance about for the little "no back" chair —

"How can you ask me to stay out here talking with you, when you know ——"

"Oh, I know," Mr Turner interrupted quickly. "I know how very thoughtful and considerate you are for those people, Miss Hungerford. I know what lofty ideas you have just now of consecrating yourself to the work of refining and elevating the Wallencampers. I know how coolly you can fix your eyes on a certain goal and stumble indiscriminately over everything that comes in your way. I know what a deucedly superior state of mind you've gotten into. I know too about Miss B's school, and Miss L's school, and the Seminary at Mount Blank, and the winters in New York."

There was triumph at the last, in Mr. Turner's tone.

"You have taken pains to collect a great deal of information about me," I replied, virtuously concluding that I should disappoint the fisherman more by not appearing vexed.

"Is it strange?" he continued earnestly, with an unconscious parody on his usually suave and insinuating manner. "You will allow, Miss Hungerford, that you might strike one, at first, as not being exactly in the ordinary line of home missionaries, that is, as not having been trained for the work, exactly, a sort of novitiate, I mean — Confound it! You will allow that you might strike one at first, as being deucedly new in that role."

After this, I smiled with a faintly malicious sense of satisfaction at Mr. Turner's confusion, though I felt that I had been cut to the heart.

"And when I spoke about having found out about your past life," he went on, struggling desperately with his lost cause, " I did n't mean that there was anything bad, you know, only that you sought pleasant diversions in common with the rest of humanity and enjoyed the Heaven-born instinct of knowing how to have a good time, and were n't always the ambitious recluse and religious devotee that you choose to be just at present, though I've sometimes wished that I could turn saint so all of a sudden, but I could n't," added the fisherman despondently; "if I should go to the ends of the earth in that capacity, nobody 'd take any stock in me, whatever; and, after all, what does it amount to?"

"This is n't what I meant to say, any of it;" he sighed angrily. "It's just what I meant *not* to say — Confound it! You've done gloriously; you've played the thing through to perfection; you've made an inimitable success of it; but Wallencamp does n't offer scope wide enough for your powers. I offer you a field hitherto untilled, left to the wandering winds and the birds of the air, extensive enough in its forlorn iniquity, I assure you, to engage your patient and continued efforts. It may prove productive of good results yet, who knows? Is it my fault that I did n't know you sooner? "

I did not mistake the change in Mr. Turner's tone, nor the meaning in his eyes, but as we stood there by the window, in the full moonlight, I caught a glimpse of another face outside, vanishing up the lane,—almost like a ghostly apparition it seemed to me — the handsome, pale young face. I guessed instinctively whose it was, and suffered a pang of sharp, unconfessed pain, while the fisherman was murmuring in my ear.

"Don't speak to me again of missions!" I cried with the strong and tragic air of consciously blighted aspirations. "I shall go on no more missions, great or small. It is very true what you have tried so delicately to intimate. I was not fit for the work I undertook to do. I have only made mistakes all the way along. Possibly I have been only ' playing a part.' What does it amount to, indeed! What does it amount to!"

"Heavens!" said Mr. Turner, "play a part, by all means; never be sincere in anything you do. I never tried it but once, and I've made a desperate mess of it. Can't you understand that what I said was only in the purest sort of self-defence? You weigh my words so nicely. Well, you are considerate enough, God knows, of those dirty brats and ignorant louts — coddling that girl, Ethel, who is a good-hearted creature enough, but not fit for respectable people to touch their hands to, and associating with such conceited boors as that George Olver, and that grinning clown, Noah, and that poor fool, Noel Norris, and that what-d'ye-call-him—that fiddling young devil with the bird-like name — "

Mr. Turner stopped suddenly.

"You might make allowances for a man in a passion," he said, "instead of dissecting his words in that cold-blooded way."

"I have no notion of dissecting your words," I said, provoked into a desperate honesty; "I believe them, as a whole, to be utterly false."

"From the very beginning," said Mr. Turner, "thank you; so I can begin all over again; meanwhile,—you will forgive me? Imagine that I'm one of those dirty little beggars that go to school to you. If one of them should come to you and say that he was sorry —?"

"I should only be intensely surprised," I said; "they never do such things."

"Then I have a superior claim on your clemency," said the fisherman, "for I am sorry and humiliate my soul to the lowest depths of the confessional."

It was the voice of the plausible, easy-going fisherman again.

My hand was on the latch. "I am not angry; I would rather be friends," I said with averted face, as we were returning through the dark "keepin'-rooms."

"When you get out of this realm of myths and missions, and general dread and discomfort," said Mr. Turner, "on to comprehensible soil again where ordinary sinners are sure of some sort of a footing,— and bad as a fellow is, he knows there are plenty more like him,—then I shan't appear to you in such a deucedly poor light as I do now, a doubtful sort of pearl in a setting of isolated cedars, with my beauty and my genius and my heavenly aspirations all unappreciated, or made to descend as a greater measure of condemnation on my devoted auburn head. Truly, I believe that an evil star attends my course in Wallencamp. My own ideas seem strange to me. I cannot grasp them. My language is wild and disconnected, I fancy, like that of the early Norse poets. When I meet you in the world, I shall hope to recover some of the old-

time coherence and felicity of speech which I remember to have heard practiced among the world's people,
and it is n't long now, thank Heaven ! before you 'll leave
Wallencamp behind you. When you go home—"

When I should go home, indeed ! I had hardly
dared to cherish the thought. I stifled the rising flood
of exultation in my breast — but how pale and interesting I should look ! And, then, I would describe
Wallencamp to my own loving friends as it really
was, and what a lion they would make of me ! Had
they not always lionized my virtuous efforts to the
fullest extent !

My face must have been very happy in the dark.
I felt even almost kindly towards Mr. Turner. We
were at the last door. As we entered the lighted
room, Grandma's broad face began to beam with slow
surprise. "Why," said she, "where's the little no-
back chair ? "

Mr. Turner's resources in such extremities usually
bespoke a life-time of patient and adroit application,
but, now, he hesitated. The accumulated glory of
years seemed likely to be wrecked on the phantom of
a little no-back chair.

"Moonstruck? Eh, Mr. Turner ?" inquired Noah.

The fisherman regarded Noah with a smile of quiet
and amused sufferance.

"Ah ! Mrs. Spicer," said he, with a graceful bow in
Grandma's direction, "Mrs. Ithamer did me the
honor when I came in, to ask me to stand up with the
singers at the melodeon, a position which I shall be
most happy to take, although I fear that my vocal
powers are of an exceptionally poor order."

The fisherman turned over the leaves of the despised Moody and Sankey hymnal for Abagail, was pro- foundly attentive while the singing was going on, and made suave and affable remarks here and there during the intervals, then glanced at his watch with an ex- pression of highly affected concern, bade an elaborate adieu to the company, and retired from the scene.

" Oh, I think that Mr. Turner is so elegant, don't yew ? " said Mrs. Norris. " Oh, yes ; I think he's so genteel ! "

" *I* don't think so at all," said Noel. " *I* don't, certainly. *I* don't think so."

" He ain't got much voice," said Mrs. Norris, clasp- ing her hands in raptured appreciation of her match- less Noel.

Finally, Grandpa, with a haggard smile on his features, stumbled across the little landing of the stair- way, between the parlor and the kitchen, bearing with him a pan of much scorched and battered pop-corn.

"Oh, *aint* them beautiful ! " arose Mrs. Norris's re- assuring cry.

Grandma had already set an example to her guests by making a convenient receptacle of her capacious lap, and pouring some of the corn into it, an example which the fortunate scions of the skirted tribe, now ar- ranged in rows on one side of the room, followed, each in turn. Of the male species on the other side of the room, Noel happened to be first in line. As the corn came nearer and nearer to him, he began to look about wildly, and to cough. His legs trembled violently with the effort he was making to keep them close to- gether. He accepted the pan of pop-corn with a ges-

ture of feverish haste, and proceeded to pour the contents into his lap, but, as he poured, they disappeared,
and the faster he poured the faster they disappeared,
and the more strenuous exertions he made to keep his
legs close together, the wider seemed to grow the
chasm through which the corn went rattling down on
to the floor, until Noel's eyes began to whirl in their
orbits and drops of sweat stood out upon his forehead.

Noah, who appreciated the situation and was bursting with a desire to roar out his mirthful emotions,
showed a kind heart above all, and turned the tables
nicely in poor Noel's behalf.

"Look here, Noel!" he cried, "that's a pretty trick
to play on us fellows, you rascal! you'd better let up
on that, now!"

Noel grasped at the idea as a drowning man might
grasp at a good substantial raft that should come
floating down his way.

"T-that's so," he stammered. "It is too bad, Noah. It-t-t is, certainly, but anything for a j-joke, you
know. Here, take it yourself, Noah, t-take it; take
it, quick!"

And Noel got down on his knees as though he
would have rendered dumb thanks to Heaven for
his unexpected deliverance, and proceeded to gather up
the corn with glad alacrity.

After this, the water was passed, and, at such times,
it was always comforting to consider how bountiful
nature had been in this respect to Wallencamp, and
that the demand could never be quite equal to the
supply.

Then the company began to disperse with many

hand-shakings and "why don't ye all drop into my house," etc., etc.

Noel Norris came back twice to shake hands with me and returning the third time, got lost, somehow, in the general confusion, and shook hands very fervently with his mother, who was standing in the door.

I heard one of the departing visitors exclaim : "Why where's Ben? I should a thought he'd a dropped in, sure !"

And another answered : "Oh, he's got some new notion into his head, I reckon ! goin' on a cruise, maybe !"

Ethel was going out with a girl companion, talking rather loudly. I was moved to take her hand a moment, gently detaining her. She looked exceedingly bright and pretty. Her physical beauty was perfect, yet I believed that the soul was only half awakened in the girl.

So as I held her hand a moment, with the others taking noisy leave about us, I looked into her face with what she might have read as :—" Were n't you laughing rather loudly, my dear? I can see now, that you are not as happy as you would have people believe. Why not confide in me, and let me straighten your difficulty out for you ?"

But Ethel's eyes were downcast, and her cheeks crimson. She let her hand slip passively out of mine, and passed on, without a word.

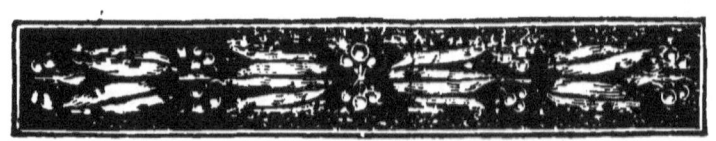

CHAPTER IX.

NOEL "POPS THE QUESTION."

ONE morning, ere we had breakfasted at the Ark, Noel Norris, like some new-fangled orb of day, was seen to surmount the ruddy verge of the horizon. He bore a gun upon his shoulders, and advanced with a singularly martial and self-confident tread. As he entered the Ark, he placed the gun against the wall, and sat down and folded his arms, and looked as though he could be brave without it.

"Well, Abagail," said he, with a determined gaze fixed straight before him on vacuity, and with a desperate affectation of spontaneity in his tone. "Well, Abagail, mother and father have gone to Aunt Larcia's, *I* suppose to spend a week, *I* suppose—ahem !—ahem !—*I* suppose so."

"You don't say so, Noel!" exclaimed Abagail. "And what 'll poor Robin do now, Noel? Oh, what 'll poor Robin do now?"

"Yes," said he gravely, "that's what *they* thought, ahem ! *They* thought they should stay a week, *they* thought so, certainly."

"Wall, I declar' for 't, Noel," said Grandma. "Now's the time you'd ought to have a wife. Jest to think how comf'table 'twould be fu ye, now, instead of stayin' there all alone, if ye only had a nice little wife to home, to cook for ye, and watch for ye, and keep ye company, and——"

"*I* think so," exclaimed Noel, giving a quick glance backward in the direction of his gun. "Certainly, ahem ! *I* think so. *I* do."

"Lookin' for game ? Eh, Noel ?" enquired Grandpa.

"Pa," said Grandma, solemnly, "I wish you'd put another stick of wood in the stove."

Grandpa was awake, now, and a youthful and satanic gleam shone from under his shaggy eyebrows ; he glanced at me, too, as was his habit on such occasions, as though I had a sort of sympathy for and fellowship with him in his bold iniquities of speech.

But the guileless Noel interpreted not the deeper meaning of Grandpa's words.

"I think some of it, Cap'n," he answered unsmilingly, and then continued. "It's been — ahem ! —it's been a very mild winter on the — ahem ! — I should say on the Cape. It's been a very mild winter on the Cape, Miss Hungerford."

Noel's nervous glance falling again on his gun, took me in wildly on the way.

I had been directing some letters that I expected to have an opportunity to send that morning.

"I beg your pardon," I said looking up. "Yes, you don't often have such mild winters on the Cape, Mr. Norris !"

"No 'm we don't," said Noel, "not very often, ahem !" He moved his chair a peg nearer the gun. Quite a —

ahem!—quite a little fall of snow we had last night, Miss Hungerford."

"Any deer tracks? Eh, Noel?" enquired Grandpa.

"Pa," said Grandma. "I wish you'd fill Abigail—seems to me she smells sorter dry."

"She ain't, for sartin', ma," replied Grandpa, giving the tea-kettle a shake to verify his assertions, "and Rachel's chock full!"

Grandma then gave Grandpa a meaning look, and put her fingers on her lips.

"Well, Cap'n, I saw more rabbit tracks," replied Noel, innocently amused at the ludicrousness of the old Captain's speech. "I did, rather—ahem!—yes, I saw more rabbit tracks—ahem!—ahem!" He gave his chair a desperate hitch gunward. "I don't suppose they ever do such a thing, where you live, Miss Hungerford, as to go —ahem!—to go sleigh riding, now, do they, Miss Hungerford?"

"Why yes," I said. "They always do in the winter, and I haven't been home through the winter for a year or two past, but I remember what splendid times we used to have."

I was thinking particularly of a certain snow-fall, that came when I was seventeen years old, and John Cable had just returned from College, with a moustache and patriarchal airs.

Some grinning recollections of the past were also floating through Grandpa's mind. The look of reprehensible mirth was still in his eyes, and he showed his teeth which gleamed oddly white and strong in contrast with his grizzled countenance.

"I remember"—he began.

" Pa," said Grandma, with an expressive wink of one eye, and only part of her face visible around the corner of the door-way, through which Abagail had already disappeared.

" Pa — I wish you'd come out here a minute, now — I want to see ye."

" Wall, wall, can't ye see me here, ma? What makes ye so dreadful anxious to see me all of a sudden'?" enquired Grandpa. But his face did not lose its thoughtful illumination. "Wall, as I was a tellin' ye, teacher," he went on. "I was only a little shaver then — a little shaver — and my father had one of those 'ere pungs, as we used to call 'em, that he used to ride around in — and he was a dreadful man to swear, my father was, teacher — Lordy, how he would swear! ——"

" Pa!" said the great calm voice at the door. " I'm a' awaitin' for you to come out, so 't I can shet the door."

" Wall, wall, ma, shet the door if ye want to, I've no objections to havin' the door shet —— and we had an old hoss, teacher. Lordy, how lean he was, lean as a skate, and ——"

"Hoggarty Spicer!"

" Yis, yis, I'm a' comin', ma, I'm a' comin'." And wonderful indeed, I thought must have been the tale, which, even under these exasperating circumstances, kept Grandpa's face a-grin as he ran and shuffled towards the door.

The door was quickly closed behind him by other hands than his own, and then I observed that Noel's chair had been drawn into frightfully close proximity to his gun.

"I — I think it's pleasanter, that is — I — I sometimes think it's warmer for t-t-two in a sleigh, than — a—'tis — for one, don't you, Miss Hungerford?" said Noel, and gasped for breath and continued. "Now I think of it, you— you wouldn't think of such a thing as going to ride with me to-night, would you, Miss Hungerford? You—you would n't think of such a thing, would you, now?"

"Why—if you are kind enough to invite me to go sleigh riding with you, Mr. Norris?"

"I think so," said Noel, grasping his gun, and becoming immediately pale, though composed. "Yes 'm, *I* think so, certainly, *I* do."

"Thank you, I will go with pleasure," I said.

"Thank you, Miss Hungerford," said Noel, rising hurriedly. "I wish you a pleasant day—*I* do, with pleasure, and I hope that nothing will happen to prevent!"

And Noel marched back across the fields as valiantly as a man may, who, on occasions of doubt and peril, takes the precaution to go suitably armed.

During the day the Wallencampers indulged in a mode of recreation, suggestive of that unique sort of inspiration to which they not unfrequently fell victims.

They attached a horse to a boat, a demoralized old boat, which had hitherto occupied a modest place amid the débris surrounding the Ark, and thus equipped, they rode or sailed up and down the lane.

It proved a stormy sea, and often as the boat capsized, the air was rent with screams of mock terror and yells of unaffected delight.

Thus the youth of Wallencamp, yes, and those who heeded not the swift decline of years, by reason of the immortal freshness of their spirits, disported themselves. And I was not amazed, catching a glimpse through the school-house windows of this joyous boat on one of her return voyages up the lane, to see Grandma Spicer swaying wildly in the stern.

Meanwhile, I managed to keep my flock indoors. But when, at four o'clock, I took my ruler in hand to give the usual signal of dismissal, the Phenomenon's heels had already vanished through the window, and the repressed animal spirits of a whole barbaric epoch sounded in the whoop with which the Modoc shot through the door.

Finally, I, myself, rode up the lane in the boat. The path was well worn by this time, and there was no danger of a catastrophe. It seemed to me a novel performance enough, but I had not yet been to ride in Noel's sleigh.

Noel came very early, and preferred to wait outside until I had finished eating my supper. Then, with that deep self-satisfaction which predominated in my soul, even over its appreciation of the novel and amusing, I donned my seal brown cloak, and stepping out of the door, gathered up my skirts, and smiled at Mr. Noel with a pair of seal brown eyes, and was not surprised to hear him ejaculate, coughing slightly, " Ahem ! *I* think so, certainly, yes 'm, *I* think so ; *I* do."

Noel's was the only sleigh in Wallencamp, and, as he informed me, it was one that he had himself constructed. It ha⸱, indeed, already suggested to my mind the workings of no ordinary intellect. Perhaps its most impressive features were its lowness and its height — the general lowness and length of its body, into which one could step easily, the floor being covered with a carpet of straw suggesting field mice, and the unusual height to which it rose in the back, being surmounted by two glittering knobs, like those on the head-board of an old-fashioned bedstead. Half-way down the back of this imposing structure the arms or wings sprouted out, giving to the whole the appearance of an immense Pterodactyl, or some other fossil bird of fabulous proportions, and effectually shutting in the occupants of the sleigh from any contemplation of the possible charms of the scenery. The seat was made very low, and it was, perhaps, on this account that the horse seemed so abnormally high. It was a white horse, and from our lowly position, there seemed to be something awful and shadowy in the motions of its legs. The red of sunset had not gone out of the sky when we started, and a pale young moon was already getting up in the heavens, but we could see neither fading sky nor rising moon, nor rock, nor tree, nor snowy expanse, nought but the gigantic hoof-falls of our phantom steed.

Being thus hopelessly debarred from any communication with external nature, and fearing to give myself up to my own thoughts, which were of a somewhat danger-ous character, I endeavored to engage my companion in lively and cheerful converse by the way ; but he was in a position of actual physical suffering, for the reins were short — too short, that is, to form a happy connect-ing link between him and the horse, and poor Noel was obliged to lean forward at an acute angle in order to grasp them at all. Whenever the ghostly quadruped made a plunge forward, as he not unfrequently did, Noel was thrust violently down into the straw, and throughout all this he comported himself with such firm and hopeless dignity that, with the respect due to suffering, I was moved to witness the struggle, at length, with silent commiseration. Once, having kept his seat for a longer time than usual, Noel said :

"I'll give you a riddle, Miss Hungerford, *I* will. Ahem ! 'why — why does a hen go around the road,' Miss Hungerford ? "

I posed my head in an attitude of deep thought.

" Because," Noel hastened to say, " because she can't go across — no, that wasn't right — why — ahem ! why does a hen go *across* the road, Miss Hungerford?" and the next instant he was wallowing in the straw at my feet.

My soul was filled with unutterable compassion for him.

"Because" I ventured, when Noel reappeared again, affecting a tone of lively inspiration, "because she can't go around it?"

"You —you' ve heard it before!" gravely protested Noel.

" I confess," said I, " that I have.   It used to be my favorite riddle."

" It — it used to be mine, too," said Noel. "It *used* to be, Miss Hungerford —ahem!   It *used* to be —. You —you could n't tell what I was thinking of when I —ahem — when I started from home to-night, now, could you, Miss Hungerford ?" said Noel, at length.

" I'm sure I could n't, Mr. Norris," said I, " but I hope it was something very agreeable."

" But it was n't," said Noel, "that is, not very, Miss Hungerford ; ahem ! not very.   I was —I was — ahem ! I was thinking of it, you know, of — of such a thing as getting married, you know."

"I hope," said I, cheerfully, after a pause, "that as you consider the subject longer, it will be a less painful one to you."

"*I* hope so, Miss Hungerford," said Noel. "Ahem ! *I* hope so, certainly ; " but there was little of that sanguine quality expressed in his tones.

The great white horse made another plunge forward, and Noel recovered himself with a desperate effort.

"What should you think now, Miss Hungerford," he continued, moistening his parched lips, "if I should do such a thing as to — ahem ! — as to speak of such a thing as — ahem ! — as something of that sort to you, now, Miss Hungerford? Now, what should you think of such a thing? now, really?"

"I should think you were very inconsiderate," I said, "and would probably regret your rashness afterwards."

"*I* think so," said Noel; ahem ! *I* think so, Miss Hungerford ; *I* do, certainly."

After this it seemed as though a weight had been lifted from Noel's mind. He kept his seat better. His was not a buoyant spirit, but there was, on this occasion, an air of repressed cheerfulness about him such as I had never before seen him exhibit. I tried to think that it was a joyous mental rebound from the contemplation of those dark riddles which trouble humanity, "why does the hen go across the road," etc.

After a brief pause, Noel said, "You — you wouldn't mind if I should sing a little now, now would you, Miss Hungerford?"

I assured him that I should be very glad to have him do so, and he sang, I remember, all the rest of the way home. At the gate, I thanked him for the ride and its cheerful vocal accompaniment, and Noel said, "Do you like to hear me sing, now? Do you — do you, really, now, Miss Hungerford?" and turned away with a smile on his face to seek his home by the sea.

But Noel was not long lonely for, in less than a week, his father and mother returned from their visit at Aunt Larcia's and brought to Noel a wife.

Mrs. Norris herself informed me that "it was an awful shock to him, at first, oh, dreadful! but he'd made up his mind to get married, and he'd never a' done it in the world, if we had n't took it into our own hands. She was a good girl, and we knew it, and Noel was n't no more fit to pick out a wife, anyway, than a chicken, not a bit more fit than a chicken!"

This girl lived in the same town with Aunt Larcia, and was confidently recommended by her to Noel's parents as one who would be likely to make him a wise and suitable help-meet, and was, indeed, an uncommonly fair and wholesome looking individual. She had a mind, too, whose clear, practical common sense had never been obscured by the idle theories of romance. She was pure and hearty, and substantial. She was neither diffident, nor slow of speech, nor vacillating. She came, at the invitation of Noel's parents, to marry Noel, and if he had refused, she would have boxed his ears as a wholesome means of correction, and married him on the spot.

So Noel's destined wife was brought home to him in the morning, and in the afternoon of that same day, the connubial knot was tied.

Half an hour after the arrival of the bride, it was known throughout the length and breadth of Wallen-camp, to every one, I believe, save Noel himself, who was gathering drift-wood a mile or two **down the beach,** that Noel was going to be married !

At three o-clock P. M., brother Mark Norris **was** despatched to West Wallen for a minister.

Small scouts had been sent out to watch, where the road from the beach winds into the main road, and when word was brought back that " Mark had gone by," the Wallencampers proceeded to make all due preparations ; and soon might have been seen winding in a body towards the scene of interest.

The small paraphernalia of invitations **and wedding** cards were unknown in Wallencamp. The Wallencampers would have considered that there was little virtue in a ceremony of any sort, performed without the sanction and approval of their united presence.

In regard to the particular nature of this entertainment, there was some snickering in the corners of the room, but the general aspect was funereal.

The season during which, with Noel at one end of the room, and the bride at the other, we sat waiting the arrival of the minister, was as solemn as anything I have ever known.

I made a congratulatory remark, in a low tone, to Mrs. Norris, who sat at my side with her hands clasped, gazing first at Noel and then at the bride, but I was forced to experience the uncomfortable sensation of one who has inadvertently spoken out loud in meeting. No one said anything.

The helpless snicker which started occasionally from Noah's corner, and was echoed faintly from other quarters of the room, only heightened, by contrast, the effect of the succeeding gloom.

The bride was perfectly composed, with a high natural color in her cheeks, and an air of being duly impressed with the importance of the occasion.

She had assumed a large white bonnet, though I do not think that she and Noel took so much as a stroll to the beach after the ceremony—and her plump and shapely hands were encased in a pair of green kid gloves. She gazed, thoughtfully, at each occupant of the room in turn, not omitting Noel, who never once stirred or lifted his eyes.

Mr. William Norris was silently passing the water, when brother Mark arrived with the minister.

That grave dignitary advanced with measured tread to a small stand, draped with a long white sheet, that had been prepared for him in the centre of the room.

He took off his gloves, and folded them; he took off his overcoat, and laid it on the back of a chair; and if he had then reached down into his pockets and taken out a rope, and proceeded to adjust a slipper-noose, his audience could not have shown a more ghastly and breathless interest in his performance.

"Will the parties"—his sonorous voice resounded through the awful stillness, "Will the parties — about — to be joined—in holy wedlock—now — come forward?"

As Noel then arose and walked, with an automatic hitch in his legs, across the room to his bride, there was about him all the stiffness and pallor of the grave without its smile of peace.

"Noel and Nancy"—arose the deep intonation — "will you—now—join hands?"

It was a warm strong hand in the green kid glove. Its grasp might have sent a thrill of life through Noel's rigid frame, for when the minister enquired:

"And do you, Noel, take this woman?" etc., etc.

Noel bent his body, moved his lips, and replied in a strange, far away tone, "yes'm, *I* think so. *I* do, certainly."

But when the question was put to the bride, she, Nancy, promised to take Noel to be her wedded husband, to love and cherish, yes, and to cleave to, with a round full "I do," that left no possible room for doubt in the mind of anyone present, and seemed to send back the flood of frozen terror to Noel's veins.

Noel and Nancy were pronounced man and wife, and Nancy then divested herself of her bonnet and gloves, and joined in the festivities which followed with a hearty good will, that proved her to be quite at home among the Wallencampers, and won at once their affection and esteem. The manner, particularly, in which she carried beans from her plate to her mouth, gracefully balanced on the extreme verge of her knife, as an adroit and finished work of art, provoked the wonder and admiration of all those whose beans sometimes wandered and fell off by the way.

And all the while, Mrs. Norris's adjectives flowed in a full and copious stream.

"Oh, Noel had been so wild," she said to me. "Oh, dreadful! But did n't I think he looked like a husband now? So quick, too! Oh, yes, was n't it beautiful! Abbie Ann said he looked as though he'd been a husband fifteen years!"

After the ceremony, Noel had taken his pipe and retired a little from the active scenes which were being enacted around him.

I saw him, as I was going away, standing in the door and looking out upon the bay. I held out my hand to him, in passing. "I congratulate you, Mr. Norris," 1 said. Noel put his hand to his mouth and coughed slightly several times, as though he were striving to think of the polite thing to say. Then he replied, "I—I—ahem I I wish you the same, Miss Hungerford. *I* do, certainly."

Noel was not so pale as he had been, but looked very serious and pensive with his eyes fixed on the mysterious depths of the ocean. Noel had propounded riddles to me, but never before had I caught such a glimpse of the deeply philosophical workings of his mind.

"When you come to think of it, life—ahem—life is very uncertain, Miss Hungerford."

I replied that it was very uncertain.

"And short, too, when you come to think of it. It's very short, too, Miss Hungerford."

"Oh, yes," I answered, "very."

"Ahem ! It was—it was dreadful sudden, somehow," said Noel.

"I suppose so, Mr. Norris," I replied gravely, "great and unexpected joys are sometimes said to be as benumbing in their first effects as griefs coming in the same way."

"*I* think so," said Noel. "Ahem ! *I* think so, Miss Hungerford, *I* do, certainly."

Adelaide joined me at the door, and I bade Noel goodnight.

We clambered down the cliffs, walking a little while along on the beach on our way homeward.

It was growing dark and the voice of the ocean was infinitely mournful and sublime. No wonder, I thought, that life had seemed very short and uncertain to Noel as he stood in the door listening to the waves.

What a little thing it seemed indeed, comparatively — this life with its fears and hopes, its poor idle jests and fleeting shows.

"And there shall be no more sea"— but this poor human soul that looks out so blindly, and utters itself so feebly through the senses shall live for ever and ever.

"Noel's folks have picked out a good wife for him, anyhow," said Abagail, briskly. "She's got a sight more sense than anybody *he'd* ever a' picked out."

I crept back into my shell again. "I think so, certainly, Addie," said I, smiling at having unconsciously repeated Noel's own favorite phrase.

"She'll make Noel all over, and get some new ideas into him, I can tell you," said Abagail.

And though I did not stay in Wallencamp long enough to witness with my own eyes the fulfilment of this prophecy, I know that it was abundantly fulfilled — that Noel soon recovered from the shock incident to his wedding, that under the influence of his wholesome active wife and with the weight of greater responsibilities, he grew more manly and admirable in character, as well as happier, with each succeeding year; and that Noel's children — a joyful and robust group, adored of Mrs. Norris, senior — play on the "broad window seat" that looks off towards the sea.

CHAPTER X.

A LETTER FROM THE FISHERMAN.

THE fisherman had gone back to Providence.

Ethel, herself, returning from the Post Office at West Wallen, brought me a letter distinguished by its peculiar dashing chirography. As she handed it to me, the girl, whose glance had been downcast of late, gave me a clear, straight-forward, unembarrassed look.

" Do you like him, teacher? " she said.

" Oh, I tolerate him, my dear," I answered. " We 're not expected to entertain a particular like or dislike for everybody we know. There are a great many people we must just simply tolerate."

Ethel's eyes fell again. " He won't harm you, teacher," she said, "for you was used to folks. Sometime you might remember — I was n't used to folks."

Occupied with my own thoughts, I passed lightly over the girl's slow, trembling speech. She turned away, and I bent to the complacent perusal of my letter. In my then composed and exalted frame of mind, its contents were not calculated to create in me either great emotion or surprise. And not because the mere fact of the fisherman's absence had suddenly rendered him more desirable in my eyes, but as the result of a recent determination on my part to take an utterly worldly and practical view of life, I resolved to give this letter the most careful and serious consideration.

The fisherman was of good family, and he was rich; these statements, artistically interwoven by him with the lighter fabric of his letter, were confirmed by an acquaintance of mine in Providence, of whom, in writing, I had incidentally enquired concerning the gentleman.

Respectability and wealth — items not supposed to weigh too heavily with the romantic mind of youth — but I believed that I was no longer either young or romantic. Moreover, I was slowly realizing the fact that school-teaching in Wallencamp was not likely to furnish me the means for making an excessively brilliant personal display, nor for carrying out to any extent my subordinate plans for a world-wide philanthropy.

" Perhaps, after all then," I argued, " it is only left for me to give up my ideas about being unique and independent and sublime, 'take up with a good offer,' and step resolutely, without any sentimental awe, into the great orderly ranks of the married sister-hood."

My life had been but a varied list of surprises to my family and acquaintances, why not effect the crowning surprise of all, by doing something they might have expected of me?

Well, I had dreamed of higher things — but this was a strange, restless, disappointing world. If one saw a plain path open before one's feet, one might as well walk quietly along that way. There were thorns in every path, and it would be nice to be rich, very rich.

My thoughts wandered through a wide field of imagin-

ary delight, encountering only one serious obstacle in the
way of their elysium, and that was the fisherman himself,
considered as a life-long escort and companion.

In my youthful dreams, I had cherished, to be sure,
a score of mild Arthur Greys and stern Stephen Montgomerys.   My Arthurs had all died of inherited consumption.   I had taken leave of their departing spirits
under the most thrilling circumstances, having frequently
been married to them at their death-beds, and had lived
but to plant flowers on their graves, and wear crape for
them ever afterwards; and my dark browed Stephen
Montgomerys had all gone to swell the avenging tide
of righteous war, and had been fatally shot, while
I remained to shed tears of unavailing grief over the
locks of raven hair they left with me on the morning of their departure.   But to marry a real, live,
omnipresent man—a man, with red hair, sound lungs,
and no wars to go to ! My aspiring soul shrank from
the realistic vision.

And all the while a tenderer vision would rise before my
eyes, clothed with its pitiful romance—the Cradlebow,
like some sadly out-of-fashion guest, arising unsolicited
out of a half-forgotten dream-land, passing indeed both
the ideal strength of the war-like Stephen and the gentleness of the saintly Arthur, but, alas ! so crude, so
unworldly, so ridiculously poor ! And the vision extended
and then narrowed helplessly to a home in one of the
forlorn houses in Wallencamp by the sea, with its dingy
walls and bare floors, its general confusion of objects and
misery, and my lord's grand eyes obscured, perchance,
behind clouds of tobacco smoke, while I set the scanty
table and fried the briny herrings.

With a shudder for romance, I returned to the contemplation of wealth and respectability; and took up graciously, once more, the briefly abandoned idea of duty.

I had often been told that it was my duty to accommodate myself to other people's views. Perhaps I should accomplish my designs for self-immolation, and thus, in one sense, effect my highest spiritual good by marrying the fisherman and accommodating myself to his views — ah! but how could that be, I reflected, unsmilingly, when my views were so infinitely superior to his!

I wondered, for one thing, why he should have entertained, of late, such an excessive dislike for Wallencamp and its inhabitants. The natural beauty of Wallencamp had impressed me daily more and more, and the people were harmless, to say the least. I thought he should have enjoyed them; he had a humorous vein; he was not too snobbish; and he seemed of a nature to wish to make himself generally agreeable to people, but for these special objects of my care, he had expressed only derision and contempt, with often a touch of positive malice; and had not been able to abstain from giving me a hard cut or two on my mission, barely avoiding it in his letter, and rejoicing with what seemed to me an unwarrantable warmth in the hope that I should soon quit forever the abominable place.

Then, in my miserable short-sightedness, my thoughts wandered indirectly to Ethel. I wondered if she had taken to heart anything in the acquaintance she was said to have had with Mr. Turner, before I came to Wallencamp, which had caused the change in her. I did not believe she had. The girl was too artless and simple to have concealed so completely the resentment she would naturally have cherished — too childish to have borne it so silently. As far as the fisherman was implicated in the affair, even if he had trifled a little for his own amusement with the vague impulses, possibly the affections, of this unso-phisticated girl, the act was by no means unprecedented among people of wealth and respectability. It was a diversion in which Arthur Grey and Stephen Montgom-ery would not have indulged, perhaps, "but this," I mused, " is a sadly common-place sort of world, viewed in the broad daylight of wisdom and experience (and with such penetrating rays I felt my own optics to be only too wearily oppressed) ; we must give up our high ideals, take people as we find them, and submit gracefully to the inevitable."

Still I was in as much of a quandary as ever as to what I should choose to consider the inevitable in my own path. It never occurred to me in this dilemma to seek advice from the elder members of my own family. They knew nothing really of my situation in Wallencamp, and even if they had been informed more truthfully in regard to it, I thought they could hardly be expected to appre-ciate the peculiarly trying circumstances in which I was placed just at present.

Mothers were excellent for mending gloves, taking ink stains out of white dresses with lemon juice, etc., etc., but there were certain exigencies in the remote and exalted life of those who go on "missions" which their humble though loving skill must ever fail to reach.

I did write home, by the way, for more spending-money. I had been obliged to send to Boston for a few of the latest novels, fresh ribbons, cologne water, and various other articles indispensable to the career of a truly devoted propagandist. I preferred my request no longer as the dependent offspring seeking gifts from a fond and indulgent parent, but as the solicitor of a mere temporary loan, until I should be able to draw on my salary at the close of the term.

One morning, having inured myself to extreme worldliness of soul and begun a deliberately reckless response to the fisherman's letter, I looked out through my window to see the Cradlebow trudging manfully down the lane, with a grotesquely antiquated portemanteau in his hand, and the general air of one who has started a-foot on a journey.

With a singular readiness to be diverted, I found that the picture was, somehow, not conducive to further worldliness of meditation; and when, in the evening, Mrs. Cradlebow came in to call, in her mantilla, the impression thus made on my mind was inexpressibly deepened.

Mrs Cradlebow was not a frequent caller. She had almost earned among the Wallencampers the direful anathema of "not being neighborly."

She informed me, while the singers were gathered, as usual, at the Ark, that Benney had gone to make farewell visits on his friends. He had three married sisters living in different parts of the State. They had children. The children were very fond of him, and he was going on such a long voyage. Mrs. Cradlebow was looking beyond the singers, her eyes shining clear and sad above the pathetic smile on her lips.

"And he says he shan't come back again until he comes to give me such pleasure as I never dreamed of."

Those words come to me now, either as part of the

endless mockery of life, or as strains of hidden music, deep and true, running ever beneath the world's dull misinterpretation.

Afterwards, the choir of voices in the room formed an effectual shield for confidential conversation.

" You don't know what a good boy he's always been to me, teacher," Mrs. Cradlebow continued, with a manner unusual to her, I thought, as of one seeking for sympathy, " so that I've learned to depend so much on him, more, I think, than on anybody else. Some boys, when they're growing up so, they feel independent and they answer you back short, but the older he grew, the gentler he was to me, always, and if he had any trouble, it never made him cross to me, and I think it's harder to see anybody so than if they was cross, for he's quick in ways, I know, but when things go real hard against him, he's patient."   -

" He ought not to know much about trouble yet," I answered hopefully, with the consciousness of one who has fathomed all the mysteries of grief and can yet speak gaily of the forlorn background.

" He doesn't know enough about the world, I'm afraid," said Mrs. Cradlebow, and her eyes, fixed on my face, seemed to me to be looking gently into my inmost heart. " He expects so much, and he never looks out for himself. I wish he'd be content to go fishing with the other boys — they always come back in the autumn — and not want to sail so far."

I was almost angry because of the embarrassment I felt under that clear glance.

" Don't you think, Mrs. Cradlebow," I said nervously, " that young people are never content until they find out the world for themselves?" It was an interrogation, but it was sagely uttered.

"I know, I know," she said. "Perhaps it's best he should go." She spoke very quietly and with uncommon composure of demeanor. She withdrew her eyes from my face but the smile trembled on her lips, and I knew that her heart was breaking over the words, for Benney was her darling.

I wished, almost impatiently, for my own part, that it might all have happened differently, that I might leave everything in Wallencamp just as I had found it, so delightfully happy and peaceful it had seemed to me. I could not bear, in looking back, to think of one face as wearing upon it any unaccustomed grief. At all events, I felt that my thoughts had been hopelessly turned from their prescribed channel, and the fisherman's letter remained from day to day, still unanswered.

Meanwhile, winter was vanishing at the Cape. As salient points in its quaint and cherished memory, I recall the frequent clamming excursions, when we rattled down to the beach, at low-tide, in a cart whose groaning members lacked every element of elasticity. Often there were as many as sixteen persons in one cart, and the same number of hoes and baskets — the baskets being filled with small children as a means of keeping both them and the children stationary.

Grandma was always present on these occasions, and the hilarity of the Wallencampers, as they were jounced and joggled over the stones, in a manner which to some might have been productive of great bodily agony, concealed, with them, no undercurrent of nervous dread or pain. They were kind enough to regard the presence of

.ne "Teacher" as indispensable to their complete enjoyment, while I was ready to congratulate myself that my
society alone was the object desired, for though I brought
my near-sighted vision to bear faithfully upon the sands, I
never succeeded in capturing a clam.

I heard that Bachelor Rae had confided aside to Captain Benney that "Teacher 'd ought to bring a hook and
line. The clams ud go for it in a minute if she 'd only
bring a hook and line ;" and, stung by the unsheathed
sarcasm of this remark, I was accustomed afterwards
to wander off towards "Steeple Rock." The rock was
accessible at low-tide, and from thence I could watch
the ocean on one side, and the clam-diggers on the
other ; could see Grandma on her hands and knees, a
dot of broad good nature in the distance, always
remaining apparently in the one place, and always,
somehow, getting her basket full of clams as she gradually
sank deeper and deeper into the briny soil, but no
true Wallencampers ever caught cold by soaking in the
brine.

I could distinguish Abagail wandering lightly about
among the rocks, scraping off mussels with her hoe, and
the Modoc, the champion clam-digger of all, spreading
her tentacles, here and there, and never failing to come
up with a bivalve. It was a picturesque scene, viewed
from the great rock ; and when the tide began to sweep
in again, George Olver sent a piercing whistle along
shore, to call the stragglers together ; clams, children, and
all were loaded into the cart, and jostled gaily homeward
chased by the fresh sea breezes.

For the chowder, which in due course of events arose
to take its place among the viands on the Ark board,

I would leave it to that sacred and tenfold mystery with which, to my mind, it was ever enshrouded.

* * * * *

I recall the exhibitions held at the school-house, confined exclusively to the native talent of Wallencamp, at which the old and young were assembled to speak pieces.

It was then that Aunt Rhoda and Aunt Cinthia, matrons of portly frame and perilous foothold, engaged in a metrical dialogue concerning the robbing of a bird's nest, in which lively diversion they assumed to have participated. And Bachelor Rae rendered "my beautiful Annabel Lee" with unique effect, and Grandma Spicer spoke mysteriously though hopefully of

> " Hope and Hannah
> Double decked schooner
> Cap'n John Homer
> Marster and owner
> Bound for Bermudy."

The strange effect produced upon me by the first of these rhetorical entertainments, is still as fresh in my mind as though it had been yesterday, so luminous was the night with stars; so loud and prolonged the preliminary blowing of the horn; so festive the appearance of the school-house, loaded as it was with evergreens; so abnormal the proportions of the stage, which had been extended to comprise nearly two-thirds of the school-room.

It comes to me again, the first shock of surprise at finding all Wallencamp on the stage, Grandpa and I, alone, being left like ostracized owls among the shrubbery of the auditorium. Our sense of isolation was only

intensified by hearing the sounds of mirth which proceeded from the other side of the curtain, and seeing
a foot or an elbow occasionally thrust out into our own
green though silent realm.

Thrice Aunt Rhoda appeared before the curtain to
proclaim in pregnant tones, "we are now awaiting for
Josiah and Annie."

Josiah, by the way, had married a Wallencamp girl
and taken her to West Wallen to live, yet the two were
ever faithful attendants at the Wallencamp festivities.

"Declaration" after "declaration" was announced by
Aunt Rhoda, and as the declaimers finished their parts,
they descended to sit with us, until at last the curtain
was drawn aside, revealing Abagail, alone upon the
stage, seated at her "music."

She opened the Hymnal, and struck the leading
chord, and straightway, from the Wallencampers, all
gathered now below, there arose a burst of melody as it
had been one mighty voice.

CHAPTER XI.

A WALLENCAMP FUNERAL.

R. 'Lihu Alden– Noah's father—lay dying, and all the Wallencampers were assembled in and about the house.

It was night, and one was going out from among them to launch his lonely bark on a deeper, more mysterious ocean than that whose moan came up to them from behind the cedars. There was awe on their faces, and a touch of terror, too, but above all there was a strange, child-like wonder.

They had seen death before. It might come to them at any time, they knew. Its spirit sounded in the dirges of the waves along the shore, yet, none the less, for time or fate, or moan of solemn wave, grew this exceeding mystery.

Was it like a cold black flood, to die at night, and no stars shining—a cold flood creeping more and more above the heart? Oh, the wonder on those poor faces, if there might be, indeed, some fairer harbor lights beyond death's tide, and gentler music lulling the dread surge, so that the voyager, with untold joy at last, felt the worn boat-keel loosen on the strand and drift off from this shore!

Emily and Aunt Cinthia were alone in the room with the dying man. They were his sisters. His wife had been dead for years.

In the adjoining room sat a group of females, a single candle burning dimly on a table in their midst. Grandma Bartlett was there, and Grandma Spicer, and Aunt Susannah Cradlebow.

Occasionally, a whisper from one of these three pierced the gloom, a whisper appropriately sepulchral in tone, but more penetrating than any voice of buoyant life and hope.

I sat in the door with Abagail, Ethel on the step below, very still and thoughtful.

The men and the young people, for the most part, were waiting about outside.

I caught the low murmur of a discussion between Captain Sartell and Bachelor Rae, who were sitting on the fence, and knew by the attitude of the listeners gathered around them, that the subject was one of no ordinary interest. I could not help wondering what these two argued concerning death and the immortality of the soul.

The tick! tick! tick! of the clock sounded with persistent distinctness in the room where the women sat, and Grandma Bartlett sighed, and then came the awful whisper.

"Ah, death's vary sahd — vary sahd."

Grandma Bartlett, superannuated as she was, was the most trite of the Wallencampers.

Aunt Susannah Cradlebow accepted the lifeless phrase with something almost like a smile of disdain in her magnificent eyes.

" Oh, it's like everything else," she whispered. " It's a mixter ! It's a mixter ! "

Once, the door of the little bedroom opened softly and Emily appeared on the scene.

" He's got most to the end of *his* rope," she said drily, in answer to the enquiring faces lifted to her own. There was an unnatural brightness in Emily's tearless eyes, and her tone was as sprightly as ever.

" He don't see nothin', and he don't feel nothin', and he don't hear nothin'," she continued, " and it's sech poor work a' breathin', he's most give that up, too. It might stop any minute and he not know it. Cinthy's cryin', I don't see nothin' to cry about. It'll storm before to-morrow, likely — it's dark enough, Lord knows — and them east winds always hurt him so. 'I don't know whether he's worse off, or better off, Cinthy,' says I, 'or whether he's off entirely. But I don't believe a righteous God'll make poor 'Lihu suffer any worse than he has in the last ten weeks.' But it's strange, all the time I was a' sittin' there by him, when he was worst, it kept comin' up before me, jest as he was when he was a little boy. I hadn't thought on him so for years, but seemed jest as though 't was back in New Hampshire, where we was born, a playin' around the old mill again. Him and me was the youngest, we was always together, and I couldn't a' called him up so before me, to save me, but there he was, as plain as life, with his little blue checked apron on, a' skippin' along towards me over the logs, and his eyes a' dancin', and the wind a' blowin' his

hair out ; and all the while I could n't help a' knowin'
that 'Lihu was a man grown a' dyin' there before me on
the bed.

" ' Seems as though a man that's been a' wearin' out as
long as he has had ought to die easier, Cinthy,' says I.
'It's pretty hard to have forty years consumption, and
then go off with a fever.'   ' We can't question the Lord's
doin's,' says Cinthy.   But for all that, she would n't
stay in the room to see him.   He could n't ke:ch his
breath and he was as crazy as a loon.   Lord, how he
worried !   All day, yesterday, he was a loadin' ship down
to the shore.   It would a' made your bones ache to hear him
workin' so ; and all night long he was a loadin', and a
loadin.'   Thinks I, won't there never be no end to this,
for I felt hard, and him a loadin' and a loadin' all
through them long hours, jest as faithful as life, with his
eyes like blood, and the sweat a rollin' off'n him.   He
could n't stand that forever.   This mornin' the pain
sorter left him, but there was that one idee on his mind.
The ship was all loaded, and he'd got to wait for high
tide to git it off, and he wanted to go to sleep, but he
could n't, because he'd got to watch the tide.

" ' Oh, if I could only rest, now,' he kep' a' sayin',
weak and slow.   'If I could only go to sleep now,' and
so he moaned and moaned.

" So I got close to his ear and I says, 'You go to sleep,
now, 'Lihu, and I'll watch,' I says, 'I'll wake you up
when it's high tide,' I says, but he only shook his head.
So then, I says, ' Aint there none o' the folks you can
trust to watch?'   And he shook his head, and so he
moaned and moaned.

" By and by, all of a sudden, 'Lihu looked up at me

different, with his eyes wide open, so that for a minute, I was most fool enough to think 'Lihu was gittin' well, and he smiled as though he wanted to say something. So I leant over, ' I — know — somebody,' he says, as slow as that, for he was all worn out. 'Who, then, 'Lihu?' says I. ' Jesus,' says he, with that queer, smilin' look, as though it was the naturalist thing on earth. ' He 'll — wake — me — up — when —,' and he could n't wait no longer, his head fell over as heavy as a log, and that 's the way he 's been ever since, sleepin' like death.

" Wall, Cinthy thinks somebody 'd ought to come in and make a prayer. 'He was n't a perfessor,' says she. 'Lord knows, if he had a been,' says I, ' there 'd be more need on 't !' 'Anyway,' says I, 'he can't hear nothin', it won 't do him no harm.' So I thought I'd come out and see. It 'll make Cinthy feel easier."

There was a whispered consultation among the women, but Emily came over to where I sat.

"Come, teacher," said she. "Your voice ain 't as raspin' as some, and you 've got a knack o' stringin' words together, that sound likely, and don 't hit nobody — you come in."

" Hush ! " I cried, grasping the woman's hand, think-ing only, then, that it would seem like sacrilege for any-one to speak aloud in the room where one was waiting for Christ to wake him. I had forgotten at that moment, that I was out of the habit of praying, even for myself. Emily's tale had moved me so, it seemed only its sweet and fitting consummation, and nothing incredible to my mind then, that Christ should come down out of the starless sky to touch that heavy sleeper's brow.

It was finally decided that there should be a quiet little

.prayer meeting in the room where the women sat, in behalf of Mr. 'Lihu's soul ; but before all the preliminary steps had been taken, and the men and youth noiselessly ingathered, Mr. 'Lihu's breathing had ceased, without a parting pang or gasp, and the tide was at its full.

Noah had been standing with a group near the door. Once at some irrelevancy in the proceedings, while the women were organizing the prayer meeting, I heard his irrepressible little giggle creeping in, but when the words so mysteriously uttered were passed out to him —"'Lihu's gone !"—the poor boy, realizing only at that instant their terrible meaning, that his father had indeed gone, gone away from him forever, ran forward a pace or two, and then fell, with his face to the ground.

So he lay, shaking and sobbing helplessly.

Grandma Bartlett, standing in the door, studied him for some moments with her fossilized eyes :

" Fatherless and motherless, now," said she. " Poor creetur, humph ! vary sahd."

Then she blinked, and, simultaneously, the subject seemed to have slipped from her mind, and she to have become vaguely contemplative concerning worlds and ages remote.

The boy was still lying prone on the ground, when I left the place of mourning with Grandma and Abagail. I spoke to him, and shrank instinctively from his face as he turned it towards me. It was swollen and disfigured with weeping. He had bruised it, too, in falling. He rose, trembling, and walked with me. For my own part, the emotional had given place to feelings of a more sustained and ordinary nature.

I strove to impress upon Noah's mind the beautiful

and poetic manner in which his father had been released from his sufferings.

I reminded him of the shortness of life, "even from your point of view, Noah," and the necessity there was always, for not allowing ourselves to be overcome by our griefs or passions, or diverted from the supreme satisfaction of performing our appointed tasks, etc.

And Noah listened patiently throughout, and said, "good-night," with a brave attempt at a smile, and a sob still choking in his throat.

I turned an instant, to look at him as he walked away. He wore, generally, a coat of ministerial form and complexion ; this, taken in connection with his round, laughing face, his boyish figure, and propensity for playing tricks, had often made me smile, hitherto.

But, now, there was something in the attitude of those long, black tails that brought the tears to my eyes.

It occurred to me, indirectly, what Emily had said about my stringing words together, and I marveled if possibly my exhortation had soared over poor Noah's head and left his heart aching for an ordinary word of sympathy, or a simple reference to One who as a man of sorrows, was best fitted to understand and console his grief. To any sentiments of the latter nature, Noah was particularly susceptible.

"Children, all of them !" Thus gently apostrophizing the Wallencampers, I dismissed the cause of my brief mental discomfiture, with a half-pitying smile.

The day after Mr. 'Lihu's death, I looked down from my desk in school to see the infant Sophronia weeping bitterly.

"What is the matter, Sophronia?" I said.

"Carietta's been to see the cops twice," she sobbed; "and I ain't been any."

I only gathered from this that Carietta was somehow implicated as being the cause of the infant Sophronia's sufferings.

" Now," said I gravely, " tell me what you mean? "

"She means the cops!" cried Carietta, her small face distorted with a leer of the most horrid satisfaction. " 'Lihu's cops. 'Phrony means the —"

" 'That will do," I said. " I understand you perfectly. I understand you only too well. This is about as bad," I reflected, " as anything in my experience."

After admonishing my pupils with that sincere emotion to which the occasion had given rise, that they should speak always respectfully of their elders, but especially in the most tender and solemn tones of the dead ; after pointing out to them the perniciousness of a low and vulgar curiosity, and expatiating on the vastness and superiority of the spiritual life, compared with the earthly and carnal, I paused, only to give, further on, a fuller illustration to my words, and said :

" Now, Sophronia, you have an immortal soul? "

There was evidence of some faint hankering in Sophronia's face as she mentally ran over the list of her possessions.

" No 'm," said she, " I hain't—but I've got a cornycopia !"

I think it was then and there that my hopes for the elevation of juvenile Wallencamp received their death blow, and my labors, which had before been cheered by a dream of partially satisfying success, at least, took on an utterly goal-less and prosaical form.

These children, I was forced to admit, regarded the day of Mr. 'Lihu's funeral as a holiday of rare and special interest, mysteriously bestowed by Heaven.

Aunt Rhoda had previously informed me that it was expected I would have no school that afternoon.

The West Wallen minister officiated on the occasion with an aspect neither more nor less funereal than he had worn at Noel's wedding. He spoke in such a labored, trumpet-like tone of voice that the Wallencampers seemed, at first, inspired with a lively hope, expecting momentarily that his breath would give out, but in this they were doomed to ever increasing disappointment.

At length, Captain Sartell drew a bucketful of fresh water from the well, and passed it around the room, winking expansively at each individual in turn, by way of silent encouragement and support.

Grandma Bartlett, observing the generally tearless aspect of the community, conscientiously attempted to weep, but being entirely out of tears, at her time of life, she only succeeded in screwing her face up into what, in earlier years, might have appeared as a lachrymose expression, but now took the shape of a fixed and ogreish grin.

The infant Sophronia was seated on a bench of an exceedingly temporary nature, between Grandma Spicer and Aunt Pucinda, both persons of weight, and it so chanced, or, rather, it followed as a matter of course, an equal pressure being applied to both sides, that the board sustaining the three, broke directly under that diminutive victim of fate, awaking her thereby from feverish slumber; and whether the infant Sophronia had an immortal soul or not, no one there present could doubt that she possessed an uncommon pair of lungs.

14

The little room where we sat was hot and overcrowded, and the thought was running in my mind continually, "Poor, restless Wallencampers! and how happy Mr. 'Lihu is not to have any connection with his funeral."

When the procession was about to start for the burying-ground, the request was made to me that I would blow the horn, even as the bell is usually tolled on such occasions, for it would seem inappropriate for one of the Wallencampers to do so, they all having been related to the deceased.

At such a time, I could not refuse, though the emotions with which I crossed over to the school-house to perform this grim duty, were of a nature best known to, and appreciated by, myself. My terror of the Wallencamp horn had waxed daily. I believed that there was nothing in the whole world of inanimate things on which I would not sooner have attempted to sound a funeral dirge. Though capable of some variety of expression, it had never yet been seduced into emitting any sound in the least indicative of the designs struggling in the mind of the blower. The human was paralyzed before it—a mere machine to blow into it and let come what would. And, now, for the first time in my experience, it took on a jubilant strain. I blew slowly; I blew solemnly. Still, it sounded like nothing less than a glad, exultant, rallying call.

I paused, horrified. From the rear of the moving procession, Aunt Patty, with a yell and a frantic gesture of the hands, entreated me to "keep a blowin'!"

And, as I stood thus on the steps of the deserted school-house and blew, only to hear the wild lamentations of my soul translated into strains of fiendish mirth through

the medium of the horn, the Turkey Mogul, arrived on
his second visit of examination to the Wallencamp
school, seemed to be descending before my eyes, in a
vortex of the giddy atmosphere. In fact, he was alight-
ing from his buggy, and a grim, though reassuring smile
sat on his features.

"I see! I see!" he nodded his head. "You've
given them a good start," he added, succinctly, indicating
the direction of the Wallencampers, "Humph! yes!
they are always up to something!"

He thrust his hands in his pockets, and, maintaining the
same sardonic grin, he, too, stood and watched that receding column.

It was an odd combination of circumstances. I had
ceased my mad though involuntary jubilate, on the horn,
and was slowly aspiring to that equanimity of mind which
the exigencies of the case seemed to require, when the
Turkey Mogul turned abruptly and, without speaking a
word, handed me a soiled and wrinkled little sheet of
paper, the contents of which caused my heart, for an instant, to cease beating, and then set it throbbing with a
wild joy and exultation.

It was simply a petition—wrought out of whose brain
I know not, but most curiously inscribed in Aunt Patty's
own hand, and signed by all the Wallencampers with
"CAPTAIN SARTELL," at the head, and "b. ny"
at the foot — to the effect that it was their desire that my
labors might be longer continued among them.

Only one, who, having made a play-day of life, turns, at
last, to attempt some earnest work, and fails, as he believes, utterly, and then catches a glimpse of unexpected
light in the darkness, can understand the impulse given

me by that dirty little scroll. It was such happiness as I had never felt before. It made me strangely weak.

"You'll stay," said the Turkey Mogul, at length, "another term, or we'll consider this term extended, if you please."

"I'll stay a few more weeks, anyway," I said, and the Turkey Mogul must have marveled at the childish faith and joy with which I clung to this new found rock of my salvation, "but I had n't thought of it before," I added, a little faintly, thinking of home.

"You're tired !" said the Turkey Mogul, almost sympathetically, "and hungry !" he subjoined, quickly, in a different tone.

I knew by this time that the Turkey Mogul's eyes were dangerously prone to have twinkles in the corners of them, yet I believe I met their derisive questioning with a simple seriousness in my own.

"Well, that 's right !" he exclaimed. "Stick to 'em ! Stick to 'em ! I'll be down to conduct another — humph ! another examination in a week or two. Good bye !" and he gave me his hand, and was off almost before the little line of mourners had disappeared over the crest of the hill. Yet I remember that Grandma Bartlett, who had been deterred by the infirmity of age from joining the procession, and had remained at the window, alone, regaled the Wallencampers, on their return, with a choice fancy, in which the Turkey Mogul and I had stood "talkin' and chatterin' on the school-house steps, for an hour or more." Grandma Bartlett, though not actively disposed to work mischief, nor possessed, indeed, of any animate quality, still cherished a few of the dry formulas of scandal, which she applied to any seemingly

favorable combination of circumstances. The Wallencampers, at any time, paid but little attention to her
words.

And, at the close of this strange day, I sat alone, in my
little room in the Ark, and indited a letter to the following effect :—

" Having received gratifying overtures from the people
of my change, I had decided, for reasons which I could
not then explain, to remain at Wallencamp until May, to
which time I looked forward with the delightful hope of
seeing my dear ones once more.

" Meanwhile, I hoped they would not consider it
strange, or ungracious of me to say that I should very
much prefer not to have brother Will, or any one else
come to Wallencamp to look after me, as brother Will
and some others had kindly suggested doing. It would
seem to imply that I was not capable of taking care of
myself, a mania which I trusted no longer held possession
of the family brain. Moreover, Wallencamp, though so
charming a place, had but few facilities for the accommo-
dation of guests. I should draw on my salary, now, very
shortly, and would then remit the sums I had borrowed
in mere temporary embarrassment," etc.

CHAPTER XII.

HE Wallencamp bonfire, like Christmas or a Fourth of July celebration in less ingenious and erratic communities, came only once a year.

It was kindled on Eagle Hill, that runs out from the main land of Wallencamp into Herrin' River,— the Wallencampers called the Hill an island,— and from most points of view it answered to the geographical description of "Land entirely surrounded by water," seeming, indeed, to stand solitary in the river, with an air of infinite repose on its broad, sloping sides ; green and gold, so I remember it ever, with the sun setting over it in the spring time,— green and gold, in a crimson river !

It had an air of sublimity, too, looking over and beyond the cedars to the bay, and down the length of the winding stream that fretted at its feet or lapped them quietly.

There I planned to build a house, in some bright future day, that should be in effective keeping with the natural grandeur of the place,—quaint, lordly, substantial, with the appearance of having fallen somewhat into disuse, ivy growing over the dark stone walls, and moss in the winding drives, and carved lions at the gate.

The hill was a favorite resort of mine, and Ethel had generally accompanied me on my excursions thither.

Once she said — it was in the days when she had been happier — "I guess *this* place is just as God made it to begin with."

Ethel had been struck with and had retained an idea which she had probably heard promulgated sometime at the West Wallen Sunday School, that, at the time of man's spiritual fall, the earth also, with all terrestrial things, had undergone a general mixing up. Her own idea in regard to Eagle Hill she expressed very modestly, looking off with a childish content and assurance in her eyes. And I was delighted with her.

" You are always thinking such things as that," I exclaimed, enthusiastically. " I know you are ! "

Ethel blushed, smiling, and shook her head.

" I ain't often sure," she said.

I think I told her then that when I had my house on the hill, she should be the house-keeper to guard my keys and conduct my affairs, " that is, my dear, attend to all the little practical details connected with living," and Ethel, to whom my castles on the Hill were never castles in the air, but who believed most implicitly that I would, sooner or later, perform all things that ever I dreamed of doing, accepted her prospective matronship with a becoming sense of its advantage and dignity.

Eagle Hill was haunted by a horse, a pure white horse — not Noel's — with a flowing mane and tail, and a beautiful arched neck. His motions, the Wallen-

campers said, were most fiery and graceful. Occasionally he paused and fell back, quivering on his
haunches, looked this way and that, and then, with
a wild plunge, swept on again, swifter than before,
Every true Wallencamper could both see and hear the
" white horse " when at night, clearly outlined against the
sky, he galloped back and forth along the very summit of
the hill.

It was on one of the blackest nights of the season that
the fuel, which less grand and poetic souls would doubtless have reserved for another winter's use, was borne
in jubilant triumph by the Wallencampers up the sides of
this sacred and illustrious steep, and there consumed
in a most glorious conflagration. The spectacle was
appalling. At intervals in the roaring and crackling of
the flames, was heard the roar of the near ocean, while
the familiar features of the landscape, the faces of the
encircling spectators, stood out with unreal and terrible
distinctness in the hellish light.

Emily, who had coughed all the way climbing up the
hill, stood stirring the fire with a long pole, and making reckless and facetious remarks the while, which,
uttered in the midst of that unearthly scene, struck
me cold with horror.

" Come, Bachelder," said she, " git onto the end
of my pole, and I'll hold ye over there a while. Ye
might as well be gittin used to it ! "

" Heh ! yes," said Bachelor Rae. " But what I'm
a thinkin', is you'd ought to have a subordinate. I never
heered — heh ! — of putting a person of such importance
in the Kingdom — heh ! — however efficient — into the
position of Fire Tender ! "

" Crazy Silvy " was at the bonfire. I had never seen her before. Silvy did not go out on ordinary occasions. I watched her as she stood with a scant, thin shawl thrown over her head, looking intently into the flames, shivering often, and smiling as she moved her lips in apparently delightful conversation with herself.

Some of the children essayed to tease her ; she seemed quite unconscious of their efforts, but I turned and spoke to them rather sharply. The next time I looked up, her strange, smiling eyes were fixed full on my face. I glanced away quickly, with a nervous shiver, and moved a little farther off. As I did so, Silvy, regarding me in that same dreamily contemplative manner, walked toward me a step or two, and as I continued to move away, she walked slowly after me.

My acquaintance with the unconfined insane had not been extensive enough to allow me to regard her motions with that mingled amusement and curiosity, which was the only sentiment expressed on the countenances of the Wallencampers who stood watching us ; but I concluded that it was better to face about, and meet my pursuer with an air of fearlessness. I did so, and held out my hand to her as she came up.

" How do you do, Silvy ? " I said.

" Oh, no ! " said Silvy, thrusting her hands behind her, laughing softly, and shaking her head. " Not with the queen of Heaven ! Not with the queen of Heaven ! "

I thought I detected Emily's derisive influence in this, poor, simple creature's words. Silvy was so perfectly mild and harmless in appearance, however, that I began to feel reassured.

" I've heard about you, Silvy," I continued, cheerfully.

"I'm the teacher, you know. You've heard them speak of the teacher?"

"So glad," continued Silvy, in that same low, cooing tone, "so glad to meet the queen of Heaven."

"Hush!" said I then. "You mustn't say that again. Draw your shawl up tighter." For in spite of the bonfire, the wind was blowing cold on the hill.

While I spoke Silvy had become absorbed in watching the fire again. I would have walked quietly away, but as I turned to go, she thrust her head towards me quickly and whispered:

"Wait! don't — you — ever — tell?"

Silvy put her hand to her lips.

"No," said I, smiling.

"Silvy never told," she went on, "except to you. You've got a key. Silvy's got a key. She keeps things all locked up, Silvy does. Emily don't have any key. She talks — she talks all over — don't you tell — but Silvy lives with Emily — so bad," said Silvy, heaving a gentle sigh and speaking in a tone of the deepest confidence, "so bad not to have any key."

"That's true, I think," said I, beginning to find my strange companion rather interesting.

"Yes." Silvy nodded her head several times as though we understood, we two, and she was delighted to have discovered the fact.

Then her eyes wandered again to the fire, and she resumed her happy, smiling conversation with herself.

I thought she had forgotten me, or concluded not to unlock anything with her key, when she turned slowly and looked at me, and seemed to gather up the lost train of her ideas in my face.

"Silvy watched the fishermen at Emily's," she went on. "They said, ' Poor Silvy !' ' See you again next time, Silvy !' They are very p'lite, thank you, and they laugh once. 'Ha ! ha !' But Eliot Turner, he laughs twice. 'Ha ! ha !' and behind his sleeve, too. Such things are damnable !"

Silvy's dulcet tones ran over that hard word with the mildest and softest of accents.

"And they bring wine," she continued. "Silvy cl'ared off the table one night. She heard ' em sing, and they says to him, ' what about pretty Eth ?' and he says ' we must have a little fun, you know, ha ! ha !' and then, 'ha ! ha !' behind his sleeve. Now if Silvy could keep it all together, you 'd straighten it out maybe. Silvy can't straighten it out. Where did she hear so much, I wonder ! She hears too much, Silvy does."

She knitted her brows in pitiful perplexity.

"You were talking about the fisherman," said I.

"No," said Silvy, shaking her head, " about Eth. She never says, ' Crazy Silvy ! There she goes ! Look at Silvy !' She says, ' Come and see me, Silvy,' so. So soft spoken. Silvy loves her."

" I love her, too," I said, gently, for Silvy had paused again, and was knitting her brows in that painful manner, as though the effort to think gave her actual physical suffering.

"Silvy knows ! Silvy knows !" She exclaimed suddenly, her face all smooth and softly smiling now. "Never—you— trust a neat man," impressively. "Never you trust 'em — for why? They was n't made so. God made 'em. God made 'em to clutter. And there was that Eliot Turner. He was always a' hangin' things up. He was always foldin' of 'em. He was always a hangin' 'em up in his room. Silvy knows. But there was a piece of writin' got over behind the bury. And it did n't fall. But it stuck. Silvy knows. She reads writin'. She reads it over and over. He did n't love Eth any more. But he 's afraid. And he 'll give money. 'Oh, go anywhere ! Only keep still, Eth. For Heaven's sake, keep still.' Why, she would n't hurt him ! Eth would n't hurt him," said Silvy in a slow tone full of wonder.

"He need n't be afraid. But Silvy won 't tell him so. Why not? Oh, she likes to be amused. Silvy likes to be amused ! "

"Silvy knows ! Silvy knows ! " She continued, after another terrible pause. " She set eyes on you, standin' there. That 's the one, she says, and she says it a long time. That 's the queen of Heaven. She would n't hurt Silvy, poor Silvy ! She 's got a key. So she 'll straighten it out, maybe. Silvy can't, she 's so tired. When Silvy got up in the morning, it was early. Oh, so still ! And a bird was flyin' up—up. Silvy could n't see—so far to Heaven. It made Silvy cry. So strange not to be any tired in the mornin'."

Silvy made a last painful effort to collect her thoughts, before her face resumed its habitual, far away, half smiling expression.

Then she said, "Silvy comes up the hill all alone. Not the way them others, and she see the fire burnin'. But it was dark in the bush. Silvy heard 'em talkin' terribly. It was Eth and George Olver. 'I 'll make an honest home for you Eth.' And she says, terribly, she no deserve. And he says, she better than him, and

won't she come?   And she cries so, ' My heart is broke!'
And how good to live with him she knows, now — so
honest and true — but she no fit, and, oh, ' My heart is
broke ! my heart is broke !' ' "

The scene, the vividness of these words had not yet
faded in the least from Silvy's memory.

" 'Then," said she, "they keep on talkin', terribly.
But Silvy—she hears so much—poor Silvy ! She goes
'round very still, 'nother way. Silvy's tired."

And, as unceremoniously as she had approached me,
she turned and walked slowly back to her old position
before the fire. She did not look at me. She seemed to
have become utterly unconscious of my presence. The
scant, thin shawl had fallen back from her head. She
shivered as she stood gazing into the flames, but the
dreamy expression was ever in her eyes and the soft
laugh on her lips, as she continued murmuring to herself.

The Wallencampers were not content to let the fire
go out after the first grand illumination. They were
bringing up more brush from the landward side of the hill,
amid a confusion of wild shouts and excited laughter.

I found Ethel among a group of girls.

" When you go home to-night," I said, " I want you
to step in and see me. Come up to my room."

" Yes " said Ethel, and I noticed how pale she turned
in the fire light. I did not say any more to her, then.

After hearing Silvy's story, I believed that Mr. Turner
had acted a heartless and unmanly part towards Ethel,
made love to her which he could not doubt the poor girl
took in earnest, and even promises which he knew he
should lightly break sometime, and then, for his own
purposes, he begged her to keep silence. I thought

I understood, and resolved to instruct Ethel to forget the red haired fisherman, to be " sensible," and " marry good, honest George Olver," who loved her so devotedly.

Benney had come home, and was one among the many figures at this brilliant fête.   Indeed, the bonfire had been deferred until later than usual in the season, by reason of his absence, and now he was noticeably the lion of the evening, in a brave dark blue cravat, that was borne outward by the wind, or fluttered becomingly under his chin, to the envy and despair of all the Wallencamp youth. He exchanged a pleasant greeting with every one, and brought the largest young tree of all up the hill on his broad shoulders.

When, at length, the Wallencampers had permitted the fire to burn low, they joined hands in a ring around the embers, and sang the saddest and sweetest songs in the Hymnal.   I sat on a rock near by, engaged as I had been much of the time since my arrival in Wallencamp, in trying to realize the situation — the awful gloom of the night, the river now invisible, below, the sound of the surf farther off, that made my heart sick, and with it the strange mingling of those religious songs, the lonely hill, the smouldering fire, the fantastic group gathered around.

When I got back to the Ark, I found Ethel waiting for me.   She followed me up to my room, and I closed the door.

" You see I waited long enough for you to come of your own accord," I said laughing.   Then I drew a chair in front of her.   She sat at the foot of the bed, and I addressed her gravely.

" Now, Ethel, something is the matter.   You are not

the merry, light hearted girl you were, when I first knew you. And I can help you perhaps. I will help you. Tell me what the trouble is ! "

I thought I should see the tears gathering in Ethel's eyes, but she looked, instead, so stonily disconsolate, that I was rather dismayed.

" I'm going to tell you," said she, " but you can't help me. They'll all know before long, I guess. I don't care. You talk good, but you don't say much about God. I guess you don't believe there 's none. I don't. I can't understand. I'm like I'd got lost, somehow, and when they found me, they 'd stone me — I don't care. I 've felt enough. I don't feel no more. I 've cried so much, I guess I can't cry no more. If I could it ud be now, tellin' you.

" When Miss Taite came here to teach, I had n't ever had no friend except the girls here, and they was n't bad, but we was always runnin' wild around in the lots, and down to shore, and always laughin' and plaguin' the teacher in school. And when Miss Taite came, she was n't like you, nor she did n't have such clothes, nor such ways as yours. I did n't love her very much, but she used to talk to me, and wanted me to be a Christian. And she did n't tell me all it was to be a Christian like you have, or I would n't a' been such a fool to think I could be ; but she talked like it was n't anything to understand, only to want Christ in your heart, and try to be good, and, first, I did n't pretend to mind much what she said, and used to tell the girls, and they 'd tell me, too, and we 'd laugh. Only one time, she was talkin' to me, and it seemed as though I could n't hold out no longer, and I cried and cried, and when

I got up, I felt happy. Just as though He was there. Seemed as though He was all around everywhere, and goin' down the lane, there was a whip-poor-will singin', and it sounded like it never had before — so strange and happy — and I always loved 'em after that — but I never shall again.

"And I tried to be good, and quieter, and have the other girls and the children at home; and when Father was drunk and noisy, and some of the folks laughed, I would n't give up — quite. Oh, I did n't feel like I was bad then! I did n't! You might remember that. I had n't much manners, but I never thought anything bad. Sometime you might remember that.

"Then Mr. Turner came, and he might a killed me, and it ud been a' kindness; but he had n't no such kind heart as that. He used to make excuses for meetin' me. He would n't look at any of the other girls. He said he could n't see no beauty in anybody else. He said I was the only one on earth he loved. He said he would n't care what became of him if I was n't good to him.

"I thought George never talked to me so much as that, and I trusted him every word. It was all so different. I thought I loved him, too. He talked about how he should take me to Providence, and I said I had n't much manners or education, and they'd laugh at me. He said there was n't another such a face there, and if he was suited, they might laugh. And he used to talk about how I'd look all dressed up in his house, down there — and I don't see! I don't see! I trusted every word.

"It would n't have been no different, anyway. I loved you when you came. When he went with you, I tried to hate you. I hated him, but I never hated you! In my heart, teacher, I never hated you. You might think of that, sometime ——"

"Well, my dear little girl," I interrupted her, "it seems we have both been somewhat deceived in the fisherman, but doubtless, we shall recover in time. You don't like him, neither do I. We'll dismiss the subject from our minds, forever. There's a good, honest boy here in Wallencamp, that a girl I know, ought to busy her head about. Why trouble ourselves with disagreeable things?"

"You might think, sometime," Ethel went on, with the same hopeless expression, and in the same tense voice, "I never knew that about not trustin' anybody till you told me. I had n't never be'n away from here. I was n't brought up like you, and I was n't so strong as you — you might think, sometime — but not now. I don't ask to have you now — you don't see. I knew you wouldn't — you can forget — you 're so happy — think of that, sometime, how happy you was, sittin' there — but I never can forget any more. I say it 'ud be'n better if I'd a died. It 's the sin and the shame. I've nothin' but to bear 'em, now, as long as I live. Oh, you might think what it was not to have no hope anywheres!"

"What do you mean?" I cried, as it rushed over me in that instant. I had been too heedless and slow to comprehend the possible wretched meaning of her words.

"What do you mean?" rising and standing over her, with a terrible sense of power to convict.

"Oh, Ethel, you did n't mean that — worst?"

"Yes," said she, with no visible change on her poor, set face — "yes — I do."

"I wish you would go out of my room, and leave me !" I exclaimed, then, "I am not used to such people as you ! Do you suppose I would have been with you all these weeks if I had known? Don't you see how you have wronged me? I never want to see you again, never ! Go ! go ! and leave me alone ! "

I shall never forget the look with which Ethel rose wearily, and went to the door — not an angry look, not a look of terror nor even of pleading reproach, but it was as if her soul, sinful, crushed and bleeding though it was, in that one moment, rose above my soul and con- demned it with sorrowful, clear eyes.

I listened to her step going down the stairs. I did not call her back. I heard her latch the outer door of the Ark. No thought of pity for her wrong, or com- miseration for her desolation moved me. I thought only in my proud selfish passion, how miserably, how bitterly I had been deceived.

I sought out the fisherman's letter, before retiring, and the one I had begun in answer, and tore them both into shreds, believing that I should as easily rid my mind of the whole miserable affair with which I had been unwittingly complicated

CHAPTER XIII.

A MILD WINTER ON THE CAPE.

"IT'S be'n a mild winter on the Cape," the Wallencampers congratulated one another, blinking, with a delicious sense of warmtk and comfort, in the rays of a strong March sun.

The Wallencampers were not, perhaps, generally incited by that love of stern, unceasing and vigorous exertion which is, geographically considered, one of the chief characteristics of our hardy northern races. True poets and idealists they were lazy, and they had but few clothes, both excellent reasons for inclining kindly to the warm weather.

And yet, notwithstanding this, they had grown used to a wild ruggedness of nature and condition, a terrible, sublime uncertainty about life and things in general when the wind blew, missing which, in this earthly state, they would have pined most sadly. And I do not believe that they would have exchanged their rugged, storm swept, wind-beleaguered little section of Cape Cod, for a

realm in sunny Italy itself; no, not even if the waves
of that bright clime had rippled over sands of literal
gold, and their winter had been nine months in the year
instead of the customary six and a half.

"A mild winter on the Cape." Grandpa Spicer often
repeated the words, and, sitting by the fire at night, his
eyes grew big and wild, and his tones took on a terrible
impressiveness as he told of *rough* winters on the Cape,
when the snow lay drifted high across the fences in the
lane, and "every time she came in yender—" pointing in
the direction of the Bay—"she licked off a slice or two
o' bank, and the old Ark whirled and shuk — o' Lordy,
teacher ! — as ef she 'd slipped her moorin's and gone off
on a high sea, and ef you 'd a heerd the wind a
screechin' inter them winders, you 'd a thought the —"

"Hoggarty Spicer ! " Grandma Spicer spoke. She
said no more. It was enough.

"You 'd a thought something had got loose, sure,"
concluded Grandpa, with a keen glance aside at me that
revealed, as with tenfold significance, the obstructed
force of his narrative.

In the daytime, Grandpa was now much out of doors.
He had most frequent and loving recourse to an interesting looking pile of rubbish at the south end of the
barn. There he sat, and napped, and nodded, and em-
ployed the brief interims of wakefulness in whittling
bean poles, preparatory for another year's supply of that
dreaded and inexorable crop. Earth's disturbing voices,
Grandma Spicer, herself, seldom reached him there.

Early, too, I saw him in the garden, leaning pensively
on his hoe — a becalmed and striking figure in a ragged
snuff-colored coat, and a hat marked by numerous small

orifices, through which, here and there, strands from his silvery fringe of hair strayed and waved in the breezes.

It was Grandma and Grandpa Spicer's custom at the first approach of spring to detach themselves from Abagail's household, and to form a separate and complete establishment of their own in the sunny kitchen, away out at the end of the Ark. I was still, nominally, Abagail's boarder and sat at the table with her and the little Spicers ; but the impulses of my heart were ever guiding my feet to that other dear resort, where doors and hearts seemed always open to receive me, and an inexpressible warmth and light and comfort pervaded the atmosphere.

It was early in March, when, returning from school one day at the noon-tide intermission, I found Grandma standing without the Ark, singularly occupied. The sun was shining on her uncovered head, and the tranquil glow on her face was clearly the exponent of no fictitious happiness. In her apron she had a quantity of empty egg shells, so carefully drained of their contents as to present an almost perfect external appearance, and these she was arranging on the twigs of a large bush that grew just outside the window.

I was glad, afterwards, that I intruded then no skeptical questions as to her purpose, for, as I stood and looked at her, her action gradually lost for me the tinge of eccentricity, with which it had at first seemed imbued. I realized that there was something grander than reason, more exalted than philosophy.

"I suppose you've heerd about egg plants, teacher," said she, at length, turning to me, while the sun in her face broke up into scintillant beams that penetrated my being, and quickened my very soul. "'This 'ere old bush

ain't bore nothin' for years, and it looked so bare and
sorrerful, somehow, standin' out here all alone, and
everything else a kinder wakin' up in the spring, I thought
I'd try to sorter liven it up a little;" and she resumed
her placid occupation.

"Blessed Grandma," I could only murmur, as I turned
to enter the Ark, "inspired, delightful soul!"

It was in March that the Wallencamp sun-bonnets
came forth, all in a single day, a curious and startling
pageant. The Modoc, who had gone bare-headed
through the winter, assumed hers as a turban of impressive altitude, while the diminutive Carietta and the
infant Sophronia appeared but as vagrant telescopes on
insufficient pegs.

In March, the "pipers" lifted up their homesick notes
at night-fall, in the meadows. On the last day of that
month, I found arbutus in bloom under the leaves in the
cedar woods.

Scarcely had the first faint signs of herbage appeared
on the earth ere the Wallencamp cows and horses were
given over exclusively to the guardianship of nature, and
to wander whithersoever they would, for the Wallencamp
fences had ceased to present themselves as obstacles in
the way. Indeed, some portions of them had been
utterly obliterated; and this was easily traced to a habit
prevalent among the Wallencampers of resorting to them
for fuel when, on some winter night, other resources
were found to be low.

Other portions of them were decayed, or blown over
in the wind, so that there was just enough left to sit on
for private soliloquy, or social debate, and to give a picturesque charm to the landscape; yet, it was a fact

which I found worthy of notice, that, in going from one place to another, no true Wallencamper ever walked over a broken-down part of the fence, or went through a gap in the fence; he always selected an upright part of the fence to climb over, even going a little out of the way, if necessary, to effect this purpose.

The Wallencampers were staunch on the matter of individual rights; they turned each his own horse and cow into his own door yard. Animated, doubtless, by something of the same principle, those attenuated animals having made an impartial detour of the premises, congregated, as of one accord, along the highway, especially in that part of the lane between the Ark and the schoolhouse.

I made my way through these new perils from day to-day, in safety, until the deepening green of the hills and fields called the herd away to wider pastures.

Dr. Abernethy, however, remained behind. Dr. Abernethy as he was termed by the Wallencampers was a horse of peculiar and distinguished parts. Among his other eccentric gifts, he had a harmless habit of chasing beings of a superior race. In what manner this propensity had first manifested itself, I do not know, but it had been eagerly seized upon as ground for further development by the juvenile element of Wallencamp, and especially by the Modoc, under whose lively tuition the animal had reached an almost strategic ability in the art.

Dr. Abernethy was truly of the mildest disposition imaginable. He had never been known to kick. He had never even been known to open his mouth and snap at a fly, but the expression of his countenance, if it might be so called, when he was on the chase, was vicious and de-

termined in the extreme, and by no means betrayed the
purely facetious nature of his intentions.   During school
hours he seldom wandered from the immediate vicinity of
the school-house, where he appeared to be waiting for the
children to come out to play.   Often have I looked up
to see him gazing in at the windows with a gleam of evil
expectancy in his melancholy dun brown eye.

With the joyful advent of the Spring came, also,
Tommy's tame owl and " Happy Moses."   Tommy's owl
emerged from his winter quarters, and took up his daily
post of observation on the fence on the shady side of the
school-house.   He was blind in one eye, which eye was
always open, the other was always closed.   Yet with that
one glassy, unblinking orb, Tommy's owl seemed to me,
as I lifted my eyes to the window, to be reviewing the
past with an indifference, as calm and all embracing as
that with which he sent his inexorable gaze into the future,
and to take in me and the passing events of the school-
room as a mere speck in his kaleidoscopic vision of the
ages.

What was the winter's thraldom from which Happy
Moses had escaped, I never learned.   He was a broad
shouldered fellow, six feet in height, with a beard like flax,
and a sunny, ingenuous countenance.   What term should
have been applied to his eccentricities in politer circles I
cannot say, but in Wallencamp, he was artlessly designated as " the fool."   Whether it was on this account, that
with a certain rashness of perception peculiar to the Wallencampers, they always prefixed the adjective " happy "
to his name, or merely on account of the transparent
sunniness of his disposition, I cannot say, either.

Happy Moses played with the children.   He reg rded me, as one of the class of those who presume to te ach, with mingled scorn and aversion. When I went to tl e door to blow the children in from their play, he invariably turned his back upon me, cocked his hat on the side of his head, and walked away with an air that was palpably reckless, defiant and jaunty.

When he reappeared, it was usually with his knitting-work, to which he devoted himself in a desultory way, reclining on the school-house steps. But sometimes he sat on the fence with the owl, and then it was noticeable that while the gaze of the one was transient and silly, the gaze of the other seemed to grow the more unutterably searching and profound. So, at last, the new term was fairly established with these three — Dr. Abernethy, Happy Moses and the owl.

Hulled corn and beans had now become but as a dream of the past in Wallencamp, and for a brief season before the accession of lobsters, life was mainly supported on winter-green-berries, or box-berries, as they were called. These grew in large quantities at "Black Ground" a section of the woods which had been burned over. Daily I met happy groups of Wallencampers, with baskets and pails in their hands, going "boxberry plummin.'"

We had boxberry bread, boxberry stews and pies, and one day, I caught a glimpse of Grandma, in her part of the Ark, frying boxberry griddle-cakes.

Grandpa, when I met him, at this time, wore an air of deep dejection ; yet he bore his woes in silence, doubtless avoiding any concession that should suggest the need of another clarification of his system. Once, when nobody was looking, he cautiously withdrew a handful of scraped birch bark, from his pocket and gave it to me, remarking that he thought it was " a little more bracin' than them tarnal woodsy plums."

Next in the order of events, as the Modoc stood in her place in the reading class and slowly enunciated each separate syllable of the lesson in a tone as remarkable for its distinctness as it was for a total lack of meaning and modulation, from that side of her dress which had been sagging most heavily, something fell with a crash to the floor. It was a boiled lobster of anomalous proportions. The pocket had given way at last under its overpowering burden, and now appeared ignominiously upborne on the claws of its former prisoner. The Modoc seized the crustacean with glittering defiance in her eyes, and at recess, I saw that turbaned Amazon devouring it, with a group of wishful and admiring faces gathered round. The boys were out in the bay "setting pots" and "trolling for bait." Soon, not a child at Wallencamp was lobsterless. I discovered two under the infant Sophronia's desk one morning, and afterwards kept a sharp eye in that direction. Sophronia's conduct throughout the session was in an unusual degree exemplary. I detected no guilty blush on her countenance, I heard not the crackling of a claw, but when she went out, I observed that she took no lobsters with her.

Investigating the place where she had been sitting, I found a wild confusion of claws and shells, as carefully denuded of meat as though they had been turned inside out for that purpose.

What was my surprise and mortification to find a like collection at nearly every seat in the school-room, and all the while my flock had seemed unusually silent and attentive, such proficiency had those children acquired in the art of dissecting lobsters.

I saw how many they devoured day by day, and how much water they drank, and I fancied that they themselves grew to partake more and more of the form and character of marine animals. I believed that they could have existed equally well crawling at the bottom of the deep, or swimming on its surface.

We had lobsters, too, at the Ark. For the first day or two of this dispensation, Grandpa's face perceptibly brightened. At the end of two weeks it was longer than ever before.

He came over from his potato patch, I remember, and leaned on the fence, as I was going by to school.

" It 's be'n a mild winter on the Cape, teacher," he observed, studying the heavens with an air of utter abstraction. Then his glance fell as it were inadvertently in the direction of the house, and he immediately continued with a peculiar spark of animation kindling in his eye, " I 've et so many o' them 'tarnal critturs, teacher, that I swon if I don't feel like a 'tarnal, long fingered, sprawlin' shell-fish, myself ! But it 's comin' nigh time for ale-whops. They 're very good, teacher, ale-whops are — very good, though they 're bony as the — they 're 'tarnal bony, teacher. They 're what we call herrins' in the winter."

Grandpa then laughed a little, and showed his teeth.

" I was goin' to tell ye, Bachelder Rae, here," he went on, " he was a askin' Captain Sartell what kind o' fish them was that it 's recorded in the Scriptures to a' fed the multitude, and then took up so many baskets full o' leavin's, and the Captain told him that as to exactly what manner of fish them was, he had n't sufficient acquaintance with the book of Jonah to say, but, as near as he could calk'late, he reckoned they was ale-whops.

"And the Bachelder told him that it seemed to him, he was right, and had solved a mystery, for it stood to reason that there wa'n't no other fish but an ale-whop, that they could feed five thousand folks out of seven little ones and then take up twelve bushel baskets full of bones !

"And the Captain was pleased, and kind o' half owned up that he had n't felt no ways sure as to his surmise to begin with, but he said when the question was put to him, he did n't think no man ought to hesitate to come down strong on a doctrinal p'int.

Wall, as I was a sayin', teacher," concluded Grandpa his teeth still skinned and gleaming, "it's be'n a mild winter on the Cape."

CHAPTER XIV.

RESCUED BY THE CRADLEBOW

THE ship in which the Cradlebow expected to take flight was to sail from New Bedford on the twentieth of June. Meantime, having abjured my friendly relations with Ethel, and missing the quiet sustenance hitherto supplied my vanity in the girl's thoughtful devotion, I found a measure of relief for my wounded spirit in the companionship of this other — my boyish and ardent ex-pupil.

Many times, after my last interview with Ethel, had I regretted that I did not leave Wallencamp at the close of the first term. The school grew continually more irksome to me. I was not so strong as when I had first undertaken it, and no longer overlooked the discomforts of my situation in the delight I had then experienced in its novelty. Often I longed to get away from it all, to rid myself abruptly of the perplexities and distasteful duties which bound me, and yet, all the while, there was a truer impulse, a deeper longing within me, to stay. Had I not been, all my life so far, forsaking my unfinished tasks, quitting an object as soon as it seemed any the less attractive. I willed to stay, and labored, still blindly, under the conviction that my regenerating work among the Wallencampers (not theirs in me; ah, no!) was not yet accomplished.

Toward Ethel, I had not softened. I was bitterly disappointed in her. She had been the formless, pliable clay, on which I had purposed to prove my pet theories for development and culture. I had taken her as a perfectly fresh and untainted being, naively unconscious, even of the elements, either good or bad, of which her own nature was composed, waiting only for the hand of a wise and skillful modeller, like myself, to bring her up to the highest condition of manners and morals.

This elegant superstructure, a purely mental product of my own, had fallen away, revealing the erring, passionate nature beneath. But, deeply as I mourned the fall of my idol, I felt still more keenly a sense of personal injury, because the inner structure on which I had been building, had not spoken out and said, " I shall contaminate you. I am not fit for the touch of your fine hands."

Clearly there could no longer be any sympathy between Ethel and me. I avoided any occasion for private interview with the girl. Meeting her casually in the lane, or at the neighbors' houses, I acknowledged her presence with a nod or a smile, colder, I knew, than as if I had ignored her utterly.

She understood; she was quiet and unobtrusive. She made no attempt to break down the wall thus established between us. And I was determined, on the whole, to be more than just with Ethel. I would be kind to her in her disgrace. I would palliate her weakness as far as I could consistently with a pure and high standard of action. I even congratulated myself on the magnanimity of my intentions, except when I met the clear, sad gaze of those dispassionate eyes. Then I experienced an unaccountable sensation, as though I had received a blow inwardly, that staggered me, for an instant, in my fine conceptions of honor, and set my conclusions out of order.

The Wallencampers were quick to note the estrangement between us, and affirmed that " Eth was mad, and would n't speak to Teacher, along o' Teacher's goin' with Eth's beau."

This gratuitous solution of the mystery was not evolved in my presence. Still I knew, that all through those lonely, suffering days, it was often repeated to Ethel; that those who had borne the girl any grudge, or deemed that she was taking airs above them, took pains, now, that the taunt should reach her ears ; and even the children, who had always loved her, uttered it before her with childish thoughtlessness.

But, for the Cradlebow ; his bright dream of seeking his fortune over wide seas and in distant lands, his dreadless enthusiasm in the belief that he should find so much waiting for him in that unsounded world, his determination, above all, to acquit himself truthfully and bravely — all these made him, to my mind, ever an object of more inspiring and romantic interest.

He seemed, somehow, to have divested himself entirely of the old, heedless irresolution. His speech expressed little of doubt or hesitancy. It was full of a bold, bright affirmation ; and his step, in these days, had none of the ordinary slow, smiling, philosophical Wallencamp shuffle. He brought to my weariness and dejection, such an at-

mosphere of vigorous, tireless life ; he was so cor fident,
helpful, unselfish ; I was so faithless and dishe rtened
a burden-bearer, that I grew almost unconsciously to
find for myself a certain rest in his strength, which, whatever high and heroic qualities it may have lacked, devel-
oped, at least, rare resources of patience, constancy, and
forbearance.

He did not say. "You have changed your mind ;
you will wait for me, teacher, till I come back from over
the seas?" but his eyes were eloquent. What if I was
moved, I had grown so weak, to answer their question, at last, with a half-involuntary admission in my
own—

Ah, no ! I assured myself that my attitude towards
the Cradlebow was sisterly—sisterly, merely—although
I might have reflected that the yearnings of that amiable
affection had never, hitherto, in the ordinary walks of life,
constrained me to hem so many as a dozen pocket-hand-
kerchiefs for my brothers, which irksome task I cheerfully
performed as a surprise for the sailor boy, not to speak of
a pair of scarlet hose which I had already begun to knit,
under Grandma's tuition.

And now the life in Wallencamp seemed never like
real life to me, even in the broadest daylight. It was
like a dream — the sweet, warm, brightening of the landscape ; the vines growing over the low, brown houses ;
the lazy, summer voices in the air ; the skies, too, were a
dream — and Benney, with his ideally beautiful face and
his quaintness and ardor and unworldliness, was a part
of the dream. I knew that when he went away, I should
follow him long in my thoughts, and wonder much concerning him ; that at home again with my own people,

in gayer, different scenes, I should never hear the wind blowing up strong at night, or see the winter settling down gloomily, or watch the opening of another spring-time, without following him afar and wondering, with a vague, sorrowful, tender regret, what chance was befalling him in the world.

Then an incident occurred which changed, not me, perhaps, but the complexion of my dream.

One afternoon, at low tide, I wandered down to the beach and ensconced myself comfortably, with book and shawl, on the roof of Steeple Rock. The rock was an old acquaintance of mine, by this time.

There was a group of children playing, a little farther down the beach. My eyes turned ever to them from the written page, following them with a languid pleasure, as they revelled in the sand at the water's edge with their bare, brown feet and legs. I had a sense of safety, too, in their proximity. I knew that they generally returned home passing by the place where I was.

It was warm on the rock. I was very tired. As I lay there, I became only conscious, at length, that my book was slipping out of my hand, and down the shelving side of the rock, and I was too listless to attempt to re-claim it. I heard a little, dull thud on the ground below, and a faint flutter of leaves — and the long, white beach, the ragged cliffs, the laughing children, had faded from my sight.

Then I dreamed, indeed, in the ordinary sense of the word; I was back again in Newtown, in my own home, in my own white bed, and I was very glad, looking at the pictures on the wall, and out on the familiar hills. I was glad to hear my sister playing for me down stairs, only it was the same tune always, and I wished that she would play more softly.

And the pillow was hard, but I did not mind that so much, for my mother stood over me, looking very sweet and grave, and she said : " Why did n't you tell us that the pillow was hard ? "

My father was there, too, and repeated the same question, and my brothers,— they all kept saying : "Why did n't you tell us that the pillow was hard ? " and seemed to be pitying me and admiring me at the same time, until John Cable came in, friend of the old Newtown days, and his face was hard and stern.

" Why did n't you tell me the pillow was hard ? " he said : " Now, I can't wake you ! Don't you see, I can't wake you, now ? " and he shook his head and would not look at me. So they took him out of the room, and went on pitying and admiring me, but my sister kept playing louder and louder, and it troubled me so that I could not rest. Then I heard a voice, that was not in my dream, calling to me in a sharp, clear, cheering tone, " Teacher ! Teacher ! " and I looked up to see Benney coming towards me in a boat, his face aglow with excitement.

This first — before I realized that I had fallen asleep on the rock, and that what I had dreamed was my sister, playing, was the sound of the tide coming in, and that I was already sprinkled from head to foot with the spray. The Cradlebow continued calling to me cheerily, and would not give me time to consider the terrors of the situation then, nor afterwards, when I strove, in my half-stunned condition of mind, to weigh and appreciate the peril from which I had been rescued.

The children had wandered a mile or more along the beach and had gone home by another road. It was not yet dark. No alarm had been occasioned in Wallencamp as to my absence, but the Cradlebow, knowing that I had gone in the direction of the beach, had been moved to search for me, and had discovered me on the rock, where, in a few moments more, I should have waked to find myself at the mercy of the waves.

My deliverer laughed reassuringly, sending the boat leaping upon the shore, holding out his hand to me, as though this were merely an every-day occurrence, the close of some ordinary excursion, but, to me, life had suddenly grown significant.

The strong warm hand which clasped mine, weak and trembling, as I stepped from the boat, I must recognize henceforth, I knew, as the link between me and the living world.

For several days afterwards, I considered the matter of my relation to the Cradlebow in a new and serious light, especially in the light of present gratitude, with a sense of life-long obligation, but the Cradlebow was too generous and noble to recognize the obligation, or take advantage of the gratitude. He loved me, I knew. He had watched for me. He had saved my life. He should know, I resolved, that if he wished it still, I would wait for him.

And the idea was not foreign to my heart, but it grew, at last, too light of wing, and disposed to take up permanent abode in the realm of fancy. A poor, handsome young lover, seeking his fortune at the ends of the earth, and the future — ah, it did send a little stab to my conscience, to think that the uncertainty of that lover's future should so have heightened, to my mind, the romance of the picture. However, meeting him in the lane one evening, as I was returning from one of my parochial calls — it was just at dusk, I remember, and we stood under the balm-of-Gilead tree, in front of Emily's gate—I said very gravely and with none of that embarrassment which the occasion might seem to have warranted :

" Benney, although I seem to myself much older than you, we are really, I suppose, of about the same age. I have known very happy attachments where inconsistencies of birth, habit, education were far greater, perhaps, than with us. I have made up my mind that, if you still desire it, I will wait for you."

"Wait for me, teacher !" exclaimed the Cradlebow, opening his eyes with a solemn, wide surprise, " Why, of course ! "

" Why, of course? " I questioned faintly, not knowing whether to smile at being thus abruptly disarmed, or to feel the least little bit piqued at the youth's unconscious audacity.

"What else should two people do who love each other ? " There was nothing either of doubt or arraignment in the Cradlebow's serious eyes. "Besides," he continued, " I've known it all along. See here, teacher ! " and he took from his pocket, and carefully unfolded, a sheet of paper, against the background of which there lay revealed a dainty star fish, most curiously twisted about with some rare and beautiful sea vine.

" You wont find that vine washed up on this beach every day," he said, eagerly. " When I showed it to Granny — ' If Heaven itself had spoken, boy,' says she,

'I should be no surer it was a fair voyage waiting you than I be now,' though I was thinking of something besides the voyage, teacher, but it's all the same, it means good luck ; and would n't you like to keep it for us ? "

" Oh, no ! " I answered, laughingly refusing the delicate talisman. " I should blast its good intentions. I should stifle it with my cold unbelief."

The Cradlebow tenderly replaced his treasure, and laughed with me good naturedly.

" It is n't your fault, teacher," said he, " that you were n't better brought up. If you 'd always lived with our people, down here, you 'd be more believing."

At all events, my severe and protracted mental exertions had proved quite unnecessary, I thought, although after this there was, in some respects, a tacitly admitted change in our converse with each other. A sort of vague venturesome house building for the future, in which the Cradlebow seemed to wish that I would oftener show an interest in the feminine details within doors, while I had a grand and absorbing predilection for constructing imaginary grades and turrets and mediæval door-posts, receiving any thoughtful suggestions as to tin kettles and pantry shelves with gracious and smiling forbearance.

The Cradlebow seemed particularly pleased, when he came into the Ark of an evening, if I chanced to be knitting on the scarlet stockings. I did have a new and not unpleasant sense of housewifely dignity while engaged at this task, and undoubtedly assumed an air calculated to serve as an impressive exponent to my emotion. The poor scarlet stockings lengthened, meanwhile, but it was a disheartening and almost imperceptible growth. Where the article should have been most voluminous, at the calf of the leg, it grew, in spite of me, more alarmingly narrow at every round. This was after I had graduated from under Grandma Spicer's tuition, and assumed my own responsibility in the matter, so that I disdained to appeal to her for assistance in the dilemma, but thoughtfully devised means of my own for widening the stocking.

"I'll tell ye what it is, teacher," said Grandpa, who had been regarding me with that wild look which sometimes visited the old man's face when a problem seemed well nigh insoluble, "I'm afeerd, teacher, I'm afeerd that that ere stockin' ain't a goin' to fit nobody! I'll tell ye what it makes me think on. It make me think o' one o' these 'ere accordians that ye open and shet. I'm afeerd, teacher, that it ain't a go'n' to fit!"

"Thar! 'sh! 'sh! pa," said Grandma, with all the unction of holy disapproval; but, for once, my ever dear friend and champion was compelled to turn her back upon the scene.

In this position, she exclaimed in a low, broken tone of voice, "There may be legs, pa, as we don't know on!"

Grandpa was curiously aroused.

"I tell ye, I've traveled to the four quarters of the 'arth, ma," said he, "and set eyes on the tarnalest critters under God's canopy, but I never see anybody yit that 'ud fit into that 'ere. Besides," he added, knowingly, in a milder tone, "I reckin that 'ere stockin's meant for somebody nearer hum, and a pretty straight-legged fellow, too."

I was enabled to judge something still farther of the speculations waking in the Cradlebow brain, when, having to keep Henry G. after school, one night, as a means of discipline, he bawled out:

"Ye don't keep Simmy B. after school no more ! and why not?" continued the aggrieved infant, at the same time framing for himself an answer of malicious significance : — "Oh, cause he's Ben Cradlebow's brother!"

Social converse was at its high tide, now, in Wallencamp among the birds in the trees and the fowls in the door-yards, and quite as naturally and harmlessly so, for the most part, I think, among the beings of a superior order. They had little other recreation.

The bonfire had marked the close of the gay epoch in Wallencamp. It was too warm now, for the livelier recreations of the winter. Religious interest, especially, was at a low ebb. At the evening prayer meetings, the number of worshippers appeared but as a handful compared with the number of the unconcerned who lingered outside in the pleasant moonlight. Conspicuous among these latter, replacing the fervid debates of the winter with a calm philosophy befitting a warmer season, were Captain Sartell and Bachelor Rae.

The old songs held the same charm for them all, however. They sang them ever with pathos in their voices and tears in their eyes.

The little unpremeditated chats by gate and road-side, the neighborly "droppings-in," grew more and more frequent.

But when poor Ethel was taken up on the tide of social wonder and debate, and I heard whisperings concerning her and knew that an evil suspicion had taken hold of the mind of the little community and when finally, Emily said to me, "I guess you done about right shirking off Eth, teacher. I guess she ain't no better than she ought to be," in spite of what I felt to be my own unblemished conscience in the matter and the justice of the retribution which was overtaking Ethel, I went often to my little room and cried bitterly for her, as well as for myself.

CHAPTER XV.

ELIOT TURNER IN THE SCHOOL-ROOM.

RS. Ithamer Spicer grew kind. At first, especially while the fisherman was in Wallencamp, her demeanor towards me had been marked by a decided touch of coldness and mistrust. She suspected me, I thought, of trifling with the Cradlebow; now, she invariably deferred to me as a person worthy of all honor and consideration — of congratulation even, in an eminent degree.

She assumed to be on the most frank and confiding terms with me. She found a thousand little ways for promoting my physical comfort that had never occurred to her before.

So I was the more surprised, when after school, one Friday afternoon, as I was sitting in my room, this same Abagail suddenly appeared before me with her eyes glittering, her lips compressed, and her complexion of that positive green hue which it always wore when she was in a high passion.

"There 's a gentleman down stairs, waiting to see you, teacher," she said, with a peculiarly dark inflection on the

word gentleman. "Oh, he's got on an awful interesting
look!" snapped out Abagail, with a spiteful little laugh,
"and a suit of light clothes, and a new spring overcoat,
and he looked at me as though I was a pane of window
glass, and he says, 'Oh — ah — yes — Is Miss Hungerford in?' I wonder if he's come back to make his farewell calls —" with another unpleasant laugh. "One thing
I can tell him, he'd better steer clear of George Olver!"

Was ever a zealous young devotee, I pondered, more
perplexed!

"Come this way, please," I said; holding out my hand
to Abagail, and leaning back in my chair with unaffected
weariness, at least, "Is Mr. Turner down stairs?"

They call him that, I believe," said Abagail, sententiously, "things don't always get their right names
in this world."

"Well, you may tell him," I said, "that I can't see
him."

Abagail's countenance changed wonderfully in an
instant. She gave me a bright look, and without waiting
for another word, ran down the stairs.

When she came back, her tongue ran on glibly:

"I told him," said she, "that you couldn't see him,
and he kept on in that window-glass way of looking, and
his head as high as ever, and he took his hat and 'I'm
very sorry,' he says, 'that Miss Hungerford is indisposed,
and I hope I shall have an opportunity of seeing her
this evening.'

"He said he came to-day, and was going away to-
morrow morning, and he had something of importance
to communicate, and I knew he expected I'd go up and
see you again about it, but I didn't. So he said he'd

call again this evening or to-morrow morning, just which 'd be most agreeable, and expected I'd budge then, sure, but I didn't show any signs of it; and I told him rightly, I guessed one time would be about as agreeable as another; and I suppose he thought he would n't show mad before such common bred folks. He smiled that window-glass looking smile of his, and says, 'Ah, thank you; now I won't detain you any longer, Mrs. Spicer;' and out he went.

"I suppose he's come down to smooth everything over, and have it hushed up with Eth and her folks. Well, money 'll do a good deal for a man, but it would n't stand him much if he got into George Olver's hands. However, teacher," concluded Abagail, in a sprightly tone, "give the Devil his due. It's better'n as if he'd run off and never showed his head again; and I don't suppose he 'll get much satisfaction out of you, if you do see him, teacher. It's better to trust honest folks than rogues, and nobody knows that better than the rogues themselves."

I knew that this last clause was not designed as a personal thrust by Abagail, yet I could not help musing a little over it, smilingly, after she had gone. The fiction, of which I was living a part, in Wallencamp, was taking on, it seemed to me, a tinge even of the tragic — perplexities were deepening. I was becoming, more than ever, the suffering though exalted heroine of a romance.

I rose, and dressed myself before the glass, I remember, with particular care. I did not know why I should dread or avoid seeing the fisherman in the evening, since the part I had to sustain in the interview was so distinctly calm, dispassionate and spiritually remote. At the same

time, I wished that my cheeks had not grown so pale and
my eyes so dark-rimmed and hollow. They bespoke
the interesting part I had to play in the world's tragedy,
but were not, otherwise, so becoming as I could have
wished.

Earlier, the fisherman had sent me books from Providence. I would rather, I thought, that he should take
them back again. I remembered that I had left one of
them in my desk at the school-house, and put on my hat
to go after it.

" Going out to spend the evening, teacher ? " said Abagail, as I opened the door of the Ark, giving me at the
same time a gay and knowing look.

'· No," I said, gravely tolerant of the little woman's
surveillance, " I 'm only going to the school-house for a
book that I want.   I shall be back in a few moments."

It was hardly dusk then.

Aunt Patty, as usual after school on Friday, had swept
the room and put down the dark and dingy paper curtains.

I opened the door and stood an instant looking into
the gloom before entering.   Then I saw that there was
some one sitting in my chair — a man with his head bent
forward and buried in his arms, which were folded on the
desk.

It was Mr. Turner, and before I had time to retreat,
he lifted his head and saw me standing in the door.

I had expected that the first revelation of that glance
would contain something of grief, wretchedness, remorse.
The fisherman's countenance wore a shadow of annoyance, but it was expressive, above all, of a childish petul-
ance and irritation.

"Oh!" he exclaimed, speaking with the utmost abruptness, and rising from the chair, " if you had only left this place at the end of the first term, it would have saved the whole of this abominable misadventure ! "

" I don't think I understand you," I said, freezing now in sober earnest.

" Because in your eyes only, it is a misadventure," he continued rapidly, with growing excitement. " You came to this miserable hole — this Wallencamp — resolved to view everything in a new light — the light of unselfish devotion to great ends, and exalted aspiration, and ideal perfection, and all that. Well, how has the wretched, giggling, conniving little community shown out in that light? I suppose there's one — that larking Cradlebow — who has stood the test and come out creditably, by reason of an uncommonly artistic shock of hair and a Raphaelite countenance. As for me, taken in the ordinary sense, I'm no worse than a thousand others, but I say that it was a decidedly unfortunate light to put me in ! It was a decidedly unfair light ! "

"I have no wish to judge you in any light," I said, and explaining briefly my errand to the school-house, I expressed regret at having interrupted the fisherman's meditations, and turned to go.

" Miss Hungerford !" he exclaimed, with a gesture of whimsical force and impatience, " it's my last chance for an explanation. Don't, for God's sake, cut it short at this point. You might know — you might *know*, that I'm not a bad fellow at heart. But you will never see the best side of me — there's fate in it. I never wanted to seem specially contrite but I must set myself jumping like a Jack-in-the-box for your infernally cold amusement !

I had an explanation at my tongue's end. D—n it! I don't remember a word of it."

" I don't think it is necessary," I said.

" Oh, no !" he continued in a deeply aggrieved, almost a whining tone ; "nothing's necessary that would set me out in a little better shape ! Anything 'll do for these grovelling Wallencamp, but just as soon as it comes to me, all the extenuating circumstances of my life — that I was left so early orphaned, sisterless, brotherless, my nearest of kin a wicked, carousing old uncle ; taken to see the world here, and to see the world there ; home-less, if ever one was homeless ; never trained to any cor-rect way of thinking, or settled manner of life, but just to spend my money and aim at enjoying myself—they all amount to nothing in my case.

" Well, I used to come to Wallencamp just for that same purpose — to have a good time ; it was such a jolly, wild place to let the Old Nick loose in ; and now it seems that 's to be taken for a man's natural level, and the best that he 's capable of ! Then I met you. You would voluntarily give up ease and luxury, for a time, for the sake of an abstract idea — whether misguided or not, I will not say, the fact remains the same — and I swear it was a new revelation to me. It was strange and perverse and it was deuced taking ! Then I tried to get you to include *me* among the objects of your mission, to accept *me* as a candidate for temporal leniency and final salva-tion, and you wouldn't. It's only the happy, ragged, unconscious heathen that are looked out for in this world ; the real ones don't get any sympathy."

The fisherman paused.

" I should be glad to give you the first lesson in the

code of salvation," I said — "that the fate of souls is not left to human hands."

"Oh, I've heard that formula somewhere before I" exclaimed the fisherman impatiently, with a little sneer in his laugh. "Why don't you tell me that God will help me? Perhaps you will even remember me in your prayers, sometime."

At those last words an unbearable pang of self-conviction and remorse shot through my heart. I, who had not felt greatly the need of any supernatural aid, but rather that I was able to manage my own affairs with becoming discretion — of what saving power and grace could I speak to one who was weak enough to fall, and for whom there was no help in himself? In the dark school-room I involuntarily lifted my hands to my face. When I heard the fisherman's voice again, he had come a step or two nearer to me down the aisle.

"Let me tell you what I was thinking about when you came in," he said, in an altered tone. "Rather, how I was allowing my imagination to run away with itself, for my own particular delectation. I was imagining, when you opened the door and stood revealed there in the light, how you might come to me, indeed, as the angel of some better life and hope, offering me a forgiveness as full as it was unmerited."

"It is not I who have to forgive you," I repeated.

"It is you, if any one," replied the fisherman, quickly. "I tell you, you feel that girl Ethel's fault ten times more deeply than she feels it for herself. You should never have come to this place. It was deucedly odd and entertaining, but it was a step in the wrong direction. You put yourself in the place of these people and translate all their possible moods and tenses according to your own. It's a mistake. That girl, Ethel, would stare in perfect bewilderment if she could know of some of the thoughts and emotions you doubtless attribute to her. She might even laugh at you for your pains."

"I do not believe you," I said, not angrily nor resentfully, as might have been earlier in our acquaintance, but with a painful, slow positiveness. "Perhaps I was wrong in assuming the place I did in Wallencamp, but it was not in the way you think. I don't know — I can't see the way myself, clearly — always, but I believe that what you have said is utterly false !"

"At least," continued the fisherman, in the old gay frivolous tone, which I heard now for the first time during this conversation, "I can make her tenfold and abundant reparation — ah, you don't know — I say you don't understand these people. It's a disagreeable subject; let it go ! But I'm very rich, you know," with an easy laugh, and the air of a man only conscious at last, of his good worldly fortune, and the exquisite fit of his clothes. "Oh, I've got no end of money. After all, that's the chief thing in this world. If a fellow's ordinarily clever and good natured, with a good reputation in town, what's a little row in the suburban districts ! It's an awfully insignificant affair, anyway, it seems to me. We may as well talk sense, and the plainer the better. People don't employ lens for short sightedness in that particular — common sense, I mean. You walk without seeing, Miss Hungerford, and you 're bound to get infernally cheated, in some shape. Why not me, I say, as well as another?"

Still, the fisherman's words roused no bitterness in me.

His hardened recklessness of speech served rather to strengthen me in the part I had to play of the unapproachably sublime.

" I can not consider that question," I said, with my hand on the door.

He swept my face with a keen glance that had lost none of its derisive quality.

" So it 's true, then ! " he said. " The ultimatum has been reached, at last, in the possessor of a pretty face and a broken fiddle ! and dreams for the restoration of the race, are to end in a broken-down hovel by the sea, in darning the Cradlebow's socks, and dressing the clams for dinner, while the bucolic George Olver and the versatile Noah, and all the rest of the awkward, moon-gazing crew, take turns in sitting on the door step, and dilating on the weather ! ravishing idyl ! but it lacks substantiality. It lacks seriousness."

I heard that mocking laugh again without emotion, except it might be for a faint, far off echo in my breast of the fisherman's own scorn. Above all, I was weary, and willing to make my escape.

" We can not help each other by standing here talking," I said, and added a "good bye."

It was the last time, probably, that I should see the fisherman's face; but he refused the valediction with a toss of the head.

"Oh, no ! " he said, " it is n't time for my obsequies. I shall return to town for a few days or weeks only ; this detestable place has always thrown a spell over me. I can't rid myself of it. Like the natives of Wallencamp, I always drift back to it again."

It was growing dark. I found Abagail waiting for me

in the lane.   Somewhat piqued at the persistency of the
little woman's ministrations, I informed her briefly, that I
had found the fisherman in the school-house, and had
been conversing with him there ; but she put her hand in
my arm with an air of unshaken confidence.

CHAPTER XVI.

GEORGE OLVER'S LOVE FOR ETHEL.

"I 'D like to see you alone a few minutes, teacher, if you please."

It was George Olver who spoke, in his sturdy, resolute bass. The words hardly took on the form of a suave request; they were uttered in too earnest, grave, and intent a tone.

I had dismissed my school for the day. The roar of the young lions just released from bondage had not died away when George Olver entered the school-room, closed the door behind him, and stood in a manly and self-reliant attitude, his hat in his hand.

"No ma'am," he said, in answer to some gesture of mine, "I'll be much obleeged if *you'll* set down in the chair."

"There's times, teacher," he then went on, gravely and steadily, "when ordinary friends, like you and me, meetin' each other in the road, or in a neighbor's house, maybe, we say 'How d'ye do?' or 'It's a pleasant day,' or the like o' that, and all well and good. It's a fair understandin', and enough said 'twixt you and me; and then agin, there's times when the wind blows up rough, as ye might say, and oncommon dark, and some harm a befallin' of us, when we git closter together and more a dependin' on each other, and then them old words ain't o' much account to us, but to speak out different what need be without fear or shame."

"Yes," I said, much impressed by George Olver's manner. He was held somewhat in awe among the Wallencampers, and regarded generally as a "close-mouthed" fellow.

"I hear," he resumed, "that El' Turner has been down this way agin. They say it was lucky for him I wasn't to home that day; maybe so. Ef he'd a turned up suddenly in my path — I can't say — I might a trod on him. I never done anythin' like that for the fun on't. I'd rather go round one any time than step on't, but if I'd a come on him so onexpected, I can't say for what might a been the consequences. Wall, he comes down here, and he goes to her with money ! Her, that ain't used to all the devilish ways o' the world, nor as fine clo's as some, but that's got a lady's heart in her, for all that, and she told him — I know just how she said it, in that quiet way she's had along lately — that it was the last thing he could do to hurt her — but he'd made a mistake if he thought she could take that.

"So, then, as I've heered, he went to her father, a tryin' to make it appear, as nigh as I can make out, that he'd got suthin' in the shape of a conscience that he wanted to whiten over a little more to his own satisfaction afore he went away.

"Wall, Bede and his daughter used to be called about one piece for temper, though I don't reckon that temper's lackin' allays cause it don't show.   There's them as Jest keeps the steam down a workin' the whole machinery patient and stiddy;   but Bede, he's allays a histin' the cover, and lettin' on't out in one general bust, and I reckon that was what he did when he was a talkin' with the fisherman ; he histed up the cover and let off a good deal of onnecessary steam, but he come to the right point in the end ; that the fisherman had made a mistake thar, too, and — as near as I can make out — this El' Turner was kind o' took back and disappointed.   He had n't calkilated that the folks down here had any sech feelin's as his sort o' folks.

"Thar ain't any use in talkin' about him.   I feel hard thar, I confess, but that can't help her none, now.   What I want is to help her.   I tell ye, teacher,"—the strong voice trembled slightly — "there's been times when I've felt as though I've been a sinkin', as ye might say, and a wantin' to call out for help ! help ! like any weak, drowning fool, instead o' swimmin' above it strong, and helpin' them as was weaker than me.

" No shame for me to say, teacher, I've allays had it in my mind that Ethel'd marry me.   It grew up with me. I never thought o' no other girl but she.   Ye see she'd always knowed me, and it was more like a brother, she said.   She had n't thought o' *that.*   So, I says, I 'll bide my time patient, but I believed she'd turn to me.

" When   El' Turner began to hang around there, I did n't feel exactly kindly towards him, I don't pretend. The folks, they tried to set me on.   It 'ud a been mighty easy to a gone on !   I guess there ain't nobody as knows us two 'ud deny I could handle four o' such as him, but a man has got to say, fa'r play ! fa'r play ! and not put

himself in other folks' light.   Thinks I, if his intentions
are all squar and honorable — and I had n't no reason,
then, to say they wa' n't — and them two take a fancy to
each other, why, it ain't no more than nateral !

" She was handsome enough for a queen, and he had
different manners from us fellows down here, and purtier
ways o' talkin' and lookin' at a girl, as though if she
did n't have him, it was goin' to knock im straight, and
she 'd lived with such different folks, it made it vary interestin' ; that was nateral.   Thinks I, a man in my place
had ought to have sense enough to back out quiet.

" You know what he done, teacher.   He took the best,
and when he got tired on 't, he threw it away," — the
brawny hand at George Olver's side was clinched so as
to appear almost colorless, yet there was little discom-
posure in his voice — " but cursin' him ain't a goin' to
help us now.   When a thing that 's allays been precious
to us has once fell, we can't never make it quite like it
was afore, but we can keep care on 't patient, a waitin'
God Almighty's time to make it whole.   I know what
folks say.   I know, but I don't keer.   She ain't no less
precious to me, now, than she was afore, only it 's more
for her, now, maybe, and less for myself.   And she sees,
now.   She does keer for me, now.   Ay, I know what
they 'll say, but they don't know that girl as well as I do,
teacher.   They ain't nothin' would a wrung them words
from her ef they had n't a be'n true ; no, not ef it had
been savin' her life to say 'em.   She does keer, now, but
she won't never take me now, she says, because it ud be
wrongin' me, and I might a knowed what she 'd a said,
what it was nateral and noble for her to say.

" But," continued George Olver, with a flash of magnifi-

cent fire in his eyes, and thrusting his arm out straight,
"what's right atween me and my God need n't be afeard
o' no man's face ! I want to take that girl and keer for
her, and keep her from meddlin' tongues. Let 'em say
what they choose to me ; they must be keerful what they
say afore her, that's all.

"I 've waited a good while. I could bide my time,
but not now, when she's heart broke and sufferin', and
nobody ter put out a hand to help her. There's be'n a
look on her face, lately, that I don't like to see. It's
afore my eyes all the time, and it werries me night and
day—as though she did n't hold herself o' no account
and might make away wi' herself.

"Teacher, you 've got a woman's heart, and you can
save that other woman ! It's a task that they need n't
nobody be ashamed on, for the Lord Jesus himself set
the example. I guess she thinks you 've turned agin her,
too, but I knew that could n't be, for no friend 'ud leave
another when they was perishin', not even if they was
more to fault than she was ; and she was apt to mind ye
more than any one. I thought if you 'd go in and speak
to her as a woman could, and tell her she 'd got a right to
hope, and tell her her friends would not forsake her,
least of all would it be likely God would forsake her, and
tell her—"

George Olver seemed both to be looking at me
and beyond me with his beautiful, brave eyes, "Tell her
thar's somebody that don't find any cause to be sorry for
havin' loved her, but knows how she 's been werrited,
and suffers along with her, and 'ud be more glad and
content than of anythin' else in his heart this minute, to
protect her and keer for her as it 's right — yis, tell her

as it 's right that she should let him do, and if she asks
from whom that comes "— George Olver smiled brightly,
with that far-seeing look still in his eyes — "why, it 's
no secret from whom it comes.   Will you go, teacher?"

"Yes," said I, with a vague sense of having caught a
glimpse of a hitherto unknown world, " I will go."

George Olver came forward, gave my hand a firm
grasp, and then turned resolutely and walked out.

Left to myself and my own thoughts, I dreaded more
and more the concession there would seem to be in my
seeking Ethel now, for the poor girl could hardly be expected, I thought, to appreciate the magnanimity of such
an act.

I deferred going to see her until evening, and even
thought of writing a letter instead of going at all, signifying my willingness to take her back into my favor, in a
limited sort of way, and reinforcing her with a share of
that counsel and advice which she must have missed so
sadly of late, but I was conscious of the fact that I
should not thus be keeping my promise to George Olver.

After supper, the singers came in and wailed some
peculiarly touching songs about rescuing the fallen and
the erring.   As Grandma Spicer was preparing to go on
an errand of mercy down the lane, I joined her, and
stopped at Bede Alden's door.

Aunt Patty, Ethel's mother, appeared in answer to my
knock.   Her glances had fallen rather reproachfully on
me, of late.   Seeing me now, she cast down her eyes, a
steely expression gathering about her mouth.

"You 've come too late, teacher," said she, her voice
breaking suddenly into a sob, as she lifted her apron to
her eyes.

In that instant it flashed through my mind,— the fear George Olver had expressed lest Ethel should make away with herself. I fancied that I turned terribly pale.

"Come in, teacher!" Aunt Patty exclaimed, with a quick motion of her hand, and she continued rapidly:

" Ethel went away this afternoon. She's gone to Taunton. She did n't tell nobody but me. If you 'd a come sooner, you might a kep' her, teacher. She's gone to Becky Merideth's that works thar in the shops, and Eth used to know her. She hires a room, and Eth she 's saved a little money cranberryin'. She says she 's a goin' to stay thar as long as it holds out, and ' maybe, she says, ' I can git work;' she says thar ain't nobody here cares for her but me. 'And it 's only a trouble to you mother,' she says, ' and, maybe, I shan't never come back again.' If you could a' seen how she looked. Oh, my God!" As the poor woman held her hands to her face, I saw the tears springing out between her fingers. "There 's nobody knows how I feel this night! She wa'n't a bad girl, my Ethel wa'n't. She was deceived, but it'll make her bad, everybody turnin' agin her so — and that Becky, she was sech a wild girl! Oh, I 'm afeard! I 'm afeard!"

" But we 'll have Ethel back again, Mrs.Alden," I said, intensely relieved, even at this state of things, "and, more than that, we shall see her very happy yet. I will write to her, myself, to-night."

" I don't know,"—Aunt Patty shook her head sadly— "she might think I 'd got you to do it. I seen she took it to heart, you're turnin' agin her so, and I did n't believe you 'd a done it if you'd known all. I wanted to go up and see yer, for I knew you 'd soften, but no, she

would n't let me.   She said she'd never forgive me ef I
did.   No ; she'd think I'd been a puttin' ye up to it."
Aunt Patty dried her tears, helplessly.

"You ought to have come to me !" I exclaimed witr
grave emphasis, "whether she wanted you to or not !"

"Perhaps I had, teacher," said Aunt Patty meekly,
"but you could n't a gone agin her ef you'd been in my
place.   She was n't vexed, teacher, but she was awful
set, and she looked so wore out !   I couldn't go agin
her."

"All the more reason," I continued, fortifying myself
with new confidence, "why you should have been firm
with her.   She is not fit to go off by herself in that way.
She's a child ! a child !   She needs some one to tell her
what to do."

"I know that ; that's what worries me !" cried Aunt
Patty, bursting into tears, "but what could I do, teacher?
what could I do?"   .

"Well, never mind," I said, assuming with readiness
the attitude of the consoler, "we will have Ethel home
again in a very short time.   I will write this evening, and
if she does not come, why, we shall have to go after her,
that's all !"

This last I was able to utter almost gaily, looking into
Aunt Patty's face.

The woman's poor, worn hand placed in mine, the look
of confidence upturned to me in her tearful eyes, her
readiness to forgive, to forget any resentment which she
might have cherished towards me, all touched me deeply
and strengthened me in a sincere determination to win
Ethel back.

"She made me promise I would n't let George Olver

know where she was, teacher," said Aunt Patty, breath-
lessly, as I was going out of the door. "She had her
reasons; we'd ought to respec 'em some. I wouldn't be
deceiving her entirely."

On my way homeward, I reflected how altogether bur-
densome it was to one half of humanity that the other
half was not better calculated to take care of itself, and
resolved that my letter to Ethel should be at once dignified, imperative, and kind.

CHAPTER XVII.

TEACHER HAS THE FEVER.—DEATH OF LITTLE BESSIE.

HERE were oppressive days in Wallencamp, when no fresh winds were borne to us from the ocean. The sun shone hot on the stunted cedars. The tides crept in lazily. All one weary afternoon, in the hum and stir of the dusty school-room, little Bessie Alden — Captain Sartell's youngest, and his darling — sat stringing lilac blossoms together in a chain. She was such a cunning edition of the big Captain. She had the same strong Saxon physique in miniature, the same clear pink and white complexion, eyes hardly more limpidly blue than his, and hair that was sunniest flax, like the ends of the Captain's beard. And how patient the chubby little fingers were at their task. What small, charmingly despairing sighs escaped the child when some link fell out in the chain of purple flowers ! I was struck with her air of weary, patient endeavor — so important it seemed—so important that the chain should be finished before school was out. And, at last, little Bessie lifted it to wear upon her neck, and it broke and fell in pieces on the floor.

Then there was a look of gentle dismay in the blue eyes, a tear or two, and Bessie folded her arms on the desk, her head sank slowly down on them, and she fell asleep.

She was still sleeping when I dismissed the school. The sound of the others going out did not wake her; the Phenomenon, disappearing through the door, pointed a finger at her, his face full of scornful merriment — so incredible was it to him that any one should sleep when school was out.

I went down to Bessie and woke her gently. She looked at me, at first, with startled, feverish eyes, as though she did not know me, and screamed in pain or terror. I noticed then that the color on her cheeks was unnaturally bright. I put my hand on her pulse. It was throbbing violently. I was thoroughly frightened.

"Come, Bess," I said, as winningly and soothingly as I could, "come home with teacher, now. Teacher will lead you, all the way."

For answer, the child's head fell heavily to one side. I tried to take her in my arms, but she was very heavy. I found one of the small boys lingering outside the schoolhouse and sent him for Bessie's father.

I shall never forget the look with which Captain Sartell 'ifted his baby in his arms. He had seven other children; he was a poor man, a Wallencamper, but one would have thought him a king, and that the only hope of his line lay treasured in the mass of flaxen curls pressed against his shoulder,.as he carried her home.

The next morning, early, Captain Sartell appeared
at the Ark with a blanched face.   Bess had been growing
worse, he said.   They feared it was a fever.   He was
going to West Wallen for a doctor.   "She thinks," he
continued, with absolute white bewilderment on his features, "that she's in school all the while, and it's a gittin'
late, and the teacher ain't there, and so she keeps a
callin' for the teacher; and I would n't ask ye to go up,
teacher, if you was anyways afeard, but it 'ud break your
heart to hear her."

For one of my years, I knew singularly little, either of
sickness or death, so I was the more readily susceptible
to the slight disrespect the Captain seemed to have cast
on my wisdom and fortitude.

"Certainly I will go and see her," I said "why should
I be afraid?"

"I was only thinkin' it was fair to say," said the Captain " she was took so sudden and so violent like, it
might be — might be — suthin'— suthin' kitchin' perhaps.
They was a case or two o' scarlet fever up to Wallen, but
she was n't exposed no way that we know on.   She was n't
exposed."

The Captain, regarding me intently, repeated the
words, thrusting his neck out with a pitiful gulp, his hand
on the latch.   Observing him, the expression of my face
changed; he groaned as he went out, closing the door
silently.

My first impulse then was to pack my trunk and start
for home, but the wailing of Mrs. Abagail and of the
other women who had followed the Captain in, lamenting
one with another in an agony of helpless fear, appealed
to my courage and presence of mind, and had a strangely

sustaining and quieting effect upon me. I suggested after a few moments reflection, that very likely the case was not so bad as Captain Sartell supposed. I determined to have no school that day, and advised the women what they should do, in case their children had been already exposed to a contagious disease. Then a happy thought struck me. I went out in the other part of the Ark to seek Grandma Spicer. I wondered why we had not thought of her, before.

She entered the room where the women sat. Calm and sunshine was Grandma Spicer — calm and sunshine breaking through a storm.

If it was scarlet fever, she knew just what to do. She and pa had had it years ago, and they 'd lived through it; but she did n't believe that it was nothin' half so bad, and "What if it is, you poor critturs, you," said Grandma in such a tone as she would have used to soothe a frightened child, " every time there's a squall must we go to takin' on as though it was our doin's? The Lord, He makes the squalls, and He don't put it on 'us to manage 'em ; but up thar in His fa'r weather, He looks down on the storms that we know not whither, but are only drivin' of us landward safe, and 'keep ye still,' He says, 'jest keep ye still ! ' No need o' strainin' eyes, but fix 'em thar, on Him. I 've seen a many times when no words but them would do."

The tears stood in Grandma's eyes. Beautiful soul ! Whatever storms she might have known in her life's voyage, she only seemed to lie at anchor now, in a sure haven ; and all the while, her heart was going out in the tenderest sympathy to those still tossing on the seas and striving to make perilous passages, even to those watching

false harbor lights in the distance. She had had an experience wide enough for all. She had found where it
was still. She longed to draw all others into that stillness.

Soon Grandma was on her way to give help and consolation where it was most needed — in Captain Sartell's
household. She did not come back until near mid-day.
Mrs. Ithamer's children were kept carefully out of the
room when she entered.

"'The Lord is a goin' to take that little one to Himself,
teacher," she said to me, very impressively.

Captain Sartell had not yet returned with the doctor.
Possibly he had been obliged to drive to the next town.
Poor Mrs. Sartell was nearly distracted. Bessie's fever
had gone to her brain.

" We couldn't quiet her, no way," Grandma continued,
" and she's a growin' weak, but when them spells come
on, she's ravin', first about one thing and then another,
but mostly it's school, school. 'It's a gittin' so late in
school and the teacher not there' —and then she screams
and moans so ! Poor, sufferin' darlin' ! ye can't ease her
no way."

With a desperate determination not to yield myself to
my own thoughts, I informed Mrs. Ithamer that I was
going to live with Grandma a while, that I should not
go through that part of the Ark where she and the children were, and she must keep the little door at the foot
of the stairway locked, and not let the children follow
me ; and I sprinkled myself with camphor and went
back with Grandma to Captain Sartell's house.

Mrs. Sartell was alone in the room with Bess. I
expected that she would meet me with an almost reproachful look, but there was only sorrow in her face, a

sorrow that seemed intensified by the smile she lifted to us as we entered. The air in the room was very pure and sweet. The bed on which Bess lay was as white as snow. But what a change a day had wrought in the little face pressed against the pillow.

"Teacher's come," said Grandma Spicer, with soft, pathetic cheer, bending over the child.

"Would she care, now?" I thought. "Would she know me?"

Just once she opened her eyes wide, smiled, and threw her arms towards me feebly. I would have taken her then, I thought, if it had been my death.

They wrapped a shawl around her, and I took her in my arms, rocked her gently and sung to her, very softly, the songs she loved best. She moved a little restlessly, and then lay very still with her head on my breast.

So I rocked and sang to Bess, and the two women moved noiselessly about the room until Grandma Spicer came and looked down very intently into the little one's face.

"She's asleep," I murmured, placing a finger on my lips.

"Yes, she's asleep," said Grandma, in a trembling voice, solemnly. "Sweet, purty little one," she went on, with tears running down her cheeks, and she turned to the mother—"Thank God, you!" she exclaimed, with sudden strength and firmness in her voice, that was yet thrilled with emotion, "From sorrowin' and from pain forevermore, the Lord has took His lamb!"

Aye, life's chain of dewy morning flowers was broken! The baby fingers had dropped those purple fragments without grief or dismay, now — only the peace of some sweet unfolding mystery over the veiled blue eyes!

18

Still, she seemed to me asleep — only asleep. I felt no shrinking from the dead child in my arms. When they took her away from me and laid her on the bed, I looked at her tranquil face, and the mother's passionate grief seemed out of place. Why should one wish to wake another from such repose? I could not comprehend the mother's aching sense of loss. But later, when we heard the sound of wheels and saw Captain Sartell and the doctor driving very fast up the lane, I went down the stairs and passed out before them. I could not bear to watch the strong man's face when he should find his baby dead.

Little Bess was buried under the lilac blossoms. The fever which had so soon smitten her down was not properly a contagious one. I went on with my school again, missing the sweet face of the dead child more and more each succeeding day.

Not one of the children with whom she had played was taken sick, but it was scarcely two weeks after her death that I was taken sick as she had been. In the interval George Olver had come to me and I had written to Ethel, but Ethel had not come back to Wallencamp nor answered my letter. I was more anxious and troubled about her than I dared confess to any one. Then suddenly, I ceased to care for any of those things Of my last afternoon in school I could recall very little afterwards, except that the clock on the shelf back of me seemed to be ticking in my brain, and the voices in the room sounded indistinct. My own voice sounded to me like that of some one else speaking from a long way off.

And at evening, in the Ark, I put my little room in perfect order, my head growing heavy with pain. I felt

that I must finish this task before I lay down, and there
was another intention to which I clung with a painful per-
tinacity of mind.

I sat down at my table and wrote half a dozen or more
brief letters home. These were filled with irrelevant
anecdotes pertaining to my experience among the
Wallencampers, a few desultory descriptions of character
and scenery, with a philosophical digression or two.

To one not intimately acquainted with the epistolary
products of my pen, these letters would have undoubtedly suggested the workings of a crazed and feverish
brain, but they were not calculated to arouse any particular alarm in the minds of my friends at home, unless,
indeed, it was by reason of the unusual care and pains-
taking evinced in their chirography and the punctilious
manner in which they were dated. The first one I dated .
for the evening on which I was writing. The next for a
time several days in advance of that, and so on, performing
this strange act with utter indifference to the presumption
of it.

When it was finished, I seemed to have forgotten what
next to do. Grandma Spicer told me afterwards, that I
went to the head of the stairs and called to her, that she
came up, and I told her very gravely that I was going to
be sick, but I knew I was not going to die, and adjured
her with a look in my eyes which she said, " I could n't
go ag'inst, teacher, for it was more convincin' than
health," not to write to my friends of my sickness, and
instructed her how to send the letters which I had sealed,
stamped, directed, and methodically arranged on the
table, in their proper order to the Post.

For the rest, all through the pain and impotence and

vague mental wanderings of the days that followed, I had a restful, comforting consciousness that a kind, loving face, like the lamp of my salvation, was hanging ever over me — always it was Grandma Spicer's face, though it seemed to have grown strangely young and fair, and the eyes that followed me with such a lovingly tireless, wistful expression in them were like other eyes that I had known, and the watcher's voice was clear and musical, with a youthful repression in it. Still, somehow, it was Grandma's face, *her* eyes, *her* voice — and when at last, I woke one morning very weak, but able to recognize clearly all the familiar objects in the room, it was Grandma Spicer indeed, who sat by my bed, beaming gloriously upon me.

" Is it most school time, Grandma? " I inquired, feebly, slowly concentrating my gaze on her face.

" Oh, laws, no ! " said Grandma, with cheerful emphasis, and then continued talking in her quiet monotone. I hardly heard what she said. I was painfully endeavoring to pick up the lost thread of my consciousness where I had left it on that night when I put my room in order and went so wearily to bed. At last I inquired, still vaguely, " How long? "

Grandma understood. She smiled reassuringly.

" Only a little while, teacher," she said. " You 've only been sick a little while — a few days, may be," and she immediately proffered me some broth which was a triumph of the good soul's art, and seemed to partake of her own comfortable and sustaining nature. I lay back on the pillows, contented to be very still for a little while.

When I next looked up and recognized that familiar figure sitting by the bed, I said, " Has Ethel come back? "

" Yis, Ethel's come back ! " said Grandma, in a tone

which seemed to imply, in the very best faith, that during my illness, the world had been running on excellently well. "You take some more broth now, teacher, and keep r'al slow minded and easy, and hev' a good night's rest, and to-morrer I 'll tell ye all about it ! "

But I persisted ; so Grandma continued gently :

" Wall, it wa'n't much to tell, only the doctor said ye was n't to be talked to much, nor worked up ; but I reckon a little pleasant news ain't a gonter hurt nobody. Ye see, when you was took sick, George Olver, he got a hold of where Ethel was ; he had a mistrustin of it, some- how — and he went and told her, and it brought her, hearin you was dangerous, and she calculated she might be o' use to ye now, for *some*, they *be* sich friends ! " said Grandma, making this observation with the most guileless enthusiasm. " And Ethel, she wa'n't much brought up, and used to be as wild and harum-scarum as any of 'em ; but I allus said that there was a good deal to Ethel, after all. Wall, George Olver, he re*cog*nized where she was and he went down thar and found her, and they was n't anybody ventured to say a word, and what need? for everybody respec's George Olver, knowin' he 's uncom- mon ser'ous and high minded, and the very same hour they came home, Ethel, she come up here, and she turned me right out of the room, as ye might say. ' It 's my place, Grandma,' says she, and ' I 'm better able than you. I understand. It's my place.' And she was n't vary strong, but she would n't give up to nobody, and only run home a little while between spells to rest, and watched and and tended ye as faithful as though she was keepin' count of every breath ; and when the fever turned a' Monday night, and you fell off into a kind of a nateral sleep, the doctor, he says to her, what it ain't a very common thing for a doctor to say. ' It 's you saved her life ! ' he says. ' She was vary sick.' And he shook his head the way they do. ' You 've tended vary faithful,' he says, and Ethel, she hardly spoke, but I seen when she looked up that her eyes was a shinin', and that happy look that she 's had somehow, sence she came back — I can't tell ye exactly, teacher, but it 's most like as ef somebody should have a bad dream, and be wakin' up kinder surprised and thankful — but when the doctor said them words, I 'll never forget how her eyes went a shinin', and she says to me, ' I 'm goin' home now, and never you tell her, when she wakes up, for she thought it was you watchin' with her all the time, and kep' a callin ' Grandma ! Grandma !' says she, ' and don't you tell her ! don't you ! for it would seem as though I was obligin' her, and if she forgives me and is friendly I don't want it to be for that.' And I did n't say as I should or should n't tell," said Grandma, smilingly unconscious of the two large tears that were stealing down her cheeks, " but I knowed pretty well what I had on my mind ! "

Grandma ceased speaking, and began to busy herself about the room, humming softly her favorite refrain :

" The Light of the World is Jesus."

I lay very still, thinking —

"Once I was blind, but now I can see ! "

That low, glad, tremulous murmur brought no peace to my troubled heart.

When Grandma Spicer looked at me again, I fancied she met a helpless, appealing, almost an aggrieved expression in my eyes.

"I want to see her," I said. "I want to see Ethel, of course."

"Yis, yis," said Grandma, " to-morrer. You 'd want to talk, and you 've had enough for one day I 'll tell her, and she 'll understand."

" But I want to see her now," I persisted.

"They 's some folks just come in to inquire," continued Grandma, giving an easeful touch to the pillows. "They 's been a good many in to inquire. May be, she's amongst 'em. I 'll go down and see."

Soon I heard the old, girlish, familiar step on the stairs. Ethel hesitated, standing an instant on the threshold. In spite of the new and loftier soul looking out of her eyes, in spite of the new and womanly dignity which she bore so reposefully, she read my face with that quick, intuitive glance I had learned to know so well.

Then coming towards me, she put her arm gently around my neck, kissed me, understanding all, hushing all, forgiving all, and smiling a tender prohibition in her eyes, put her finger on my lips.

Sobbing inwardly, I accepted this divine retaliation in silence, and rested a while in that loving, warm embrace.

CHAPTER XVIII.

BENNEY GIVES THE TEACHER A NEW CHAIR.

NE morning, early in my convalescence, I was startled by a mighty rumbling and scraping sound on the narrow stairway, as of some unwieldly object pushed steadily upward. The summit reached, I heard the retreat of manly feet, and this leviathan presented itself with Grandma Spicer as an animating force, breathless and smiling, in the rear.

"He did n't have time to paint it, teacher," she began joyfully, "but it 'll be jest as comf'table to set in. He 's been explainin' of it to me — Ben has — ye see, it 's a cheer. He made it for ye, himself. And all you 've got to do is to turn this 'ere crank, here—" Grandma's countenance was radiant with wonder and approval — "and up it 'll go — so — as high as ye want it ! and this 'ere can be shoved in and out for ye to put yer feet on, and this 'ere back can be let anyways ye want it. He seen a picture o' one in a paper, once, and he went and made this by his own eye, and all the hinges and cranks, and everythin' as slick as a pin ! He did n't say anythin'," Grandma continued, in a slightly lowered, insinuating tone of voice, "about likin' to come up and see ye, when ye was able to set up, and you know, teacher, as I don't believe in meddlin' in young folks affairs, but it appeared to me, havin' had so much exper'ence with the men folks as I have, that may be he was kind o' hangin' around waitin' for an invitation,— for ye see, they 're goin' to sail now, in a vary few days."

So, a little later, I sat up in my new chair and received the Cradlebow, in a loose, trailing gown of rich material, heavily embroidered. In the midst of my narrow and humble surrounding I had an exiled princess sort of consciousness, and recognized with a new pleasure the Cradlebow's lordly face and bearing, as he stooped on entering the little red door.

Living in a reverie, still,—a fancy, a day dream, strangely vivid and life-like, but not real,— not real, I was so far softened by my illness that, with the delicious sense of returning health and strength, I was content, for a time, to live simply in the present, to dismiss the stern warden, Duty, from my thoughts, and that ever grave necessity for maintaining a mental and moral superiority which had so oppressed me.

It had been weary work living on the heights, and what had it all amounted to? I asked myself, with a reckless-ness too tranquil, now, to be converted into bitterness. "It was so much easier and safer, lower down." But while I doubted and almost gave up the struggle, the Cradlebow aspired ever to greater faith, and hope in life, and enthusiasm for life's work.

And with all this, it was evident that there had been with him an inward struggle and preparation, a silent con-

quering of self. With a vain discontent for my own failure,
I marvelled at the glory which had crowned his humble
efforts. " This, too," I thought, " is a sort of heroism,"
and my spirit of condescension towards the youth took on
something new, like reverence.

It was even with pride that I reflected, "Here is a
strength I may rely upon by and by," and I was proud
that my lover's kiss was so pure upon my lips, his breath
on my cheek — ah, foolish, sleeping heart !   It was well
that the dream should grow passionate, even intense, for
the awakening was near.

In the bewildered and feverish condition of mind in
which I had last left the Kedarville school-house, I had
been consciously impressed, at least, with the idea that
I should probably never enter those familiar walls again,
never again as the teacher. And now, I had no intention of resuming my labors there.

But I did not wish to flaunt my boasted independence
before the family circle at Newtown, until my eyes should
have assumed a little more nearly their usual proportions,
and my manner of going up and down stairs should have
become less strikingly feeble.

I decided to remain in Wallencamp a few days to
recuperate. I was not impatient nor especially chagrined
on account of this necessity. Secretly willing to await
the departure of the Cradlebow's ship, to have a brief
season of rest from all care and responsibility among the
scenes of my past labors — a little breathing space in
which to study those people quietly, to exchange unhur-
ried kindly words with them before I should go away from
them forever — I was glad to have it so.

Such welcomings and congratulations as I received

from the Wallencampers when I was able to get down
the stairs once more ! I felt very happy, almost humble,
sitting where the sunlight poured in at the open door of
Grandma's living-room.

That picture is still before my mind : The bare, shining
floor, the unpainted table, the chimney-shelf and a clock,
the successful working of whose machinery demanded a
crazily tilted attitude ; a Bible on the shelf, too, and
Grandma's spectacles lying askew. Then, a commodious
lounge of exceedingly simple construction set up straight
against the wall and extending the whole length of the
room. The original framework of this lounge, by the way,
disclosed itself in many bold and striking instances, under
a unique method of upholstery. It was stuffed sectionally.
There was the "old paper corner," within whose rustling
precincts Noel was reputed once to have endured agonies,
during a religious meeting held at the Ark. There was the
" sawdust " section, substantial, but by no means billowy to
the touch, and the "dried yarb" section, of a nature
similar to the sawdust ; and, omitting the "old clothes
section " with its insidious buttons, and the " corn-cob "
section, and the "cotton-wood bark " section, there was
the "feather corner," at the other end, generally conceded
to be luxurious, but silently avoided, as having given, on
more than one occasion, a sharp suggestion of quills.
Over the whole, depressions and excrescences, was
stretched a faded chintz cover. But woe to the luckless
wight who thought to find repose by throwing himself
carelessly down on this hitherto untried structure !
It was reserved only to the knowing few to find a comfortable seat on the lounge.

The cat, without having subjected herself to those trials

which some of us endured, had discovered, with true
feline instinct, wherein the deepest rest lay, and had
established herself on a suspended bridge of chintz between two overhanging systems.

There were a few chairs in the room besides, but the
doorsteps were wide. Grandpa sat always in the south
door, Grandma on the steps looking towards the lane,
and it was at this latter inviting spot, that the neighbors,
the "passers by," paused most frequently and disposed
themselves, with a grateful air.

I listened to their talk, while the birds struggled to
make noisy interruptions and cast their fleeting shadows
in the sunlight on the floor, and the peach blossoms outside were falling noiselessly.

Grandma Spicer had been telling me in a happy,
droning voice, though gravely enough, of the "awakenin'"
that was going on in Wallencamp — how "a good many
o' the young folks was impressed," and "Cap'n Sartell
had been seekin', ever since little Bessie died, and some
that had seemed to be forgitful and backslidin' had come
forward and told where they stood, until it seemed as
though the Lord was a sendin' a blessin' down, jest as
soft and beautiful as them blossoms," and Grandma's
eyes wandered towards the peach tree with a tearful fervor in them.

Aunt Patty was a temporary occupant of the steps.
Her anxious, care-lined face was turned indoors, away
from the light and the falling blossoms. There was an
anxious, restless ring in her voice, too.

" I 'm glad to hev such a time, I 'm sure," said she.
" We need it bad enough, any time, Lord knows I — but
it seems a queer season o' the year for 't. When we 've

had 'em before it's generally been along in the winter. I never heered of an awakenin' before right in the midst o' tater-buggin'.''

Aunt Patty was not intentionally irreverent. Life, with her, had been so narrow and hard pressed, always a painful reckoning of times and seasons.

The allusion to "tater-buggin'" gave Grandpa an opportunity of a sort of which he had not been slow to avail himself lately — to engage in a little old-time, secular conversation. His voice, however, as it sounded from the south doorway, was impressive enough for any subject.

"Grists on 'em, this year!" he said.

"Heaps!" Aunt Patty responded readily. "I don't see how ever the children could be speered to go to school now, anyway. Randal had all eight o' hisn out yesterday, with a four-quart pail apiece, and him and Lucindy pickin' into the half-bushel besides; and Rodney told Bede, for the livin' truth, he'd seen a lantern movin' around last night right in the dead o' night, and he looked out and it was the Dean and Abbie Ann out tater-buggin', and everybody knows they wasn't out in the daytime it was so dreadful hot. I'm sure we never had such queer weather afore. But them bugs are the hardest critturs to kill. It's almost impossible to dispose on 'em; and it does seem enough, what with ploughin' and plantin' and harrowin' and hoein' to git a few potatoes, and like enough, wet weather to rot 'em, without havin' to fight over 'em, for the last chance, with a whole army of varmint. I'm sure this 'ere way o' gittin' a livin', as old Grandther Skewer used to say, ' It costs more than it's wuth.'"

Led by the screams of the little Spicers in Abagail's apartment, Grandma had left the room for a moment, and Grandpa cleared his throat and began, hopefully :

"Talkin' about tater bugs," he said, and he glanced at me with a preliminary gleam in his eye, " Bachelder Rae was tellin' me the other mornin,— he said he was eddicatin' a couple on 'em. He said thar wa'n't no other way to get rid on 'em, but to appeal to their moral natur', and he said when he 'd got 'em eddicated up to the highest pint o' morality, he was a goin' to send 'em out as missionaries ter convart the rest. Bachelder said he 'd got 'em fur enough along, now, so 't they 'd pass examination along o' average folks that wa'n't admitted church members —"

" Hoggarty Spicer !"

Grandma, unexpectedly returning, had caught the last word only of Grandpa's discourse, but taking this in connection with the bright and mirthful expression of his countenance, she judged that his sentiments had been of an unusually reprehensible nature.

"Wall, wall, ma," said Grandpa, with an evident notion of continuing his narration, " what now, ma?"

" I hope, pa, " said Grandma, giving one the impression that she felt she could n't put the case too strongly, " that you are as innocent o' what you 've be'n a sayin' as the babe unborn, and to your credit, pa, I believe you be ! "

" Wall, wall, ma," said Grandpa, now mentally lost and bewildered, " I guess I know what I 'm talkin' about ! "

"And if you do, pa," said Grandma, with a solemnity that was unutterably conclusive, "you know more than I do ! "

Then, while the women talked, Grandpa, sitting alone in the south door, sighed and whittled, and abstractedly scanned the horizon. Once, he made a singularly bold attempt to entice Aunt Patty again into the channels of profane conversation, by an introductory speculation as to the prospect of the bean crop; but Grandma Spicer nipped this reckless and irreverent adventure in the bud, by replying in a calm, vast tone :

"Pa, it r'aly seems to me that for a vain creetur in a fleetin' world, and a perfesser besides, there 'd ought to be more things to talk about than beans !"

Grandpa Spicer sighed still more deeply, gazed wistfully towards the barn, as though he would fain have shuffled out in that direction; but the weather being so warm, he refrained. He glanced at me with a feeble, helpless smile, his head fell backward, his eyes gradually closed, and, in spite of the iniquities which covered his ancient head, he fell into a slumber that had all the semblance of child-like and unblemished innocence.

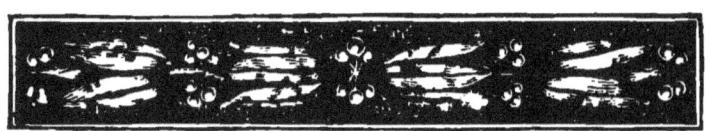

CHAPTER XIX.

DEATH OF THE CRADLEBOW.

HILE Grandpa Spicer dozed peacefully, Emily Gaskell, also "passin' by," joined the group of women on the door-steps of the Ark.

Emily, by the way, was regarded as a hopeful subject of the "awakenin'." She had been to see a doctor in Farmouth, who told her she could not live through another winter "with that cough on her." She sat very still in the meetings, it was said, and seemed "tetched and wonderful," whereas she had been wont formerly, on occasions of this solemn nature, to evince many signs of restlessness, and even to engage in droll and sly diversions for the greater delectation of the "unconsarned."

Emily herself was particularly unreserved on the subject of her spiritual condition. Her tone had lost none of its former bright vivacity, though I thought I saw frequently now, while she was talking, a softer shadow steal over the restless, consuming fire in her blue eyes.

"I know what some on 'em say," said she; "I know what I might a said, jest as like as not, if it had been somebody else in my place. Oh, she's afraid she ain't a goin' to git well, and so she 's a seekin' religion. She 's scart into it !

" Wall, if folks that know me are a mind to say that, they may ; though if it comes to bein' scart into religion by what the doctors said, I should a jined the church twenty times over !

" It ain't because I 'm afraid o' what 'll happen to me after I 'm all dead and .peaceable. It 's because I want a little more comfort while I 'm a livin'. Seems to me there 's more comfort needed for the livin'.

"And ever since my brother 'Lihu died, seems as though them last words o' hisn have been a ringin' in my ears. ' I know somebody that'll watch. Who? Jesus will ! Jesus will !' over and over again. And when I get to worryin' about things, and can't see no way through, or whoever 's a goin' to straighten 'em out, it keeps a goin', 'Who, then? Jesus will I Jesus will !' over and over. And 'Lihu was n't a professor, neither ; and maybe he had n't no right to take the comfort out o' them words that he did ; and maybe I hain't no right, and it 's only like a string o' music that 'll keep a runnin' in a body's head sometimes and they not thinkin' nor meanin' any-thin'.

" I don't see any further into it than I did afore. I don't know as I 'm what you'd call any more believin', but when I 've laid till after midnight with my eyes as wide open as daylight, and no shut to 'em, thinkin' and worryin' and coughin', I 've seen it agin, jest the way he rolled and tossed that night, and then them words come to him, and he smiled and went to sleep peacefuller nor any child ; and so *I've* said 'em, and faith or no faith,

believin' or no believin', they 've set me a cryin', time
and agin, and they 've put me to sleep ! thar, they 've put
me to sleep ! "

"And who else could they 'a be'n meant for but him
and you?" cried Grandma, in a gush of sympathy, " him
and you, and anybody else as you seen needed them
words and could give 'em to 'em to quiet 'em ; for, dear
woman ! there ain't none on us that see into it, but jest
to say it over. Dear woman ! we don't know no more.
It's what's a restin' all on us. It's what's a restin' all
on us ! "

I looked up and saw tears in Abagail's eyes. I had
not heard Abagail spoken of as among the number of
the impressed. There were tears in my own eyes, I
knew ; there had grown to be such a pathos in those
women's voices.

A little later, Emily lapsed into a strain of sprightly
gossip.

"And who do you think 's kitin' around in this region
agin?" she began. "Somebody you'd expect least of
all, I reckon ; wall, it's Eliot Turner," and she nodded
her head quickly and expressively at the others.

" I don't mean," she continued, "that he's been in
Wallencamp, but Levi was down from Wallen this
mornin,' and he said they stopped last night in Wallen
Harbor—him and some other fellers, mighty stylish
lookin', but he said it was Eliot Turner's yacht, as fine
and fancy-rigged as ever he see, and there was some that
looked like common sailors, and they all come ashore,
and the common ones was the quietest. But he reckoned the fisherman was off on 'a time,' and stopped there
jest for fun, and to show off, maybe.

" Wall, Levi told me that, and to-day, 'long about the middle o' the forenoon, my man come up to the house — he's down to shore, you know, along o' Cap'n Sartell and George Olver and Ben Cradlebow and all the rest, down there a mendin' up the old schooner, 'cause Cap'n wanted Ben to see to it afore he went away. My man come up for a wrench and ' who do you think 's a scootin' around down on the Bay ? ' says he. ' Wall, it 's Eliot Turner,' says he, ' in the purtiest little craft, that runs jest like a picter,' and he said they could n't see but two men aboard of her then ; he guessed they wa'n't many. It was jest like Eliot Turner to take a run from Wallen down this way to show what he could do alone, for he was always braggin' about bein' so stiddy on his sea-legs and how 't he understood this shore better 'n any o' the old uns.

" My man said they did n't know who 't was out there, at first, for it ain't the kind o' vessel often seen, and it skimmed along on the edge o' the water, Jim said, like a bird, in and out amongst the rocks, so 't anybody 'd a thought, not knowin' who they was — and them, may be, not knowin' the shore — that they was drunk or gone crazy, and Jim said they hollered to 'em to look out for the rocks, and they heered a kind of a laugh on the water, and somebody shouted back :

" Stow your gab, land lubbers ! " and they knew from the voice, it was Eliot Turner.

" He was probably meanin' to put in there, and might a come ashore may be, — he was wild enough — but he seen our men and that kind o' hendered him ; he did n't want to turn around and put right back neither, lookin' as though he was scared, so he kep' on, and Jim said

they watched 'em clean out o' sight; 'but,' says he, 'I
never seen a man turn whiter 'n George Olver did for a
minute, and then he onclinched his fist and went to
work agin, harder than ever, for you can allays depend
on 'im, somehow — George Olver — but he 's a dreadful
close-mouthed fellow !' "

During the recital of this narrative, recalling so much
to my mind, I experienced more than anything else a
feeling of annoyance, almost of resentment, that the fisherman should appear, however remotely, to disturb the
serenity of these last few days in which I had to live out
my Wallencamp idyl.

For the others the story seemed to have created a
momentary excitement, but they regarded it, on the
whole, as of little consequence.

Aunt Patty had passed on to the doorway of another
neighbor, and George Olver 's relations with Ethel soon
constituted the theme of a more general and lively discourse, in which the remarks concerning Ethel were
mostly kind and considerate, and the praise of George
Olver 's conduct enthusiastic; and, at the close of
which, I remember, Grandma said that "the higher
minded folks gits to be, the pitifuller they be a'most
always ! "

The fact of the fisherman's transient appearance on
the Bay was not again alluded to, nor do I think the
mind of any one present reverted to it, when, Grandpa
Spicer, looking up with that utterly dazed and bewildered
air, which betokened a decisive awakening on his part,
cast his eye along the horizon, and observed gravely:

"Storm a brewin', ma."

"You've been asleep, pa," said Grandma in sweetly

mollifying tones; and Emily Gaskell, almost involuntarily, glanced up at me with a mischievous, anticipative
wink.

"Asleep, ma," said Grandpa Spicer, "no, I hain't
be'n asleep, neither! And what if I had, ma? That
don't hender a storm's brewin', does it?"

"We've be'n seein' them little wind clouds passin'
afore the sun for half an hour past," explained Grandma
Spicer composedly.

But Grandpa scanned the sky with a dark, keen
glance — the air of an old voyager on stormy and literal
seas, and he shook his head, sagely.

"Wall, wall, ma," he said, "It don't make no difference whether it's a wind storm or a rain storm that I
know on, but a tempest it's brewin', sartin sure. I
remember once we'd had a spell o' weather jest like this,
and it begun to gether up in the same way. It was in
the same latitude, teacher, same latitude. I was off
cruisin' with Bob Henchy — whew! that ar' was a singin'
gale! I remember it as well as yesterday. I was off
with Bob —"

"Are you sure it was Bob ye was off with, pa," interrupted Grandma. "I could a'most write a book, pa,
while you was tellin' a story."

"Wall, wall, ma! Write a book, if ye want to!" exclaimed Grandpa with sweeping force. "I'm sure
nobody wants to hender yer writing a book if ye want to,
ma!"

Grandma Spicer heeded not those derisive words
Her mind was bent on pursuits of a far loftier and more
engrossing nature. In respect to the weather — except
on Sabbath mornings when it was impossible to credit

Grandpa with perfect fairness and impartiality of judgment — Grandma, it must be said, had real faith in the
old sea-captain's prognostications.

"It does look like a shower, and a mighty sudden
one," said Emily. She thrust her knitting work in her
pocket, donned her sun bonnet, and departed with other
chance occupants of the doorsteps. And Grandma too,
admitted the prospect of foul weather by throwing a
handkerchief over her head and going out to fetch the
milk-pans.

Since early spring Grandma Spicer had put her milk-
pans to dry in the sun on a bench half way up the "Pas-
tur-Hill." Why she should choose to place them at such
a seemingly capricious and unnecessary distance from
the house, for it was really no inconsiderable journey
for Grandma, taking into account her peculiar style of
locomotion, whether she considered that the rays of the
morning sun visited them more directly on that plane, or
that the elevation exposed them to peculiar atmospheric
advantages, these were questions which the curious mind
was left to solve for itself, for the grave office of carrying
out and bringing in the milk-pans was performed by
Grandma with an air of mysterious calm, which admitted
of no profane comment or speculation.

Abagail laughed, watching her, the musical notes
ringing out with a touch of insane gaiety.

"If ma knew it was Judgment Day," said she, "she'd
carry those milk-pans up the hill to dry, and if she knew
it was Judgment Hour she'd go to fetch 'em."

The scene grew rapidly weird as the sky darkened.
A low sigh, like a premonition, crept through the heavy
atmosphere and shivered among the peach blossoms.

The first gust of wind seized Grandma, returning with the milk pans. It was a zephyr compared with the blasts that followed, but it had the effect of giving to that good soul's usually composed and reassuring presence, something of the appearance of a crazy and dismantled ship, rolling in a high sea.

Grandpa was quick at detecting the resemblance, and hailed her approach in thrilling nautical terms, such as : "why did n't ye reef yer top-gallant, ma !" when the handkerchief was torn off her head ; and "hang to the main royal, ma," as Grandma's apron was caught up and borne, wildly fluttering, about her ears ; and "keep your ballast, ma ;" with frequent ejaculations of "lor, how she pitches ! how she pitches !"

These were not thrown out as light shafts of ridicule. It was no occasion for such. There was an awful earnestness in Grandpa Spicer's eye and in the tone that invested his words with due solemnity. Grandma, struggling with the wind, had not heard them. She entered the Ark, however, cheerful though panting.

"Hoggarty Spicer," said she, in accents of real affection, "I would n't have you out in that wind for no money — not for no money, nor our teacher, neither. Why, no stronger than she is now, it 'ud take the breath right out of our teacher's body ! Why, ef it had n't been for the cargo I had on board, pa," continued Grandma, naturally falling into the same train of ideas we had followed, while watching her battle with the elements, "I should a' slipped moorin's, sure !"

A casual listener might have smiled at this, in view of Grandma's substantial physique.

Presently she said, as though the thought had just

struck her, "I hope fisherman's got back to Wallen Harbor, pa."

"And if he ain't, ma," replied Grandpa Spicer, sententiously, "he'll know what it is to be out in a squall! but I reckon he's looked out for himself."

The old captain's face grew graver; his eyes, in that closed room, which had grown so suddenly dark, took on an intensely solemn look. He did not attempt the narration of any stormy adventures of old.   Perhaps the scenes of the past rose too vividly before his eyes.   But, as the fiercest gusts came, he kept muttering:

"I knew what it meant—mild winter on the Cape! There's the Devil in the old Cape weather, teacher, and he never skipped four seasons yit! If it ain't one time, it must be another. Yis, yis! mild winter on the Cape, and no March to speak on, and a hurricane in summer! Wall, we're both on us right ma, and we're both on us wrong. It ain't neither wind nor rain, but the heavens let loose, and God a'mighty's own power a blowin' of it. Yis, yis! I had my misgivin's all along; thinks I, better a little more weather now, than to blast every livin' thing by and by; but I hadn't no idee o' this! The Lord ha' mercy. The Lord ha' mercy!"

For all that one could see through the windows was a great black sheet of driving rain, and the roar of the storm was terrible. The Ark shook. It seemed, at each successive blast, as though the walls would fall in over our heads. One could easily imagine the whole crazy structure borne onward before the resistless tempest, to take a final wild leap from the cliffs.

"Wallencamp's a gittin' all mixed up," said Grandpa,

without the faintest tinge of humor, now. "We sha'n't know where to find ourselves when we git out o' this 'ere, ef we ever do git out on't. Lord a' mercy!"

Abagail sat very white and still, resting her chin on her hands, her great eyes staring out.

Grandma held the two frightened children in her lap. She was rocking and singing to them in a low, crooning tone. Though she was pale and her lips trembled, there was still about her a soothing atmosphere of peace.

I was frightened, like the children. I longed to cry out as they had done; to bury my head away from the terrors somewhere, as they did in Grandma's lap.

"That was the blackest squall," said Grandpa Spicer, afterwards, "that ever swep' across the Cape!"

Terrible as it had been, it died quickly. The transition seemed miraculous from the sullen roar of the wind and torrent-fall of rain, to the renewed chirping of the birds, the quiet dripping of the eaves, and sunshine over all.

But the young peach tree that had stood by the window of the Ark and sent its fragrance into my little room above, lay prone upon the ground. When she saw that, Grandma Spicer moaned heart-brokenly, as though it had been some fair human life stripped suddenly of its promise and left to wither fruitlessly.

There were traces of the storm everywhere. Trees that had stood isolated in the fields lay, some of them, with roots exposed; others were broken off at the trunk, left with only a branch or two, helpless figures with outstretched arms, to give a weird desolation to the landscape by and by, I thought with a shudder, when winter should come again to Wallencamp.

The fences — what remained of them from former depredations — had either fallen utterly to the ground, or assumed a strikingly precarious position.

Part of the roof of Mr. Randal's house had been blown off, and the chimneys of several of the Wallencamp houses demolished, and Grandpa's barn twisted and distorted almost beyond recognition.

That poor old gentleman put on his hat and stepped out of the door cautiously, looking about him like one in a dream.

The Ark had stood firm, apparently, in its old resting place. Grandma and Abagail proceeded to sweep out the rain which had been driven in through the cracks, and then it was that little Henry G. came running, with a white face, to the door. He had an air of childish importance, too, as being the first to bear tidings of some strange and dreadful event, and eager to hasten to other doors.

"Where's the rest?" he gasped, seeing only me in the room. "You tell 'em, teacher, Benney's drowned!" and the boy disappeared, without another word.

I was already faint from the reaction of the excitement incident to the storm, weak with the effort I had made to "hold myself still." I heard Grandma calling quickly, "Child! child!" I saw her coming towards me, and then I lost consciousness.

*   *   *   *   *   *

At evening, while the sun went down over the hill by which the transfigured river flowed, Captain Sartell sat in the door of the Ark, and told the story.

The marvellous light was on his face, too. It fell, in shafts of glory, on the bright foliage of the fallen tree.

Grandma was at Godfrey Cradlebow's, but Grandpa Spicer was within the Ark, and Abagail caressing her children with a new fondness. There were a few of the neighbors present; they looked neither frightened nor curious, but ineffably exalted.

"We'd got our work about done," said Captain Sartell, speaking mechanically and with little of his customary hesitation of manner. "As near as I calk'late, there wa'n't a half hour's more work to do on the old craft, and it had got to be sometime arter noon, but says the boys, 'Let's finish her off, now we've got so near through, and not have to come back agin. They was always a cheery set — especially *him* — when they took hold of a job, to put it through.

"We'd seen them sailin' fellows go by a while before; and we knew Turner was one of 'em. They was n't but two, as we could see, managin' the craft; and they was full sail, clippin' it lively. I calk'late there ain't many knows this shore better 'n me, but I would n't a durst skirted along the adge down thar at sech a rate, not in the finest day blowin'. First we thought it was somebody did n't know what they was about. When we made out it was Turner, we knew, if he *was* drunk, he was tol'able well acquainted with the rocks along shore, and 'ud probably put further out when he got through showin' off. We did n't worry about 'em, nor think no more about 'em, in special. The boys did n't want to talk to rile George Olver.

"So we kep' to work, and in a minute, cheery agin' with the hammers click, clickin'—and every now and then the boys 'ud strike up a singin somethin', 'Beyond the River,' and 'Homeward Bound.'

"It sounded dredful purty down thar by the water, with the water and the wideness all around sorter soft-enin' of it. It made a man feel curious and wishful, somehow.

" Well, by and by, him and George Olver struck up a song. I 've heern 'em sing it before, them two. As nigh as I calk'late, it 's about findin' rest in Jesus, and one a askin' questions, all fa'r and squar', to know the way and whether it 's a goin' to lead thar straight or not, and the other answerîn'. And *he*—he was a tinkerin', 'way up on the foremast, George Olver and the rest on us was astern,—and I 'll hear to my dyin' day how his voice came a floatin down to us thar—chantin' like it was—cl'ar and fearless and slow. So he asks, for findin' Jesus, ef thar 's any marks to foller by ; and George Olver, he answers about them bleedin' nail prints, and the great one in His side. So then that voice comes down agin, askin' if thar's any crown, like other kings, to tell Him by ; and George Olver, he answers straight about that crown o' thorns. Then says that other voice, floatin' so strong and cl'ar, and if he gin up all and follered, what should he have ? what now ?

"So George Olver, he sings deep o' the trial and the sorrowin' But that other voice never shook, a askin' and what if he helt to Him to the end, what then should it be, what then ? George Olver answers : ' Forever-more, the sorrowin' ended — Death gone over.'

" Then he sings out, like his mind was all made up, ' And if he undertook it, would he likely be turned away ? '

" ' And it 's likelier,' George Olver answers him, ' That heaven and earth shall pass.'

"So 1'll hear it to my dyin' day — his voice a floatin' down to me from up above thar, somewhar, askin' them questions that nobody could ever answer like, so soon, he answered 'em for himself — and when I looked up, thar was Noah, with his hammer dropped, and his mouth wide open, a starin' up thar, and the tears rollin' down his cheeks like he was a baby.

"They did n't sing no more, after that. They was still for about five minutes, I calk'late.   Noah, he was still, too; but pretty soon, he wakes up and says, 'Gad, boys!   Did ye ever see sech a queer look in the sky?   I believe thar 's a September gale brewin."

"' It 's a little wind storm, I reckon,' says Bachelder. Bachelder was settin', with his legs curled up under him, mendin' sail, and he begun to spin one o' them yarns o' his'n, with his voice pitched up middlin' high, and the boys, they begun to laugh and cheer.

"Then Noah says, ' I 'll run up to head quarters, and find out about the weather,' and clim' up the main mast as limber as a squirrel, and when he came back, thar was Tommy's hat stickin' way up top o' the mast; so Tommy, he promised to pay him — them two was always foolin' together, but good natered enough."   The captain introduced this little incident, in the midst of his narration, with a dull, pathetic gravity.   " It was the last thing we thought on, o' bein' fearful, or calk'latin' any danger.   We reckoned it was a brisk little shower comin' up, may be, and the boys was runnin' one another about gittin' into the cabin, and runnin' on about the old craft.

"Then thar come, all of a sudden, sech a strange feelin,' as ef the 'arth and the water was a tremblin', and a dreadful moanin' sound runnin' through 'em. Seemed as though it came swirlin' across the bay. Then it bust on us in a fury.

"He was out, sorter lookin' around him, Bachelder was, and the wind took Bachelder up, and keeled 'im over two or three times runnin'.

"Black it grew as the Jedgment day. Then come no sich rain as ever I see, even the pourin'est, but the clouds fallin' all to once, and the wind a scatterin' of 'em, and up on the cliffs, we could jest hear a creakin' and a bendin' whar the trees was turned as white as ghosts in that 'ere blackness, and the old Bay, in sech a minute, was spinnin' into foam.

"We was shelterin' around the old craft now, sure enough, and nobody speakin' a word, but jest a holdin' our breaths a waitin', when, in among them other noises, thar come, out on the water, sech a low, dull sound as sent the awful truth on us in a minute, and, for a minute, that ar right hand of mine was numb.

"Then Noah, he had hold o' me, a pintin' out, and whether he spoke a word or not, I seen it — through wind and rain and foam, all in my eyes to once, I seen — reelin' and tossin' and pitchin', out thar on the Bay, lost, lost for sure — I seen that fancy ship !

"Thar wa'n't no hand on 'arth could guide it, now. Every second was like to see it keeled squar' over, or slipped and driv in straight on to the rocks.

"We're used to other 'n fa'r weather along this shore. I calk 'late we ain't used to frighten at a little danger, but knowin' the sea so well, we know the helplessness a'most o' puttin' out in sech a gale as that.

"I heerd the sound. It only came but once ; and Seth hissed through his teeth, a cryin' too, a'most :

'Ain't thar no other way to werry us, but they must come in here to drown afore our very eyes ! A fool's ventur' ! what could ye expect but a fool's end ! Ef he must drown, let the red haired devil drown !'

"But when they heered it, them two, *him* and George Olver. I knowed how it would be. I hardly durst to look. I seen them flash at one another with their great eyes, as ef it wa'n't enough to do man's work, but when thar come a chance, they must go act like God ! I seen in jest that flash, them two agreein' solemnly.

"Then it was all done in a minute's space, like you'll live yer life through sometimes, in a dream. They had Bill Norris's eight oar ready. They pushed us back. They'd a gone alone, them two. I kep' the third place. Olver and Tommy scuffled, in a breath, and Noah, he thrust Tommy back, and we was off.

"God knows I never expected we 'd come back again. You heern the wind. You can calk'late what it was out thar with the rain a drivin', and the salt foam blowed into our eyes. I calk'late we never fetched a harder pull, no, nor a blinder one.

"And she, the cursed thing, mad with twitchin' at her cable, lay over to one side. But she was dyin' mad. I tell ye she **was** dyin' mad. Thar was them two a hangin' to her — thar had n't be'n but them. So we hauled Turner in, but that other one, when he seen us, the chance o' bein' saved, it crazed him, and he sent up a quick, glad sort of a yell and throwed his arms out straight, and back he fell, like lead, into the water. And Turner, crouchin' thar and shiverin' ' He could n't swim ! He's sunk ! he's sunk !' he says. Then *he*, he ris up in a flash, and out he dove into that hell.

"Then come another gust, a blindin', blindin', blindin'. 'He 'll weather it ! He 'll weather it !' George Olver kep' a mutterin', but his teeth was set ; his eyes shot through me like a tiger's—them two was brothers, and more 'n brothers, always. But when thar come a half lull so 't we could see, and we looked out and seen him risin' on the wave, grippin' that other one, in spite o' hope I scurse believed my eyes, and what a shout they sent up from that boat !

"Aye, thar they was, for sure but—God, how fur away ! Not much for common weather, but then they looked as fur to me as arth from heaven. Ef we could reach 'em afore the next sweel come ; and every man, it seemed as though he put his livin' soul into his arms. 'Pull ! pull !' says George, and seemed to git the strength of seven, but still we went too slow. We missed *him* at the oar. And *he*, he was the strongest swimmer that I ever knowed, but who could live in the like o' that ? We pulled for life or death, and that brave head kep' risin' on the wave.

" Ef we could a had another minute afore the next sweel come ! George Olver felt it. He sent the rope out with a giant's throw. Then all and more than we could do to hold the boat agin the wind. It come so fast ye scurse could see them next ye in the boat. 'He's grappled it ! he 's thar ! he 's thar !' says they, and when they pulled it in, thar was that other one helt fast, and only him.

"God knows ! I calk'late he made sure o' the other first, and thar wa'n't jest the breath's time left for him, blinded so sudden may be, and fell death faint. I 've knowed it be so with the strongest ; no wonder thar ; the

wonder was in what he done. He was the strongest
swimmer that I ever knowed, the strongest and the fear-
lessest !

"George Olver never'll be content. He would a
gone in after *him*. We'd be'n driv a furlong back, I
reckon, and every mark was lost. It 'ud be'n naught
but to swaller him, too. He lost his sense. We had to
holt him back. He raved thar, like a madman. It
blew a bitter spell. longest of all, and when it helt a bit
so we could take our bearin's some'at, what hope ! what
hope !

"But poor George, of a suddint he grew quiet as a
lamb, and set a lookin' out, with his hand light on the oar,
as ef 'twas pleasant weather, and he could see *him* ridin'
in thar easy on the wave ; and his eyes was fur off and
smilin', but they looked as though they died. Mebbe—
I know no more.

"We found him arterwards. Thar wa n t no mark nor
stain on him. You think I talk dry-eyed. Go you and
look at him. Somehow it don't leave ary breath for
cryin'. It's like as ef he knowed. It's more than
quietness, seemin' to say, for all he loved his life and
fou't so hard out thar, ter lose his own at last—givin'
or losin', he never missed o' naught ! he never missed
o' naught !

"I can't tell what's the thought come nighest to ye
when ye look at him. I hain't got high enough for that,
but I can tell ye what's the furderest—weepin' and
sorrowin'. Since I seen him and my little Bessie fell
asleep, please God I die a half so trustful or so brave,
I make no fear o' death !"

The Captain sighed a long, ecstatic sigh and rose, the

after-glow still shining on his face. In passing through the room, he pressed something softly into my hand.

"We found it in the breast-pocket of his coat, teacher," he said. "The coat lay in the bottom o' the boat, and was soaked with brine. It had your name on 't."

When I unfolded it, it was the little star-fish the Cradlebow had showed me, days before, still folded close in its delicate vine wreath.

CHAPTER XX.

GEORGE OLVER'S ORATION.

THE Wallencampers gathered at the Ark, singing a calm and high farewell to earth that alone was meet for the untroubled lips of that silent singer in their midst.

They gathered at the Ark. No other place seemed to them sacred enough for such a meeting, now; no other place dear enough for the celebration of such a solemn, long farewell.

Over the threshold, where he had come so often bounding in his life, they brought the dead; there was the same strange look of exaltation on their faces that I had noticed while Captain Sartell told the story of the storm; stricken and white, the poor faces, yet touched with some daring, unutterable hope — so clear a message they read on that wondrously still and reconciled face, so without fear the dead lips spoke to them.

To me, the message was one of infinite pathos and rebuke, speaking of a heroism beyond my poor conception, of a height of glory of which I had not dreamed.

"Farewell, forevermore," the fathomless far voice murmured to my despair, and slowly and repeatedly, "Farewell, forevermore. I am beyond the need of your poor love."

And my heart turned to stone, with all the passionate, pure sorrow that might have been, the tears in which I might have found relief.

Granuma Spicer's sacred "keepin' rooms" were open d wide for the reception of this guest, yet the sunshine stole in with a hallowed light, the entering breeze sighed low and softly. The children, always present, were, on this occasion, attentively still.

There were no external signs of woe for the poor Wallen campers to assume; they made no mad demonstrations of their grief; the suffering and the wonder were too deep.

Lydia — they all knew how she had loved this son. When they returned from their perilous quest in the storm, the first words Captain Sartell said were, " Who must go up now, and break Lyddy's heart?"

She stood among the others, very still, the old faded mantilla folded decently over her shoulders, the great dark eyes, *his* eyes, shining out even kindly from the worn face on those who came to speak to her.

Godfrey Cradlebow stood at the outer door, and addressed the people as they entered. Some said, afterwards, that he had been drinking; others declared he had not touched a drop for days.

In the room where I stood, I heard his musical, deep tones now swelling with the fervor of his harangue, now broken and trembling with emotion.

"Enter, my friends!" said this strange man. "Go in,

and look on quietness. What do we seek for most, my friends? Look out on the world. It's a whole world of seekers. How they jostle against one another! how they sweat! how they strive! how they toil! and why all this? What seek they for? For quietness, my friends, even so — the quietness of wealth to gain, may be, or competence; may be, the quietness of some renown. And some go seeking over land and sea for their lost health, and quietness from pain.

"My friends, within there was as restless a seeker as I ever knew. Pity the old, my friends, but pity more the young! Never such dreams of rest! Never such restlessness! Hush! when he heard, he answered well. He put all by. Somehow, we think he has obtained — wealth, honor, perfect health. My friends, pass in! behold this wonder!

"My friends, you look up at the sky. Ah, what a sky! purple and deep! Yet I see something in your eyes that is not quietness; for storms will come, too well you know, and the cold blasts of winter; but if you knew that never any sorrowful, hard wind could sweep across yon blue — then, my friends, you would look as he looks who lies within there. Pass in! pass in! behold this wonder."

Within, Grandma Spicer stood with closed eyes and folded hands. Her cheeks were wet. She wore a heavenly, trustful expression of countenance. Her lips moved as if in prayer.

Aunt Susannah Cradlebow rose in her place — majestic and weird she looked, like some old Eastern prophetess, a grand forecasting in her shadowy eyes.

"Gether in the sheaves," she began, "the bright

sheaves, early ripe and ready for the harvestin'; and begrudge not the Master of His harvestin'. Why, oh
Lord, Lord, this sheaf, while there be them that stand,
late harvest day, bowed and witherin' in the cornfield?
Because He reckons not o' time. Glory, glory to the
Lord o' the harvestin' ! But gether in for me, He says,
my bright sheaves, early ripe ! my sheaves o' the golden
wine !

" It was the night but two before my grandson died, I
seen a death sign in a dream, and so I speaks to my
son's wife, but ' Fear you not,' I says ; ' it was the blessed
sign o' blessed death ;' and thought o' some one old
and helpless, sick maybe, gettin' release thereby. Why
this sheaf, oh Lord?—Glory, glory to the Lord o' the
harvestin' ! For I dreamt there was a bird ketched in
my room, and flutterin' here and there, and beatin'
'ginst the window with its wings. And dreamin' I ris up,
and there was such a light along the floor as never any
moonlight that I see was half so solemn or so beautiful.
But when I stretched my hand to free the poor, blind,
flutterin' bird, it ris away from me, and spread its wings,
snow-white, and out it flew, and sharp and clear along
that shinin' track. Then when I woke, I knew it was the
sign o' blessed death, nor ever feared. And God will
bear me true, it was the very night they brought my
grandson home that, lyin' down to rest a while from
watchin' with the rest, nor ever wonderin' nor layin' it to
mind what I had dreamed afore, but tired and heart-broke
only, I seen the long, bright shinin' track agin', a pourin'
through the window ; and ' My son's son ! ' I cries, ' dear
boy ! dear boy ! '—for it was like him playin' on his
violin—' What tunes must be,' I cries, ' that you play so,

and scarce a day in heaven !' But when I ris up, callin',
it grew dim along the track, and thar was mornin' in the
room, and then I heered them cryin' where they watched

"Why this sheaf, oh Lord?—gether in the sheaves, oh
Lord, the bright sheaves, early ripe and ready for the
harvestin'. Glory, glory to the Lord o' the harvestin' !"

Then the Wallencampers sang tremblingly of the
"Harvest Home." They were glad when they saw
George Olver stand up in their midst — George Olver,
least subject of them all to dreams or ecstasies, but with
his slow, labored speech, and his sorrowful, bowed head.
He took his place beside the coffin of his friend, looked
gently at that face, and squared his shoulders for a
moment then, and held his head with the old manly air :

"When Uncle 'Lihu died," said he, " my friend and
me walked home together from the funeral, and Benney
says to me : ' I want you to promise me, George, that if I
shed die, you would n't have that man to preach over me,'
meanin' the minister, though he was kindly to him, ' and
he means well,' says he, ' but he don't understand us ; he
knows naught about us 'ceptin' that now we 're dead, and
not bein' used to them long texts o' hisn, it frets our
folks,' says he. ' They weary on 't, so long a string they
har'ly understand ; but I would rather,' Benney says, ' have
some one amongst my folks that knowed me well, git up
and speak, ef it was only : *This was my friend lies here ;
I loved him.* And promise me, George, ef I shed die,
you 'd hev no stranger preachin' over me, but speak some
such easy words yourself for love o' me.' And I felt with
him thar, and promised him, and he me ; but I remember
thinkin', as I looked at him, it 's little likely I 'll ever
stand above your grave.

"Enough said. 'This was our friend lies here. We loved him.' We thank him for them words. Better nor more, they cl'ar it all up on this side twixt him and us. No need ter tell o' what he was, or what he done. "T'ain't likely we'll forgit. He didn't say ter praise him. He wanted none o' that, but jest we knowed and loved him—

"And so it might a' been enough, but now, my God! my God! as I stand here aside o' him, he bids me, plain as day, to speak a word beyent; ef I could only name it, ef I could only name it, what looks so cl'ar and beautiful thar on his face.

"'Hold strong' he says, 'below thar. Keep heart and make cl'ar reckonin', for it's losin' all may be, in this 'ere mystery, makes cl'arest gain o' all. There's fairer day to rest ye arter storm. All's well! all's well!' he says, 'all's well beyent. ll's well along this shore!'"

Here George Olver's husky voice failed him; sobs rose in the room.

Then the "farewell" was sung, and bravely; but at the last, I heard only Abagail's voice, it grew so surpassingly clear and sweet; it seemed to float solitary in the room, and to play triumphantly about the silent sleeper's lips—the voice, indeed, of a free spirit in its bliss, thrilled only with some plaintive memory of human woe and loss.

*   *   *   *

> "Farewell, ye dreams of night;
>   Jesus is mine!
> Lost in this dawning bright;
>   Jesus is mine!
> All that my soul has tried,
> Left but a dismal void;
> Jesus has satisfied.
>   Jesus is mine!

Farewell, mortality;
  Jesus is mine!
Welcome, eternity.
  Jesus is mine!

Welcome, the loved and blest!
Welcome, bright scenes of rest ·
Welcome, my Saviour's breast.
  Jesus is mine! "

Scarcely had the leaves of the fallen peach tree by the window begun to wither, when the strong bearers passed out with their beautiful, stainless burden, while slowly, reverently, the little community of mourners followed to the grave.

CHAPTER XXI.

FAREWELL TO WALLENCAMP.

ET another week passed in Wallencamp before I was able to complete the preparations for my departure.

One day, I set myself with a sort of listless fidelity to the summing up of my accounts. I found, on deducting the amount of my actual expenses from the sum total of my earnings in Wallencamp, that I had sixty-two cents left !

The revelation caused me some surprise; strangely little perturbation of spirit. I thought what tragic tales might sometimes lie hidden beneath a seemingly dry and senseless combination of figures, while, in my own case, I was merely struck with the justice of those figures.

For such eccentric and distracted services as I had rendered in Wallencamp, the superintendent of schools had paid me in full at the price stipulated, eight dollars per week.

On the other hand, the column of insolvency, I considered that the West Wallen Doctor's bill was an expression of modesty itself. The sum due my dear Abagail for "board" at two dollars and a half per week, though I trusted it was some compensation for the merely temporal advantages to be enjoyed in Kedarville, did not appear as an astounding aggregate. The list of "minor details" was well portrayed, and presented an aspect of clear use and value.

My once fond dream of a "private bank account" had gradually faded from my memory. I saw the last spar in that fair wreck go down, now, without a sigh. And the "loans solicited," in labored phrase, as "mere temporary conveniences" from the friends at home — these, I was satisfied, must remain only as the sweet continuation of a life-long debt. But how was I to get home?

The combined fares on that route, I remembered, had amounted to something over nine dollars! So the question haunted me, not restlessly, but with a vague, tranquil, melancholy interest, as pertaining to the history of some one who had lived and died a few years before; so long indeed, it seemed to me, since I had performed the journey to Wallencamp.

I had not written home as to the day of my probable arrival, in this yielding passively to the force of habit, which had ever constrained me to plan my returns as "surprises" to my family and friends.

But for myself, I had fixed the day of my departure from Wallencamp and, in spite of the discovery made in regard to the insufficient state of my finances, looked forward to that event without any trepidation, so that,

I remember — it was actually the day before the one fixed on, and still no hope had dawned on the financial horizon — when Grandma Spicer embraced me with some tender words premonitory of our parting, I kissed her gratefully, musing at the same time in dreamy, untroubled fashion : " yes, I must be going home to-morrow."

It was on this same day that we drove to " Wallen Town," Grandma and Abagail and Ethel and I. The excursion was one Grandma had planned several weeks before, and I had no intention of making it the opportunity which I finally did.

As we were passing a dingy looking establishment, where some doubtful articles of virtu appeared in the window, an idea seized me, as new as it was comprehensive of my difficulties.

I went in, ostensibly to purchase a watch key, really to engage in negotiations of a more serious and complicated nature.

The proprieter of the shop became the temporary guardian of my watch, while I was invested with the funds necessary for my homeward journey.

I learned, afterwards, that this man had made an exception in the usually limited range of his operations in my favor, his establishment not being, by any means, that of a pawn-broker, but, in every sense, of the most highly moral and respectable nature.

He gave me such " ready cash " as his coffers would yield, with an improvised pawn-broker's check, at the composition of which we had both seriously and ingeniously labored. I can testify both to his honesty and obligingness. He insisted on my taking with me, "jest to tell the time o' day," a very large watch, in a tarnished silver case.

Not wishing to seem to cast any disparagement on his wares, I became the helpless recipient of this favor. The article in question was far too large for my watch-pocket, and had a persistent habit of holding its mouth wide open like a too weary shell-fish. On the interior of the case, one on either side, were pasted photographs of individuals to me unknown, male and female, their countenances such as the blinded eye of affection alone, I thought, could have rendered mutually entertaining, and the watch maintained, on all occasions, a system of chronology peculiarly its own.

As we drove back to Wallencamp, Grandma Spicer, her great heart close to Nature that sunny afternoon, beguiled the way with a gentle hilarity which never shocked or offended, but Ethel put her hand often in mine, looking up with the old helpless, pleading expression in her eyes—Ethel, I knew, would remember longest.

Sometimes, as my hand wandered almost unconsciously to caress the precious coin in my pocket, instead of the wild tract of stunted cedars through which our road lay, I fancied I saw the great elms of Newton, the wide straight street, the familiar house, an open door, and— ah ! it wasn't the first time that I had been taken in at that door, the survivor of wrecked ambition and misguided hope, only to hear my shortcomings made tenderly light of, my most desperate follies lovingly ignored and forgiven.

But I had meant that it should be so different this time ! I had gone out as a missionary ; and deeper than ever in my consciousness, I must feel the want and woe of the

returning prodigal ; the same old story, the ever recurring
failure.   It seemed as though all the wonder and impatience might well go out of my despair.

Then as I lent myself more and more to the contemplation of that home picture, how restful, and happy it
grew ! but poor old Wallencamp — for we were nearing
the little settlement now, and the sun was fast westering
— poor, squalid, solitary, beautiful, Wallencamp, as I
looked down upon it from the brow of Stony Hill, thrilled
me with a troubled sense of some diviner, some half-
comprehended glory.

The crimson glow had not quite faded in the sky when
I took my last walk across the fields to where the new
grave had been made on the hillside.   This is the new
burying ground of the Wallencampers ; the old one lies
a mile farther up the river, near the Indian encampment.
Here I saw more than one simple slab, bearing the name
of Cradlebow.   Here little Bess lies, too.   The hill,
meet for such sublime repose, looks ever calmly on the
humble, straggling homes of the Wallencampers below,
and sees the lonely river winding near, and hears, by
night and day, the monody of deeper waters.

I thought the voice of that great ocean of restlessness
sounding along the shore might quiet my unrest, but the
beat of the waves, the growing gloom of that still evening
hour, oppressed me with a feeling unutterably sad.
I could not bear it, at last.   It seemed as though
another deep was rising and breaking in my heart,
the flood of proud, half-stifled passion waking in one
awful moment to overwhelm me.   No light upon that
sea — but hope wronged, the mockery of death for yearn-
ing love, the unguided clash of drifting human lives !

An agony of blindness swam before my eyes. I felt my weak hands clutching at the grass, and gasped, as though it had been indeed in the blindness and pain of physical death, the prayer wrung from my selfish need. But the answer was of infinite love and compassion. It came to me then — not as some grave revelation of truth to the " enlightened seeker," but like the kiss of peace to a tired child, a door mysteriously opened to the self-bound captive, to one ignorant the light shining along a plain, straight way. And the doubt and terror and anguish went out of the world ; even the sorrowless farewell of frozen lips changed to tender benediction.

When I looked up at last, wondering, peaceful, my face wet with happy tears, the stars had come out in the sky and, down below, the windows of the Ark were shining. The faint murmur of a song was borne up to me. The Wallencampers had gathered at the Ark to celebrate our last " meeting " together, and I went down to join them.

* * * * * *

At what ghostly hour of the next morning Grandma Spicer awoke Grandpa to the unusual exigencies of the occasion, I cannot say. It was necessary for me to start very early from the Ark to take the train at West Wallen, but when I descended the stairs, by candle light, Grandpa Spicer had been already washed and dyed and arrayed, as for the Sabbath, in his best. Yes, and I was constrained to believe that he had even been instructed in the mysteries of Sunday school lore, for there was about him an air of haggard and feverish excitement, and he glared at my familiar presence with wild, unseeing eyes.

Memorable were the colloquies held that morning
between Grandma and Grandpa Spicer; Grandpa's
tragic assumption of manly consequence, and solemn
fears lest we should miss the train, directed in astute
syllables of warning towards Grandma Spicer; Grandma's increased deliberation, and imperturbable quietude
of soul.

I recall the strange, unearthly aspect of the scenes
enacted in the Ark at that early hour, the fleeting vision of
a morning repast which formed some accidental part in
the chaos of vaster proceedings.

Then when the first faint signs of dawn were beginning
to break through the grey in the eastern sky, I bade farewell to the Ark forever, lingering a moment on the
old familiar door-step for a last word with those of
the neighbors who had gathered there to see us off, for the
whole Spicer family accompanied me to the station.

There were others waiting at the gate to say good-bye
and at various posts all the way down the lane. At
the big white house Emily came running out, breathless.
She whispered hurriedly in my ear, " There was a
message left. Ye was n't well. I reckon 'twas a message.
When fisherman and that other one came up from
the shore, day o' the storm, he came to our house for Jim
to take him to Wallen. He said it was better to be
the dead one than him. He was awful white, and Jim
got harnessed, and just as fisherman was goin' out,
he left a message along o' me, though there wa'n't
no names mentioned, and he talked queer; but he
wanted as somebody should know that he realized it all
now, and he could n't make up for it, never; but it
was go'n' to be new or nothin' for him, and they should n't

want for nothin', never, and kep' a sayin' more, and
no message, exactly, as ye could call a message, but I
reckoned — I thought — may be —— "

Emily's glowing eyes, fixed on my face, grew very wide
and grave. I could only press her hand in parting, for
Grandpa, growing impatient, had succeeded in clucking
Fanny on again.

We drove along the river road, and, passing through the
Indian encampment, there were more good-byes exchanged by the roadside.

Then climbing up "Sandy Slope," beyond the settlement, we heard the shrill "Hullo !" of a familiar voice,
and looking back, saw Bachelor Rae running after us
very swiftly, his head destitute of covering, and his little
wizened face glowing red as the celestial Mars in the distance. He looked like some odd, fantastic toy that had
been wound up and set going.

So he came up with us, and trying to conceal his
breathlessness in polite little " hms and haws," delivered
aside, he offered me a huge bouquet composed, I should
think, of every sort of wild flower available on the Cape
at that season, and showing, in its arrangement, marks of
the most arduous striving after artistic effect. In the
other hand, he held out to me a basket of large, selected
boxberries.

I accepted the gifts with unaffected ˙delight, and
thanked Bachelor Rae warmly. I looked back at him,
trudging cheerfully homeward through the sand, so withered and small, with the grey in his hair, and his coat so
much too long for him — back to the poor brown house,
which no tender love had ever hallowed, or merry waiting laugh made bright for him ; and I wondered, along

his life's way which looked so sad and desolate, what hidden wild flowers God had strewed for him, that he seemed always so humbly cheerful and content, and brought his best of offerings with a smile to bless the happier lot of others.

For the rest of the way, the wild untenanted stretch was unbroken by any incident; yet I remember no tedium by the way; and I believe that a trip taken with Grandma and Grandpa Spicer through the most trackless desert would inevitably have been made to teem with diversion. Those blessed souls! I smile, looking back, but through tears, and with a reverence and tenderness far deeper than the smile.

By the time we reached the West Wallen depôt, the sky had clouded over.

" A little shower comin' up," Grandma said, but Grandpa shook his head and prophesied " a long, stiddy spell o' weather."

I persuaded my friends not to wait with me for the arrival of the train which, owing to some discrepancy in the matter of time between Wallencamp and West Wallen, would not be due for an hour or more.

I watched them out of sight, the last of my Wallencamp ! How deeply, how utterly it had grown into my life, so that now, in spite of the secret, glad exultation I felt at the thought of going home, my heart went running out after that quaint, receding vehicle, and aching sensibly.

On board the train at last, I began to experience something of the sensation of one who awakens from long sleep to the half-forgotten ways of men and life with a vague, untroubled wonder as to the latest styles in dress;

or, like a traveller from a strange country, weary, and way-worn, and out of date, who yet can smile hugging in his breast the happy secret of boundless wealth in the gold mine he has discovered far away.

I had neither umbrella, portmanteau, nor shawl-strap; such ordinary paraphernalia of travel I remembered once to have possessed, and tried in vain to recall the particular occasions on which they had been wrecked in Wallencamp. I bore with me my bouquet, my basket of boxberries, some small cedar trees for transplanting, and half of the largest clam shell the shores of Cape Cod had ever produced; this last a parting gift from Noel Norris.

I was far from being troubled with the consciousness of anything quaint or *bizarre* in my appearance. I felt no mortification on account of these treasures so intrinsically dear to my heart; but Grandma Spicer had insisted on binding a mustard paste on my chest. It was a parting request—I could not have refused—but in the close air of the car, the physical torture began to be extreme. Tears fell on the cedar spray at my side, yet was I withal strangely, peacefully happy.

It was raining when I passed through Boston. Once more in the din of a city, jolting noisily over the rough uneven pavements, I found myself wondering continually if the Spicers had reached home, and imagining how the rain was falling gently, quietly, on the roof of the Ark.

At the next stage, at Hartford, I was half afraid that I should meet brother or sister or some member of the family, and so have the complete effect of my "surprise" destroyed; but I saw none of them. There were few passengers on board the Newton-bound train. It was raining still. I was growing more and more glad at heart and looking out with my arm pressed against the window, when I heard a voice right over me — a soft, pitiful, thrilling exclamation :

"Great Heavens !"

I looked up and saw John Cable.

He sank slowly down into the seat in front of me and, for a moment, neither of us spoke. I did not mind meeting John. I had not thought of including him in the surprise. The sight of his familiar, friendly face gave me a positive thrill of pleasure, but there was something in his manner that kept me silent.

I said : "I 'm going to surprise them, John."

There was nothing offensive in the grave, swift glance with which John Cable then took me in, me and my bouquet of wilted wild flowers and my small cedar trees, only a slow, solemn distinctness in his tone.

"You will succeed," he said. "Undoubtedly you will succeed."

Still I felt no resentment. A gentle, sorrowful perplexity filled my breast.

"Why, do — I — look — very — very — unusual, John?" I questioned, and looking in his face I wondered why, in the old days of careless jest and repartee, he had never seemed so moved.

More words he said, but I could not bear them then, and tears from an inward pain fell on the cedar spray, yet I was glad that I had not grown so unusual that people would never like me any more.

Next, the surprise was a success, as John Cable had predicted, but that was the one point in my career in which my genius had never failed me. My surprises, though inclined to take something of the nature of an accumulation of calamities, had never lacked the great element of awe-producing wonder.

For the rest, I had known that I should be forgiven, and received with the usual *eclat* of the returned prodigal into the family bosom — but to be held up on successive days as an object of ever increasing marvel and interest, as one whose words and acts were endowed with a peculiar significance, as the light of the social fireside, the enchanter of small spell-bound audiences! Well, I had been spoiled so early in life that little was needed to complete the wreck. I felt a deeper satisfaction when, as I was meekly beseeching our Bridget's instruction in some particular branch of the culinary art, that majestic female observed, as she folded her arms and looked down on me complacently:

"There's one thing I like better about you, than I used to, miss — you do have to wade through a great deal o' flour to larn a little plain cookin', but Job himself, could n't a be'n no patienter." And it was indeed true that my " graham gems " never quite reached perfection, though they bore with them marks of earnest and faithful endeavor.

I found new sources of interest everywhere, and in ways which I had formerly regarded with aversion and disdain.

At the " Newton Ladies' Charitable Sewing Society " I was elevated from among the common stitchers and sewers, for faithfulness in service,— I believe, though malicious fingers would point to the distortion of the legs of little heathens' trousers,— to a place on the " cutting circle." From the cutting circle, it is needless to say, I was speedily exalted to a presidential chair of easeful observation and general vague superintendency.

Later, there was a revival of the "Literary Club."
There John Cable and I shone once more amid a group
of familiar and undimmed luminaries.   John Cable never
took up the exact thread of the discourse broken off
so abruptly on the day of my return in the cars, but it was
when coming home from the club one evening that
he expressed himself to the effect that I had always
been a great burden on his mind, even since the first day
he led me to school, and, to be sure, I had shown signs of
improvement lately, but there was always a pardonable
doubt as to what I might do next, and it was wearing on
him, and would I set his mind at rest by allowing him, in
some sense, to take the direction of my life into his
own hands?

John, though of adverse views, had been heatedly discussing the merits of the Capital Punishment question at
the club, so I was not surprised at the unusual grace and
flow of his address.

Years have passed since that evening.   I have been
very happy as John's wife.   If I wander in my story, be it
said that little John is running a model express train
on the floor over my head.   Little John, when not dreaming, exercises a vast amount of destructive physical force.

*   *   *   *   *   *

A little more than a year after I left Wallencamp, I
heard of Grandma and Grandpa Spicer's death.   "Very
quiet and peaceful," they said concerning Grandma, but
I had known what sort of a death-bed hers would be.
Scarcely a week after she had passed away, Grandpa
Spicer followed her.   I had it from good authority that
he kept about the house till the last.   There was a "rainy

spell," and he stood often gazing out of the window "with a lost look on his face," and once he said with a wistful, broken utterance and a pathetic longing in his eyes that did away forever with any opprobrium there might have been in connection with the term, that "it was gittin' to be very lonely about the house without ma pesterin' on him."

Since then, I have not heard from Wallencamp. It is doubtful whether I ever get another letter from that source. Though singularly gifted in the epistolary art, it is but a dull and faint means of expression to the souls of the Wallencampers — and *they* will not forget. From the storms that shake their earthly habitations, they pass to their sweet, wild rest beside the sea; and by and by, when I meet them, I shall hear them sing.

A LIST OF BOOKS

PUBLISHED BY

A. WILLIAMS & COMPANY,

283 WASHINGTON STREET, BOSTON.

ANDREW. The Errors of Prohibition. An Argument on the Matter of License and Prohibition. By the late JOHN A. ANDREW, Governor of Massachusetts. Paper. 8vo. 50 cents. *Tenth thousand.*

ATKINSON. Our National Domain: A Graphical and Statistical Chart. By EDWARD ATKINSON. Printed in colors and enclosed between handsome board covers. 50 cents.
☞ It can be obtained, if desired, mounted on rollers and varnished, suitable for hanging on the wall. Price, $1.25.

ATKINSON. What is a Bank? What Service does a Bank Perform? By EDWARD ATKINSON. 8vo. Pamphlet. 25 cents.

ATKINSON, Edward. The Railroads of the United States: their Effects on Farming and Production in that Country and Great Britain. By EDW RD ATKINSON. 8vo. Pamphlet, with chart. 50 cents.

ATKINSON. Comparative Geography: the Area of the Political Divisions of the world shown graphically in colors. By EDWARD ATKINSON. On roller. For the use of schools. $3.00. *In preparation.*

ATWATER'S History of the Colony of New Haven. 8vo. 611 pp. $4.00.

BAILEY. The Book of Ensilage; or, the New Dispensation for Farmers. By JOHN M. BAILEY. 8vo. Cloth. 202 pages. Portrait and illustrations. $1.00 Paper, 50 cents.
*** A work of incalculable importance to the farmer, treating the new system of feeding cattle.

BATES. "Risk," and other Poems. By CHARLOTTE FISKE BATES, editor of the "Longfellow Birthday Book." 16mo. Red edges. $1.00. *Little Classic style.*
*** "Crystallizations of subtle thoughts and fancies." — *John G. Whittier.*

BIGELOW. Litholapaxy or Rapid Lithotrity with Evacuation. By HENRY J. BIGELOW, M.D. 8vo. Cloth. Illustrated. $1.00.

BOTH. Small-Pox. The Predisposing Conditions, and their Prevention. By Dr. CARL BOTH. 12mo. Paper. 50 pages. Price, 25 cents.

BOTH. Consumption. By Dr. CARL BOTH. 8vo. Cloth. $2.00.

BOWDITCH. Suffo'k Surnames. (Surnames of Suffolk County, Massachusetts.) By NATHANIEL INGERSOLL BOWDITCH. 8vo. Cloth. 383 pages. $2.00. *Second edition, enlarged.*

BOYCE. The Art of Lettering, and Sign Painter's Manual. A Complete and Practical Illustration of the Art of Sign-Painting. Oblong 4to. By A. P. BOYCE. 36 plain and colored plates. $3.50. *Fourth edition.*

BOYCE. Modern Ornamentor and Interior Decorator. A Complete and Practical Illustration of the Art of Scroll, Arabesque, and Ornamental Painting. By A. P. BOYCE. Oblong 4to. 22 plain and colored plates. Cloth. $3.50.

BUTTS. Tinman's Manual, and Builder's and Mechanics' Handbook, designed for Tinmen, Japanners, Coppersmiths, Engineers, Mechanics, Builders, Wheelwrights, Smiths, Masons, &c. *Sixth edition.* 12mo. Cloth. 120 pages $1.20.

BUTTS. The New Business-Man's Assistant, and Ready Reckoner, for the use of the Merchant, Mechanic, and Farmer, consisting of Legal Forms and Instructions indispensable in Business Transactions, and a great variety of Useful Tables. By I. R. BUTTS. 1 vol. 12mo. 132 pages. 50 cents.
*** It would be difficult to find a more comprehensive manual for every-day use, than this valuable Assistant.

CAPE COD FOLKS. A Novel. Illustrated. 12mo. Cloth. $1.50.
*** A powerfully written story, depicting the characteristics of a class conspicuous the world over for keenness, originality, and humor.

CHANDLER. A Bicycle Tour in England. By A. D. CHANDLER. 1 vol. Small 4to. *In preparation.*
*** Full of views of out-of-the-way nooks, castles, country seats, unsurpassed for clearness and beauty.

CUPPLES. The Deserted Ship: a Story of the Atlantic. By GEO CUPPLES, author of "The Green Hand." Illustrated. 12mo. $1.50. *Fourth edition.*

CUPPLES. Driven to Sea; or, the Adventures of Norrie Seton. By Mrs. GEORGE CUPPLES. Illustrated. 12mo. Cloth. $1.50. *Second thousand.*

CUPPLES. Singular Creatures; or, Stories from a Scotch Parish. By Mrs. GEORGE CUPPLES. Illustrated. 12mo. Cloth. $1.50. *Second thousand.*
*** "The tenderness and humor of the volume are simply exquisite."—*E. P. Whipple.*

DERBY. Anthracite and Health. By GEO. DERBY, M.D. Harv. 12mo. 76 pages. Cloth, limp. 50 cents. *Second edition, enlarged.*

DES CARS. A Treatise on Pruning of Fruit and Ornamental Trees. Translated by C. S. SARGENT (Harvard). Engravings. 12mo. Cloth 75 cents.

DIRECTORY OF BOSTON CHARITABLE INSTITUTIONS. 12mo. Cloth. 182 pages. 50 cents, *net.*

DRAKE. Memorials of the Society of the Cincinnati of Massachusetts. By F. S. DRAKE. Royal 8vo. Cloth. 584 pages. Many steel engravings. $13.00 *net.*

ELLIS. The Evacuation of Boston, with a Chronicle of the Siege. By GEORGE E. ELLIS, LL.D., author of "The Life of Count Rumford," &c., &c. With steel engravings, full-page heliotype *fac-similes*, maps, &c. 1 vol., imperial 8vo. $3.00.
*** A monument of historical research and industry. Only a few copies now remain.

FIRST HELP IN ACCIDENTS AND SICKNESS. A Guide in the absence or before the arrival of Medical Assistance. Illustrated with numerous cuts. 12mo. Cloth. 265 pages. $1.50.
" A very useful book, devoid of the quackery which characterizes so many of the health manuals." — *Am Med. Ob.*

FIRST LESSONS IN THE ARTICLES OF OUR FAITH, And Questions upon Our Church Doctrines, and upon the Life of Christ, with their Answers from Scripture. For young learners. With introduction by Rev. PHILLIPS BROOKS, D.D.. 2 vols. Boards. 70 cents.

FISHER. Plain Talk About Insanity. Its Causes, Forms, Symptoms, and Treatment of Mental Diseases. With Remarks on Hospitals, Asylums, and the Medico-Legal Aspect of Insanity. By T W. FISHER, M.D., late of the Boston Hospital for the Insane. 8vo. Cloth. $1 50.

FOLSOM. Disease of the Mind. Notes on the Early Management, European and American Progress, Modern Methods, &c., in the Treatment of Insanity. By CHARLES F. FOLSOM, M.D., Secretary of the Massachusetts Board of Health. Illustrated. 8vo. Cloth. $1.25.

FOLSOM. The Four Gospels, from the Text of Tischendorf. By N. S. FOLSOM. 12mo. Cloth. 486 pages. $2.50. *Third edition.*

GODDARD. Newspapers and Newspaper Writers in New England, 1787-1815. By D. A. GODDARD, editor of *Boston Daily Advertiser.* 8vo. Pamphlet. 50 cents.

GRANT. The Confessions of a Frivolous Girl. A Story of Fashionable Life. Edited by ROBERT GRANT, author "The Little Tin Gods-on-Wheels." With vignette illustrations by L. S. Ipsen. 16mo. Cloth, extra, $1 25. Paper, 75 cents. *Tenth thousand.*
* "A charming novel, abounding in clever comment, good-natured sarcasm, and witty reflection." — *Saturday Evening Gazette.*

GREEN. Early Records of Groton, Massachusetts. By SAMUEL A. GREEN. 8vo. Cloth. 201 pages. $2.00.

GREENE. The Blazing Star: with an Appendix treating of the Jewish Kabbala. Also a Tract on the Philosophy of Mr. Herbert Spencer, and one on New England Transcendentalism. By W. B. GREENE. 12mo. Cloth. 180 pages. $1.25.

GUARD (DE LA). The Simple Cobler of Aggawam in America. By THEODORE DE LA GUARD. 16mo. Pamphlet. 50 cents.
* A *fac-simile* reprint of the London edition of 1647.

HALL. Masonic Prayers. 4to. Large type. Limp. Cloth. $1.25.

HALL. Master Key to the Treasures of the Royal Arch. A complete guide to the Degrees of Mark Master, Past Master, M. G. Master, and Royal Arch. Approved and adopted throughout the United States. By JOHN K HALL. Morocco. tuck. 75 cents.

HALL. Master Workman of the Entered Apprentice Fellow- Craft, and Master Mason's Degrees By JOHN K. HALL, P. H. P. of St. Paul's R. A. Chapter, Boston, Mass., and P. D. Gr. H. P. of the Grand Chap. of Mass. Morocco, tuck. 75 cents.

HASKINS. Selections from the Scriptures. For Families and Schools. By Rev. D. G. HASKINS. 1 vol. 24mo. 402 pages. $1.50.

HOWE. Science of Language; or Seven-Hour System of Grammar. By Professor D. P. HOWE. Pamphlet. 50 cents. *Thirtieth thousand.*

HUBBARD. Summer Vacations at Moosehead Lake and Vicinity. A Practical Guide-book, by L. L. HUBBARD. With maps and twenty beautiful photograph illustrations done in heliotype. 16mo. Cloth. 114 pages. $1.50. Paper covers. 50 cents.

JEFFRIES. Diseases of the Skin. The Recent Advances in their Pathology and Treatment, being the Boylston Prize Essay for 1871. By B. Joy JEFFRIES, A.M., M.D. 8vo. Cloth. $1.00.

JEFFRIES. The Animal and Vegetable Parasites of the Human Skin and Hair, and False Parasites of the Human Body. By B. JOY JEFFRIES, A.M., M.D. 12mo. Cloth. $1.00.

KING. The War-Ships and Navies of the World. Containing a complete and concise description of the Construction, Motive Power, and Armaments of Modern War-Ships of all the Navies of the World, Naval Artillery, Marine Engines, Boilers, Torpedoes, and Torpedo-Boats. By Chief Engineer J. W. KING, U S. Navy, author of "King's Notes on the Steam-Engine." 1 vol. 8vo. 500 pages. 64 full-page illustrations. $7.00.
₊ "The ablest, most interesting, and most complete work on the subject in the English language." — *Edinburgh Review.*

KING. Handbook of Boston. By MOSES KING. Profusely illustrated. 12mo. 296 pages. Paper, 60 cents. Cloth, $1.00.

KING. Harvard and its Surroundings. Copiously illustrated with heliotypes, wood engravings, and etchings. Small 4to. $1.50. Paper, $1.00.

KNAPP. My Work and Ministry, with Six Essays. By Rev. W. H. KNAPP. 16mo. 327 pages. $1.50. *Third ed.tion.*

LAIGHTON. Poems by ALBERT LAIGHTON. Frontispiece. 16mo. Cloth, gilt. 125 pages. $1.00.
₊ The author is a native of Portsmouth, N. H., and this little volume is of special interest to natives of that ancient city.

LEIGH. Modern Cotton Spinning. By EVAN LEIGH, C. E. 2 vols. Quarto. Profusely illustrated. Price $30.00. *Second and enlarged edition*

"LET NOT YOUR HEART BE TROUBLED." Square 12mo. Leaflet, tied. 48 pages. Printed in two colors. Illuminated cover. 75 cents. *Fourth thousand.*

LITTLE. Early New England Interiors. By ARTHUR LITTLE. A Volume of Sketches in old New-England places. Thick oblong quarto. $5.00
₊ "To those far distant, unfamiliar with the nooks and corners of New England, and prone to consider the work of Puritanical colonists, noticeable only for its lack of taste, and conspicuous for green blinds and white painted walls, this work will be a revelation." — *Boston Daily Advertiser.*

LOVING WORDS FOR LONELY HOURS. Oblong, leaflet, tied. 22 pages. Printed in two colors. 50 cents. *Sixth thousand.*

LOVING WORDS FOR LONELY HOURS. Second series. 22 pages. 50 cents. *Second thousand*

LÜCKE. Surgical Diagnosis of Tumors. By A. LÜCKE (Strasburg). Translated by A. T. CABOT, M D. 16mo. Pamphlet. 25 cents.

MALLOCK. Every Man His Own Poet; or, The Inspired Singer's Recipe Book. 16mo. Paper. Price, 25 cents. *Fifth thousand.*
₊ A most enjoyable piece of satire, witty, clever, and refined. In society its success, here and abroad, has been immense.

MITCHELL. A Manual for the Use of Clergymen and Others Preparing Classes for Confirmation. By Rev. W. MITCHELL. Pamphlet. 10 cents.

MORRIS. The Autobiography of Commodore Charles Morris. With heliotype portrait after ARY SCHEFFER. 1 vol. 8vo. 111 pages. $1.00.
₊ A valuable addition to the literature of American history and biography from the pen of one who, in the words of Admiral Farragut, was "America's grandest seaman."

MORRISON. History of Morison and Morrison Families. 468 pages. 8vo. $3 00.

NANTUCKET RECEIPTS. Collected chiefly from Nantucket sources 16mo. Pamphlet. 40 pages. 25 cents.

NEWTON. Essays of To-Day. Religious and Theological. By Rev. WM. W. NEWTON, Rector of St. Paul's Church, Boston. 12mo. Cloth 253 pages. $2.00.

PARKER. The Battle of Mobile Bay and the Capture of Forts Powell, Gaines, and Morgan. By Commodore FOXHALL A. PARKER. 8vo. Cloth, elegant. 136 pages. Portrait and two colored charts. $2.50.

PEABODY. Æsthetic Papers. Edited by ELIZABETH P. PEABODY. 1 vol. 8vo. Pamphlet. 248 pages. $2.00. Boston, 1849.
₌ A rare pamphlet, of which but a few copies remain for sale. It contains early papers by EMERSON, HAWTHORNE, PARKE GODWIN, THOREAU, and others.

PREBLE. A History of the Flag of the United States of America, and of the Naval and Yacht Club Signals, Seals, and Arms, and principal National Songs. With a Chronicle of the Symbols, Standards, Banners, and Flags of Ancient and Modern Nations. By Rear Admiral GEORGE HENRY PREBLE, U. S. Navy. 1 vol. 8vo. Price, $7.00.
₌ A masterly and encyclopedic production, absolutely without a rival, conveying to the general reader, in a manner eminently readable, a fund of information on the naval and military history of the country. It is profusely illustrated.

ROLLO'S JOURNEY TO CAMBRIDGE. A Tale of the Adventures of the Historic Holiday Family at Harvard under the new régime. With twenty-six illustrations, full-page frontispiece, and an illuminated cover of striking gorgeousness, by FRANCIS G. ATTWOOD. 1 vol. Imp. 8vo. Limp. London toy book style. Price, 50 cents. *Third and enlarged edition.*
₌ " All will certainly relish the delicious satire in both text and illustrations." — *Boston Traveller.*
₌ " A brilliant and witty piece of fun." — *Chicago Tribune.*

RÜDINGER. Atlas of the Ossean Anatomy of the Human Ear. Comprising a portion of the Atlas of the Human Ear. By N. RÜDINGER. Translated and edited, with notes and an additional plate, by CLARENCE J. BLAKE, M.D. 9 plates. 4to. Cloth, extra. $3.50.
₌ The plates are the same as in the German edition, and were imported specially for this edition.

SMITH. Myths and Idyls of the Present ; or, Stories and Dialogues in Prose and Verse, for Young and Old Hearts. By ELIZA WINCHELL SMITH. 278 pages. Square 12mo. Cloth. $1.50.
₌ Deserving of being widely known and extensively circulated amongst those who have healthy appetites for books free from sentimentalism, goodiness, and slang.

SPALDING. The Ordinance of Confirmation : its History and Significance. By the Rev. J. F. SPALDING. 8vo. Paper. 21 pages. 15 cents.

SPRAGUE. Poetical and Prose Writings of Charles Sprague. New edition, with steel portrait and biographical sketch. 12mo. Cloth. 207 pages. $1.50.

STEVENS. Fly Fishing in Maine Lakes ; or, Camp Life in the Wilderness. By C. W. STEVENS. With 38 vignette illustrations, and colored frontispiece, showing the best killing flies in vogue. Square 12mo. Cloth. $1.25.
₌ A bright and attractive book for every angler and sportsman, full of breezy sketches replete with incidents. It is as practical as it is humorous.

STEVENS. On Ensilage of Green Forage Crops in Silos. Experience with Ensilage at Echo Dale Farm. Also the Practical Experience of Twenty-five Practical Farmers with Ensilage and Silos. By H. R. STEVENS. 1 vol. 8vo. Cloth. 50 cents.

STEVENS. Revelations of a Boston Physician. By CHARLES WISTAR STEVENS, M.D. 12mo. Cloth. 252 pages. $1.00.
₌ A work that does for Boston what Warren in his " Diary of a Physician " did for London.

STONE. Domesticated Trout. How to Breed and Grow them. By LIVINGSTON STONE. 12mo. 367 pages. $2.00. *Third edition.* Revised and enlarged.

STURTEVANT. The Dairy Cow. A Monograph on the Ayrshire Breed of Cattle. With an Appendix on Ayrshire, Jersey, and Dutch Milks; their Formation and Peculiarities. By E. LEWIS, M.D., and JAMES N. STURTE-VANT. 12mo. 252 pages. Illustrated. $2.00.

THE GAS CONSUMER'S GUIDE. Illustrated. 12mo. Cloth, $1 00. Paper, 75 cents.

TOWER. Modern American Bridge Building. Illustrated. 1 vol. 8vo. Cloth. $2.00.

UNDERWOOD. History of the 33d Massachusetts Regiment. By Gen. A. B UNDERWOOD. 8vo. 340 pages. $3.00.
⁎ A Regimental history without a dull chapter.

VILLE. High Farming without Manure. Six Lectures on Agriculture. By GEORGE VILLE. Published under the direction of the Massachusetts Society for the Promotion of Agriculture. 16mo. 108 pages. Price, 25 cents.
⁎ A wonderfully cheap edition of a famous book.

WARE. Hints to Young Men on the True Relations of the Sexes. By JOHN WARE, M.D. 16mo. Cloth, limp. 50 cents. *Twentieth thousand.*
⁎ Accurate, clear, truthful, and in no way offensive to modesty.

WARREN. Surgical Observations with Cases and Operations. By T. MASON WARREN, M.D. With fine colored illustrations and many wood engravings. 8vo. Cloth. 630 pages. $3.50.
⁎ The last published work of this eminent surgeon.

WATSON. A Course of Descriptive Geometry. For the use of Colleges and Scientific Schools. With an Appendix containing Stereoscopic Views of the Solutions in Space of the Principal Problems. By WILLIAM WATSON, Ph.D. Plates. Quarto. Cloth. $3.00.

WATSON. European System of Instruction: Studio and Atelier. With the most approved Models and Appliances recently selected from the Technical Schools of France, Germany, and Austria. By WILLIAM WATSON, Ph.D. 8vo. Boards. 50 cents.

WHEELWRIGHT. A New "Chance Acquaintance." A Trifle served up on Twelve Plates, by J. T. WHEELWRIGHT. Illustrated by F. G. ATTWOOD. 12mo. Paper. 25 cents.
⁎ A Boston *jeu d'esprit* in verse. Very clever and witty.

WHITEFIELD. The Homes of our Forefathers. Being a collection of the oldest and the most interesting buildings in Massachusetts. From original drawings in colors by E. WHITEFIELD. With Historical Memoranda. 1 vol., oblong quarto, cloth, neat, gilt edges, bevelled, $5.00.
⁎ A work that gives, with the faithfulness of a photograph, the curious, picturesque and always interesting relics of colonial days that still remain to Massachusetts.

WHITNEY—CLARKE. A Compendium of the most important Drugs with their Doses, according to the Metric System. By W. F. WHITNEY, M.D. and F. H. CLARKE. 32mo. 40 pages. 25 cents. *Specially made to fit the Vest Pocket.*

WINES. The State of Prisons and of Child-Saving Institutions in the Civilized World. By E. C. WINES, D.D., LL.D. 1 vol. Large 8vo. 719 pages. $5.00.
⁎ A vast repository of facts, and the most extensive work issued in any language, on matters relating to prison discipline and penal justice.

WORCESTER. History of Hollis, New Hampshire. By S. T. WORCESTER. Maps and engravings. 8vo. 394 pages. $2.50.

For sale by all booksellers, or mailed, postage paid, on receipt of price.

A. WILLIAMS & COMPANY,

PUBLISHERS, BOSTON.

The Land of Gold.

A Tale of '49. Illustrated. By GEORGE G. SPURR.
12 mo. Cloth. $1.50.

Dr. Howell's Family.

By MRS. A. B. GOODWIN. 16mo. Cloth. $1.00.

Christine's Fortune.

By MRS. H. B. GOODWIN. 16mo. Cloth. $1.00.

Rollo's Journey to Cambridge.

ILLUSTRATED

By FRANCIS G. ATTWOOD. 50 CENTS.

James A. Garfield.

TRIBUTES FROM OVER THE SEA.

Being selections from Foreign Testimonials to the late
President Garfield. Sm. 4to. 50 Cents.

Myths and Idyls of the Present;

Or Stories and Dialogues in Prose and Verse for Young and Old Hearts.

By ELIZA W. SMITH. 12mo. Cloth. $1.50.

Driven to Sea;

OR, THE ADVENTURES OF NORRIE SETON.

By Mrs. GEORGE CUPPLES.

The Deserted Ship.
A STORY OF THE ATLANTIC.
By GEORGE CUPPLES.

Author of " The Green Hand," " The Sunken Rock," etc. Illustrated. 12mo. Cloth. Brilliant binding. $1.50. Fourth thousand. New and improved edition. Now ready.

Southern Rambles.

By OWEN NOX.

With many illustrations. Small quarto. Paper covers, 50 cents. Cloth, $1.00.

A humorous and dashing brochure, detailing the adventures and mishaps of two gentlemen in Florida, *a la* Mark Twain.

Sent, postage paid, on receipt of price.

A. WILLIAMS & CO., Publishers, Boston.